THE BROTHERS STRYFE

J.A. BULLEN

© 2020 Jacob A. Bullen
Published by Team Daddashygan Creations
an imprint of Pages Promotions, LLC
Edited by Diana Kathryn Plopa
www.PagesPromotions.com

All Rights Reserved
First Edition

Print ISBN: 978-1628282412
E-book ISBN: 978-1628282429
Library of Congress Control Number: Pending

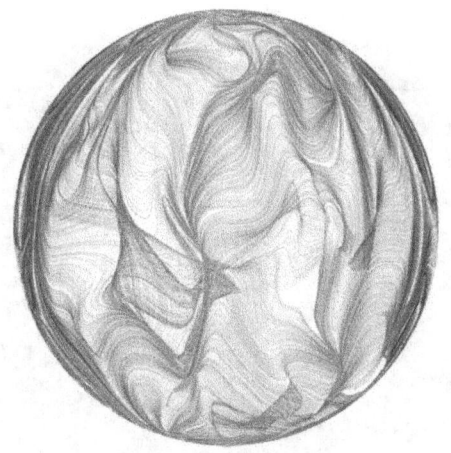

DEDICATION

To the builders, who paved the way for tomorrow's children. Who gave it all, leaving nothing behind. May our constructs prove to enrich their lives and never hinder. May our progeny seize their destinies and achieve today's impossibilities.

As always, thank you to my family for their unwavering belief.

To Diana, thank you for your kind words and your support.

Prologue

In the deserted, moonlit streets of Lothren, three cloaked figures entered the desolate courtyard at the center of the Noble's sector. The hoods of their cloaks were held tightly to their faces, concealing their identities from any who might recognize them. Stepping off to an isolated corner, they waited in the shadows until a fourth figure drew near.

"What took you so long?" One man among the three figures growled. "Why did you not appear at the specified place and time?"

"There were complications." A genderless voice answered, the sound filtered through the use of magic.

"Complications? You, an asset of the Court, waylaid by complications? Be serious. You do understand what is at stake, do you not?" While the three forms held an aggressor's stance, the slightly smaller form remained relaxed.

"Yes, complications. Considering each of you is aware of what I have done to serve this Kingdom, I trust you will refrain from questioning my judgment on the matter further."

"Fine. Fine." The figure replied, once more scanning the field for any eavesdroppers. "Have you obtained the item?" A ball wrapped in heavy cloth was produced from some invisible fold in the late comer's robes. Extending a hand, the cloaked form accepted the wad.

"Is everything else in place?" The man, now holding the bundle, asked.

"It is." The form nodded. "None suspect the object has been tampered with. Are you certain your target shall come into contact with it?"

"You have asked us not to question your judgments. I would advise with equal tension for you to avoid the same mistake." The lone figure bowed its head deeply.

"As you wish, my Lords. Far be it for this humble servant to question your motives. If all is in order and my Lords, pleased, I shall take my leave." Turning and walking from the men, the mysterious man sighed with relief as he looked to the concealed knives in his hands. Returning them to their sheaths, he stopped at the sight of another shadowy figure.

"Is it done?" A young man spoke.

"It is. Why do you insist on prying in such matters?" Stepping away from the wall, the cloaked figure walked alongside the assassin as he resumed his stroll.

"You know how Her Majesty is. Besides, I hear my brother is going to be attending that school soon. I only want the best for him." The assassin stopped and eyed his young companion.

"Brotherly love, is it?" he mused. "How interesting."

"Hardly." The young man responded, absently waving his hands. A flash of moonlight showed a longsword on his back and a crude, twisted knife at his waist. The knife was curved at the edge, taking more of a small axe's likeness than a dagger. The older man took note of this as they walked.

"What will you do now?" he asked. "What is it your Queen demands, now?" Placing both hands behind his head, the youth walked without care.

"Nothing for the moment. Things have been a bit quiet for me. Gives me plenty of time to have some fun. That is why I decided to help you deliver that present."

"Wouldn't the bane of Eternia be a hindrance to your Queen's plans? Surely, she does not plan to rule alongside another." The smaller figure slowed in pace as it allowed silence to linger a moment.

"My Queen has a greater agenda, which extends far beyond that woman's ambitions. As I said, this is purely for my entertainment." They continued to saunter, though the man's curiosity deepened hopelessly.

"And what does the Grey Mother have to do with your brother?"

"Not a thing. However, knowing him the way I do, it would take a miracle to keep him from becoming involved." Curious about the boy, who radiated with a dangerous aura, the assassin relied on his instincts, which told him to inquire no further.

He was glad to see the boy leave his company, shortly after leaving the churchyard. An assassin who had the fortune of living to see his late years, the man still shivered at the thought of the young man. Something about the boy always left him ill at ease.

"I would hate to have any connection to that boy's brother." He whispered only to himself, looking out over the sea, where the mystical island and castle awaited all those who possessed the gift of the Amaranthine.

The wind howled as he thought upon the atrocity he helped to commit, salty air blowing through his garments with a wintry chill. Pulling his robes tightly to himself, he considered the orders of his employer and vanished silently into the night, with his guilt for comfort.

J.A. Bullen

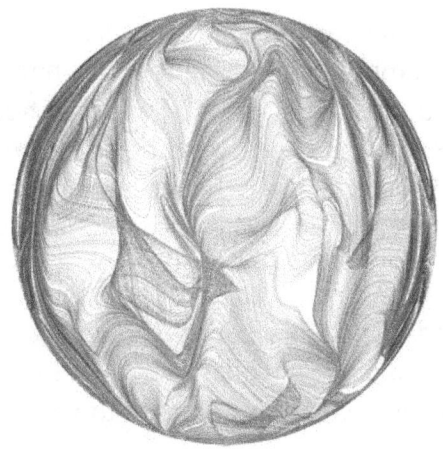

CHAPTER ONE

Before their father left on his ill-fated trip to Lothren, Gael and Gabriel had just been accepted to attend the Cabal, where they could learn to control their natural-born gifts of sorcery. Despite their unique origins, the boys would be allowed to overcome their world's great prejudices.

The sons of a fabled war hero and monster slayer, the brothers were among a select few students to join the school, despite possessing no tangible relation to nobility. Spending the majority of their young lives hearing the countless tales of their father's vast travels and contributions to the Nation of Altair, neither could wait to start their own legend. To them, there could be nowhere better to start than where their father studied, the Magic Academy on Cabal Island.

Before their father was branded a traitor to the realm and became the tipping point of a war between the Kingdoms of Altair and Dalmorithia, he had managed to reach out to loyal friends from his former life. These friends, who even after Tristan's fall from grace, felt their old bonds. With promises of vast, latent potential and strong-willed, eager students, the sons of Tristan Stryfe were welcomed with open arms.

Their letters had arrived midday, whilst they tended to their daily chores that summer. At first, neither boy had thought much of the wind. Rosalind, their caretaker and a former healer of the Cabal, stood off to one side of the field, hand pressed to her growing belly. She had assured them that the baby would not come until winter, though both brothers stared at the woman uneasily.

She gave them a reassuring smile, as she turned back to her patch of their garden, pulling weeds and planting their late-season crops. Shana worked diligently near to them, as well. Looking to their baskets, Gael increased his efforts at the sight of Shana's filled basket.

"Let me help you." Gabriel chirped, trotting across the field to take the heavy basket for his friend. Gael shook his head at his brother, while the young girl thanked the mousy, blonde-haired boy.

It was then, wiping the sweat from his brow, that Gael noticed a peculiarity in the distance. A small trail of dust rising in the air, he focused his eyes before reaching for his hoe. As though sensing his brother's tension, Gabriel also turned about. The entire family was soon on alert, prepared for whatever manner of bandit or traveler had wandered so far away from the nearby town of Leones.

The mirage conjured by the wind quickly dispersed, and a glowing beast appeared. Neither taking flight nor running, the ominously shaped creature floated towards them, as though propelled by the wind. Even as the boys braced themselves, Rosalind smiled.

"So, they've finally arrived." She sighed with bittersweet pride, at last making out the sight of the glittering cloud of birds. At last seen for what they were, the birds dispersed, broadening out into several ribbons of vibrant red plumes and yellow feathers.

Cautiously watching the bizarre occurrence, the brothers stood shoulder to shoulder. As the birds continued their wild swirl, two envelopes appeared above them. Slowly floating to their outstretched hands, the brothers eyed the parchment paper envelopes, staring at the olive branch seal.

As they read the acceptance letter, and running to Rosalind, their eyes grew bright. "They came!" Gabriel cheered, holding the parchment high into the air. "They actually came!" Turning to Shana, who sat her things down by the porch side, the young girl excitedly looked at the letter.

"You're going to get to learn how to cast magic," she exclaimed, looking to Rosalind, who continued to smile.

"Come now, boys. Let us write a letter to Sir Tristan and the others. They will want to know immediately." None of them were aware in that single moment of happiness, that their peaceful lives had come to an end.

****

The first of the winter snowdrifts coated the mountain tops, leaving behind a gentle sprinkling of evergreens. Falling from the majestic, white-capped peaks, the drifts lapped at the King's Highway. His home far from sight, Gael sighed and turned back from the window.

"Do not worry, young Master," Garis said, looking back at the young, plain-faced boy.

Gael turned away, blowing a few stray brown locks from in front of his eyes. "I am not worried," he grumbled as his blonde-haired brother, Gabriel, slept in his seat.

"Your brother has the right idea," laughed Garis, the curved edges of his silver-tipped mustache, touched by the snow. "It was from these very mountains, the Gargesh descended upon Lothren, nearly conquering the realm."

Gael looked back out the window, eyeing the mountains. "I don't see anything," he complained, staring at the seemingly lifeless mountain, despite the highest peaks being consumed in a shrouded swirl of snow clouds.

"Well, they do not live there anymore. No one does." The elder man chuckled. "I imagine the Gargesh are the only ones who ever could."

"How much longer to the ferry?" Gael asked, shifting uncomfortably in his seat.

"Ah, well, we should be in Lothren soon. It is not far to Bay City from there. However, I must ask that you and your brother stay close to me until the drop off point. You may do as you please once we meet with Sir Tarkan. Low Town is no place for youth."

"Are there many ruffians?"

"I suppose so, amongst other things. Let us just say that it is best to avoid it, altogether." Gael did not pursue the topic after Garis dropped it.

"Who is this, Sir Tarkan, that we are to meet with?"

"I am not rightly sure. However, it would appear that he is someone the Cabal trusts."

Garis shivered as he stared to the southeast, where beyond the mountains, lay the ocean. "Is the cold getting to you?" Gael asked.

Garis looked back to him, at a loss a moment, and smiled. "Ah, none at all, young Master. I was merely thinking of those sorcerers up there, in their almighty tower, conjuring world storms and demons as they look down upon us mortal folk."

"You do not like sorcerers?" Again, Garis smirked.

"Love them, to be true. The alliance with the Cabal has been good for Altair. However, it cannot be helped that they live near forever and can remake a kingdom in a season."

"But Mister Garis," Gabriel, freshly woken, spoke. "Only in the legends have there ever existed sorcerers of such power."

"Ah, young Master, Gabriel." Garis cheered. "Pay this superstitious old man no mind. I mean no harm. You boys must be eager to begin your studies."

"Quite," Gabriel chirped, the boy immediately perking up. "We have been studying with Rosalind for over a year now. I cannot wait to meet my instructors and start learning real magic."

Garis laughed at the young man's enthusiasm as Gael continued to stare out the window, dismissively. "Aye, as you should be, young Master." The driver eyed back with a broad smile. "I do not know much of what you will practice once you are within the walls of the Cabal, but I wish you the best."

Their words traveled off a distance as Gael's attention drifted further out across the endless landscape. Their view of the mountain pass faded, opening his gaze to the ocean and to Lothren. Immediately, Gabriel shot to his brother's side, peering out the window.

"Ah, there you have it, lads. The very heart of Altair; Lothren, in all of her splendor." The two young men, dressed in their winter cloaks and furs, sat as close to the window as possible, watching in awe as the massive city filled the panoramic scope of their vision.

Lothren, tall, bright, and gleaming in the morning sun, shined like a beacon. Beyond the gleam of its many buildings, high, white stone pillars, and paved streets, they could see the castle. High up and buried into the face of the next mountain peak, the castle watched over the city's many districts.

Garis steered the coach to the south of the main road, leading the coach down a second road, which traced along the mountain's face, descending towards the districts below. As Gael and Gabriel continued to watch out the window, their view of the ocean and the cities nestled beneath Lothren came into view. Lower Lothren, where the city's serfdom, lower class, and villainy dwelled; and the lustrous Bay City, which nestled next to the bay, and floated upon the river.

"Gabriel, look. You can see the Alistair Bridge from down here." Gael said, pointing skyward towards the monolithic bridge that served as the sole connection between the castle and the city.

"And look at the pier!" Gabriel clamored back, pointing over his brother's shoulder, at the port of Bay City.

"Are those houses or boats?" Gael asked, looking down at the many structures beneath them, which floated off from the bank of the river.

"They are both, young Master," Garis replied. "In Bay City, houses, shops, and all other manner of buildings are anchored to the pier. You might say that the entire city, with few exceptions, simply floats as one, singular vessel."

"An entire city, floating on the water?" Gabriel sighed. "Gael, we have not even arrived at the Cabal, and already, we see such marvelous things."

"What happens when it is high tide, or when the storms roll in?"

"Ah, worry not, lad. The folk below are not without their own protections. Those buildings were all built by master ship builders. Nestled so deeply into the bay, they fear not the massive waves one meets out on the broader ocean.

"Besides, any wave which might approach, oft breaks its back on Cabal Island. If you look carefully on a clear day, you can see the shore of the island from the pier." Both brothers trained their eyes out over the water, hoping to see their destination.

"I would not suspect you to be able to see it now." The driver said. "Far too much spray in the air. Fog's rolling in and a storm not far beyond it. No, it is safe to say you will not see it until you arrive." Both boys, clearly disappointed, sat back in their seats as the carriage continued down the mountain's slope and through Lower Lothren. As their transport came to a stop, the boys leaned forward.

"Have we arrived?" Gael asked.

"Aye. We are outside of the meeting point. Hold a moment while I unload your belongings. Then, we will go inside together. It would not do to have come all this way, just to have the two of you lost to vandals." They could hear the creaking of the driver's seat as Garis rose and leapt from the side of his post.

The sound of their trunks, sliding from above, told them that it was nearly time for them to meet Tarkan. Grabbing up his dark, emerald, traveling bag, Gael handed the navy blue over to his brother. The carriage door swung open, bringing in a burst of chill air as Garis smiled at them from behind his snow-covered mustache.

"Might I take your bags?" he offered, holding out his arms.

"I can carry it," Gael said, clutching the bag closer to his chest.

"We thank you, all the same, Garis." Gabriel smiled.

The middle-aged man smiled at them as he nodded. "As you wish. Be sure to bundle up, young Masters. There is a small bite in the air. Do not worry, though. Once inside, we will get you two some cocoa and a meal to warm your insides." Garis walked away, resuming his whistling tune as he followed two men who carried their trunks. As the men carried their belongings towards the

---

tavern's back entrance, Garis walked to the front door.

"The Underbridge?" Gael read aloud as they approached the tavern. Gabriel pointed towards the Alistair bridge, which could be seen, looming high above them.

"Aye, the lift is just around those buildings there," Garis said, stopping to point at a small cropping of buildings, where near a dozen guards stood. "Easiest way to transport goods to the city above." He finished his explanation as he walked inside.

Adjusting his pack, Gael followed his brother and the driver, taking a brief moment to examine his surroundings. He saw numerous rough-looking passersby, tending to their daily affairs. From men with prosthetic hooks for hands, or long jagged scars from the previous war, to fierce faced women bartering in the streets, everyone he saw would surely be noticed out in Leones.

"Only a day away and already so far from home," Gael whispered to himself. Turning about, he walked inside. Immediately, the smell of ale, hot gruel, and the Amaranthine knows what else assaulted his nostrils. The near dizzying haze of odors served as introduction to the various individuals he saw within.

All around, men and women of various sizes and colors, wearing exotic clothing, filled the tables and bar. Carefully, he walked across the old, oak floorboards, watching as each individual he passed, bore a different tale on just their appearance.

"It is because of the upcoming games," Garis said, gently patting Gael on the shoulder.

Catching the occasional word from the dozens of conversations around, they confirmed Garis's words. "It is a shame that we will not be here to see them," Gael said solemnly. "I would have liked to watch."

Garis smiled. "Hoping to see your father contend?" he asked, stopping at an empty, somewhat clean table in the corner.

"Tristan is not our father, Garis," Gabriel corrected, pulling up a chair and seating himself. "He took us both in when we were still young. Our father has no legitimate children."

"Well, now that he has resigned himself to settling down with the fair Lady Talamarian, perhaps matters will change. Who knows, boys? Come this time next year, you might just be venturing home, to await the arrival of a new family member." Neither of them made any notion of care, one way or the other. After a moment, Garis flagged down a waitress, who, while young and supple, looked most distraught.

"Heading to the Cabal, are we?" she said, without making eye contact; her eyes otherwise busy, scanning the room nervously.

"These two young men are indeed." Garis chuckled, gesturing towards the two. "None other than the sons of Sir Tristan Stryfe, himself." To this, the young woman's eyes left her surroundings.

"Sir Tristan Stryfe, the Monster Slayer?"

"One and the same!" Garis cheered with pride. "Why, I can still remember when my father and I first delivered the man to the Cabal. Wondrous times, I tell you. I am certain one day soon, I will be telling others of the day I delivered you two." He laughed again, gently rapping on the table.

"Good afternoon, dear lady." Gael began after clearing his throat. "Might my brother, our escort and I ask what is on the menu for today? We have been traveling the length of the day and are quite hungry." Realizing that she was, in fact, the server of the establishment, she snapped back to attention.

"Of course. At present, the cook has cod stew and roasted potatoes prepared for the small army of guests we are expecting.

Would you care for some?"

"Ah, anything to warm these three travelers, young miss," said Garis. "Also, perhaps some cocoa for the boys and something with a bit more spirit for myself."

"I know just the thing." She smiled, quickly walking away from the table, her eyes again searching about the crowded tavern.

"Do not worry, young Masters." Garis said, leaning back in his chair. "They seem like unruly folk here, but the majority of them are seeking honest work. Were this the slums of The Wall, you may have reason to worry."

"I thought you said that Lower Lothren was a dangerous place for the young to wander about?" Gabriel asked.

"Aye, it still is. There are a great many vices here, seeking to take sway over young and old, alike. We will be just fine, so long as we stay here. Captain Tarkan shouldn't be too much longer."

"Captain Tarkan?" Gael asked.

"Aye. He is supposed to meet us here. While we wait, why don't you tell me what you plan on studying."

"I want to learn more about sorcery!" Gabriel chirped excitedly, causing a few eyes to wander over him.

Gael sat, half turned away in his seat as Gabriel and Garis, continued their conversation. After a moment, their waitress returned with food and drinks but was quickly lost amongst the crowd.

"Gael, are you going to eat?" Gabriel asked, tearing a roll in half and dipping it into his stew.

Gael grunted at his brother, his eyes still drifting away towards another table across the room.

There were two figures, one large and one small, clad in blackened leather, seated at the opposite table. Their hoods were pulled up over their heads, hiding their faces. Noticing that the boy was watching, one of the two figures stiffened in his seat.

As the figure stared at him, Gael felt a chill rising in the room. He turned to look at his brother and Garis, both of whom seemed undisturbed by the cold He shivered, and exhaled, noticing the frosty stream of his breath. A small smile crept across his face at the strange magic he was experiencing. It had not occurred to him that he should be concerned. Instead, he smiled wider, waved to those across the room, and returned to his stew.

"I see you have finally brought yourself from your daydream." Garis chuckled. "Whatever took you away?"

"The two hooded ones in the back of the room. They must be sorcerers."

Gabriel turned around and spotting the two, waved. "Do you think they are headed to the Cabal, same as us?"

"It is quite possible," Garis said. "Either they are preparing to leave, or they are just arriving. Not much opportunity for a Magus in the games, though. I would guess they are leaving on the same boat as you two."

"I am sure we will find out sooner or later. When is Tarkan supposed to arrive?"

"I believe that he just did," Gabriel said, pointing towards the door.

Turning to face the doorway, Gael saw a lone figure wearing a tanned leather cuirass with steel greaves and gauntlets. Crimson red cloth could be seen along the armor joints, with a dark hood, which concealed the figure's face.

Captain Tarkan, Gael presumed, was of average height with firm, rounded shoulders. The clank and jingle of the figure's armor echoed through the room as it marched towards the back of the room where the hooded Mages sat. As Tarkan passed, Gael caught the glimmer of a blood-red ruby, set in the pommel of the Captain's longsword.

As the Captain walked through the tavern, all eyes watched. Stepping in front of the hooded figures, they rose. The larger of the two hooded figures clasped wrists with the armored figure, while the smallest of the three bowed.

"Should we go and introduce ourselves?" Gabriel asked.

"I believe it would be best for us to wait," Garis suggested. Each continued to watch the exchange between the three until the taller two clasped forearms once more and separated.

As Captain Tarkan walked from the table, the small, hooded figure followed. Before their departure from the table began, however, Gael noticed the Captain's skilled and steady hand, resting upon the pommel of the longsword. Before any of the three men knew they were still staring, both figures approached their table.

"Are you the sons of Tristan Stryfe?" A neutral, genderless voice slithered within Gael's mind, making his skin crawl. Gabriel sat wide-eyed, fingers clenching the table as Garis sat in ignorance. Looking at his brother, Gael nodded his head.

"Follow me," the voice returned. Gael, Gabriel, and Garis, each stood as Tarkan looked to Garis, with a face still concealed by a hood.

"I shall take these two from your custody," the figure said, producing a folded piece of parchment from its side, handing it over to the coachman.

Garis accepted the paper, unfolding it several times, before reading. "All appears to be in order," he said, tucking the paper away and standing. "All of their belongings are..."

"Already loaded, I assure you," the voice said, then turned to the boys. "If you would follow me, we can be on our way." Captain Tarkan said, moving past them, the small, hooded figure behind.

"Thank you, Garis." Gabriel said, waving to the man energetically as they left.

"Thank you," Gael muttered.

Garis smiled in response. "Make us all proud, young masters. I plan on telling your story, too."

"We will." Gabriel cheered, only moving after Gael tugged gently on his collar.

Stepping outside, they were greeted by a sudden burst of wintry chill. Clutching their cloaks tightly to their bodies, they followed the Captain. She continued to lead them through Lower Lothren but stopped briefly as they entered Bay City.

"Hail!" A rough-looking group of men said as they drew near. Each was thickly muscled, with rough callused hands, which hung unerringly close to their swords.

"We are returning to the Cabal, now," Tarkan said. "It appears that there are only these three. Keep two trustworthy men behind to watch for late corners. I will return come the morrow."

"Of course, Battlemage," a well dressed sailor who appeared to be in charge, said. "A shame you cannot open one of them fancy portals." He laughed. "Though, I might need to find a new client, if you could."

"We each excel at and possess different specialties, Captain Blaze." Tarkan responded to the sailor with an aggressive tone. "I trust that discretion remains yours?"

Captain Blaze smirked and inclined his head. "Of course. This way, please. The *Gallows' Mare* awaits." He said, gesturing towards a massive, black stained vessel. Large, silver sails stretched out between masts the size of oak trees. All other vessels in the harbor paled in comparison to the ship.

Gael, Gabriel, Captain Tarkan, and the small, robed figure all followed the Captain of the *Gallows' Mare* and her crew, walking up to the steeply inclined plank to the upper deck.

Onboard, droves of people worked to prepare the ship. Others still, stood, arms at the ready, prepping mighty ballistae that peppered the deck. Four more children, only slightly older than Gael, stood towards the back of the galleon.

"Are those other students?" Gabriel asked, pointing at the youths, who were entering a cabin door, leading to the lower decks.

"Second years," Tarkan answered. "Most students keep to their own classmen, an exception being combat practice, specialized courses and such."

"Specialized studies?" Gabriel asked.

"Combat practice?" Gael added.

Tarkan stopped to turn their hidden face towards them. Studying the two for a moment, the Captain continued. "Yes, at the Cabal, you will be introduced to various fields of study. Every student shall undergo various aptitude tests to help determine where you will be best suited. You will receive more in-depth explanations once you begin your instruction. For now, I would advise the three of you to head down, below."

"Is it alright if we explore?" Gabriel asked. "I have never been on a ship before."

Tarkan continued to stare, pointing down towards the door. "Of course, you can. Below deck. Do try to stay out of trouble. Keep an eye on one another. Not all return students enjoy seeing competition in their midst."

Begrudgingly. Gael and Gabriel looked back to the third student and shrugged.

"Hello, I am Gabriel," the mousy haired boy said, extending his hand. The shrouded figure, opposed to returning the gesture, simply pressed between the two and walked past.

"Nice to meet you," Gael called, waving to their back as they slammed the door. "She seems friendly," he laughed.

"She?" Gabriel asked. Gael eyed his brother.

"You didn't notice? I thought it was obvious." Gael said, raising an eyebrow. "Long strands of violet hair, clinging to her clothes and stretching out of her hood. Then, there is her posture and..." He emphasized with a smile. "Did you happen to notice her small hands or smell her perfume?" Gabriel shook his head, irritable frown on his face.

"Obviously not, Gael," he sighed. "You are certain that Sir Tristan is not your real father?" They shared a laugh as they entered the hold.

Inside, a series of blue glowing flames encased in old fashioned lanterns guided them. Moving through the surprisingly well-lit decks, the brothers took the time to look upon those around them. They were passed by the occasional sailor, making their way between decks, carrying various supplies. In general, the halls proved to be barren.

"Where do you think everyone is?" Gabriel asked, looking back and forth.

"I am not sure. Let's go down another deck." Gael suggested, leading them further on. The growing murmur of voices and activity led them to the stairwell. Traversing downward, they rounded out at the second lower deck, where several more students could be seen.

Many of the students wore colors consistent with the higher born families of Altair. Green, silver, and bronze for Stromholdt; burgundy and gold for Reynald. Other noble families were present, though to which family they belonged, Gael could not be certain. They laughed and conversed in unison with some members shying away from the greater whole.

Eager to make new friends, Gabriel stepped close to the greater cluster of students and bowed his head respectfully. "Good afternoon, are you all headed for Cabal Island, as well?" A slow turning collection of irritable faces halted their conversations as they reared on the two.

"Everyone on this Gods blasted vessel is headed for the Cabal, you invalid," one of the boys, a handsome faced, raven-haired noble, bearing the colors of the Reynald family, seethed. "Pray tell which rabble family have you hailed from?"

Gael attempted to grapple Gabriel's arm, before he could further alienate himself, but failed.

"The Stryfe family," he smiled proudly, extending his arm. "Gabriel and Gael Stryfe," he added, motioning to his brother. "We look forward to studying with you." He allowed his sentence to trail off, waiting for the other boy to introduce himself. However, the raven-haired boy eyed them, whether with disdain or amusement, Gale could not be sure.

"From the house of Stryfe," the boy mused. "As in Torran Stryfe, Shield of Altair?"

"Yes, he is our uncle. Tristan Stryfe is our adoptive father." As the edges of the boy's lips curled, Gael recognized the formation of a cruel smile.

"Do you hear that, everyone?" he laughed, mockingly. "These two are the adoptive sons of the tramp hound, himself." Gael balled his fists as Gabriel continued to stare in confusion. "Please tell us what form of magic you two are adept with?" He sneered as a broad-shouldered, lean-framed boy approached.

" now, Reynald?" the boy began. "Can we keep your father's petty jealousies out of this? Some of us have come to the Cabal to shine on our own, with talent mind you and not our parents' money." Gael felt a slight tug on his shoulder as the boy pressed past him.

"And why have you come, Ruthger?" the cruel faced boy spat. Ruthger smiled.

"What can I say? Not all of us can build a life riding on our forebearers' coattails. No, I rather strike out on my own. Go where I please, when I wish it. It suits me better than having my orders relayed to me through my pampering servants." Neither of the boys knew the history between the two but the result was clear as a vein on the young Reynald's temple flared. The raven-haired boy's hands flashed with magic, as an off, icy blue hue radiated from his fingertips, and a strange, runic circle formed beneath his feet.

"A summoning it is, then?" Ruthger laughed, producing a pallid green light and matching rune of his own. While the two pushed their individual energies into their spells, the crowd of observers, swelled.

"A wood summoning." Reynald snuffed. "Predictable choice for someone on a ship."

"I see you have opted for a water type." Reynald's grin only broadened at his opponent's comment.

"Check again, you color-blind, illiterate oaf." Following the boy's suggestion, Ruthger's eyes widened at the darkening circle.

"Reynald! You would summon a Darkling in an enclosed space?"

"Just for you, I would," he answered. "Also, my family has a score to settle with the Stryfes. Two birds, one hungry demon." A bright light burst into the center of the room, causing everyone present to groan in anguish. A second later, Captain Tarkan stood at the center of the confrontation, both challengers on the floor.

"Do my eyes deceive me or do we have ourselves an unsanctioned duel?" The Battlemage boomed. An excited smile crossed Gael's lips, comparable to the one Gabriel displayed earlier. The term 'unsanctioned duel' proved music to his ears as he considered there must be sanctioned ones. Lying on the ground, Ruthger merely laughed.

"My apologies, Captain. It was just a small show for the newcomers, here. Reynald and I weren't going through with it. I do not even think he could summon a Darkling."

Tarkan spun on a heel to glare at the raven-haired, quite pale-faced boy. "Is this true, Duncan?" she growled as she stared at the terrified boy.

"Y...y...yes, Captain," the boy stammered. "I would never dream of it. They are too dangerous." He continued to play along with the other boy's ruse, despite the deathly looks he shot.

Tarkan's gaze shifted from one boy to the next, until the soldier's posture eased. "Very well. I would strongly advise both of you to remain in your cabins. In fact, it would not be a terrible idea for the lot of you to leave for your cabins." Tarkan turned on her heel in military fashion, before leaving the compartment.

"This is far from finished," Reynald growled, pointing directly at the brothers. "Ruthger cannot save you every time." The boy stamped away with his entourage, leaving the brothers in disbelief.

"Do not pay any attention to him," Ruthger laughed, dusting off his clothes. "He just likes to believe he is better than everyone else. In truth, his family is the only reason anyone takes him seriously."

"Thank you for your help, Ruthger." Gabriel said, extending his hand.

"Call me CJ," the boy replied, clasping wrists with each brother. They exchanged greetings before the larger boy waved as he walked away. They stared at the boy's back until he vanished into his cabin.

"Come on, Gabriel. Let's have a look about the ship," Gael suggested, enthusiastically.

His brother whirled around on him, eyes wide, head already shaking in answer. "Captain Tarkan said that we should stay in our cabins, until we arrive."

"But not that we had to," Gael added. "This is our first big adventure and you would rather just stay in the cabin?"

"We're heading to the Cabal, Gael. We are going to learn to manipulate the forces that make up the world and study the Convergence. We will have plenty of adventures."

"Fine," Gael sighed. "Suit yourself, but I am going up on the top deck." He walked away from his brother, scaling the stairs to the main deck. He passed few souls on his way, none of which paid him any mind as he walked by. Thrusting open another door, he filled his lungs with the salty air.

"What are you doing here?" Gael spun about to see a lone, tall figure looming over the door.

"I just wanted to look about the ship. I have never been on a vessel such as this before."

"Not that. Why have you returned?"

"Returned? I have hardly left." Gael answered in confusion.

The figure leaned forward, revealing a face too malformed to be considered human. "The flow of souls is constant." The halfling muttered to himself, his robes shifting uneasily. "Never too fast nor too slow, yet you've returned early." The man continued to mutter unintelligibly as Gael stared on.

Robes parting, the halfling reached out towards Gael with a blackened hand, which looked more elemental in composition than flesh. Fingers liking to ensnaring brambles reached towards him. Too stunned to move away or defend himself, he watched as one of the 'fingertips' touched his forehead.

A series of images flashed before his eyes. Fields of green, fetid, and died before his eyes. Flames engulfed cities, which stood tall as mountains. Children laughed and played with their parents, joyously until dark clouds loomed overhead. Over and again, the scenes of death flashed, until with a light jostling, he was back aboard the *Gallow's Mare*, anxiously shuffling from the tall, thin halfling.

Quick to distance himself from the halfling, Gael shook himself fervently, before stepping away. He stumbled about the swaying deck, eagerly dodging the sailors as they jeered and teased him. Not wanting to be trodden upon, he opted to move across the deck from the halfling and clutched the railing.

Staring out over the water, he attempted to peer through the thick wall of fog, which had formed. He could hear the floorboards of the deck groan as the sailors moved back and forth across them. Doing his best, he worked to make himself invisible between a stack of crates and fishing nets.

He sat in silence, listening to the angry waves as they crashed across the deck of the ship. His gaze drifted off somewhere far beyond the waves. A memory came to him of a much younger him, dirt-smeared face and innocent grin. He looked upon the unfamiliar child for a time, before the image flickered and he instead found the child covered in crimson with doll's eyes.

The spray of the waves splashed him in the face, recovering his senses. Sputtering from the chill, he rose to his feet and made for the lower deck. Seeing the halfling from before, still haunting the stairs to the lower level, he moved to those on the opposite side of the ship and made his way below.

As before, the lower deck was dimly lit. The blue lanterns provided the sole lighting as the fog-darkened sky allowed little into the portholes of the Gallow's Mare. Mindful of his footing, Gael descended the swaying stairs. Making his way beyond the lower levels where his and his brother's cabin awaited, he heard a sharp voice beside him.

"I am glad I found you." Gabriel chirped, bent in half as he attempted to catch his breath. "You need to see this."

Curious, Gael followed his brother as he sped further down the stairs, to the lowest level of the boat.

There was no crew below. Several crates and barrels were strewn about, sliding within the confines of the netting, which surrounded the cargo. Staring at the back of his brother's head, Gael followed Gabriel through a narrow walkway that traversed the gap between.

"Where are we going?" Gael asked.

"Shh." Gabriel responded, irritably, finger pressed firmly to his lips. "We do not want to be seen," He said nervously, carefully looking around. In the brief silence that came with his careful observations, they heard the gentle thud of boots striking the wooden planks.

Without sound or warning, Gael snatched his brother's collar and dragged him back behind the cargo netting. The boy quickly clasped his hands over his own mouth as he yelped from surprise. Carefully tucking themselves away behind a collection of crates and barrels, they listened carefully as not one but two pairs of boots, marched past their hiding place.

"Is this not an unnecessary risk?" a high-pitched voice whispered as the troupe marched through the cargo hold. "Can this not wait, until we've arrived?"

"I am afraid not." The voice was genderless, ominous; though Gael's sensitive ears could tell it was different from Tarkan's. "The girl's power draws forth the creatures lurking beneath the waves. It is a perfect opportunity for her to hone her gifts."

"Gifts? Surely, you mean curse?" The pitchy voice resumed. The footsteps continued until they were drowned out by the sound of a swinging door. Carefully, the brothers peeked out from their hiding place and stepped into the aisleway.

"We should head back." Gabriel groaned, turning back towards certain safety.

"Suit yourself." Gael grumbled, moving in the opposing direction. "I'm going to look."

"Gael," Gabriel cursed lightly under his breath. Following his brother, they both stopped another twenty paces down the narrow hall, where a heavy, oaken door awaited them. A small portcullis rested in the upper center of the door, allowing trace amounts of light from within the cargo hold to seep in. As Gabriel loomed closer, he found his brother already peering through a small corner of it.

Gently slapping his brother on the side, Gabriel glared into his smiling face, even as his own knees wobbled. "Are you trying to get caught?" He attempted to relay his frustration through a series of silent, hand gestures their father had taught them. Rolling his eyes at the cowardly boy, Gael returned his gaze to the room within.

Five figures stood within the room, their backs all turned towards the curious brothers. Four of the hooded persons stood within arm's reach of the door, while the fifth knelt at the room's center. Surrounding the kneeling form, a series of chalk lines were drawn within a large circle, which was outlined with blue flamed candles.

"A summoning circle," Gabriel whispered delicately into his brother's ear. With a large, though subtle wave of his arm, Gael shrugged off his brother.

"I am not an idiot. I remember my lessons."

Raising both hands in the air, Gabriel returned his gaze to the next room. A gentle glow of blue light was now emanating from the candles. The tiny figure within the circle shuffled lightly, though the other four remained inanimate.

The penitent person began swaying slightly as they poured over the chalk lines on the floor. Both brothers held their hands over their faces to conceal the sound of their breathing. They watched diligently, like statues, as the light provided by the flames rose higher, emanating from the lines of the summoning circle.

As Gael stared into the azure flames, he was no longer certain if he was breathing or not. Something lurking within the flames came forth, as if wishing to meet him. It hummed in his ears, even before bearing a physical form.

A hand reached from within the center ring of the circle, a hair's breadth from where the hooded figure knelt. A gust of wind assailed the room, despite the lack of breezeway. Everyone, save the summoner, braced themselves, keeping their concealing clothes in position. Violet hair fell free from its linen confines and the face of Tarkan's third ward came into view.

Startled, Gabriel gasped lightly as he stepped back. Gael however, remained fixated on the circle the same as each of the individuals on the other side of the door. Slowly, a hand crept out from the circle, reaching towards the girl's frozen form.

Her eyes were closed as a long, gangly arm met her at eye level. Adrenaline began to flood Gael's body as he dared to shove his shoulder into the door, toppling the nearest two of the cloaked observers. However, as though responding to his very concerns, both figures stepped forward.

The hooked fingers of the creature reached out, touching an invisible barrier. The nails grated against it, creating a sound, not unlike that of talons scraping on stone. The hand retracted slightly, while more of the unworldly beasts rose from the circle.

"That's a Drowner," Gabriel whined, sinking away once more. "They're a type of Darkling that's particular to the water."

Waving his hand irritably to silence the boy, Gael watched on as a scaly, fish-like head and torso were pulled through the *Gallow's Mare*'s woodworking.

"Gael?" Gabriel moaned, stepping away as the ritual continued, with the unidentified assistants pushing back against the creature. "Can we go, now? I don't think we are supposed to be seeing this."

Gael grumbled in the pit of his throat, watching even as the girl's hands pressed against the creature, forcing it deeper into the hole. Once the beast was back beneath the lower deck, he sighed.

"Fine," he relented. "But I get to pick what we see, next." As the light in the room faded, they heard the door hinges creak. Without a word, both brothers dashed to their hiding places behind the crates. They peered through a small gap in the cargo as the figures in the room left, one by one.

As their classmate shuffled past them, they could see the fatigue on her face. Sweat decorated her brow as she dragged her feet behind her. Once the entourage had left, only did the brothers resurface.

"That was close," Gabriel breathed.

Patting his brother on the shoulder, Gael led them away.

Peering out over the railing of the top deck, Gael attempted to see through the thick fog, which had set in. The world beyond the one hundred paces of visibility remained a mystery to him as the *Gallow's Mare* carried on faithfully forward. An aversion to the cold had turned his brother away, though Gael suspected more that what they had witnessed below was the true reason.

He shivered at the thought of the visions they had seen before, their new mysterious friend shut herself away. He heard a call high above from the crow's nest. Tilting his head towards the source, he saw the vague outline of a sailor, pointing out to sea.

Gale turned his head back towards the bow. Narrowing his eyes, he focused through the fog wall and smiled. Jagged fangs rose out from the depths, guiding them further towards a landing, which stretched onward, before fading. They had arrived at Cabal Island.

Chapter Two

Within moments of the island coming into view, Gael heard the booming growl of Tarkan's voice. Per the voice's instructions, he rushed back towards the entrance to the lower deck and growled at the sight of the sentry. Looking for a manageable entrance, he sighed when one did not appear.

"Excuse me, sir," he attempted, though the voice paid him no mind. "Pardon me, sir. The Captain needs me below." The dead-eyed guard grunted at him, once again motioning towards him with his necrotic hand.

"Get below, then," the man growled, stepping to the side. Gael silently thanked his luck as he passed the man unmolested. Below deck, hosts of people shifted about, gathering their things as they prepared to disembark

Moving through the lower decks, Gael quickly found his brother, who was fast at work, grabbing their belongings. They felt a shift as the ship came to a stop. Allowing themselves to grow used to the change in momentum, Gabriel threw his brother's pack to him.

"I was wondering if you were coming back." Gabriel smiled as he worked to fasten his cloak. "What do you think we'll see, next?"

"Hopefully, some action." Gael responded with some unnecessary enthusiasm.

Several of the older students laughed at him as they moved past them. Shrugging off their chortling, Gael continued looking about, the exit far from near enough. He noticed their new friend, CJ, up ahead, flanked by several other well-dressed students. Behind them, the young Reynald marched with scowling lackeys of his own. Glancing off to his left, he saw the young woman from earlier, still hidden beneath her hood.

"There you are." Gael smiled, moving over to the young woman. "Tarkan asked us to keep an eye on you."

"That will not be necessary," a sharp toned voice replied hastily.

"Is this your first time going to the Cabal?" Gabriel asked, moving beside his brother.

The head beneath the hood moved about nervously. "Yes, now please leave me alone," she said, continuing on her way.

"I guess she's just the unfriendly sort." Gael shrugged. "Oh well, we tried," he said, waving the incident off.

"Gael!" Gabriel grumbled in disbelief. "What if she is in some kind of trouble?"

"She is surrounded by mages, guarded by templars, on an island settled for the instruction of magic. I think that we can assume she is safe."

"That doesn't mean we should just ignore Captain Tarkan's orders!" Gabriel maintained his argument.

Ignoring his brother, Gael smiled broadly as he looked out over the vast landscape surrounding them.

Far off in the distance, they could see the outskirts of Lothren, despite not having been able to see the Cabal on the way in. Immediately, his mind blamed the happening on the magic of the island. He watched intently as the *Gallow's Mare* trailed off in the distance, off to gather their next batch of passengers, no doubt.

Their eager classmates continued to swarm off from the beach in droves, while others sat at the top of the hill, waiting. Gael growled lightly to himself as his eyes passed over the young Reynald and his gang, already making their unpleasantness known to their other schoolmates. He took pity on the trio of students who served as the noble's latest victims. Watching as Duncan and his entourage jeered and pointed at the distressed children, Gael grumbled angrily as he continued walking.

Further beyond them, he saw Cornelius, accompanied by a tall, red-haired woman and a shorter, although equally scarlet-headed man. They walked together, laughing at something CJ had done. As the group of upperclassmen passed Duncan however, they quickly plowed their way through the pack, dispersing the confrontation. Satisfied with the outcome, Gabriel stared at the back of his brother's head as he continued to follow the crowd up the hill slope.

Atop the small climb, they could see the main road, where dozens of coaches sat waiting. At the head of each coach, a strange, scaly horse was hitched. The animal stood high in the reins, it's companion, snapping lazily at it. A forked tongue lapped out at the cantankerous steed. Both brothers stopped before them, to stare in wonder.

"Dracomares," they gasped as they continued to stare. The reptilian beasts snorted and stamped impatiently as the students approached. With a helpful nudge from Tarkan, they followed her to one of the many coaches and boarded.

"Rinoa, try not to lose these two." The Captain said, motioning for the brother to be seated. The girl lunged forward in her seat, though her hood remained in place.

"Inquisitor Tarkan, I need neither an escort, nor two untrained bodyguards. I have managed by myself this far and I aim to continue as such." The mysterious young woman scoffed before turning away and faced the window.

"She makes a good point, Captain Tarkan." Gael scowled. "Usually it is better to leave the venomous ones alone. Otherwise, they force everyone around them to suffer." He imagined a slight shiver from the young woman, who continued to stare out the window. Tarkan however, continued to glare at each of them from behind the abysmal hood.

"Stay in the carriage until I collect you." The Captain growled once more, before slamming the carriage doors closed.

"At least we have a nice view," Gabriel said cheerfully. He sat across from Rinoa, though he made no initiative to prod her from her foul mood.

"I agree." Gael joined in, leaning against his brother to watch as the carriage rolled away.

"My name is Gabriel, by the way." The enthusiastic boy broke the awkward tension, extending his arm. "Pleasure to meet you, Rinoa. This is my brother, Gael," he added, receiving a cold shoulder from both his classmate and his brother, who rolled his eyes while turning to look out the window.

The hillside slopes quickly vanished, traded for a more alluring view of the mountain. As they came upon the first bend, a large hamlet came into view. Buildings made of sturdy-looking stone and topped with red clay, wood, and straw stood before them.

The village was ripe with activity. People of various sizes, colors, and occupation darted about, tending to the chores of their daily lives. The village was not quite so large as that of Leones but what they lacked in size they compensated with diversity. Several individuals garbed in thick, winter robes, stood about the center of the gathered crowds, performing feats of magic to adoring spectators.

A woman stood in the square, apathetically juggling balls of flame, seven at a time, while speaking to her adoring crowd. Across the square from her, another mage held his hands in the air, levitating large blocks of ice, carved in differing shapes. Further yet, two individuals held hands as the greenery around them grew rampantly, circling and twirling into a cascade of vines, until they formed hedges in the shapes of animals.

The brothers found themselves among the admirers as they stared with eyes wide from the vision. Their hooded riding companion stared as well. As they passed the spectacle, Gabriel turned to his brother.

"Do you think we will learn how to do things like that?"

"I would guess they learned it from somewhere."

"They are charlatans of the Cabal," Rinoa whispered. Gael and Gabriel both turned to eye her.

"How do you suppose?" Gabriel asked.

She turned to face them but quickly turned back around. "They perform lesser, yet flashier magical acts for spare coin. None of the villagers can use much magic and do not care that what they are seeing is not real."

"Just because it is an illusion, that does not make it less real," Gabriel huffed with disapproval. "I look forward to learning illusion magic."

"Suit yourself," she snuffed.

"I can see the potential uses," Gael smiled. "You could make an enemy see what is not there while hiding what is important."

"Exactly!" Gabriel yelped, glaring at the young woman, who continued to ignore him. The conversation soon died down as they took in the sights of the less developed areas. High above, they could only see the mountains and a tall, foreboding forest.

"All students, first-years, or otherwise are to remain within the carriages at all times," Tarkan ordered with a voice amplified by magic.

"Why?" Gael asked, aloud. "Is the forest dangerous?" He glanced over at his brother, who smiled.

"I knew you didn't read *The History of the Cabal*, he said, shaking his head. "The entire forest is filled with dangerous beasts and an unnatural mist that causes confusion to those who do not have proper protection against it."

Gael raised an eyebrow to his brother. "I thought that was why I keep you around? Bookworm," he teased as Gabriel narrowed his eyes.

"A few more brains and a little less brawn would not hurt you any," Gael shrugged at his brother with a smile on his face.

"I read, too. I just do not make a habit of studying everything." Gabriel shook his head and returned his attention to the view. The large, far-reaching branches of the trees scraped and scratched at the top of their carriage. They could hear the irritable snort of one of their dracomares as their burden grew harder.

Gael's eyes widened with anticipation as the sight of the confusing mists rolled ahead of them. Within the mist, he imagined he saw frightful forms prancing between the cover of the trees. The steeds snorted once more, before a bright light shined all around

---

them. He continued to watch in awe as the mists began to recede and the forms he had only thought he imagined, retreated. One after another, bright lights erupted from the following carriages that arched off to the left, down the steep path. Again, the brothers were in awe of the simple, yet grandiose uses for magic they had yet to discover.

"Did you read about that, as well?" Gael asked.

"No, not exactly," he replied, shock in his voice. "There was no real detail for what manner of enchantment that is used to move through the forest."

"Probably better for security that way," Gael whispered. "The majority of the world still hates us. Suppose you cannot allow just anyone to reach the Cabal." Rinoa shivered as they spoke, though further prodding did nothing for them.

They continued through the slow, winding paths through the forest, jolting at every bump in the night that drew close enough for the dracomares to snort at. With a few added scares, they reached the edge of the forest. The moment they broke through the tree line, all three gasped. High up above them, built into the mountain pass, was the Cabal.

A large, gothic castle rising from three shelves, stood the archaic structure, built from a combination of magic, masonry, and sacrifice. They imagined the countless secrets the structure housed, their mouths drying at the thought. Smiles crept across their faces as they continued their journey.

Coming up to the top of the hill, they came in sight of the massive iron portcullis, which sat open, high above great oaken doors. Before them, the lead carriages lined up, as one by one, wisping trails of smoke drew near, springing the doors open. The doors sprung, students slowly stepped out from the carriages and filed into the castle courtyard.

"I hope we are allowed to eat soon," Gael grumbled, patting his growling stomach.

"Me too," Gabriel chimed in, looking over to Rinoa, whose hands slowly crept over her own stomach.

Their carriage came to a halt. A moment after, a thick, smoky vapor smeared against the carriage windows. Curious, Gael leaned in closer. A face appeared in the mist, a woman's kind smile, which winked at him.

With a gentle *click*, the door slowly opened. Exhilarated, he turned back towards his riding companions, who had pressed their bodies firmly to the opposing wall. He chuckled at them, his sense of adventure tickled.

"Come on, you two. You do not want to stay here tonight, do you?" He rose to his feet and pressing the door open, stepped into the mist. Dancing wisps, giggling merrily, flew around him. Ghostly visages of men and women, dressed in elegant ball formal garb, floated about him, waving and laughing merrily. He continued forward, following their phantasmal parade towards the castle gates.

"Wait for me, you maniac," Gabriel yelled, trailing behind as he looked up at the many spirits warily.

"Hurry up!" Gael yelled back, a spritely tone in his voice. "Keep falling behind this way and Sir Tristan is bound to be disappointed."

At this, Gabriel's lip twisted. A few seconds later and his brother was again at his side. Rinoa stayed close to them, her concealing hood, shifting between the festive ghosts.

As they entered the great hall, they were caught in awe by the flashing panels of enchanted stone, which shifted from one scene to the next. He stopped to admire a star map, which had appeared. A ripple appeared in the panel, a river of twinkling lights dancing until they spread the length of the hall.

Stepping into the reflection of the illusionary ripple, a Highlands elk, with four, sturdy posts of antlers, stared out at them. It's eyes trailed Gael as he passed by. He smiled again as another wonder appeared in the next room.

Having followed the halls to a second set of massive, oaken doors, he stepped out into the great hall. A large arched, cathedral ceiling, lit with thousands of floating lights, twinkled above them. Large chandeliers hung at equal lengths down the ceiling in four lines, illuminated by brightly glowing candles.

Long tables sat end on end, stationed in between rows of chandeliers. He had entered the castle alongside a crowd of people. Now that they reached the hall, he looked about sadly at the seemingly empty room. After a quick scan, he counted roughly fifty heads.

"There are so few," Gabriel said.

"There will be more after winter has passed. Only those who wish to get ahead of their studies come during winter." A small, kindly-faced woman with bright pink hair said from behind them.

"Are you a student here, as well?" Gabriel asked, just as soon as his heart settled back into position.

The amber eyes of the woman grew wide as she laughed with a surprisingly deep guffaw. "Me? A student?" She laughed again, a slight trill to the tone this time. "My dear boy, I like you already." She continued to giggle as Tarkan approached.

"Madam Zerenia, I did not realize that you would be joining us for the winter classes?"

"Ah, Aurelia! What a pleasure to see you, my dear. However, I must protest the ghastly Inquisitor's armor you wear. Terrible lot, the Inquisition. Why you feel fit to continue wearing that ensemble is well beyond me." Noticing both Gael and Gabriel staring in confusion, Madam Zerenia smiled. "To answer your question, lovely boy," she said, reaching up to ruffle Gabriel's hair; "No, I am not a student. I shall be one of your teachers."

"An Artificier, to be precise," a tall, curvaceous woman, with long flowing hair of midnight said, as she drew near.

"Ah, Rowena Crowl," Zerenia said through gritted teeth. "What a pleasure to see that you are still here. How long has it been? Two, maybe three decades, now?"

The brothers turned their gaze upon the sinister-looking woman, who looked no older than their father. Aware of the secret to their father's youthful appearance, however, neither brother questioned Madam Zerenia.

"I do not see what matter the number holds," Rowena Crowl responded, clucking her tongue as she examined the ever-youthful back of her hand. "What are decades to a sorceress? I see that you too, have changed little since you graduated." To this, Zerenia smiled.

"Well, you know us gnomes. We may not count years in decades or beyond, but we still outlive most of the other races."

"Yes, it would appear so." The sorceress spoke with little actual care in her voice. "My question is, what has brought the Inquisition's fallen Battlemage to the Cabal?" she continued, glancing over Gael, Gabriel and Rinoa as she stared directly at Tarkan.

"That is between me and the council," Tarkan answered in her hollow, genderless tone. "Beyond that, Professor Crowl, it is none of your concern." The woman's eyes narrowed slightly before she sighed and stared up, through the shifting collages on the ceiling.

"Fair enough. If you would be so kind as to excuse me. I have matters I wish to attend before the evening is over." She turned from the group, quickly fading amongst the rest of the crowd.

"As if her leaving us was anything but a blessing," Zerenia grumbled as she looked to the brothers, kindly. "Alright then, dears. You have best be off to join the others. There is bound to be an announcement sooner or later." She smirked and then turned to Tarkan, placing her arm around the Battlemage's hips, which were at the level of her shoulders.

"I must say, dear, it is truly wonderful to see you, again. So, tell me all the latest gossip. I have been away from Altair for so long now, and I do wish you would catch me up."

"It would be my pleasure," Tarkan responded, looking back to her charges. "Rinoa. I want you to stay with those two," she commanded, more so than suggested. "I shall be back in short order."

"I do not require a babysitter!" The young girl growled, vehemently, her body trembling angrily.

Out of the corner of his eye, Gael noticed a minor, white twinkling emanate from her sleeve cuffs.

"All the same, do as I ask," the Captain responded, continuing to walk with the gnome. "So then, Madam Zerenia, where would you like me to begin?"

"By taking off that detestable hood," grumbled the pink-haired gnome. They could hear the sound of Tarkan's gravel-toned laugh as the two walked away.

"So..." Gael broke the silence amidst their entourage. "I suppose that we should go and have a seat, then?"

"Do as you wish, but leave me alone," Rinoa grumbled, stomping away from the others.

"What do you suppose is her problem?" Gael growled. "I would dare guess that she wants everyone to hate her." She paused briefly, before continuing her leave.

"I think she heard you," Gabriel sighed, glancing at his brother with disappointment.

"Like I care? We have been nothing but nice up to this point. She wants to be alone." He turned his gaze away from her retreating form and stubbornly crossed his arms.

"Then what do you want to do?" Gabriel asked. "I'm starving." Gael placed his right hand over his stomach as it answered for him.

"Let's still stay close to her If Tarkan is watching over us, while we are here. I would rather deal with a spoiled noble than an angry battlemage." He walked in the direction Rinoa had fled and seeing her in a secluded corner, dropped his pack beside the table several seats down. Gabriel sat beside his brother as the young woman glared at them.

"I am not going to be your friend and I do not appreciate the two of you attempting to be friendly." She growled at them as Gael looked anywhere else in the room.

"I wonder what and when we can start studying?" he said to Gabriel, who was digging around inside his bag. Noticing this, he leaned in closer. "Any more food?"

"You already ate it!" his brother grouched, withdrawing a small, woven kerchief from his bag. He felt the multicolored, silky smooth material, before depositing it in his pocket.

"That the one Shayna made for you?" Gabriel blushed slightly, before nodding his head.

"I am going to miss her." He mumbled.

"Me too. At least she will join us, next year. Plus, the Commander made sure that we could write as often as we wanted. I would not be surprised if we receive two or more letters per week." Gael said, encouragingly, patting his brother on the shoulder.

Gabriel smiled as he considered the thought. "You know what? You are right. I want to learn as much as I can, so we can show everyone when we get home."

Gael smiled at his brother's change in spirit. "And I have to get stronger, so I can join the Commander's band. A new adventure every day. See the world. Protect the Kingdom." A loud, mocking laugh interrupted his train of thought. The brothers turned to see Duncan and his entourage.

"You hear that, everyone?" He laughed as he looked back at the cruel smiles of the seven girls and boys who followed him. "This tramp actually believes it will make some use of itself in the world. I doubt they would even allow him a post at The Wall, let alone anything of importance." Gael rose to his feet, ears already tinged with red.

"Gael!" Gabriel spoke up, catching his brother's attention.

"See, there's a good boy." The cruel faced boy laughed, staring at Gabriel. "He knows when to back down to his betters."

"I just do not want him getting expelled," Gabriel muttered, though the others paid no attention.

"What is it going to be, tramp?" The boy continued his prodding. "Are you going to acknowledge your betters, or are you going to have a problem?"

"I would much prefer neither at this point." A soft, elegant voice spoke from behind them. All eyes turned towards a fair, dark-skinned woman with bright, hazel eyes. She wore long flowing robes, which reminded Gael of a desert oasis. He knew at once that she was from one of the many tribes of the Southern Continent.

"And who are you?" Reynald asked, a high sprung huff in his tone.

"My name is Niferi, and I am in my third year of study, here at the Cabal. While it is my desire for a peaceful resolution, I am required as a disciplinary member to remind you that only through battle practice, do we allow any fighting, here." Though no one had at first noticed, a thin sheet of ice had begun to spread from the woman's feet. Two of Reynald's entourage noticing this, tapped their leader's shoulder. Eyes growing wild with an irritable flicker, the Count's son glanced back at Gael, before addressing Niferi.

"There is no problem. Just bringing to light a few time-honored truths to our new friends. We were just leaving," he finished, carefully walking away to avoid tripping, though each of them slid, helplessly.

"And are you of the same mind?" Niferi asked, setting her eyes on the three still at the table.

"Yes, there is no problem."

Niferi raised an eyebrow to Gael as he answered. "Just remember not to catch yourself on my list," she said, coldly. "I do not enjoy collecting ill-behaved students. Save it for the dueling circle."

"Thank you for the advice," Gael said as she walked away.

Several more figures entered the hall, wearing various expressions. Many were students, while only two others, which could be distinguished as faculty arrived. While a few of the newcomers sat at their table, none looked alert enough to cause any bother.

A sudden, intrusively loud clap interrupted the dreary peace, followed by a ring of yellow and orange flames, which burst upon the podium at the far end of the room. All eyes shot towards the center of the commotion as a disembodied voice spoke from within.

"Welcome students!" It roared as the flames leapt to life, their tongues forming various shapes, which transitioned and flowed into the next as though they were water. "Are you ready to unearth the hidden potential locked deep within yourselves? Discover and study secrets of the lost ancients?

"Others of you will learn to conquer beasts, while others yet, to gain dominion over them. Will you help uphold the peace? Or even defend the realm? Here at the Cabal, the possibilities are limitless!" The flames burst to life once more, launching flame forged stags and flocks of birds into the air. The entire hall gasped with excitement as they watched the dancing figures flying around the room.

"Honor! Glory! Riches! Fame! All can be yours if you only seize it!" Reaching out, Gale managed to draw near to a prancing stag. The animal radiated a gentle heat but did not burn him as it continued running circles around the room.

"Now, to introduce you to your instructors!" The various animals; raven, stag, ferret, and so on, changed direction and charged towards the high tables. One after another, they dashed against the tables, producing bursts of bright light.

"Professor Crowl!" the voice cried as the raven exploded. Once the light cleared, Professor Crowl sat proudly, glancing over the room.

"Clavicus Boon!" was the cry, before the boar erupted, changing into a large, broad-shouldered man, with a mane of curly black hair and matching beard. The man smiled broadly, an intimidating expression from such a man.

"Professor Zerenia!" he called as the ferret burst and the pink garbed gnome stood in her chair to be seen. She waved cheerfully as the stag moved into position.

"Battle Master, Mareena Damcian!" The blonde-haired woman stood in soldier attire, wearing the colors of Dalmorith. Upon her hip, Gael saw her rapier, which for unknown reasons, unsettled him. She bowed her head to the room, before adjusting her gaze upon the final two animals, wolf, and owl.

"Captain Aurelia Tarkan!" Instead of the Inquisitor garb they had grown accustomed to, the wolf transformed into a woman. Ghostly white hair decorated a canted face with angular grey eyes. High cheekbones further accented a breathtaking face. She stood proudly, at the far end of the raised tables. Looking to her peers, she smiled boldly as Professor Zerenia waved to her. Smoothing out the slightest wrinkle in her black and silver robes, she turned her attention to an owl, which alone, remained aloft.

"Before I introduce our final, highly esteemed Headmistress, I wish to inform you that I am the Spirit of the Hearth, and it has been my great pleasure to entertain you this evening. Now, it is time to introduce you to the wonderful, the magnificent, champion of Dagger Falls, our Headmistress..." The voice was cut short as a trail of ice shot down the center of the hall.

In an instant, a pillar of ice shot skyward, forming a large stalactite, which branched out into hundreds of small, needle-like tips. The flaming owl dashed itself head first against the column, creating an eruption of snow, which showered upon the room.

As the confusion died down, a roar of applause split the silence. Allowing his eyes a moment to adjust, Gael stared at the very center of the high tables. There, a tall, dark-skinned woman stood, hands raised high. She appeared to be in the late end of her middle years, which Gael realized made her countless years older.

"Phyllida Caramoor!" the voice of the spirit returned, igniting every candle in the room. Phyllida stood, absorbing the applause a moment, before kindly asking for silence. A moment later and several jars to the ribs of the younger students, the room grew quiet.

"Good evening, students and faculty." She spoke with a commanding voice, which radiated both power and kindness. "It warms my heart to see so many new faces in this room. While many more will be certain to join us in the coming months, it is your dedication to mastering your craft, which has brought you here.

"Work hard and live plenty. Be sure that your time here at the Cabal, is invested without regret. It is a frightful world out there and we need each of you at your best. I look forward to seeing what you all make of yourselves. But first, let us gain strength." The woman clapped her hands. In less than a single blink of an eye, she was gone and their tables were filled with food.

A steady flow of saliva had already begun to accumulate, before Gael had the opportunity to fill his plate. Large portions of roasted ham, poultry, potatoes, and freshly baked rolls, steamed with heavenly aromas. Desserts, some recognizable among other, extravagant delicacies, were piled high, tempting his every fiber.

"Finally!" Gabriel gasped, immediately tearing into the many offerings. Surprised at his brother's wolfish enthusiasm, Gael watched the usually reserved boy, savage his food a moment, before following his example. Piling their plates high, they feasted until their stomachs grew heavy. As the feasting came to a close, the flames within the hearth again roared to life.

"I hope that everyone has eaten their fill," the formless, masculine voice manifested. "It is now time for us to clear the hall. If everyone could please file behind your sponsors, we can be on our way." All around the room, students rose from the many benches and formed lines behind one of the many professors.

"I guess we should follow Captain Tarkan?" Gael suggested, mouth half-filled with food. Gabriel nodded his head as he stood, along with Rinoa. Approaching the non-existent line behind the Captain, the exotic-looking Tarkan stared at them, sternly.

"Are you three ready to see your rooms?" She asked with a command more than a question. All three answered with a single nod. "Good. Follow me, then. You will want to be well-rested for tomorrow."

"Do we start training, tomorrow?" Gael asked, excitedly. Tarkan raised an eyebrow to the boy.

"He wants to be either a Templar or a Battlemage." Gabriel explained as the lights in his brother's eyes brightened. Tarkan continued to stare.

"You will begin general studies, starting tomorrow. You will need to wait until your third year before you decide your general profession."

"General studies?" Gael repeated the phrase. "So, combat arts, monster-slaying, battle magic…" he allowed the comment to trail off.

"I was thinking mathematics, writing, history, and such." She smiled as Gael's expression sank.

"We will be learning magic still, right?" Captain Tarkan allowed her gaze to linger a moment, causing Gabriel to twitch nervously.

"Of course, along with combat practice. Do not for a moment, however, suspect that your time at the Cabal will be leisurely. Your courses will be grueling, as will be your training. You will be partaking in academic studies, alongside everything else."

"Training?" Gael asked. Tarkan sighed.

"Yes, young Stryfe. Training. Every student in the Cabal should be trained as a soldier and academic. The King's army may tolerate its share of invalids wielding deadly blades, but for those rare few gifted in the magical arts, who may very well reshape the world around them, incompetence will not suffice."

As Captain Tarkan proceeded down the smooth, shined floor, the pounding of her bootsteps echoed down the hall. Gael, Gabriel, Rinoa, and several others, who joined their party late, followed the Captain. Eyes scanning every detail in the hall, the entourage's travel through the ancient halls was slowed.

"There are a number of enchantments in this hall. I would advise all of you to show caution when channeling any spell. You never know when a stray spell or even an imbued phrase will set something off." As though to orchestrate her point, Tarkan stopped as they came close to a rather gruesome looking gargoyle, which sat upon a perch on the landing.

Leaning near to what Gael supposed served as the gargoyle's ear, Tarkan whispered. A second later, dust scattered from the surface of the statue as stone joints bent and flexed for the first time in possible ages. Next, the creature crawled along the railing of the landing, until its hooked nose was near enough to sniff the Captain's hand.

"This is Persecles. He is but one of many living gargoyles here at the Cabal. While he is friendly, there are many others who become volatile, once they are awakened. Do not take him lightly, however. If you find yourself on Persecles' bad side, you will likely not live to make amends."

The small gargoyle carefully climbed onto the Captain's outstretched arm and fastened itself around her shoulders. As it stretched itself, Gael took notice of the pointed hooks at the end of each finger and the pointed barb at the end of its one and a half arm length tail. It looked from the Battlemage to the many students, carefully examining each one.

"Can I touch him?" One of the latecomers in their group questioned. Looking to the small, timid young woman with freckled cheeks and long red hair, their instructor nodded.

"You may," she said tipping forward slightly, extending the creature forward. Persecles eyed the students cautiously, watching as slowly, the five of them drew near. Gael, the first to draw close, reached out calmly and placed his hand against the smooth, stone surface.

"He is warm," Gael gasped, lightly stroking the creature. Persecles closed his eyes in elation as it cooed. A moment later, the barbed tail uncoiled and rewound itself around Gael, whose heart pounded from surprise.

"It appears that he likes you." Tarkan smiled. "Do not be nervous. He will feed off from your energy." She allowed the gargoyle to continue its transfer from her to the elated boy. "Slowly, one at a time, now. Come now. It will be alright." Gabriel approached next, petting the heavy creature, which secured its grip on Gael's shoulders. One after the other, two more of their entourage joined in. Rinoa, who came last, shook with nervous energy. Gale winced as he felt the sharp talons gripping his shoulder.

"It is alright, Rinoa. Persecles will not hurt you. Just take it slow." Rinoa's eyes only widened as the gargoyle's gaze met her own. It opened its maw and emitted the slightest of squawks as Tarkan cleared her throat.

"That is enough for now. Come here, Gael. Place your arm over the lattice, here so he can climb down. Persecles cannot fly and you do not want him to jump down."

Gael did as instructed, placing his outstretched arm over the railing. Laying his palm down on the platform, he felt the stone tail's grasp on his arm loosen.

"Well done, Gael." Tarkan praised. "It seems you have inherited your father's gift for tending to beasts."

"Do you know the Commander?" Gabriel asked.

A kind smile still on her face, she nodded. "I do. However, that is a story for another time. Come now, children. There is still plenty more castle to see. The living quarters for the first years are this way." She added as the tour resumed. Gael looked back briefly and watched as Persecles became inanimate once more.

The rest of the castle buzzed with activity as various wisps of light skirted from place to place. They varied in color, from silver, gold, emerald, and ruby. Though they had never been much for celebrating the solstice, they were well acquainted with its intricacies.

"Are those wisps?" Gabriel asked.

"Yes, they are, Gabriel," Tarkan answered. "Excellent work identifying them. Not surprising for your upbringing."

"But why are they colored so? Are they not usually blue?"

"Typically, yes. In rare cases, they can take on a pinkish hue. However, these wisps you see here, were enchanted." The students stared at the wisps a moment as they climbed the stairwell. Every so often, one of the twinkling lights would fade away.

"Why are they disappearing?" Rinoa asked, though her question was barely audible.

"Are they dying?" The red-haired student gasped.

"No, they are not dying," Tarkan responded. "The wisps you see above are simply magically produced, festival lights. Once the magic powering them fades, then so do they."

"So, they are dying?" Gabriel asked.

"They are no more alive than a lit candlewick. They are made with a certain lifespan. Once their wick is expended, they vanish. That is all."

"Will we learn how to create such lights?" Gael asked.

"You will. They likely will not have the same shape, but a simple light spell will be part of your general studies."

"What other spells will we learn?" Gabriel gasped, his enthusiasm rekindled.

"We will wait until after your aptitude tests," Tarkan answered, reaching the top of a third staircase. Turning left on the landing, she led them across the hall. "The living quarters begin here on the third floor. It is another two floors to reach where you five will be staying." Along the walls in these halls, the décor became much more inviting.

Lavish, maroon drapes hung around the broad, frost-covered windows. Bright lights filled the hall with warmth and color. Students of varying ages marched about independently.

"Through here," Tarkan began, motioning towards a hallway to her left. "Is the common area, where you can relax and mingle with your peers. I would advise against spending much time in the other areas where you are not meant to be."

They took the next stairwell, which led to a similarly decorated room. Again, they were not permitted to see the commons as they continued around the bend in the stairwell and climbed to the higher floors.

"Here is the first year commons," Tarkan stated, turning down a long hallway on the third floor of the dormitory tower. A few other students had already arrived and stood beside their sponsors. Professor Crowl stood at the far end of a massive hall, which funneled out into numerous other hallways. She and her brood, Reynald and his friends among them, traveled down one such hall, out of sight.

The five students looked about the room, taking in the vastly colorful and warmth filled room. Two fireplaces, one at each far end of the room, roared with activity. Numerous accommodations were set before them, inviting the weary students to rest.

At one end, large, double glass doors opened to a small balcony. Staring through the windows beyond the frost, they could see snow. Hailing from the countryside, the brothers instinctively pulled their cloaks tighter.

"To the left, here, are the boys' dormitories. Girls are on the right. I would advise everyone again, to avoid going where you are not meant to be." As she spoke, another troop, led by the massive, Professor Clavicus Boon, moved about on their tour. Among them, a lanky, sleepy-eyed boy, broke away from his party. With a yawn fit for a lion, he stumbled down the hall leading to the girls' dormitory.

A moment after, a flash of light caught the attention of every student and professor present. There was a *thud*, which was followed by the *clicking* and *clacking* of boots as everyone from the boys' troop charged towards the girls' dormitory.

"Again, it is important you do not stray from where you are meant to be," Captain Tarkan said, shaking her head as Professor Boon reached out with one massive paw and as though pulling an invisible lasso, pulled the boy from the hall.

"Is he dead?" The small, dark-haired boy asked as he cowered behind the rest of the pack. The Captain stared at the boy with a raised eyebrow.

"No," she replied sharply. "The light you just saw only stuns." Taking a few, short steps forward, she guided them to face the commotion head-on.

At the far end of the hall, a stone creature not unlike Persecles, slithered about on a serpentine body. A woman's expressionless face rested upon a stone, human torso. The bust appeared covered by strips of linen, which had been carved into the stone.

The statue glanced towards them, specifically at Gael, Gabriel, and the third boy in their group. Her gaze remained fixated on them as she slithered back to the doorway. There, she pressed her body against the wall and solidified as silently as she had come to life.

"Was that a lamia?" Gael asked. Again, Tarkan raised an eyebrow.

"Keen eye, young Gael. Yes, Callia was carved into the shape of a lamia. It was a fitting form, considering her power to stun anyone of the male persuasion. Rinoa, if you and Mari wish to turn in, you may. You will find your belongings are already by your beds."

"Thank you," the newly announced Mari said as she started down the hall, cautiously stepping around the commons area and turned her gaze back to her sponsor.

"Rinoa, it will be fine. I will be back, shortly." Without a response, the young girl turned and walked away. "If you three will follow me, then," Tarkan said, turning away. "I will show you where you will be staying."

"Umm, Professor?" Mari returned, an embarrassed look upon her face.

"Yes, Ms. Tallow?" She said, turning about to face her charge. The young girl looked to the floor, wringing her hands with embarrassment.

"I didn't bring anything besides this," she sighed, clasping protectively to a roughly woven bag in her hands. Tarkan's gaze softened, before responding.

"Liberties were taken to ensure you had what you required. You will find your name upon them beside your bed." The girl's eyes shone brightly as relief washed over her.

"Thank you, so much," she exclaimed, charging back down the hallway, flying past Rinoa, who huffed.

"Boys, if you would follow me, please." Tarkan resumed her tour without further pause.

They walked towards the far end of the room, where Professor Crowl had vanished earlier. Moving down the hall, they found the warmly decorated hall welcoming. At the far end, a statue similar to the one guarding the girls' dormitory stood. This one eyed them carefully, canted eyes embedded within the face of a goat. It stood on two legs, which ended in hooves. As the others stared carefully, Gael smiled.

"Satyr," he said, confidently.

"Again, it seems as though your father has taught you well," their guide mused.

"Rosalind handled most of our schooling,." Gabriel chimed in. "The Commander mostly drilled us on our defensive lessons."

"Hopefully, those lessons stuck, then. You will find yourself at a disadvantage otherwise. Here, we do not waste time playing catch up. You either have what it takes, or you do not," she said, stopping halfway down the hall. "Here you are. All your things are awaiting you upon your beds. Yours, as well, Mr. Mathers," she said, looking to the mousy boy who continued to cower in the back of the troop. He nodded his head, nervously as he retreated down the hall.

"Thank you, Professor," Gabriel called, before retreating down the hall. Tarkan inclined her head as the other two boys exchanged their thanks. They paid no attention to any further details as they shuffled into the dormitory and found their beds.

As Tarkan had said, they found their trunks already on their beds. Not even bothering to unpack, they sat their belongings on the floor and climbed into their beds. No sooner had Gael landed upon the soft mattress, did he fall asleep.

J.A. Bullen

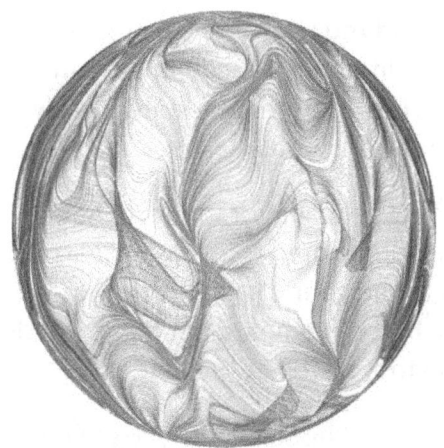

CHAPTER THREE

They awoke the following morning to the sight of a white sheet, which fell from the sky. Dim flames had ignited on sconces scattered about the room of their accord. Using that light, Gael took his first glances about the room.

Each student had been assigned a four-post bed, which was decorated with a vibrant, crimson bedspread. The bed, nearly twice Gael's size, formed around him, unlike anything he had experienced previously. Peeling himself from the bed, he looked at the others in the room.

His brother was still asleep, lying in the bed opposite from him. The boy had not even noticed the torch lights, one of which was mounted near to him. Turning himself about, he stared through the vastly empty room. The other boy in their group still slept, as well. Looking at the initials on the boy's trunk, Gael sighed.

"Suppose I might as well have a look around," he said aloud, before rising from the bed. Eying his traveling clothes, which he still wore, he stripped down and exchanged for fresh. Donning an emerald tunic and tan breeches, he reached for a sweater, which Rosalind had sewn for him. Assured that he was ready to begin his day, he exited the room.

First, he found the restroom, located at the far end of the boy's dormitories. Within, he found himself amazed by the running water the facilities incorporated. He stared in awe several minutes, before utilizing the washroom.

Rejuvenated, he made for the first year commons. Stepping into the room, he approached the nearby hearth. Sitting opposite of Rinoa, he looked to the gentle roar of the flames. A few, silent moments passed, before he heard her make the slightest of irritable scoffs, though she too, stared at the flames.

"Good morning," he said softly, stretching himself.

"Do you intend to follow me for the length of our stay?" She turned her head to look at him and he saw his first true glance at the young woman.

Her violet hair was worn in gentle curls, which dropped past her shoulders. Her eyes, a deep, dark blue, stared at him inquisitively as he continued to examine her. Her features were immature for her age and her lips pursed unattractively as she continued to glare.

"Those intentions ceased some time ago," he answered, a cold tone in his voice. "I try not to invest too much of my time with unpleasantries. That is a nobleman's job."

"And yet, here you are," she stated.

"Can we just agree that neither of us desires the other's company? I only wished to enjoy the fire. I can visit another hearth." She rose as he spoke and stared more intently.

"No. It is fine. I had lost interest long before you arrived," she replied angrily, her tone trembling slightly. As she stamped away. Gael shrugged the happening off. As he sat in front of the fire, he thought of his family.

"I will have to write them a letter tonight," he thought aloud to himself. Continuing to stare at the fire, he listened as several of the other first-year students arrived.

"I wondered where you had gone to," Gabriel said, taking the seat where Rinoa had been. "Couldn't sleep?"

"No, I slept just fine. You just oversleep."

Gabriel smiled at the comment. He too, sat staring at the flames, fingers tapping on the cover of the massive book in his lap.

"Good morning, boys," the energetic dark-haired boy said as he stood between them. "Should we get on with it, then?"

"Get on with what?" they asked. "Has class already begun?" The other boy laughed.

"Of course not. Today is placement day. We will not start regular studies until after that. No, the Inquisitor is on her way up the stairwell, now. After that, she will escort us to the breakfast hall, where massive trays of food will be waiting." The boy's eyes continued to swell as he stared off absentmindedly into the stonework of the hearth.

"Are you crying?" Gabriel asked, examining his peer.

"Course I am," the boy replied proudly. "All of that delicious food. An all you can eat buffet. You'd have to be noble-born not to be moved."

"I suppose so," Gael responded. The boy eyed him.

"Do not tell me that you two are among those snotty nobles? They are all supposed to be housed in a separate wing."

"Our adoptive father was brought up in a noble family, but he holds no title. We have a farm back home, though."

"Your family has land?"

"Yes. My brother, myself, and the rest of our family all work the land together. It is hard work, but we are happy." The boy continued to stare in disbelief, shaking his head as he muttered to himself.

"Were you and your brother conscripted?"

"No," Gael laughed.

"Then why are you here?"

"Pardon?"

"If you do not have to be here, then why are you?"

"The Cabal allows military candidates but is by nature, politically neutral," Gabriel instructed their peer. "You do not need to be conscripted in order to be here. You just have to be accepted."

"And afford the entry fee," The other boy grumbled, kicking absently at the floor.

"Were you conscripted?" Gael asked. "I did not realize Altair was doing such."

"They are not, with few exceptions. I am here, because of the title and the money the King pays for servicemen. With both, I can get my mother and sisters out of The Wall." His gaze trailed off for a moment as Gael looked away.

"I suppose I do not have such a reason," he responded. "I just don't want people to live in fear of their own neighbors."

"Good morning," Mari chirped, entering the room. Her long, red hair had been pulled back into a braid, which fell over her back. As she moved to sit beside them, she smoothed out a wrinkle in her military-style garments. Her uniform was the same colors as the Altairan royal family; silver, red, and gold. She sat straight-backed upon the nearby bench, keeping a proud smile on her face.

"You were already conscripted?" the boy gasped, staring at the young woman's matching wardrobe.

"I was. I accepted my offer three weeks ago."

"But how?" he continued to pry in exasperation. "We have not even taken our placement tests."

"Klein, I already told you that a group of Cabal agents was present at my awakening."

"You mentioned that they sprung you from your cell," he replied. "You did not say that you were recruited directly after."

"Well, that is what happened. When they mentioned that I had awakened, it did not take long for the local Lord to field the order."

"What happened during your awakening?" Gabriel asked. At this, the young woman's eyes dropped, and her cheeks took on a slight blush.

"My hands and arms burst into flames and I panicked. I burnt down a couple of stalls, startled half of the town square, and nearly scalded a guard to death." Gabriel nodded his head as he listened.

"It was different for me," Gabriel sighed. "My mother was burned at the stake, while I was still small. I can barely remember her face. As far as I recall, I never had an awakening. I was able to use the gift before I could walk. At least that is what I have been told."

"I am sorry, Gabriel." The young woman spoke, turning her head downward in regret.

"I am not upset by it, now. My story is not too uncommon."

"What about you?" The young boy in the group asked, staring at Gael.

"No. I am not a sharer. When are we supposed to begin our studies?"

"Soon." All heads turned to face Tarkan, who had just entered through the opposite end of the wing. "If you would all follow me, we will begin with a trip to the Great Hall for breakfast.

"Today, I shall be escorting you to your classes to meet each of your instructors. Tomorrow, a representative shall take my place. Later tonight, each of you shall undergo divination, a process which will better guide our instruction." Without another word, Tarkan strolled back through the entrance she appeared from.

Quickly falling in line, they followed their sponsor back to the Great Hall. Again, finding themselves marveling at both the castle's magnitude and its décor, they looked at the many moving statues and ghostly portraits. Reaching the Great Hall, they witnessed many of their peers, already filing in.

Walking into the hall, they quickly found their way to their tables. While the remedial class consisted of only a few of the many students, who would be in attendance, the first several tables were filled. The various sponsors stood near their respective students, Tarkan lurking at the head of their table.

Gael looked about the massive room, observing the other instructors as they led their wards within. As they had the day before, the assembled tables quickly filled, though their occupancy was still dwarfed by the grandiose Great Hall. Without the theatrics of the day before, the teachers moved to their individual places at the head table. Unlike the night before, he noticed nearly half the seats were empty.

The instructors looked to one another, smiles on their faces as they waited for the center seat to be occupied. Soon, the doors to the hall burst wide open, and Phyllida marched into the hall, brow furrowed. Behind her, several armored forms marched for the castle exit.

Looking to her students, the creases at the corners of her mouth eased and she walked with purpose to the deep end of the hall. As she strolled, sprinklings of winter crystals floated from the ceiling. Turning, she faced the students assembled and smiled. Looking back to her fellow instructors, she cleared her throat.

"Today, you will begin your remedial studies. It is our aim to get the lot of you up to speed with your fellow classmates. Typically, you would not be allowed to join our ranks so late into the academic year."

The magical snowflakes continued to fall, accumulating across the tables and floor as their Headmistress continued her speech. The magic on the tables began to interweave, forming a rich tapestry running the tables' length, where before they had been bare.

"However, as each of you has been sponsored and received outside tutoring by alumni, we have made exceptions. I would still caution you not to be fooled. The circumstances of your entry in no way suggests that you will succeed along with your peers who are on leave.

"I believe that each of you is familiar with your instructors who have chosen to tutor you. Your sponsor shall guide you to your classes for today, your class representative, tomorrow." A small commotion rattled on the other side of the oaken doors, snatching everyone's attention. Unable to peer through the doors, their eyes returned to the Headmistress.

"I suppose it would also be prudent to remind everyone that the forest at the edge of the campus is off-limits to all students for both your safety, and the safety of this establishment. I strongly advise all of you to avoid the restricted areas."

At the sound of her last two words, Gael's attention peaked. Mind curiously wandering towards the dark corners of the Cabal, a slap to the arm from his brother brought Gael back to his senses. He flashed a glance at his brother who silently urged for him to pay attention.

"Now, children, without further interruption; breakfast." As Phyllida raised her hands to shoulder level, the piles of snow burst, revealing platters of food that ran the length of the tables. The students cried out in surprise and delight as hams, eggs, sausages, and countless other breakfast foods appeared before them.

"Food!" Klein and Mari both called, their voices scarcely audible amongst the other voices in attendance. Startled by the sudden burst of energy from their classmates, both brothers sat back in surprise. With only slightly less enthusiasm, they began filling their plates.

As they sat, platters mounded with eggs, sausages, and potatoes, Gael looked around at the others in the hall. Absently chatting to themselves between heaping mouthfuls of food, they paid him no mind as they socialized. It was at that moment, a group of students down the table caught Gael's eye.

"You from Leones?" a large, barrel chested boy with a seemingly small head and mousy hair said.

"Yeah," he grunted in response, stabbing a mouthful of eggs and shoveling them into his mouth. "So?" he continued, food still in his mouth.

"Recognized the insignia on your things. You a Stryfe?"

"Got a problem with that?" His confrontation with the Reynald boy was still fresh in his mind.

"Gael, be polite," Gabriel snapped, slapping his brother in the arm. "Yes, we are. Gabriel and Gael Stryfe." The energetic boy extended his hand, which the stranger shook.

"A pleasure, then." the boy answered, his enthusiasm uncurbed by Gael's temper. "Lionel Rolands, third son of the

Rolands family. My oldest brother fought alongside Baron Stryfe and his sons in the last excursion with the Dalmoritihians. Nice to meet you."

"The pleasure is ours, right Gael?" He kicked his brother in the shin, this time.

"Of course, it is." Gael choked, nearly spitting egg and potato down his front. "Your father is part of the King's council of advisors, is he not?"

"Well, more like my mother is a confidante of Queen Lorian, but yes." The boy turned sideways, nudging the young woman beside him, who scowled at her peer, before looking where he pointed.

"This is Emma," Lionel started. "She is from the Tisreen family."

"Belonging to the eastern province of Talis," Gabriel finished the introduction, himself. "Our brother, Nero worked a few jobs in your territory. He doesn't talk but we've heard about the host of spectres he helped with."

"Nero?" Emma began. "Tall, scary guy with a scar."

"Right across his throat. That's him." Gabriel said, happily.

"Old battle wound," Gael grumbled, continuing to show disinterest in anything but his breakfast. "He got it when he was a child."

"Along with a charming, nightmarish personality," Emma sighed. "Your whole family is not as scary as he is, are they?" The brothers looked to one another, confused looks on their faces.

"Scary?" they both asked one another aloud. Shrugging their shoulders, they left the greetings aside and continued with their lunch.

Tarkan, sharing a final laugh with her gnomish friend, moved from the high table and stopped before her students. "Are you all ready for your tour?" she asked, a lighter, more energetic air about her.

"Yes, ma'am," half the table answered as a mob voice, while rising from their seats. An angled smirk creasing the edge of her lips, she looked to the open hearth.

"Does the Spirit of the Hearth wish to serve as our guide today?" The flames at first, only flickered dully. After a brief pause, however, forked tongues leapt from the center of the hearth, forcing the students gathered around it to back away.

"Aurelia!" The voice of the Spirit roared to life as an ethereal face appeared within. "My apologies, My Lady. I was preoccupied with a matter upstairs. What can an old specter such as myself do for you?"

"I thought I might invite you to take a part in our tour today. Would that be of interest to you?"

The face within the hearth hesitated as it glanced up and away from them. "I might accompany you a moment. Lady Phyllida has made herself quite clear that she requires my attention this evening. I do suspect I might accompany your students halfway, however."

A smile creased Aurelia's lips as she reached for a candelabra with four unlit candlesticks. "Shall we, then?" the teacher said, motioning forward with a smile. What Gael continued to imagine were eyes, traced over the candelabra.

"I suppose we should be on our way," the flames said as a flare leapt from within the hearth towards Tarkan's outstretched arm. The children all jolted back as the candle wicks roared to life.

"Now, children," the voice said, emanating from the candelabra. "If you would follow us. We shall begin our tour by taking a gander about some of your classrooms." Smiling, Tarkan led on, holding the illuminating Spirit high as she walked.

"First off, on your left, you will see a lovely portrait of the High Lady Wolfren, matriarch of one of the original, Nine Noble Houses in Altair. Now, now, children. Take heart. She was much more fearsome in life than in this still."

"That doesn't keep her from giving me the willies, now." Klein stammered, teeth clattering as they looked to the fierce-eyed and strict postured woman in the painting. The slight animation of the enchanted portriat, gave her an added aspect of terror as she summarily examined each of the people in front of her, before returning her attention to her stationary.

"Ah, yes. That was indeed some time ago. I remember it like it was only last century." The Spirit's audience members quickly glanced at one another as they continued to follow. "Moving on." The candelabra resumed the tour, introducing them to various figures depicted within the paintings, ranging from famous noble family heads to the lecherous Baron of Teruza, whose wife transformed him into a dancing toad for his various indiscretions.

"Ah." The spirit interrupted its own tale, regarding a casual affair between him and a portrait of a rather disagreeable looking fellow. While the tale of their battles was cut short, they each chuckled lightly at the Hearth Spirit's regaling of setting the cantankerous man's rump on fire. "Here, we have come to the first of many classrooms, within which your eager minds shall be molded."

The tour stopped in front of the average-sized room, which at the Cabal secretly meant the room was larger than most commoner homes. Easily adequate in size to teach several dozen students, they stopped before the doors. Upon the stone floors, several large tables stood in two rows, running half the length of the room. At the far end, stood an archaic desk surrounded by cages.

"Here, we have Professor Boon's classroom. When he is not traveling about with his own troop of students, he shall serve as Beastmaster and instructor. From him, you'll learn about the anatomy of many creatures."

Turning from the room, Tarkan led them down the next hall. The Spirit introduced them to each of their classes, one by one, until early into the afternoon.

The Spirit of the Hearth had a way with storytelling that entranced even Gael. Each tale it told was vastly different from the one before and accompanied by the Spirit's own interjection of comedy and commentary. By the time they reached the stairwell leading to the third floor, half the entourage had already been brought to tears, while Gael and Rinoa both kept a protective hand over their sore abdomens.

"Well, children, Dear Aurelia," the gentle flames said to them, "I fear that I must take my leave of this thrilling venture." While the five students each emitted a groan of discontent, Tarkan bowed her head to the candelabra.

"We thank you for your time, Master of the Hearth." She began, tipping towards the nearby fireplace. The flames upon the candle wicks leapt from her hands, forcing a burst from the mantle.

"It has been my pleasure, Aurelia. If you will excuse me, students, I must return to my previous tasks." Without further warning, the face within the fireplace vanished, leaving nothing but the empty crackle of the magic flames.

"Now, students." Tarkan began, placing the candelabra back on the mantle. "There is one final room on this floor. You will visit the lower levels of the castle, tomorrow." She said, gesturing towards the room near to the start of the tour.

"Which instructor teaches here?" Gabriel asked.

"I do." All eyes jolted from the room back to their sponsor.

"What do you teach, here?" Gabriel asked, the lone body in the group curious enough to ask.

"Mostly torture and interrogation techniques. I feel it solidifies the lesson when such skills are applied upon an individual." More than one gulp rang out from her stunned audience before she laughed. "History, mostly." She revised her statement. "However, now is the time for lunch."

That afternoon, they dined on much the same as they had the day before. Freshly baked loaves of bread and platters of meat decorated the tables, alongside massive three-tiered platters of fruit.

"Are all of you finished?" Tarkan asked, looming over their table. "If so, we can be on with the tour."

Gabriel was the first to bolt upright from his chair, eager to carry on. Gael took his time standing as he looked to Mari and Klein, both trying to cram as much into their mouths as possible.

"Do you need some time?" Tarkan suggested. "We have a few moments, yet."

"No. I'm ready," Mari said through a mouthful. Rinoa looked at the two and tsked as she rose.

"Me too." Klein swallowed a mass of food, which he later assisted with several thumps on the chest. "I want to see more."

"Very well, then. This way, if you please," Tarkan smirked lightly as she led them away from the Great Hall. "First, we might as well venture out into the courtyards," she began, turning to the right as they exited the hall. Gael traced the living murals lining the exit to the castle as he had the day they arrived.

"Now, despite the heavy workload required of your remedial studies, you shall each have a bit of free time, every afternoon and evening. Once the rest of the students return and normal study sessions resume, you shall have slightly more time at your disposal. I suggest using some of that time to be outdoors."

Everyone pulled their cloaks tight to their bodies as they stepped out into the snow-filled landscape. Each of the gargoyles and hedgerows were coated with chilly, white powder, giving the castle grounds an almost festive look. The evening's storm had left along with the blistering wind, allowing them a clear vantage of the enormous grounds and its ornaments.

"This way, you will find the courtyards," Tarkan began, taking an immediate left from the castle gates. "Down this lane, leads to the first of the exterior gardens." She led on, the fieldstone path scarcely touched by the snow.

The hedgerows had been expertly shaped to form large archways shielding the path they walked. Through the breaks in the archways, one could see a growing maze of hedges not far in the distance. Leading past the enclosure, they entered another path lined with the well cared for greenery.

"Here, you will find the main courtyard," Tarkan continued, walking into the enclosure they had just passed. "The backside of the courtyard serves as a maze. While tempting, it is currently off-limits save during special events. Simply, it takes far too long to collect missing children who have lost their way within."

Without missing a beat, she continued with the tour, showing them around the main courtyard. A large fountain stood at its center, water gushing from the mouths of griffins and pegasi. The entire courtyard was lined with slabs of stone spread out in a vast circle, surrounded by benches.

"Many of you will likely find yourselves here, playing in your spare time. We ask that you avoid any unsanctioned duels, even if there seems to be plenty of space. That is not to say you cannot practice spells, however. If additional study is your aim, we shall head to the next courtyard where such things are encouraged."

The tour continued without further pause or warning. As the troop moved on, Gael, Klein, and Mari each stared at the maze, their lust for adventure calling them. Turning away from the forbidden area, they ran to keep up with the party.

As they reached the second courtyard, a series of stone steps delivered them to the center of a bowl-shaped, grassy area surrounded by stone pillars. At its lowest point, Tarkan stopped and turned to face her charges. The three stragglers eyed their surroundings as they joined the group.

"Here, you may practice basic spells and incantations. Each of these portal stones you see will repel rudimentary magic." As she spoke, Tarkan formed a claw with her hand and, speaking a short word of power, threw a streak of lightning towards the stones. Responding to the magic, a great blue wall rose within the portal, absorbing the magic.

The students stared in amazement as the professor fired shots at three more of the countless stones and archways. Each of the objects absorbed the arcane energies she emitted. Allowing the students to marvel a moment, Tarkan gently coughed into her fist.

"Alright then. Time is short. Let us carry on." Her gallant strides quickly left the students behind. Urgently, they chased after their sponsor, charging up the stone steps back towards the side of the castle.

At the top of the stairs, the hedgerows resumed, leading them to a gentle enclosure complete with a spiraling staircase leading back into the castle.

Gael could not help but stare in wonder as the snowy landscape continued far beyond the stairwell. Following his brother and peers up the stairs, he quickly found himself back on the second floor of the east wing.

"Next, I will be taking you to the planetarium, where our mages focusing on astrology and study of the convergence can be found. From there, we shall head back through to the greenhouses, observatories, and beast pens."

Moving through the hall, Tarkan led them to a pair of large doors. Holding a hand out before them, the seam in the doors split and slowly swung open. From the outside, the room appeared no deeper than the standard classroom they had visited thus far. Stepping within, the room expanded, stretching on for vast lengths.

Frozen in awe, the students halted just a few dozen paces inside. Tarkan walked to the center of the room and looked up to the ceiling. With a clap of her hands, she whispered words of power and the room burst into light.

"Woah," Gael called, falling on his rear. Staring skyward, he watched as stars soared across the ceiling. Constellations formed in front of their eyes. Suns burst with life, sprawling out and forming nebulas. While the students continued to gaze on with awe, Tarkan walked beneath the illusion.

"It has taken several years to enchant the ceiling in this room. Some spend most of their lives studying the stars and the infinite cosmos. Come along, children," she said, stepping back into the hallway as her students scrambled to their feet.

"When will we have the chance to go back in there?" Gabriel asked, walking backwards to keep his eyes on the structure. Gael absently steered his brother, keeping him from crashing into anything.

"After your second year," she answered as she moved to the far end of the hall and stepped outside. The bridge outside was covered over with glass, allowing them a clear vantage of the grounds on the backside of the castle.

Gael looked carefully as they walked through the bridge, observing as the path led them over a deep canyon on the northern side of the castle. All eyes opened wide as they stared straight down into the depths below as they walked to the north tower beyond. Pressing open the doors, they stepped inside.

The north tower seemed colder than the rest of the castle. The decorative warmth they had seen throughout the rest of the grounds was simply non-existent here. In fact, as they slowly walked through, large slashes could be seen in the stonework.

"Are these claw marks from a monster?" Gael asked, reaching up to touch the lower edges of the three rakes.

"Yes. I suspect Professor Boon was less than careful with one of his pets," Tarkan surmised. "That or they were left behind by his predecessor. I must admit I am not certain which."

"What happened to his predecessor?" Klein asked, swallowing a hard lump in his throat.

Tarkan tilted her head to the side, thoughtfully. "I cannot seem to recall," she mused, index finger tapping her chin. "Were they eaten by a beast or did they transform themselves into a beast?"

"You can transform yourself into beasts?" Klein gasped, rousing all eyes to fall on him.

"Of course, we can," Tarkan smiled. "However, the technique can become quite difficult to reverse if not done properly. I seem to recall a word that the previous Beastmaster was attempting to transmute themself into some manner of monster or hybrid or such and became lost." She considered the thought a moment, hand grasping at her chin as she did so. The others continued staring at her, until she nodded her head, smiled, and continued walking.

Meanwhile, his question answered, though presenting several more inquiries, Klein followed silently.

"And here, upon the lower level of the north tower, you will find Professor Boon's lab. I daresay, I do not anticipate you attending until your second year. However, in case you are summoned for some business or another, you know where it is."

"Professor?" Gabriel raised his hand.

"Yes, Mister Stryfe?" she said, halting the tour.

"Earlier, when you said that the professor was lost. Do you mean…" His voice quieted as he trailed off.

"Yes. His mind was gone. Taken over by that of the beast he had morphed into. It would serve each of you well to remember that any use of the Amaranthine's Blessing, be it a simple warming spell or a far more complicated one, comes with a price.

"Professor Boon's predecessor forgot this simple lesson and irrevocably changed himself into a monster. Some exchanges, unfortunately, are permanent." The students spent the brief remainder of the tour, horrified by Tarkan's story. Each considered their undertaking with added weight as they made their way to the dining hall.

"Good evening, students and faculty." The Spirit of the Hearth said as everyone gathered for the evening meal. "I hope each of you has enjoyed your tour of the castle." A loud explosion came from somewhere above them. They felt the stones rumble up above.

"Ah," the Spirit paused. "Do not mind the explosions. An experiment gone astray in the upper stratum, I am afraid. No worries, though. This sort of thing happens from time to time. Now, then, in the Headmistress's stead, it is my astute honor to present to you, your dinner."

Streaks of flame ran across each of the tables, alarming all the students. Gasps of shock erupted from every student table, while the instructors chuckled, happily. The flames rose higher, though radiated no heat. Many of the students began clapping excitedly at the Spirit's display. The smell of food came to them, wafting in from the flames. Curious, Gael reached for the flames as they wavered, revealing heaping plates of food for their feasting.

Klein bolted at the platters, grabbing food with both hands. Mari had immediately filled her plate and was face down, shoveling in as much food as her stomach could hold. Unfazed by their table manners, the brothers tucked in as well.

As both the evening meal and theatrics came to a close, the students shuffled off to their own dorms. Bellies completely stuffed from the evening and eager to begin tomorrow's activities, the brothers moved straight for bed.

CHAPTER FOUR

The following morning proved less exciting than the former and their afternoon progressed uneventfully, until it was time to conclude their studies for the day, at long last. "What do you want to do?" Gabriel asked, looking to his brother as they strolled through the halls.

"I was thinking of heading outside, stroll the courtyards, enjoy the weather, while it's still decent. You?"

"I actually have a few new spells I would like to try. The courtyard would be the perfect place for me to get some practice in."

"Wouldn't you rather practice with one of the faculty or something?"

Gabriel scrunched his face as he shook his head. "No. I'd rather practice alone. I'm not sure how well this spell will work."

Rolling his eyes, Gael waved forward. "Follow me, then," he sighed. Moving through the castle, Gabriel waved to Mari and Klein, who perked up as they came by. Quickly following in pursuit, Gabriel's cheeks began to blush.

"What are you two up to?" Mari asked, curiously staring at the inconspicuous duo.

At first, Gabriel fidgeted with an answer.

Rolling his eyes, Gael looked to them. "He wants to go practice in the courtyard and wants a few spectators. Want to join us?" The sheepish boy shot his brother an irritated glance, before slouching his shoulders.

"Sure!" Mari jolted, knocking Klein's fistful of snacks from his hand. "I could use the practice, myself," she said happily, trotting alone towards the courtyard. Klein remained at a standstill, frozen in horror as he mourned his fallen food.

"We'll see you there," Gael said, turning and leaving the stalwart boy to himself as he slowly crouched down and wiped off his roll.

The castle grounds were pristine and filled with snowcapped greenery from the freshly fallen snow. Despite the weather, the courtyard felt surprisingly warm and void of the windy chill that often settled into the mountain passes. Their boots left light trails through the snow as they moved off from the stone path leading from the castle. Other footprints already guided their way, trailing off in the same direction.

"What kind of spells are you trying out?" Mari asked excitedly, inching nearer to the boys as the intensity of her stare increased.

"Nothing too special," Gabriel responded, meekly. "I just wanted to practice some of the things we've seen, so far. I am awfully curious to see how summonings work." The eyes of all but Gael grew wider as the words left the boy's mouth.

"But that is higher level magic," Klein complained. "We won't learn about that for another year at the earliest."

"But Duncan Reynald can already summon Darklings," Gabriel retorted.

"That's extremely dangerous," Mari, the typically least cautious of the entourage interjected. "Everyone knows that you are not supposed to mess with Darklings."

"Seriously," Klein added. "Altair has a special elimination task force, specifically for that sort of thing. There is absolutely no way someone our age should be even thinking about them." He let out an involuntary shiver.

"I'm not going to summon one," Gabriel clarified, excitably. "I found this book in the library in the early learner's section. It talks about how to summon lesser elementals." Finally, the book that had been carefully tucked beneath his arm was revealed. An old, worn tome that's size was even less impressive than its dull, plain cover.

"Let me see?" Mari whined, holding her hand out for the book. "I want to try a summoning, too." The call came out louder than intended, causing the students to look about nervously for any eavesdroppers.

"Okay, then," the mousy haired Gabriel hissed. "Just be quiet, alright?" Nodding their heads, they continued their trek to the outer courtyard, where only but a few groups of students had assembled.

"Alright," Gabriel sighed, looking around to ensure no one was paying too much attention to their activities. "This spot should work just fine." He knelt low to the ground and carefully poured over the book, flipping directly to the page he needed. Forming a tight huddle around him, each of them watched intently as he held out his hand and focused on the magic he was attempting to cast.

Small waves of power leaked from him, forming a minor summoning circle on the ground.

****

"Can anyone tell me what the difference is between visualization and incantation?" Professor Tarkan asked as she paced up and down the rows of seats.

Without hesitation, Gabriel's hand soared skyward. Gael groaned inwardly at his brother's desperate attempts to please their instructor.

"Gael?" He cringed as she called out his name. "Do you know the difference?"

He rotated his head, a flabbergasted look on his face directed at his now pouting brother. "Visualization refers to casters who imagine using spells, while incantations are casting spells through speaking or chanting."

Tarkan nodded lightly as she continued walking. "Yes. You are close. Does anyone else wish to answer?" Gabriel slowly lowered his hand as Rinoa's lazily floated up.

"Oh?" Tarkan mused. "Rinoa, do you care to answer?"

"Yes. Visualization does refer to the imagining of your spell. However, it is important to imagine the effect you wish your spell to have, while considering the strength of the reaction whilst speaking your incantation. This is how actual sorcerers cast magic." She stared directly at Gael as she spoke, causing heat to rise to the boy's ears.

"Good, Rinoa. I will add that the two concepts do work harmoniously together but some mages use the two independently of one another." Gael huffed with approval, causing an annoyed reaction from his peer. Ignoring the two, Tarkan continued her explanation.

"We will discuss the complex applications of invocations versus visualizations at a later time. I will, however, advise you, students, that in your first years at the academy, stick to using invocations. There are risks involved with channeling the Blessing without a control word or phrase." Gabriel's hand launched skyward.

"Yes, Gabriel?" Tarkan paused, looking curiously to her pupil.

"If you do not wish for us to do it, why tell us?" he complained, Gael completely aware of his brother's curious nature.

Immediately, Tarkan scowled as she reached for the edges of her eyes and pinched them. "I caution you so you might know the dangers should any of you discover it on your own. Ignorance is an unacceptable excuse here at the Cabal."

"But in the hands of a fool, knowledge is even more dangerous." Again, Gael felt further infuriated as he noticed Rinoa's eyes upon him. Klein and Mari both continued to watch in fear as Tarkan sighed.

"Again, you are not mistaken, Rinoa," she answered. "Please, do not speak out of turn and avoid taunting your classmates." The young girl's scowl returned as she looked away. "If you could all open your books to the introductory chapter, I would have you read to yourselves. I will be quizzing you in due time."

Several groans escaped the collective, while Gabriel happily opened his book, instantly turning to a chapter he'd already read. Not long into their reading, Tarkan loudly cleared her throat. "I see it is time for us to move to your next lesson." She began leading her students back through the hallway.

Walking in single file through the castle halls, they slowly traveled higher up the castle towers. Their eyes studied the countless mechanisms, which piloted themselves from the moving gargoyles to the phantasmal lights floating over their heads. Seemingly of their own accord, the wisps occasionally floated absently about, bumping into the odd painting, which looked at the glowing orbs with irritation.

Reaching the landing on the fifth floor of the east wing, Gael and his peers awed at an open expanse. On the top floor, before the eastern tower, the entire eastern side of the wing faced out over the mountain pass. There was a break in the passages, providing a striking view of the snowy canyon, which ran deeper into Cabal island. To where, Gael did not know.

The sun shone in through the windows, blindingly bright as the light reflected off from the snow-covered passages. Within the center of the long hall, sat a magnanimous fountain. Several spouts sprayed out in all directions, cascading together to form ever-changing shapes.

They watched, awestruck as the patterns shifted from birds to floral patterns and morphed into animal figures, before restarting the pattern. They smiled at the fountain as they moved on with the continuation of yesterday's tour.

The next room possessed a maze of shifting stairwells and hallways. The students froze as they looked on fearfully, while Tarkan maintained her forward stroll. "Step lively, children," she instructed, turning around a corner as the stairwell moved into position.

They hustled in step, huddling close to the instructor as she scaled the shifting tower. Glancing about in wonder, Gael smiled as he recognized the inner mechanisms of the stairwell. "It's a clock," he laughed.

"Astute observation, Mister Stryfe." Tarkan stated, continuing to lead them to the lower floors. "This is called Horo's Tower or Clockwork Tower as the student's typically call it."

The procession came to an abrupt halt as they sat in marvel at the masterful craftsmanship of the shifting staircases. Mechanical gears the size of village houses, rotated in synchronicity high above them, *clinking* in a repetitious rhythm. Noticing the looks on his classmates faces Gael could sense their ease. To him however, a shiver tickled the back of his neck as an ominous specter looming about the massive tower. As his classmates slowly left him behind, he kept his gaze trained on the mechanisms above. He watched as the staircases crisscrossed endlessly, though never aligned in a pattern which allow someone to reach the top.

"Just up ahead, you will find Professor Crowl's classroom. I daresay, you shall enjoy it," She said, looking straight to Gabriel.

His attention recentered by the distant voice of his teacher, Gael hastened to catch up.

Turning down the hall, Tarkan stopped before a doorway. "I shall collect you later," she smiled, gesturing for them to enter. The students shuffled into the class, quickly finding seats among the large, empty room. At the back, they saw Professor Crowl, staring at them, impatiently.

"Find your seats. Quickly," she growled, tapping irritably as she waited for the last two stragglers. Lionel, Emma, and a few others from their group shuffled in, scuffing at the floor with their chairs as they dove into them.

"Well," she huffed as she stared down at them. "Good to see you can follow basic instructions. I am Professor Crowl. I shall be teaching you history. Our primary focus shall be on the Three Kingdoms Continent and its relation to the Cabal.

"I trust everyone has brought their books with them. Feel free to open to chapter one."

Gael felt something within him dying as the dry tone of the instructor's voice stabbed at the back of his mind. Opening his book, he focused all his energy on staying awake.

"Mister Rolands!" Crowl snapped at the sleeping boy. With a snap of her fingers, an explosion of sound erupted from behind the boy, causing him to launch himself from his seat.

"Professor?" He shrieked as he fell to the floor.

"Find your seat, Mister Rolands," she grumbled, returning to her board. Gael made certain that he was the first to the door once they were dismissed.

"Well?" Tarkan spoke from behind him, startling the boy. Turning, he saw her leaning against the wall, waiting patiently for her students alongside Professor Boon. "I trust history class was enlightening?"

"It was absolutely fascinating?" Gabriel cheered as he exited, the last to leave the room. "Some of what we learned wasn't even in the book." Tarkan raised an eyebrow to the only enthusiastic child between the two groups of students.

"He's already read most of our textbooks," Gael explained, half-dead tone to his voice.

"No harm in a committed student," Tarkan summarized as Professor Boon looked dazed. "I hope your enthusiasm holds. You may need it to get you through your cram studies."

"There's something strange about that boy," Boon whispered.

Tarkan reached back, gently tapping the man on the chest as she led her students away. "We all have some unique pupils this year," she smiled, looking back at Lionel, who was rubbing his sleepy eyes. "Come now, children. I shall show you to your final class, though you will not begin until next week."

They moved back through the castle, working their way lower, until the stonework and levity of the structure evaporated as they entered the damp, musty tunnels of the dungeons. Looking back, they saw Professor Boon and his entourage, following closely behind them.

"Worry not," the massive man, who was bent in half as they walked, chuckled. "We're not locking up anyone, today."

"Just up ahead, you will find the entrance to the arena," Tarkan explained, moving forward. "Keep up." Tarkan turned down one of the various tunnels underground. Following close behind, they could all see a bright light at the far end.

"Here we are," she breathed, holding out her arms as everyone emerged. "Here, you will undergo battle training regularly. I suggest you take your training just as seriously as you would your studies. Professor Lang does not waste time with pleasantries."

Turning on her heel, Tarkan quickly moved back into the tunnelways as Professor Boon's students remained behind. "Follow me, please," she said to her students as the other professor spoke with his students. "The hour is getting late and we must make progress."

Moving back through the tunnels, Gael noticed markings on some of the stones, along the walls. He did not recognize the runes being used but looking back, saw slightly different runes on the tunnel they had come through initially. Following the instructor's lead, they emerged from the dungeons into another tower.

"This is the Western Tower. From the arena, this will serve as the quickest path back to the dormitories." Scaling up to the third floor, they quickly found themselves on the side of the first-year commons, opposite. Quickly finding a place to rest after the substantial tour, they relaxed until Tarkan's return in the early evening.

****

"Is everyone ready for dinner?" she asked, only slightly alarmed as Klein and Mari threw themselves at her feet.

"Famished," Mari groaned.

J.A. Bullen   89

"I thought we were going to starve to death," The boy nearly had tears in his eyes.

"Alright then." The instructor spoke with no sense of alarm, stepping around and over the prone facing bodies. "If you would allow, follow me, then. I suppose we can keep the rest of you from collapse."

Returning to the main floor, they found the doors to the Great Hall already opened wide. Guiding her students to their table, she waited for each of them to be seated, before speaking. "After dinner, I shall be guiding each of you back to the commons. Starting tomorrow, your group's prefect shall tend to you."

"What do you think of everything?" Gabriel buzzed excitedly, eyeing around to the others. Rinoa remained silent as she had the entire day as Klein and Mari moaned about their empty bellies.

"I wish we could have seen more of the arena." Gael huffed, his disappointment clear. "I didn't even get a chance to look around."

"Hopefully, we'll have a chance tomorrow," Mari chirped, jabbing and kicking invisible targets. "We're going to slay dragons and fight armies of the undead," Klein shivered visibly as Lionel and Emma observed, curiously.

"You know dragons are not real, right?" A tan-skinned girl with dark hair interjected from across the room.

"You cannot prove that!" she retorted. "There are many stories about dragons roaming the land."

"Legends, you mean," another youth with red hair argued beside her friend. "Just because there is a story about it, does not mean it's true. What's that story you Northerners tell each other? Winter witch? Gravy Mother?"

"Gravy!" Klein burbled, mouth half open from the un-masticated wad in his mouth.

"The Grey Mother," Rinoa blurted from across the room. Both Klein and Mari fell silent and froze.

"Now, you've done it," Lionel rolled his eyes as Emma tensed in her chair. As the four parties started to bicker, Gale and Gabriel wandered off towards the dormitories. Sifting through their belongings, they changed clothes and turned in.

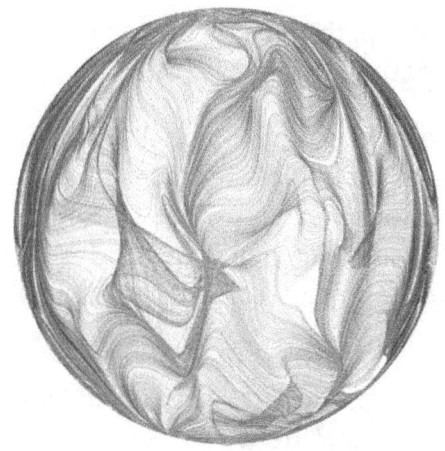

Chapter Five

"Is everyone ready?" Niferi asked, standing at the head of Gael and Gabriel's table. A loud, hysterical screeching, sounding like the grinding of sharpened stones, emitted in muffled bursts from Klein's mouth.

"I'm sorry?" Niferi's eyes squinted slightly. "Does anyone understand what he's saying?"

"He wants to know what we should be ready for?" Mari translated without looking up from her breakfast plate.

"To go to your classes," she clarified, still eyeing the boy as his animalistic consummation continued.

"But we're not done eating, yet," the boy gasped.

"Will you be finished shortly?" she asked, a worried expression on her face. Opposed to requiring Mari's translations, the boy merely nodded his head. Satisfied, Niferi waited for the two to finish before resuming.

"Right, then. If you will all follow me, we shall make ready for your first class." Niferi maintained a pace rivaling the professors. She led the lot of them, Lionel, Emma, and the others from

Professor Boon's group, through the hallways and to the first-year commons to gather their things.

Among their group, Gael, Gabriel, Mari, and Klein watched from beside Niferi as their noble-born peers struggled to maintain the woman's brisk pace. As they arrived in front of their first class, they stood outside, catching their breath before entering. Stepping into the room, they saw Professor Tarkan seated at the far end of the room.

"Good morning, students," she smiled, fingertips touching in a tent in front of her face. "Are we all eager to begin our studies?" The general enthusiasm of the room met a high point as the students rushed to their seats. Thus, their studies into the intricacies of magic continued.

As Tarkan's lecture came to its end and it was time for them to move to their next course, Niferi appeared. Guiding them through each of their classes, they walked to their final class before lunch. Rounding the corner to Professor Zerenia's room, they paused at the sight of smoke filling the hallway. "Wait here," she instructed, holding everyone back, before moving forward on her own. They could hear coughing coming from around the corner up ahead.

"Should one of us go look for a teacher?" Gabriel asked as a tiny blur of light shot past them.

Niferi appeared from around the corner. "My familiar will find them faster. Do not be alarmed," she said softly, proceeding forward. "Everything is under control. This has happened more than once." She turned back around the corner, covering her mouth as she stepped into the smoke screen.

"Has happened more than once?" Mari repeated, a broad smile on her face. "This class must be amazing."

"Or extremely dangerous," Klein murmured.

"Perhaps a bit of both," a small voice squeaked from within the cloud. Stepping forward, Zerenia appeared, waving her hand in front of her nose as she smiled through a face covered in soot. "Today's experiment went a bit awry, I'm afraid," she giggled as Niferi returned, sputtering.

"Professor, I must ask you not to maintain such an impartial air regarding this mishap." Niferi sighed, palm to the side of her face.

Another figure appeared from the curtain, as well. "Confound it all, Zerenia!" An old, grey-bearded gnome sputtered and spat as he stumbled through the cloud of smoke. "How many times am I going to be called up here to clean up another of your experiments?" He flailed his arms about as he continued to sputter, cantankerously. Walking into the fresh air, he drew in a deep breath and, holding his hands wide, blew. Immediately, the smoke sprayed down the hallway opposite the children, surging through like a rolling storm, combating the torches, which remained lit in their sconces.

Curious about the type of magic employed, the troop scuttled closer to Niferi and Zerenia and watched as the horizontal whirlwind bellowed through the hallway and out the window. Pleased with his work, the elder continued to spit and sputter as he tended to every last trace within the hallways. Looking inside Zerenia's classroom, however, his face went pale before he growled at his gnomish associate.

"Well?" Zerenia smiled, pulling a rag from her pocket and using it to wipe a pair of soot-coated glasses. "I suppose we shall take today's lesson elsewhere?" She smiled, her teeth luminous in contrast to her soot-stained face.

"Actually, I think perhaps the students shall enjoy a free period for now," Phyllida sighed.

Tarkan walked beside her, arms already crossed over her chest. "What have you done, now?" The former Inquisitor groaned before looking back to her pupils.

"Oh, you know. Tinkering with a touch of this, a pinch of that." Zerenia maintained a chipper disposition, despite the numerous eyes glowering at her. "How was I to know the relic was booby-trapped?"

"You brought an unresearched artifact into my school?" The tone in Phyllida's voice strained, her pitch nearing an inaudible octave. "Professor Zerenia, we have discussed this at some length, now. No unauthorized artifacts. Period."

"Let's say we return to the commons for a spell?" Niferi smiled awkwardly as the gnomish man returned from out of the classroom, his rampage resuming.

"I quit!" he spat, scarcely rising over the unnaturally tall Headmistress' thighs. "That does it! I can't take it anymore!"

"Now, now, Mister Deets," Phyllida cooed in a deceptively soft tone. "Please come with me to discuss these matters. I assure you this will be the last time you must tend to one of your Grandniece's messes." As they strolled down the adjacent hallway, the students remained transfixed until Niferi called once more in a gruffer tone.

****

"That was amazing!" Mari cheered back in the common room, rocking her armchair with excitement so that the front legs were consistently lifted from the floor. "How long before we get to blow stuff up, do you think?"

"You don't honestly believe that we're going to be allowed to blow things up, do you?" Rinoa asked. Half of the commons looked back to her, confirming quite the opposite. Rolling her eyes, she turned her chair to face away from the group.

The rowdy crowd continued chattering as the hour went on and Niferi returned to guide them through the rest of the day. Moving on through their classes and lunch, they found themselves yearning for battle school. Thus, the routine for their lives was set and the students counted the days until the evening of the Divination had finally arrived.

****

As instructed, that evening at dinner, the two brothers stepped aside as the tables in the hall vanished. Next, Phyllida waved her hands in a broad circle as she spoke words of power, in a language Gael could not place. A large, icy-blue rune appeared in the center of the room a moment later, a frosty mist floated out of it.

Raising trembling hands as though heaving a great burden, the Headmistress summoned twelve wide columns of ice. Gael watched in awe as the columns reached towards the ceiling. He watched as the climbing pillars and the accompanying grinding noises, ceased.

The students stared silently at the twelve pillars, awaiting instructions. Slowly, some of the braver students stepped forward, Gael among them. Looking back, he looked to Tarkan, who nodded her head.

"Students, one by one, come forth. Step within the center of the icy mirrors. It is time to take your first steps towards fate's calling."

Stepping aside to allow his eager classmates to rush ahead, he stared back towards his brother. The blonde boy remained still. Whether in awe of the magic or from the fear of what the divining might reveal, Gael did not know.

The boy remained firmly planted near Rinoa, who looked frightened. Gael moved away from the line that had formed as Tarkan gave the other two a gentle prod. Glancing back and forth between her and the pillars, they walked slowly towards Gael.

"What do you look so worried about?" Gael asked, nudging his brother, while ignoring Rinoa. "You look as though you'd rather get back on the carriage than stand in front of some ice."

"I don't know." Gabriel groaned. "I guess the thought of discovering my future scares me."

"It's not going to tell you the future. It's going to tell you all the things you could do with the abilities you have."

"Maybe he is afraid he won't live up to some expectation," Rinoa suggested, her eyes focused ahead.

"You know, for someone who tries to be as lonesome and miserable as you, you seem to interject yourself into a lot of conversations," Gael said sourly. "I didn't see you in much of a rush to get in line."

Rinoa's hands balled into tight fists as her cheeks, ears, and tips of her nose reddened. "Some of us are already aware of our potential," She growled, marching away.

Doing his best to ignore the young woman's unstable behavior, Gael turned back to his brother. "If you want, I'll be first." As he spoke, bright lights emanated from the pillars. They both stared in awe until a moment later, Klein stepped out, a broad smile on his face.

"I am going to be a Warlock!" he declared, striking an awkward pose, which made half of those present laugh.

A second flash of light came a moment after, and Mari leapt out, a ridiculous victory pose of her own. "Battlemage!" she cried for the entire world to hear.

One after another, the students took their turns. With few exceptions, no one else excitedly proclaimed what the pillars had shown, though many excitedly conversed with their friends afterwards.

"I think I'll go ahead," Gabriel murmured, swallowing the hard lump in his throat. Slapping his brother on the back, Gael watched the reluctant boy step inside. A smile crept across his face as he imagined the results of his brother's test. Already eager to discuss their profound futures together, he could hardly keep from showing annoyance, when the boy's divining took far longer than the others.

"Hey, does it normally-?" His question was cut short by a bright burst of light as Gabriel resurfaced. Smiling, Gael approached his brother, who bore a harrowed expression. "What is it?" he asked. "Didn't see what you wanted?" A shake of his head the only response. Gael shrugged his shoulders before moving to the columns.

Stopping just before the structure, he looked back and saw Klein and Mari still goofing around. Laughing, he walked inside. Stepping within, he immediately found himself within a remarkable maze of mirrors. His reflection bounced from countless angles; he slowly moved towards a slightly raised platform at the center.

Taking the two steps to the center of the room, he slowly spun himself in a circle. In front of him, he saw only himself a moment before the image began to change. A fully grown man stood before him, sad eyes staring at the blade of a well-worn sword, wreathed in a red hue. He wore mail armor with a crimson tunic and tan breeches. Looking at the man, he realized it was himself.

"The journey has been difficult, and your trials many. You have walked a solemn path, and while none might ever thank you for the work you've done, you know in your heart, you have done your best. The last man standing upon another impossible battle, none can deny your strength." As both the image and the voice faded, he stood at a loss.

Turning about, he looked at the various other mirrors, looking for an answer to show itself. Brief glimpses of himself appeared in each. While the pictures each maintained the same style outfit as the image he had first seen, none of them were the least bit distinguishable.

Peering at each reflection, he attempted to see what the fates had to say of his latent abilities. Stepping closer to another, nearby mirror, he placed his hands to either side of the frame and stared deeply within. He could see his face clearly, though the rest of his body slowly shifted in and out of focus.

He waited patiently, watching as the rest of his body finally came into view. His reflection smiled back at him and placed its hands against the glass. As the other him opened his mouth to speak, the mirror cracked and fell away.

He heard the first mirror speaking to him once more as the images on the rest of the mirrors grew increasingly blurry. As he moved to the next, the mirror broke before he had a chance to touch it. He stumbled backwards, hand brushing across the one mirror possessing a clear image. Again, something whispered to him from a distant place.

Confusion ran through Gael's mind as he sought reason for what he had seen. A word came to his mind, spoken from the lips of the image. He attempted to speak the word, tasting it on the tip of his tongue.

"Young Gael, are you alright?" He could hear Captain Tarkan.

Looking up to face her, the word slipped from his tongue. "Warden." The mirrors shined with a permeating light. He saw one thing, before both he and his instructor were blinded;-the shock on his instructor's face.

****

"Tell me what happened?" Aurelia demanded, leading Gael by the arm to the library. Pressing him forward, he managed only a quick glimpse at the monstrous room. A single room, which was larger than the entire home he had grown up in. The door to the library opened again as Phyllida entered.

"What is the matter, Professor Tarkan?" she demanded, holding her hand to the door. Speaking a few words of power, she sealed them away from any eavesdroppers.

"Come on, then, Gael," Tarkan pressed. "Inside the divination circle, what did you say?"

He looked frightfully between the two anxious-looking teachers. Already, the memory of what he saw was quickly fading. Seizing the last drips of the retreating daydream, he felt a single word. "Warden," he repeated, the title bringing back some of what had trickled away. "It was the only option. None of the other mirrors worked. Just that one with the man on the battlefield. He said he was the last standing." He desperately sought to hold on to the fading image. "He had a flaming sword."

Phyllida flashed Tarkan a quick and subtle look. With an even more modest nod of her head, Tarkan stepped forward.

"Did I do something wrong?" he asked. "Did I mess up?"

Phyllida stepped forward. "You've done nothing." She spoke as cold as her ice magic. "I wish to speak with your father soon. It seems that his sons are going to prove themselves as interesting as he."

"Is something wrong with my brother?" Gael asked.

"Not at all," Phyllida said. "You may return to the common room, now. Professor Tarkan tells me you have already met Niferi. She shall be in charge of showing you around the castle, as well as where you shall be this year."

Nodding his head, Gael slowly approached the doors. Opening them, he found his classmates waiting for him. Closing the doors behind him, Aurelia turned to her Headmistress.

"Another Warden?" she asked. "The last fell alongside the Rune King, half a century ago. Now, we have three of them in two years?"

"Not to mention another World Shaper," Phyllida mused thoughtfully. "It is clear that we will need to keep a close watch over those two. However," she began, flashing a look to the Captain, which made even her war-forged heart shiver.

"I understand, Headmistress. I will do my best to protect them from that which we have already sensed in the shadows."

Phyllida nodded her head to her subordinate. "Between them and the three heirs of the Court of Shadows," she tutted. She looked to the skies silently, forcing a clawed motion of her hand to ward against evil. "It's enough to make me wish I had never accepted this job."

"That makes two of us," Aurelia replied.

"Had you turned it down, you would still be a Witch Hunter of the Inquisition."

"Precisely. My conscience has no problem with those who've chosen their fates. These children however…" Aurelia, forgetting herself, returned the superstitious ward. "I shall not fail you," she declared. "If not for their or Tristan's sake. Then for my own."

"Be certain you do," Phyllida said as her skin sparkled, then faded, leaving only Aurelia.

CHAPTER SIX

Though they had been quite solemn the night before, the morning brought with it a revived spirit. Gael quickly rose from his bed, stepping outside to enjoy the snowy weather. Taking in a deep breath, he returned to his bed.

"You boys ready for breakfast?" Klein asked, excitedly. "I know I am." He continued without pause, as though their answers were unimportant. "I hope they have lots of eggs and potatoes. Oh, and ham," he continued as he left the room.

"Niferi said she would meet us in the common room," Gabriel said.

"Thanks," Gael grumbled as he forced himself into a clean shirt. Quickly rushing to the washroom from there, they made for the commons.

"Good morning!" Mari cheered happily, as they entered the warmth-filled room. "So, what did you pick?" she asked, anxiously. "Klein and I announced ours, but we did not get to hear the two of yours or Rinoa's."

"Niferi said we were not allowed to ask." Looking at the boy, who stared intently at the brothers anyway, Mari stuck out her tongue before returning her gaze to them. "It's alright if you tell me," she whispered, shielding her face in a vain attempt to block out eavesdroppers. "It will be our secret."

"Says the one who announced her results to the entire class-," Rinoa scoffed. "They probably did not get anything interesting, anyway-," she added, glancing back at the brothers.

His temper immediately sparked at the snide dismissal, Gael clenched his fists. "Just because you got landed with something like, "Dark Empress" or "Callous Calamity," to match your equally unpleasant personality, does not mean we did not receive awesome callings." Gael seethed, angrily.

Balling her own fists after recovering from her initial shock, Rinoa snarled. "An imbecile such as yourself-. could not pronounce my calling, let alone. comprehend it," she snapped, face redder than Mari's scarlet locks.

"Do not mistake my level of disinterest as a lack of comprehension, you vapid, distastefully black-souled wart. Shouldn't you be somewhere else, bringing about ruin to civilization, eating children, or spreading your pestilent unpleasantness?" Gael could not discern when he had gotten so worked up. Even as he stood, breathing heavily, he did not understand what drove him so berserk. By the time he noticed the stunned looks on his peers' faces, Rinoa was gone.

"That may have been taking things a bit far," Gabriel growled out the corner of his mouth.

"But still, there is no reason for her to be so rude all the time," Mari sighed.

"From the girl that refuses to mind her own business," Klein jabbed.

"You wanted to know just as badly!" she turned on him.

"Hey, you started this. Don't make this out to be my fault," the boy shrieked as he cowered. The moment she saw the tension leaving Klein, Mari slugged him in the shoulder. As the boy howled in shock, Gael turned to his brother, head bent.

"I'll apologize," he grumbled. "I don't know why she gets me so worked up." As Gabriel patted his brother on the shoulder, Niferi entered the room.

"Ah, so good to see all of you so full of energy and ready to begin." She smiled as she clapped her hands together. "If you'd all just follow me, we can head down for breakfast. Afterwards, I shall escort you to your classes." Falling in line as commanded, Gael sighed, remorseful of his behavior as they walked towards the Great Hall.

As the morning before, breakfast brought with it a great rabble as everyone at their table, greedily stuffing their faces. As they ate, they watched as, once again, tears poured from Klein's eyes with every bite. With newfound appreciation for the food in front of them, the brothers savored every bite.

Watching the nobles entering the room behind their escorts, Gael could not help but notice the young Reynald boy sneering. Nudging one of his entourage, the six-person troupe all made similar jeers towards their table. Doing his best to ignore the group, Gael returned to his eggs and potatoes.

"Look!" Mari shouted, thrusting her hand in the air. "Carrier birds." Everyone at their table turned their heads skyward as hundreds of small, red birds flooded into the room through the Great Hall doors. The creatures swarmed the hall, converging at each of the populated tables.

Gael's eyes reached to the ceiling, where a whirlwind of red and yellow formed. The swirling colors swelled as they descended towards him. Suddenly and to the alarm of the two boys, the birds burst apart, leaving behind a sealed letter, which floated down towards them.

"It must be from Rosalind!" Gabriel cheered, stepping up onto the bench and snatching the letter out of the air.

"What do you think it says?" Gael asked. Without answering, Gabriel tore into the envelope and stared lovingly at the folded parchment in his hands. As he held it, his eyes slowly widened as he considered the potential words the letter might hold.

"What if she had the baby?" he asked, panic in his voice.

"We won't know until you open it!" Gael growled, trying to snatch the letter away.

Dancing away from his brother's reach, Gabriel continued his worrying. "What if something's wrong?" he asked.

"Open it!" Gael ordered in a demanding tone.

With a final smile, Gabriel unfolded the letter and began to read. "No baby," he summarized as he continued to skim. "The Commander has been called to Lothren, as well as Uncle Torran and the others." He scanned some more. "They say they miss us."

"Anything else?" Gabriel smiled in response.

"They told me to keep you out of trouble." Gael squinted his eyes.

"No special note from your girlfriend?"

Gabriel's cheeks glowed with crimson. "It's not like that!" he shrieked, causing the others to look away from their letters. His face growing an even deeper shade of red, he folded the letter and tucked it away safely in his pocket. As the spectacle cleared and they finished breakfast, Niferi escorted them to their classes.

"Welcome, everyone!" Madam Zerenia called cheerfully, waving excitably from atop a ladder, which leaned precariously against one of many bookshelves.

The classroom was set up like a small amphitheater. Filing into one of the upper rows, Gael had a fair view of the entire room. The room was arranged as he imagined it would be; shelves, books, chairs, a desk for the instructor in front of the chalkboard. The part that threw him for a loop was the many strange, archaic-looking devices and trinkets. The enormity of the collection gave him the impression of being in a storage shed.

"Today, we will be learning a bit of magic theory. However, as you can see by the abundance of objects around me, I am an Artificier. I am a magus who specializes in the study of magical relics and artifacts." Taking another glance at the so-called "magical relics," he could not shake the opinion that all of it appeared to be junk.

"Now, I understand most of you would look at these objects and immediately write them off as little more than garbage. I'll have you know, however, many of our most important symbols are in fact, relics from a lost age." Raising her hand mid-lecture, Rinoa captured Zerenia's attention.

"Ms. Rinoa. How might I help you?"

"Didn't you say that today's lesson was on magical theory?"

Zerenia's attention trailed off as she tapped the tip of the strangely globe-like object in her hand. As a series of lights blinked in various regions on the globe, she opened her mouth. "You are absolutely correct, my dear," she smiled. "A terribly boring topic, yet fundamentally important to your development."

Gael was unsure what had transpired next. He sat tentatively, listening to Zerenia's lecture about magic when he felt his mind wandering to far-off places.

"Gael, wake up!" He jolted upright from his brother's elbow. Looking around the room, he could see his peers gathering up their things and making for the door.

"What happened?" he yelped, desperately looking about.

"You fell asleep," Gabriel grumbled in a reprimanding tone. "I cannot believe you are so lazy."

"I didn't mean to," he protested, following his brother as they joined the line of students. "Where are we headed, now?"

"Professor Zerenia trailed off to the subject of artifacts, again. Now, we are on our way to the dueling grounds."

"Why the dueling grounds?" he asked, rubbing the sleep from his eyes as he mindlessly followed his peers.

"She doesn't want to blow up her classroom, again." Lionel and Emma snickered with the rest of their band. "They only just got this one ready."

"But for the sake of the lesson, she would prefer to demonstrate her point," Mari chimed in.

"What point is that?" Gael, still confused and not fully awake, carefully checked to ensure he had all his things.

"That you should stay awake in class," Gabriel answered, smiling.

"Keep at it, wise guy," Gael grumbled. "Just wait until they split us into teams for any of our physical activities."

Gabriel's eyes narrowed, eliciting a chuckle from his brother. "Let's just say I am not helping you with your schoolwork if you are going to keep sleeping during class."

"Fair enough." Gael smiled, clapping his brother on the shoulder. The exchange quickly ended as they stepped onto a stairwell leading below ground. Tunnels pulled off on either side, though they followed Zerenia straight forward. As the tunnel before them opened, they found themselves staring in wonder at a massive room with an unbelievably high ceiling.

Parts of the ceiling were no longer intact, showcasing the snow-capped mountains surrounding the castle's north side. Looking forward, Gael peered out over what seemed to be the remnants of an old city. Several buildings lie in ruins, dilapidated shells of what used to be. Each of the students spread out, in awe at what they saw. While each saw something different, Gael smiled at the thought of large-scale duels.

"On the matter of magical theory," Madam Zerenia began. "When applied to the body versus utilizing an artifact." Already, Gael could feel his eyelids growing heavier, despite being on his feet. "Magic channeled through the body."

As she said the words, flames slowly licked her palms. "Is much more efficient than using an artifact." Reaching out for one of her coat pockets, she pulled from it a simple, claw-shaped relic. Staring down at her hand, the relic sparkled. Lifting her arm, she quickly raked it from right to left. The class rang out with an enthusiastic cheer as three streaks of violet trailed behind the movement.

"As you can see," Zerenia continued. "By making use of an artifact, one has much more control, even if the energy expended is greater." She swiped the weapon several more times, creating identical streaks of light. "For those of us with vast amounts of magical energy but little control, artifacts are a necessity."

"What about those of us without either?" Gabriel asked.

"There are low output relics, as well as high output ones. Are you thinking of the farms outside of Leones, where such devices are commonplace?"

"I was, instructor. Thank you." Smiling, the pink-haired instructor began removing several other trinkets from her robes.

"Now, I would like each of you to take one of these relics and practice. I find practical tests are far more interesting than those written monstrosities. I am assuming each of you has cast at least one spell or has some understanding of how to channel your energy." The class answered with a general nod of their heads.

At their teacher's urging, each of the children moved forward, collecting an artifact. A simple, three-fingered glove sat in front of Gael, catching his eye. Sliding the metallic glove on, he flinched at the slight pinch as the engraved runes on the back of it began to glow as it drew from his energy.

Curious, he lifted his hand and looked it over. Waving his hand about, he attempted to learn what the glove's purpose was. Around the group, the class members laughed as they created small beams of light or illusionary creatures. Considering his many options, he lifted a small rock.

"It must enhance strength," he declared, already imagining the inhuman feats he would now be able to accomplish. Squeezing the stone in his hand, he scowled when it did not shatter. Dropping the rock, he stared at his outstretched hand and formed a fist. "What could it be?" he asked aloud, lifting his hand higher.

"Hey!" He heard Klein yelp as his shirt lifted over his head. Eyebrows raised, Gael turned to see his brother making a series of luminescent butterflies. Focusing on the book tucked lovingly beneath his arm, Gael moved his hand as though he intended to bat it. Another yelp rang from the boy as his book fell to the ground.

Laughing maliciously, Gael then reached out for the book on the ground. Waiting for Gabriel to grab for it, he pushed the book out of his reach. His laughter intensifying, he moved the book three more times, before his brother turned and glared at him.

"Excellent work, young Stryfe," Zerenia said from behind him, startling the boy. "Try to bring the book back to you." Looking at his teacher, he shrugged his shoulders, before focusing on the book once more.

The book vibrated in response to his psychic touch. Pulling his arm towards himself, the book wiggled listlessly closer. Brow furrowing, he reached back out again, only to see the book scurry away. Grumbling softly to himself, he jerked his arm back harder, bringing it closer than before. Releasing his grip, he outstretched his arm, engaged his link, and repeated the process, wrenching as hard as he could manage. Having lifted his arm, the book soared high, flying on a direct course towards his face.

Yelping, he dove to the ground, forgetting to release his hold on the book. As he crashed, followed by the book landing on the back of his head, the class roared with laughter. Rubbing the small welt that was already forming, he rose to his feet, lifting the book.

"Despite that last bit, you've displayed excellent control with the telekinetic glove," Zerenia praised, reaching up to pat Gael on the shoulder. "I am surprised you were able to use it at all." Extending her hand, Gael deposited the glove. Putting it on her own hand, she used it to begin summoning the various relics back to herself. Methodically placing each one into one of her many pockets, she smiled enthusiastically.

"Now, does anyone understand the difference between the magical theory as applied to an artifact versus the body?" As everyone eyed each other in search of an answer, Rinoa raised her hand.

"Good. At least one of you does." Zerenia smiled proudly. As she turned to move away, Niferi walked out towards the center. Rinoa stared at the instructor's back, confused about the validity of the lesson.

"I thought I might find all of you here," The Cryomancer began, looking around the arena. "Professor Zerenia has a habit of abandoning her classroom."

"Or blowing them up," several students snickered in the back of the pack.

"Where are we headed next?" Mari asked, still buzzing excitedly as the last of her conjured birds faded away.

"Here, actually," Niferi responded happily. "Your next class will be here with Professor Lang." As she said it, a small woman approached, leaning on a large walking stick. "While peaceful relations have been maintained, it is important for everyone to know how to effectively defend themselves or those in their charge."

"On that note, I would advise each one of you to act as enemies, while in my tutelage," The elderly woman began in her raspy tone. "You can never be too prepared for a war."

"Will you require my assistance for class?" Niferi asked. The woman looked up at Niferi, one eye squinting at her.

"I am certain we shall manage just fine. Thank you." She inclined her head lightly. As Niferi moved off to one side to serve as a spectator and potentially medic, Lang turned to her recruits. "Looks as though I've been handed another sorry lot of recruits," she tutted, irritably. "No matter, we'll get you tulips into ship-shape condition. Line up all of you," she barked, waving her stick about.

Quickly, the group charged to form a single line. Shoulder to shoulder, they stood awkwardly, waiting for further direction from the elder. Approaching the line, she walked around each member of the group, poking and prodding each of them, until they stood exactly as she desired.

"Knees apart," she growled, whopping Gael just above his right calf. With a light snarl, he did as instructed and felt a second jab between his shoulder blades. "Back straight. Quit slouching," she commanded before moving to his front.

Having learned his lesson from witnessing Klein's inspection, he already held his head high. With only a scowl, Professor Lang grunted with minor approval.

"You all have the posture of complacent slugs," she barked, moving to the front of their formation. "However, you'll be well-trained slugs by the time I am finished with you." With that last insult, a small smile creased her lips.

"As I stated before, my objective is to teach each of you to stay alive in a combat situation. I aim to achieve this by prepping you for various battle scenarios. You will take part in stand-alone and team battles. I know you were expecting Professor Damcian. However, not a single one of you is ready for her lessons. Before that begins, I will drill each of you."

As the majority of the class took on fearful expressions, Gael and Mari grinned. This earned each of them a quick slap to the shins and a chiding from their instructor. Trying to keep his mind off his bruised shin, Gael watched as a cart full of weapons was wheeled in.

"Each of these has had its blade dulled," she began. "However, everyone shall wear armor, which I shall enchant to help better protect you. While you will not use battle-ready weapons until at least your second year, I will slowly scale back these protections."

"What good are blunted weapons going to be in combat practice?" Lionel asked, snickering to his friends once they had been set at ease. Without warning, Lang whirled around, striking the boy unexpectantly in the ribs with her cane. Though the blow was light, Lionel still doubled over and coughed from the shock.

"What good indeed," Land grumbled, unimpressed. "As you can see, they can still be used to gauge someone's battle readiness.

Any other pointless questions?" Emma, smirking at her embarrassed friend, confidently raised her hand.

"Yes? You by the joker," Lang grumbled, tapping her cane irritably.

"You suggested we would eventually move on to battle-ready weaponry," she began. "Beyond armor, what other precautions are taken?"

Rolling her eyes, Lang cleared her throat and spat to the side. "Once you are ready for Professor Damcian, and plan to partake in the dueling circles, each combatant will be given a special artifact that draws upon your energy to protect you from blows. Regardless, I would advise against allowing yourselves to be struck." At the far end of the line, Rinoa's hand rose. "Yes?" Professor Lang spoke.

"Many of us have plans to become Battlemages. Will the use of magic be permitted?"

"Eventually," The woman grunted. "For now, you will focus on your close quarters disciplines."

"But wouldn't combat magic prove far more prudent?" she continued. "A sword is not likely to cut through a powerful fire spell."

Professor Lang's eyebrow arched as she glared directly into the young woman's eyes. "Cast a spell."

Rinoa blinked twice in response. "What?"

"You heard me."

Nodding her head, Rinoa began a simple chant, moving her hands in front of herself with well-practiced motions. No sooner had the words begun to leave her mouth, Lang swung her cane around her body. Switching grip mid-swing, the professor grasped the handle with both hands and brought it down towards the startled girl's neck. Stopping within a hair's breadth of Rinoa's throat, Lang looked up at the girl.

"Sometimes, a spell will not save you." As she straightened her stance, Gael realized she had also moved to Rinoa's side, beside her trembling, outstretched arm. Digging the base of her walking stick into the dirt, the not-so-decrepit elder leaned upon it heavily. "Now, I wish for everyone to grab one of the blunted weapons I have prepared for you and equip a set of armor. Now, go." Immediately, every member of the class charged forward.

Immediately, Gael reached for a dulled blade. Swinging it to feel the balance of it, he allowed It to rest at his side as he moved to the armor rack. Several worn doublets rested on the frame; the leather ratted from regular use and lengthy exposure.

Throwing a glance at his brother, he saw Gabriel already reaching for a set. Well-versed due to Rosalind's regular training, both were quicker than their classmates at working the straps. Waiting patiently for the others, Professor Lang stopped in front of them and examined their equipment suspiciously.

"Who trained you two?" she asked, tugging on their doublets to ensure they were secure.

Ever cheerful, Gabriel smiled broadly. "Our father and Rosalind, but we've also practiced archery with Zara. Although, Rosalind was probably our best teacher."

"Evilest, more like," Gael protested, making Gabriel laugh.

"Sometimes, she would start a panic first thing in the morning, just to see how quickly we'd respond."

"And she'd thump us if we went back to sleep, instead." Gael continued to grumble, rubbing his head where he had once been whopped.

"Rosalind Hagen?" Lang asked. "Daughter of that old goat, Bors?"

"That's her!" Gabriel cheered. "You know her?"

"Not too well. I served with her father when he was still the general," she answered as the rest of the class filed in. "Congratulations slugs. You are all dead. Move quicker, next time."

****

"If we have to do that every day, I'll probably die," Mari groaned as she sank into one of the many lounge chairs in the commons. "Why are our other classes only an hour long, but we have to train for three?"

"Is it already evening?" Klein grumbled from his prone position on the floor. "After all that running and swinging, I don't even remember any other classes."

"You were there," Gabriel answered, setting down his book. "Besides, this is intended to help us catch up on everything we have missed so far. If anything, we should be glad it's difficult."

"You be happy. I'll be dead," Klein moaned through a mouthful of food.

"Are you eating?" Mari protested. "I can't even remember if we ate lunch today."

"How else am I supposed to recover my strength?"

"I mean, you had food, and you didn't bother to share?" She rose from the chair, suddenly revitalized and vengeful. "I'm starving!"

Protectively hoarding his food, Klein wrapped his body around what he was holding. "This is mine. You should have grabbed your own," he grumbled, continuing to hoard his food. Ignoring his two classmates, Gabriel returned to his book without a care to his brother's whereabouts.

****

Wandering aimlessly about the castle, Gael surveyed the long barren halls filled with ornaments and rich tapestries. Many of the images moved of their own accord, keeping their eyes on the boy. He paid them little heed as he continued his exploration.

Many of the pictures looked as though they whispered as he walked by. Though he could not hear their words, he wondered at the chance of any of them being self-aware. Every corner of the castle revealed something new. As he continued his stroll, he came upon the entrance, where a series of hushed voices forced him to stop.

Ducking down behind a banister at the top of the flight of stairs, he gently peered out. Three hooded figures, one tall and two shorter, stood before the doors. The three continued to whisper to one another, before gently pressing open the doors.

A curtain of icy snow blew in, forcing the three to tighten their cloaks around their bodies. Unable to ascertain any of their identities, he moved closer as they stepped outside. Pulling the ends of his own cloak tighter to his body, he stepped outside, too curious to return to his room.

Immediately, the chill air bit at the tip of his nose and stung at his eyes. No more than a few paces from the castle landing, he became aware of the extreme weather. Frigid gusts of wind kicked spiraling clouds of snow into the air, preventing him from seeing much further than the reach of his arm.

Shielding his face from the blustering winds, he noticed fresh laden footprints in the snow. Quickly filling in as the winds raged against the trail, Gael followed the tracks away from the school. Keeping his head down, he hastened his pace. Following the trail to the edge of the forest, he stopped.

"Why are they going in there?" he asked himself, taking his first step forward. As soon as he had made the second, a fog within the forest began to roll towards him. His eyes widened as the confounding mists encroached on the edges of his vision. Though the temperature had increased significantly, it brought little comfort as he felt his other senses dimming.

Before the fog entrapped him completely, he noticed several bright flashes of light. Watching intently, he remained focused upon it until the mist covered all traces of the beacon. Blinking in disbelief, he attempted to determine his surroundings as thick fog lapped at his heels.

As a tingling, not unlike the numbing of nerves, crawled up his limbs, he contemplated the wisdom of venturing deeper. Hot embers prodded his extremities as he moved forward. Another two steps in the direction the light had emanated from, Gael found himself further hindered by the mists as his hands grew numb.

No longer able to feel the chill on his skin, he stopped his advance. Listening to the rustlings of what lay ahead, he knelt at the base of the nearest tree and waited. It was then that he realized he heard growls, not voices.

With no weapon to defend himself, he rose as quietly as his deadened muscles would allow. Creeping back the way he came, he glanced back only once and cringed at the sight of glowing, featureless eyes, peering into his own. Heart crying with thunder, he tore through to the clearing.

Immediately, he felt relief washing over his body, though the experience had taken its toll. His limbs felt slow, sluggish as he dragged them through the snow in the act of sheer will. Three dozen paces away, he felt life returning to his legs and bit his lip to keep from howling in pain.

A metallic taste coated the inside of his mouth as he brought himself to a halt. Bent in half, he caressed his trembling legs until the stabbing pains he felt dissipated. A tear trapped in the corner of his eye, he sighed with relief and stood upright. The front gate of the castle in sight, he casually walked the last hundred paces.

"Where have you been?" He heard the smooth, unnerving voice of Professor Crowl as she snatched his collar before he reached the castle gates. Still in a panic from what he had seen, he at first kicked and flailed.

"There was something out there!" he crowed, thrusting out his hand towards the forest.

"Of course, there is something out there, foolish boy," Crowl snapped, releasing his collar. "The forest is filled with beasts and such to keep out unwanted guests. That is why students are not permitted to enter without an escort. The confounding mists would have you spinning in circles for hours before the guardians within ravage your flesh. Now, get inside before I have to punish you for breaking curfew."

Nodding his head, Gael stepped inside, glancing back into the curtain of ice and snow. As Crowl closed the door behind them, she shot Gael a menacing glance, encouraging him to turn away. Making his way up the stairwell and back to the commons, he was immediately set upon by his fellows.

"What sort of trouble have you been up to?" Gabriel asked, hands already on his hips in a paternal stance.

"I haven't been up to any," he snapped back in response. "I just wanted to look around."

"Well, it's lucky you came back when you did," Klein stated, stretching his body in front of the fireplace. "If you'd been gone any longer, you might have missed the call for dinner."

Mari poked her head out from atop the lounge chair nearest the fire. "Speaking of being gone, did you see Rinoa while you were out? She left shortly before you and has yet to come back." As all eyes turned on him, he shrugged his shoulders.

"I saw some people wander outside. Other than that, I only saw Professor Crowl."

"Alright," she sighed. "Never mind, then." As she turned back around in her chair, Niferi entered the room.

"Dinner!" Klein cheered, springing from the floor, before she ever announced herself.

"I admire your enthusiasm," she said with a smile. "If you would all follow me, then." She turned and left the room, Klein and Mari at her heels.

One eyebrow arched, Gabriel looked at his brother as he sat his book down. "Want to talk about it?" he asked.

Gael shook his head. "No. Let's just go eat," he grumbled, leaving the room. Following the group to the main floor, they noticed Rinoa, waiting before the doors, head turned down.

"There you are," Mari called happily. "I was wondering where you had run off to."

"I was merely wandering the halls," she responded coldly, falling in line. "Hardy anything worth concerning yourselves over."

Entering the hall, they returned to their lonely table in the corner as those from the nobles' class entered. Ignoring them, Gael turned to his steaming plate of roast.

"There's my favorite first years," Cornelius declared, placing himself between the brothers. How are we adjusting to life here at the Cabal?"

"We're barely through our first week, and we've got homework," Klein grumbled.

"That's just how it is during cram school. Don't worry. Once classes start back for real, it gets easier."

"Easier?" Gabriel asked, disappointment on his face. "You mean the classes get slower?"

Cornelius arched an eyebrow at the young man, his gaze lingering upon the boy for a time. "Bit of a bookworm, eh?" he asked, a small smile on his face. "I suppose you'll fit in just fine."

"What about combat training?" Gael complained. "Don't tell me that gets easier, as well."

Cornelius' smile stretched to his ears. "Now, you'll fit in quite well here. No, combat training never slows down, though I would advise you not to slack off on your studies. You'll find both are equally important."

"Hey! Cornelius!" A dark-skinned woman from his group waved at him. Suddenly alarmed, the young man rose to his feet.

"If you'll excuse me," he said, before leaving them.

Eyes quickly trailing off from the hall, Gael felt a pull on his shoulder. Turning about, he found his eyes tracing up to meet Tarkan's eyes.

"I would have a word with you," she said tensely. Nodding, he followed the woman away from the line of his peers, and into one of the far rooms.

"What were you doing outside earlier?" she asked once the doors were securely shut. She held a firm tone in her voice, suggesting she awaited only his confession, before his execution.

"I thought I saw someone go out there, and I was curious," he started, staring into Tarkan's stern face. He knew it would do him no good to lie to a member of the Inquisition, be they former or current.

"You *thought* you saw someone, or you *did* see someone?" Gael focused on his breathing; something about the woman made him uneasy. He imagined an aura flowing from the woman that made his tongue heavy and his thoughts clouded.

"I saw three people. One of them was tall. The other two were about my height."

"Alright. And you decided to follow these three?" Her eyes continued dipping beneath his skin. Goosebumps rose across his entire body as he attempted to speak through the hard wad developing in his mouth.

"I did."

"Why?"

He considered the question a moment. "The way they walked. The way they moved or barely breathed a sound. It just seemed as though something was not right."

"Be that as it may," Tarkan continued; "You will often find a great many things about this castle may pique your curiosity. That does not suggest you should traipse about, seeking trouble. Am I understood?"

"Yes, ma'am," he answered. "Is that all?"

"You may not have realized it, yet but there are those amongst us who do not want you or your brother around. There are still others who would prefer to see all common-born students removed. As conscripts of the royal family, Mari and Klein are all but guaranteed their place. Don't make you and your brother any bigger targets than you already are."

"Yes, ma'am. Good evening, ma'am," he said, more questions tormenting him now than before.

"And Mr. Stryfe," she added, causing his hand to freeze on the door latch. "Do stay out of the forest." Turning to look back at

Tarkan as she hovered over him, several thoughts, none of which were good, ran through his head. Reaching out, the instructor opened the door and motioned for him to leave.

Eager to escape from the room, he sped into the hall, rejoining his brother and peers. Despite their various questions, Gael simply shook his head as he made for his bedroom. Curious at what he had seen and angry for having been seen observing it, he lay quietly in his bed the entire evening, sleep eluding him until the early hours of the morning.

The following morning, Gael spoke to no one of what he had seen or about his conversation with their instructor. Keeping to himself, he made his way to the Great Hall for breakfast. Gabriel and his friends glanced at him awkwardly, though none attempted to pull him from his deep contemplation.

The morning mail arrived as always, carried upon the wings of enchanted birds. Their letters slowly floated down from the ceiling, landing in their recipients' eager hands. Gabriel, snatching such a letter from the air, tore into the envelope as thoughts of the Dark Forest ran through Gael's mind.

Reading the letter, Gabriel gasped at each line he read. Chin resting upon his folded arms, Gael glanced over at his brother. Smile on his face, Gabriel locked eyes with his brother.

"Rosalind had the baby!" he cheered, gaining his brother's full attention.

"Well? Is everyone alright? What did she have? Is it a brother? A sister?" Had he been any more excited, he might have stood on the table. Instead, he stood overtop his brother, breathing down on him with hastened breath, garnering chuckles from his fellows.

"It's a girl!" Gabriel cheered, holding the letter up into the air. Gael grumbled deep within his throat, having hoped for another boy in the family. Shrugging his shoulders, he looked up at the letter high in the air and cleared his throat.

"What else does it say?" he asked, gaining a smile from his brother as Gabriel filled him in on the vague details relayed in the message. Despite his brother's reassured nature, Gael felt something off in the lack of information regarding their foster father and fiancé.

****

The looming dread carried him through the afternoon but was lost by the time they reached the Great Hall for the evening meal.

"Uncle Torran was hurt and can no longer compete in the games." The young boy sighed, continuing to read the letter. "Sir Tristan has agreed to take his place. House Stryfe is sure to win," he cheered, ignorant to his brother's concerns.

Gathered about as they always did, it was of little surprise to them or the rest of their table when the room suddenly grew silent and chilly. Looking to the head table as had become routine, Gael noticed the absence of nearly all the faculty, save the class sponsors. Though they each sat calmly, Gael could sense a slight air of unease.

"Something's wrong," he muttered softly to himself.

Gabriel, who had otherwise been unaware, turned to face his brother. "What's wrong?" A mouthful of food muffled the question.

"Where are the rest of the teachers?" he asked. "It's only a few of the sponsors. Even Tarkan is missing. Look at them. They are uneasy about something."

Unconvinced by his brother's conspiracy theory, Gabriel shrugged his shoulders before resuming his meal. Looking around at his classmates, the boy quickly dismissed the incident.

An irritating sensation prodding in the back of his mind, Gael continued mulling.

"Did you hear that Inquisitors are creeping around again?" The words, uttered just above a whisper, rang as church bells in his ears.

"What was that?" he nearly pounced across the table towards his peer. Stunned, the tan-skinned, young woman across from him stared with wide eyes.

"I asked if she had heard about the Inquisitors?" she repeated mindlessly, looking over to her red-haired friend, who looked equally offset. "There were several of them talking with the Headmistress, earlier."

"What were they talking about?" Gael asked, only slightly gaining the attention of his brother.

"I do not know. As soon as we saw them, our sponsor steered us away."

"Then how do you know they were Inquisitors?" Klein asked, a typically nervous, fearful tone in his voice.

"Faculty do not usually carry swords through the halls and wear Templar insignias." She harumphed, turning her head away.

"Aura," the red-haired girl teased, nudging her friend. "You always have this unforgiving air about you." She smirked, waving her arms out in circles as though measuring the invisible *air* surrounding her friend.

As they finished their evening meal, Gael was first to leap from his seat and quickly make his way through the halls. Leaving his confused classmates behind, he scaled the steps, two at a time but was halted halfway up the second-floor stairwell.

"And what has you in such a hurry, Mr. Stryfe?" Tarkan spoke to him from the top of the stairs. He instinctively thought of an excuse, though abandoned it as he felt the air thickening around him as it often did when his instructor asked a question.

"I heard that some Templars had come to visit the Cabal." He found the loosely constructed truth easy enough to tell. "I wanted to see them, is all."

His instructor merely looked at him as she stood at the top of the flight. "Curiosity could see you tripping and taking a terrible tumble." She sighed. "Take care on the stairs, why don't you?"

"Yes, ma'am," he answered. "I will be more careful."

"As far as the Templars. I am afraid that you already missed them. They left shortly after speaking with the Headmistress."

Gael's shoulders sagged from disappointment. "What were they doing here?" he asked, walking in stride with her.

"That is the Headmistress' business and none of your concern, I would imagine."

"Do they come by often?" he prodded.

"Do you wish to become a Templar?" she asked. "Follow in your father's footsteps?"

"Sort of, I guess." He looked off to the side as they passed the portrait of the dancing frog, who removed his hat, waved. Below, he could hear the sound of his classmates catching up, though none seemed in any particular rush.

"Sort of?" Tarkan mused. "What other reason might you have for searching for Templars?"

He contemplated the complicated truth of the matter. "No other reason." He choked as he felt a tightness forming within his throat. "I just want to be a Templar." He coughed, wheezing slightly as he recovered.

Tarkan continued to stare at him, an inquisitive smirk on her face. "I see. Your father would be very proud."

Gael averted her gaze, remembering a blurry image of an Inquisitor from his childhood. His body grew tense as he recalled the man's snarl of a smile, the large scar near to his right eye, and the hollow tone of his voice. "Professor Tarkan, did you happen to see the Inquisitors?"

"I did."

"Was one of them a man with a scar on his right eye?" The tone in his voice held no life to it, no youthful exuberance.

Tarkan glanced sideways at him, though made no comment on his demeanor. "No. Not that I noticed," she answered. "Do you wish for me to inquire about one?"

Gael's head snapped to meet his teacher's eye. Slowly, he looked about the hall as they headed towards the commons. "No. Thank you," he grumbled. "I was just curious." He forcibly cleared his throat when it occurred to him that he only choked when he was dishonest. Slowly rolling his eyes back to meet Tarkan, she smiled faintly.

"When you're ready, young Stryfe," she whispered as the sound of his peers drew closer. "I believe this was your destination," she said, motioning towards the first-year commons. "Good evening."

"Good evening, Professor," he replied before retreating to the commons. Within, he solemnly walked to the far end of the room. Taking up a seat in front of the fire, he stared at the flames. He brooded, even as his friends entering the room, raised a ruckus with their cheers.

He stared deeply into the flames, though his thoughts quickly traveled far from the safe confines of the first-year commons.

He was much younger, again. Terrified and alone, crying out for his sister, whom he would never see again, as he watched his childhood home burn.

The evidence of what he had witnessed had already been washed clean by the flames and the rain. His hands had been washed and bandaged, concealing the burn wounds. As he sat, shivering, clinging tightly to his blanket, Tristan gripped his shoulder.

"Are you alright?" Gael's eyes snapped open as he turned his head to see Rinoa staring directly at him.

Startled, he looked around briefly before recovering. "Fine. Why?" His tone was harsher than intended.

She leaned back, slightly, looking at him. "Nothing. You just had a look about you. That's all. Never mind." She turned and walked away before he could say anything further.

"Want to play?" Looking behind his chair, he saw his brother and Klein engaged in a game of Warriors, Wizards, and Rogues.

"No. I'm just going to bed." He slid from his chair and shuffled his feet towards the boy's dorms.

J.A. Bullen

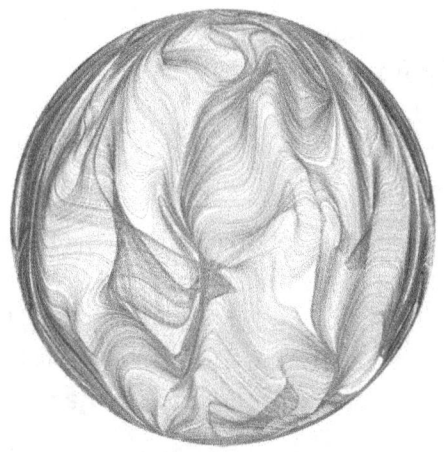

CHAPTER SEVEN

He awoke in a fit of panic that morning. His memories from the night before tormented his dreams, leaving his heart pounding when he awoke in a cold sweat. He sat upright, staring down at his lap, sorting his thoughts. As the beating of his heart steadied, he rose and walked to the washroom.

Refreshed, he changed his clothes and made for the commons, absently snatching one of his brother's books as he walked. Moving into the commons, he noticed his brother, Klein, and Mari, each assembled in front of the nearest hearth, already pouring over a table between the lounge chairs.

"What are you doing?" Gael asked, noticing the intense faces they each bore.

"Playing Warriors, Wizards, and Rogues," Mari cheered halfheartedly, contradicting herself as she lethargically raised her arm into the air. Gael glanced at the board to see Klein and Gabriel, both agonizing over their pieces.

"Who's winning?" he asked, looking at the various pieces arranged on the two boards. Both boys rolled their weary eyes up to Gael, telling all there was to know.

"You must be good at this, Mari," he commented, taking up a place not too far from the trio.

"Klein just taught me, yesterday," she sighed, rubbing the sleep from her eyes.

Slowly looking back to Klein and his brother, the boys' agonized faces confirmed Mari's story. "I'll let you all get back to it, then," Gael smiled, turning and staring at the fire. His thoughts quickly carried him away from the room, even as he absently thumbed through the pages of the book he had borrowed.

He remained alone with his thoughts until it was time to head down for breakfast. Exhausted from their ordeals at the gaming board, Klein and Gabriel returned to the dorms while he and Mari accompanied the rest of their classmates.

"You turned in early last night?" Mari asked, gently nudging him as they walked.

"I was tired," he shrugged. "You seem well-rested for having stayed up all night."

"Oh, I didn't. I actually took a rather long nap after the first few games." She smiled. "Lionel and some of the others played your brother and Klein after I turned in. I woke up early, and they were still there."

"Yeah. Gabriel loves that game." He smiled lightly. "We only have one board at home, so any chance he gets to play with more than one person, he takes."

"Do you play?" she asked, noticing Rinoa coming up alongside them as they walked. "It is a lot of fun, and they told me you can play with six people."

"On four boards. I know." He could not help but notice Rinoa listening in curiously. "I like it well enough. It can be fun when you cannot go outside, I guess."

"That makes sense." She smiled as they finished the trek to the hall. Breakfast was slightly less energetic without Klein, Gabriel, and Lionel's friends. However, out of his element, Gael found himself socializing with new faces.

"I am sorry for jumping out at you yesterday," He said over his morning porridge to the young, tan-skinned girl from the night before.

"It's alright," she smiled. "I always get excited when Templars are involved. My name is Aura, by the way. Aura Rinegar." She extended her hand with a smile.

"Gael Stryfe." He accepted her hand, shaking it. "I have never heard of the Rinegar family before."

"I'm from Renora, on the Southern Continent," she smiled. "This is my friend, Triny," she said, gesturing towards her red-headed friend.

"We've heard about your family already," Triny smiled, shaking his hand. "We look forward to attending battle school with you."

A musical chorus erupted within his ears, firmly pulling him from his foul humor. "Battle school?" he asked.

"Yes. Once the rest of the students and faculty arrive, Lang's class opens up, and we all attend together. At least that is what my older brothers told me." Triny continued. "They aren't here anymore. They are ten and twelve years older. I was something of a surprise," she smirked.

"So, in battle school," Gael began.

"Everyone shall participate together," Mari breathed, excitedly, slowly panning her vision over to Gael.

"Battlefield practice." They both grinned as the thought came to them.

"What else do you know?" Gael asked.

"Not much. Just that doing well enough in Lang's class can get you bumped up into Professor Damcian's course. Mostly, it's the military students who are funneled to her."

Suddenly, Gael's attitude for the day had been irrevocably changed.

He made certain to grab a roll and a few slices of ham for his brother, which he wrapped in a napkin. Tucking each into his pocket, he looked over to the high table. The teachers were all assembled at their usual table, though to Gael, their unease was beyond obvious. As the breakfast came to a close, a frosty chill settled into the room.

Smiling in unison, the students sat with their breathing frantic with anticipation for the morning's theatrics. Tiny, glistening flakes of snow twinkled delicately as they floated from a cloudless ceiling. Reaching up to one of the descending crystals, Gabriel startled as it burst at his touch.

The children at the table cheered as they were splashed with the glittering sprinkles of wintry magic as they scattered the length of the table. Many students began to awe in unison, effectively capturing everyone's attention as an ominous wind began gathering most of what had fallen in the center of the hall.

Whirling up from the floor as a twister, a pointed form spun as it rose, leaving a train of wintry wonder flowing behind it. The swirling reached a climax and erupted in a shower of sprinkles as Phyllida emerged from within the illusion's center. Awestruck by the show, nearly everyone erupted into applause, standing and cheering as they clapped.

Proud smile on her face, the Headmistress looked to her pupils and drew in a deep breath. "Good morning, students," Phyllida said, standing at the front of the room as the swirling snowflakes vanished from sight. "I trust you have all enjoyed your time here?" The children, Gael, and his brother included, clapped and cheered louder in response.

"Excellent. This afternoon, the returning students will join you, as they have finished their holiday. I do hope your remedial lessons have been effective, and you are all prepared for what your instructors have in store for you." Half of those in attendance groaned painfully.

"A suitable response, I suppose." She smiled, turning to her peers as they rose from their chairs. "Do not slack, now. Soon, you shall be competing against more students. You shall discover new friends and rivals to further promote one another through your magical studies."

As the Headmistress and faculty dismissed them, they rose from their chairs and made for their classes. The morning proceeded as most mornings do. They sat and listened to the lectures delivered to them by Professors Tarkan and Zerenia.

Next, they walked to the arena, where Professor Lang drilled them in combat. Bodies sore and starving for nourishment, they gathered for lunch and inhaled everything within arm's reach. Finally, as lunch came to an end, they walked to Professor Crowl's class, where Gael had the most trouble staying awake.

"And does anyone know what started the Second Magus War?" Professor Crowl asked, looming over her students who looked on fearfully. Rinoa's hand shot skyward.

"Yes," Crowl said in her gloomy tone.

"The Second Magus War was started by an invasion of Dalmorithia by forces from Neravor," she answered, to which Crowl inclined her head.

"And does anyone know why the Neravorans invaded?" Again, Rinoa's hand shot up.

"Does anyone other than Rinoa, know anything of history?"

"Oh, right here." Gabriel wriggled at his seat, hand held high for the second time. Crowl scanned over him as she had the first time. Seeing no other hands, she sighed.

"Yes. Gabriel."

"There was a large discovery of artifacts on the Dalmorithian side of the border. A network of ruins that the Neravoran King sought to control."

"A well-informed answer," she replied unhappily. "No doubt, your grandfather has schooled you on the matter."

"Yes, professor," he smiled proudly.

"Good to hear." She continued without the slightest trace of enthusiasm in her dry tone. "Then, perhaps your brother could tell us what significance the Kingdom of Altair played in this war?" Gael's eyes snapped forward, his daydream fading as Professor Crowl's evil eyes locked in on him.

"They assisted Dalmorithia?" His answer lacked all confidence. Gabriel frowned at him as Professor Crowl smirked.

"Though a dimwitted answer, you are not wrong," she replied. "Can anyone offer an educated answer?" She looked around the room, seeing only Gabriel and Rinoa's hands in the air.

"I believe the court sent agents behind Neravoran lines to help destabilize the Rune King's forces, while Altairan forces flanked their army at Garrison pass on the Dalmorithian side," Duncan interrupted, without raising his hand or being called upon. "Thus, the forces of Neravor were routed and expelled from Dalmorithia."

"An exceptional answer, Mister Reynald." Crowl smiled; a more unsettling thing than her frown. "It is heartwarming that a student takes such care with their history lessons." She turned and began waving her fingers in front of the board, which ran the length of the back wall.

Images began tracing across the blank slate, detailing a map of the region described. As she placed troops in various places along the borders and detailed the location of the contested ruins, Gabriel kicked his brother in the shin.

"How do you not remember this?" he whispered, pointing to the board. "Rosalind taught us all of this."

"She just took me by surprise, is all," Gael grumbled, folding his arms. "I remember. My mind just goes blank when she throws me on the spot. Leave it alone," he complained, turning away.

Crowl's lesson continued, calling on only select students despite others raising their hands while only praising Duncan and his cronies. The favoritism was lost on no one, which only served to stir Gael's temper further. Finally, it was time to be released, and they charged for their next class.

Moving through the changing halls and floating stairwells, they made their way from Professor Crowl's class towards Lang's arena. After another long, grueling session with the Battlemaster, they dragged their weary bodies to the commons to wash up before dinner.

Revitalized from the cool water on their faces and all their classes concluded, they prepared for the evening meal. As they left the first-year commons behind, they noticed a vast sea of bright lights hailing outside the castle's walls. The brothers made their way towards the Great Hall, only to find their way blocked by a sea of bodies, each trying to gain a better vantage of the window. Pressing their way through to the outside, they moved along the upper bannister.

"Are they here?" Gabriel chirped, excitedly, hopping up and down in an attempt to see outdoors.

"Who cares?" Gael grumbled, forcing his way past and onto the stairwell. "I'm hungry." Nodding his head, Gabriel followed after Gael, quickly finding Klein and Mari at the front of the line of students waiting to enter the Great Hall.

"Come on," Klein groaned, holding tightly to his stomach. "We're starving."

"We're dying out here," Mari chimed in, bending at the waist.

Mr. Graves, the grounds keeper, shook his head as he rolled his eyes. "I swear, children these days," he tutted. "The lot of you won't survive the next plague." He turned on his heel and forced the doors open. "Soft, this generation. Parents ruined the whole lot of them." He continued to mutter to himself as he pressed the doors wide, allowing the students to begin pouring inside.

They watched as droves of individuals representing various noble houses from three different nations, walked the halls with a distinct level of familiarity. Chatting amongst themselves, they absent-mindedly filed into the extra tables, which had been laid out for their return. It took only a few minutes, and the hall was filled with more people than ever before.

Turning in their chairs, the remedial students carefully watched those who were returning from their leave. Gael, uninterested in the goings-on, traced invisible patterns on the table with the tip of his finger. Looking up briefly, he noticed a fearful glance from Rinoa, who slouched unnaturally, her eyes barely peeking out from between her hood and arms, which rested on the table.

Eyeing her curiously, he turned his head in the direction she was facing and saw several pairs of eyes scanning the many faces. Most made eye contact with him while simply tracing over him and the others beside him. Eyebrow raised, he looked back to Rinoa, who shied away, concealing herself within her robes.

"Strange girl," he mumbled to himself. As the last of the newcomers filed in and found themselves a place to sit, Headmistress Phyllida appeared before them in her typical flash of blue light. Less inspired by the theatrics than of their classmates arrival, everyone looked to the woman, expectantly.

"Well. Perhaps I should appear in the village at the base of the mountain, instead. My reappearing act kills, down there." A dull roar erupted from the students as they humored their instructor. Smiling, she continued.

"First, I wish to welcome back all our returning students. I hope your time away was well spent." She paused a moment, allowing the students to answer in their own, rambunctious fashion. "Very good. Second, as I am certain you have all noticed, we have quite a few new faces amongst us. All of you will be working side-by-side in the coming days. I do hope we can all get along."

Despite her posture, smile, and tone, Gael could not help but sense an air of skepticism from the Headmistress. Worse, glancing at some of the favorable looks coming from Professor Crowl and some of the other instructors confirmed his suspicions. He looked from the teachers' table towards the students they were smirking at and found a gaggle of students sitting at Reynald's table, staring directly at him.

Infuriated at the growing, already sizable disadvantage he and Gabriel were at, he grumbled lightly to himself as he turned away. Again, he noticed Rinoa, carefully glancing from the gap under her hood. This time, when their eyes met, she looked away shamefully, without the scornful glance.

"Gael, are you going to eat?" his brother asked, lightly jarring him in the ribs as he motioned towards the food that had begun to appear on the table.

"Yes. Of course, I am." He distanced himself from his curiosities and tucked in. That evening, when they returned to their quarters, they found the commons only slightly more occupied than previously. Uninterested in the few new faces occupying the room, Gael moved through the commons towards the dormitory, climbed into his bed, and fell asleep.

CHAPTER EIGHT

The return of the missing students brought with it a new wave of problems and tensions. While Gael and the others grew used to the near daily taunting of Duncan Reynald and his pack of cronies, they found themselves snuffed all over again. Nobles filled every room, their noses pointed to the ceilings whenever their paths crossed. Had giving the cold shoulder proven the focus of their studies, Gael might have guessed each of the students were near graduation.

The practice of airing their superiority became a focal point in their lessons. Crowl, amongst others, showed particular interest in the familiar faces, often ignoring the remedial students. As the day progressed, the hope breaking the ice peacefully diminished.

"I thought the purpose of the remedial courses was to prepare each of you for our return?" Gael overheard one of the returning students yelling as he kicked Klein backwards during battle practice. The much smaller boy yelped as he fell to the ground but quickly sprang back to his feet.

"Klein, what have I told you about using your opponent's size as an advantage?" Lang grumbled, stepping between the two boys. Preoccupied with his session against Gabriel, he hardly noticed the professor's instruction. Instead, he turned to see the larger boy already on his rump, looking mournful.

"See? You can use your opponent's size against them." She tutted as she walked away, clicking her cane as she did so, leaving both students in bewilderment. "You may continue," she added, moving on to the next paring.

Gael looked back to his sparring partner, another young noble. His opponent lashed out at him fiercely, holding nothing back as she flailed wildly with her mace. The weapon had been significantly lightened to keep from collapsing the rib cage of anyone struck. However, Gael still felt his hands and arms growing numb from repelling countless blows.

"You're not terrible at this." The young woman pulverizing him smiled. "You might pass as a page boy in your grandfather's army."

"You're going to lecture me on nepotism?" he laughed, parrying. "You're the heir to how many titles, Tiana?"

Her eyes narrowed only slightly, though the gleam from behind her flowing hair intensified. "That is Miss or Lady Odaren to you," she grumbled, swinging with enough force to tear his head from his shoulders, practice weapon or not. "I will not be chided by a false noble." Their bout only intensified, the blows exchanged, threatening to break both their weapons.

It did not take long, before an audience of exhausted students gathered. Professors Lang and Damcian stood off to the side, talking amongst themselves as they watched. They continued moving back and forth across the field as neither managed a vantage over the other.

Arms completely numb, weapon chipping from strain, Gael smirked at his opponent. Likewise, he saw her smiling back at him as she continued swinging. Nearing his limit, Gael tipped himself out of the way of another blow, feeling Tiana's mace sliding down his blade.

He tipped sideways as he felt the mace grazing his shoulder. As he spun, ready to make his killing stroke, he noticed the slightest glint in his opponent's eye. A light emanated from behind her long bangs.

Swiftly, she rolled her shoulders, arching her back and rolling her neck, pulling herself clear from his stroke by the slightest of margins. He watched in disbelief as his blade struck nothing but the few loose strands of hair that trailed behind. His blade passed overtop her head, Gael attempted to slow his swing and recover as he felt a firm grasp on the collar of his shirt.

Adjusting her posture, she dropped her center of gravity, rapidly pulling Gael forward. The point of his weapon struck the ground, jarring it from his hand as he was thrown onto his back. Dazed, he focused his vision to see the ball of Tiana's mace resting under his chin.

"It was a worthy effort, Stryfe," she commented before turning and leaving him winded, and in disbelief. Hearing the snickers of the others in his class, he attempted to right himself.

"Right here, Stryfe," a voice called as a firm hand grasped his arm. "Let's get you up."

Looking up as stumbled to his feet, Gael locked eyes with Cornelius. "Thanks," he mumbled sheepishly, body sore from his bout. "I guess you saw that."

"You bet I did," he smiled, clapping Gael on the back. "I thought you were all talk when you were going on about wanting to practice. You're actually pretty good." He stood with his arm around Gael's shoulders, clapping him gently.

"She wiped the floor with me," he retorted, gesturing towards the mark of his body in the grass. Even as he complained, he felt an irritating grasp on his jaw as Cornelius forcibly turned his head to see Professors Lang and Damcian.

"You see them, over there?" he asked. "Know what they're saying?"

Gael, jerking his head free, looked at his upperclassman. "I have no idea," he huffed. "What are you trying to say?"

CJ muttered a few words to himself as he formed three quick hand signs.

"The entire purpose of the exercise was to test their combat abilities without using magic." Gael could hear Lang's voice, quietly speaking near his ear.

"We can debate the theory and logic of magical forms all day and night, Tannis.," Professor Damcian retorted. "However, as I have said, Tiana's abilities are not an example of casting magic."

"But one might argue that it is the result of an enchantment."

"And if invoked, a spell, correct," Damcian agreed. "However, Tiana's ability is involuntary." The voice faded away, leaving Gael staring dumbstruck at his friend.

"What were they talking about?" he asked, looking at CJ who smirked, uneasily.

"It is called *Battle Sight*, Mr. Stryfe," Professor Damcian spoke as both she and Professor Lang drew near. "It allows her a glimpse of foresight when she is in battle."

"She's a clairvoyant," Lang interjected. "She can see things before they happen."

Damcian shook her head as they began to walk away. "Battle Sight is activated by adrenaline, Tannis. It is not magic, nor is it clairvoyance. Also, CJ, espionage spells are not meant to be used against faculty. I shall see you later for your detention." The boy smiled and shook his head as he watched his instructor walk away.

"Stryfe," Lang interrupted. "It's time for you to get back to training." Looking to his classmates, who continued to struggle within the cracks of the social rift, Gael looked to his battered weapon. "Grab another and get back to it," his instructor ordered, before walking away.

Such became the general attitude of the returning students towards their remedial counterparts. However, the issue became the air of superiority the more experienced students held, and less about the coursework. In each class, Gael and his fellows found themselves segregated from their new peers, and during each battle practice, he sought to study his more experienced peers, Tiana Ordaren in particular. The separation carried on through the entirety of the day, during meals, and even recreation time.

The next several days of school progressed much the same. Professor Zerenia schooled them in the subject of Magical Theory when she was not distracted by the various artifacts strewn about the room. From there, the days consisted of basic lessons involving writing, mathematics, history, and the like. As before, Gael found great difficulty staying awake.

"Don't our classes seem too easy?" Gael asked as they made their way to his favorite class, battle practice."

"I thought it was just me, but if you're noticing it as well, then it must be the case."

"I wondered as much. Hey!" Gael snapped louder than intended, causing the other students around them to whirl about. His brother's only response was a smug smile as they formed a line, before the awaiting Professor Lang.

Their practice session that evening was as unrelenting as those that came before it. By the end, each student was drenched in sweat and ached from various welts and bruises. As had become the custom, Niferi healed their injuries one by one before sending them on their way to the mess hall.

Exhausted, Gael took a seat and looked out at the few students who were still practicing. Klein did not make it to the benches. Instead, he lay twenty paces away, sprawled out on the ground, panting.

Mari was moving back towards the ring, practically dragging Gabriel behind her. Seeing Tiana resting nearby, fighting to catch her breath, he rose. Walking to where the young woman stood, she glowered at him before he drew near.

"What do you want, Stryfe?" she spat, wiping the perspiration from her brow. "Want to get knocked down again?"

"I just wanted to tell you I think your technique is amazing. I didn't have the chance to say something before."

Tiana eyed him suspiciously. "Thanks," she grumbled in response. "You're not bad for a first-year," she added, standing and stepping away. "Keep practicing." Leaving Gael behind, she gathered with her classmates and left.

As the brothers sat that evening, demolishing whatever food was left within reach, their classmates gawked in amazement; their plates scarcely picked over. Noticing the strange break in their mealtime customs, Gael gently looked up to see several of his classmates eyeing him.

"Is something on my face?" he asked, amused as they quickly averted their gazes. With a gentle huff, he returned to his task until he received a gentle nudge in the ribs. Scowling at his brother, who stared forward in horror, Gael followed the invisible line of his vision towards the noble's tables, a place he only pretended did not exist.

Standing upon the bench, stood Duncan Reynald, broad smile on his face as he held up a poster in his hands. At first glance,

Gael merely turned to his brother with an air of disappointment at the boy's concern with their arrogant classmate. However, the image struck a chord, and he quickly returned his gaze to the parchment.

"Tristan Alistair Stryfe," Reynald read aloud, beady eyes trained on the two brothers and their horrified peers, "wanted for crimes against the Crown, murder, and treason. Extremely dangerous. Do not engage. Those who offer favorable leads to the King's army shall be rewarded handsomely. In the event of his live capture, the informant shall be rewarded with a fiefdom."

The boy's wicked eyes gleamed brightly. Catching onto his scheme, his fellows all turned in their seats, catching a glimpse of the horrified expressions on the brothers' faces. Rolling up his poster, Reynald hopped down from his perch and slowly approached them.

"Did you hear that, Stryfes? Finally, someone has caught on to the worthless garbage your father is." Gael balled his fists tightly, though Gabriel gripped his forearm, eliciting a pained reaction. Everyone gathered in the hall, rapidly centered their attention on the argument. While Gabriel's eyes searched despairingly for a friendly upperclassmen or faculty member, the flames surging through Gael, swelled.

"Personally, I hope they hang him," Duncan's smile grew. "Who knows, maybe they'll decide to teach all you common bloods your place. By the Amaranthine."

"It is unwise to invoke the Amaranthine with your childishness." Gael turned his head and stared into Rinoa's cold eyes with no small amount of shock. Despite his outrage, he could not help but feel a twinge of gratitude.

"Probably another of your family's petty schemes," Mari shouted. Klein however, did his best to shrink in his seat. His eyes flashed between the entourage of students, fearful of being dragged into the building commotion. Near to them, Lionel, Emma, and the others stared dumbstruck at the brothers.

"No, if my family has any involvement, it will be hunting down that beast and flaying him. I hope they mount his head on a pike outside of this school. Hopefully, they'll do something about that Dalmorithian wench and that Hagen trollop he keeps panting on her leash."

Despite his brother's grasp on his arm, Gael lurched free of his seat, throwing Gabriel to the floor. Pouncing upon the surprised noble, he drove his fist into the boy's jaw, paining his wrist and hand in doing so. He fell forward, overtop the squealing blonde as another leapt to his side.

"Gael!" Gabriel gasped, observing the conflict as Gael repeatedly struck at the flailing boy while his entourage came to his rescue. He paid no heed to his own bloody hands as he continued to flail with rage. Pulled aside by two of the larger boys, Gael straightened himself to throw them off when the four of them froze.

Gael felt a squeeze on his heart as the blood in his veins stopped its natural flow. Again, a large pulse echoed through the bodies of those fighting, and not even their agonized groans could escape their mouths. Immediately, the Reynald trio collapsed to the ground as Gael attempted to turn his head.

"That is enough!" Tarkan roared, hand clasping the hilt of her sword, which Gael had not seen since they had first arrived at the Cabal. The gemstone on the pommel of the weapon glowed ominously. It was the bloodstone.

A third pulse struck him hard in the chest, forcing what little air he kept from his lungs. He felt a deep burn within his body, even as ice crept over his skin. Eyes filled with panic as even the faces and voices of his nearby friends were lost to his senses, Gael turned to face his tormentor.

"Reynald, you and your friends are to report to Professor Scrowl this instant!" Her voice was clear to him, though nothing else remained in his world. She approached him, and suddenly a fog cleared around her, simply to show him the anger in her eyes.

"You. Are coming with me." Releasing her hand from the pommel of her sword, Gael felt all his vital faculties return to him at once. He gasped while the freezing of his body and burning of his organs reversed. Fighting to withhold tears, he attempted to rise, only to stumble and fall back to the ground.

"Gabriel. Help your brother," she snarled, causing the uninjured boy to yelp unceremoniously.

"Yes, ma'am," he squeaked as he quickly dropped to Gael's side and placed himself beneath his brother's arm.

"The rest of you." The entire congregation, not knowing whom she intended, went rigid. Making a quick sweep of the room, confirming their fears, she sighed. "Conclude your meals and make your way to your designated commons. An official announcement shall be made come morning regarding what you've just heard. Until then, this matter is concluded."

Turning, the former Inquisitor marched from the Great Hall, the brothers Stryfe in tow, albeit sluggishly. Shuffling behind his brother, Gael lethargically lifted his gaze to his instructor's back. They stopped in one of the many side rooms Gael had yet to explore. Turning her gaze upon the brothers, she placed her hands on her hips and glowered.

"That was quite possibly the dumbest thing I have ever seen someone in your position do," she roared, looming over Gael threateningly. Gael shrugged his brother off, lightly dropping to the nearest chair as he did so.

"He did not need to say those things about Rosalind or the Commander," he sniffled, withholding his tears. "There is no way he would betray the King of Altair."

Professor Tarkan remained silent for several moments. Turning her back towards the two boys, she placed her hands on the table, before releasing a heavy sigh. "I understand your frustrations. Believe me, I do." She turned her head to look at the two sympathetically. "I have served with your father. I understand the sort of man he is."

"Then you know he is innocent," Gael raised his voice in outrage. "You must realize it's all a hoax."

"I am afraid the world is more complicated than that," she answered softly. "Just promise me you will keep yourselves out of trouble from now on." Tarkan stood, staring at the two brothers sympathetically, she released the tension in her shoulders. "I am sorry, boys. I truly am. Just promise me." The brothers both looked to their teacher, their faces bearing the excruciating frustration they felt loudly.

"I promise, Professor Tarkan," Gabriel answered with little hesitation. Both turned their eyes upon Gael, who screwed his face in apprehension.

"I promise. To try," he grunted.

"He's like that sometimes," Gabriel chimed in. "If he sees something that doesn't sit with him, he just cannot help himself."

"I once knew someone like that," Tarkan forced a smile. "If you promise to do your best, I suppose that is all I can ask. However, there is still the matter of your punishment."

"Punishment?" Gabriel gulped.

"Yes. You did assault a classmate."

"And a noble!" Gabriel yelped. "They can hang you for that." The anxiety on his face told the tale his sweating palms and panicked quavering began.

"That is not the issue here," Tarkan assured the trembling boy. "The object of this school is to treat students according to their willingness to learn. We aim to support the balance of Anon, not the circumstances of our pupils' births."

"What is to be my punishment?" Gael sighed.

Removing a small sheaf of parchment from the folds of her robes, she handed the bundle to Gael. "Take this to Lady Strauss. She is the head librarian here. She will be the one to administer your punishment."

"You want me to report to her, now?" Gael asked in disbelief.

"Yes. Just imagine how much faster you will complete your task if you get started now." The woman bore a malicious grin, which was more in nature with the Inquisitor they had come to know. Unable to contest her judgement, Gael hung his head as he shuffled from the room.

Moving through the massive halls, he caught glances from his fellow students, who still whispered amongst themselves as they cast sharp glances. Shamed, outraged, and disgraced, he turned towards the stairwell and marched through the large halls, every bit aware of the many eyes of students and enchantments alike upon him.

His steps echoed through the halls he walked, further emphasizing the isolation he felt. He continued to seethe with anger until the large doors of the library greeted him. If the massive doors had been meant to clue him in on the size of the library, they had failed.

Within, he immediately found himself lost in a world belonging to giants. Bookcases as tall as many of the noble homes in Leones reached up towards an impossibly high ceiling. Quickly stepping back outside, he looked to the doors and quickly judged the distance to the floor above, before reentering the gargantuan room.

Upon walking inside, however, he was certain he had stepped into some illusion. Entering the room under no small amount of suspicion, he strained his neck to see the ceiling of the room. Stumbling about awkwardly, he absently walked into one of the countless bookcases and fell onto his rear.

"Quiet in the library, please." An exhausted yet no less irritated tone rang out. The voice was cold, detached. Already, he grew concerned over the fate Tarkan had prepared for his punishment. However, rising to his feet, he habitually brushed himself off and moved towards the voice's source.

A large counter stood at the corner of the room nearest to him. Approaching it, he looked to the tall, red-headed woman behind the desk, furiously stamping books. Her hair was pulled back behind her head in stereotypical fashion accenting the small-framed glasses she wore. Her eyes twitched in his general direction. Her brow creased in response, the wrinkles running along her forehead in scalelike patterns opposed to lines.

"Umm... Lady Strauss?" he asked, worriedly, reaching for the slip of paper in his pocket. Holding it up, he caught the ageless woman's attention, her eyes narrowing at the sight of it and him.

"Why does that woman always seek to waste my time?" she growled, agitated tapping coming from behind the concealment of the desk. "Fine, then. Make yourself useful and begin taking care of those stacks of books." She continued to grumble, waving in the distance towards several stacks of books taller than he.

Mouth agape, Gael looked to the books and then back to the librarian who had already returned to her previous chore of stamping books and acting as though he ceased to exist. Still, he felt some manner of relief that she had not looked at him the same way as his peers in the Great Hall. Shuffling over to the first of the many stacks, he lifted the first tome into his hands.

"Portal magic for novices: A beginner's guide to moving objects from here to there." Opening the first page of the book revealed numerous glyphs, graphs, and complicated diagrams, which he could not make sense of. Feeling a sharp stab between his eyes, he immediately closed the book and attempted to find its home.

The side of the book contained a series of numbers along the spine. He glanced from it to similar sets of numbers along the top of each of the bookcases. Wandering about the halls until he found a corresponding set of numbers, his eyes traced higher and higher until his eyes widened and watered.

"Is there a ladder somewhere?" he asked aloud. Searching many of the other aisles, he saw no sign of what he sought. He juggled the book, determining the best way to carry it. Tucking it under his arm, he carefully placed one hand onto the shelf in front of him as he stepped up onto the second.

"What are you doing?" His attention turned to Rinoa, who bore a cross expression on her face as she witnessed her peer defiling the bookcase.

"Putting the books back?" he responded with confusion. "There was no ladder."

An irritated sigh escaped the girl as she stared in disbelief at him. Lifting the book in her hands higher, she turned the book sideways. Reading the numbers upon the side of the tome aloud, she allowed the book to fall from her hands.

With jaw agape, he watched as the book, which he was sure would strike the ground with a racket, hovered just above it. As he crouched to examine the odd occurrence, the book simply soared back into the air, floating up to the sixth shelf. There, resting above his head, the tome turned spine up and wriggled itself back onto the shelf.

Continuing to stare in awe, Gael gleamed at the book as Rinoa cocked her head sideways, dumbfounded by his ignorance. "You are truly clueless to how the world you've entered works, aren't you?" she observed, shaking her head.

Broken from his appreciation of the feat she just accomplished, red crawled across Gael's cheeks as his eyes locked on Rinoa's. "You are a vile one, aren't you?"

Rinoa's face scrunched, wrinkling her nose as she scowled in response. "Fine. See if I come to help you, again," she grumbled, turning on a heel, and walked away.

"Rinoa?" he called out weakly. He heard the aggressive tapping of her boots stop as she leaned back into his field of vision.

"Yes?" The tone in her voice was softer than it had been a moment before. She looked at him with concern in her eyes.

"About..." he started, though abruptly stopped himself as the words he wished to say left him, leaving him lost in the agony of his thoughts.

"Gael. I," she paused herself, looking at the fragile look in her peer's eyes. She watched, taken off guard as his head dropped from his position and sagged between his shoulders. "I am sorry," she muttered. "I also have family I'm not proud of."

"He's innocent!" he growled, sudden pangs from an invisible red poker, sparking his vengeful side. The girl stepped back from the shock, dumbstruck. As he glared, her brow creased rigidly.

"It was a mistake talking to you. Idiot." She quickly spun and huffed as she moved away. Scoffing to himself, Gael looked to the book he held and turned it over in his hands.

"Four, twenty-three, thirty-five," he read angrily, attempting to remove the conversation from his mind. Following Rinoa's example, he dropped the book only to jump as it collided with the floor, resulting in a heavy bang.

"What are you doing?" Lady Strauss snarled, peering around the corner. He could see the woman's sharp fangs protruding over her lips as she did so.

Gael looked to the book, its high place on the bookshelf, and to the librarian in rapid succession. "Rinoa made it look so simple," he sighed pathetically.

"Well? Do not just stand there. Pick it up." The glare he was receiving carried the potential to kill, he thought to himself. Scrambling, he collected the book from the floor and looked cautiously to the instructor.

"You have to channel some energy into it first," she sighed, taking the book from his hands. Carefully, he watched as the woman's fingertips glowed lightly before she dropped the book. Watching it sail to its proper home above, Gael frowned.

"I'll try again," he proclaimed, running back to the first row of stacks. Grabbing the first tome he could reach, he wheeled around and searched the bookcases for the appropriate number.

Nearly tripping as he came to a sudden halt, he turned down the specified aisle and looked for the proper place on the shelf. Seeing the book's home just two shelves above, he stared at the tome and focused on its leathery surface. As though he were using an artifact, he attempted to force mana through his fingertips and released the book.

As before, the book fell straight to the floor, though he managed to place his foot beneath it, muffling the sound. He scrunched his face in pain as his foot throbbed beneath the heavy book. Taking deep breaths, he lifted the book from the ground and again concentrated on the energy flow leaving his fingers.

Hands vibrating with energy, he slowly released the book, wincing in advance for the crushing blow to his foot that was sure to come. Hearing no thud and feeling no resurgence of pain through his lower limb, Gael slowly peeked open his eyes and gasped with excitement. The book hovered at waist level and slowly climbed its way higher. Reaching its designation on the shelf, it nestled itself within.

Cheering silently to himself, he rushed excitedly back to the stack of unfiled books and began casting them off at the shelves, one by one. Many came crashing back to the ground upon either his feet or head, while others still, arrived at their destination on the first try. By the time he had depleted the first of the stacks, he had grown dizzy and perspired heavily from every pore of his body.

Moving back to the front of the library, he stood before Lady Strauss and smiled. "I'm all done," he said, happily.

Strauss slowly raised her gaze from her task, her eyes filled with irritation at the interruption. Looking from him to the missing stack of books, she flicked the bridge of her nose and sniffed. "Well? What are you still doing, loitering around? This is a place of learning, not a daycare. Read a book or be gone," the grouchy woman huffed, flicking her nose a second time before returning to her cataloguing.

In shock but not frozen in place, Gael peeled his widened gaze from the demi-human and made for the hall. "I almost forgot," he groaned, turning on a heel and stopping back in front of the desk.

"What is it, now?" The librarian huffed, taken from her work, again.

"I am sorry, Lady Strauss," Gael gulped, reaching into his pocket and producing Tarkan's slip of paper. "Can you please sign this, so my sponsor knows I did as you asked?"

Strauss narrowed her eyes at him as she glanced at the tiny sheet in his hand. With the speed of a striking viper, she lashed out and struck the parchment from his hand with a "thud."

Startled, he looked down at the paper on the desk and saw the librarian's stamp upon it. "Thank you," he stuttered, turning and running for the hall.

"No running," Strauss growled under her breath, returning to her task as though the boy had never visited. His pace slowed to a crawl as he closed the door behind himself. Clear of the librarian's wrath, he bolted for the common area, looking to join up with his classmates.

"It's about time you finished!" Gabriel grumbled, eyes wide with anxiety. "You've nearly missed lunch, ancient history, and combat practice." Mari laughed intrusively as Klein looked concerned.

"They can make us miss meals?" The boy gasped, silently swearing to himself to be always on his best behavior.

"No, you dolt," Mari replied, shoving him in the shoulder. "They'd still feed us. Might not be the same as what's downstairs, though." With a sigh of relief, the boy calmed himself as Gael looked to his brother.

"How could I have *almost* missed those things when I have not missed *any* of them?" His brother answered with a look of protest as he shoved a stack of papers into Gael's arms. "What are these?" he asked, snatching desperately at the pages as they fell towards the floor.

"I figured you would want some notes. You're lousy at taking them yourself." His brother stamped off down the stairwell, leaving Gael rather confused.

"He is just upset about your father," Klein added.

"What Klein said. I think he is just stressed and can't show it the same as you." Gael nodded his head as he followed his peers towards the Great Hall.

****

"Good afternoon, slugs," the tiny elder barked, slamming her staff into the ground. Gael and Gabriel smirked as Rinoa and Klein let out the smallest of yelps. "Hope you enjoyed your lunch. Today's battle practice is going to take a more practical approach." The students assembled outside, stood at attention, forming three long lines of individuals, desperately hoping not to catch the instructor's eye.

Across from them at the far end of the coliseum, Professor Damcian's students had already begun their drills. Already, they could hear grunts and groans as they attacked one another with their blunted weapons. More than once did they hear the activation of a spell as Lang continued to speak with them.

"Each of you has grown accustomed to equipping yourselves and defending yourselves with various weapons. On the battlefield, these skills will save your lives. However, if ambushed, the inability to act quickly will be your downfall."

Everyone in the class stared in confusion at the instructor as a wicked smile crept across her lips. A brief silence washed over the other class as they too, remembered the lesson their underclassmen were learning. A long pause fell upon the class, and even Niferi, stationed in her seat in the stands, shielded herself.

"And go!" she called. Slowly marching forward, the class moved for the equipment racks. "Enemy attack!" Professor Lang roared. Startled, Gael whirled about as the teacher lunged forward. "Ready yourselves or perish."

Suddenly, much lighter on her feet, Professor Lang charged across the field, staff held over her head. Reaching for a sword, Gael spun on a heel, narrowly raising his weapon in time to defend his face from Lang's staff. His hand vibrated painfully as he blocked a follow-up attack from the woman.

"Not terrible," she complimented him before turning briskly. Before his eyes managed to follow the woman's movement, he felt her heel planted deeply into his gut.

Falling on the ground, gasping violently for air, Gael scooted away from his instructor as she attacked the next student. As she floated about the grounds effortlessly, dispatching one student after another, he found his feet. Briefly remembering the exercise, he ran straight for the armor rack.

Lifting the first chest piece he could reach, he thrust his head through it. Quickly working the straps, he tightened the armor onto his torso as Lang turned her attention towards him. Stopping just inside the reach of his blade, she struck him hard in the stomach, winding him. Before he could attempt to catch his breath, he felt his legs swept from out from beneath him.

"I must admit, you did better than the others," she smiled, still pointing the end of her cane at his chest. "Still, far from good enough, however. Keep practicing." Removing her staff from the center of his chest, she allowed Gael to return to his feet.

"I would advise each of you to practice more seriously. It won't be much longer before we will be switching over to more practical combat training."

"More practical?" Rinoa asked, rubbing her shoulder where Lang had struck her.

"Correct. Starting tomorrow, you will resume practicing against one another. This will allow me to critique each of you without sending any of you to the Healing Ward. For now, we will work on form. Line up." Far from strangers to such callous treatment, the brothers quickly fell in formation, followed by Rinoa and the others.

"What is that?" Mari asked of the small grove near the center of the arena. A well worn, rust-covered sword lay plunged into the ground. The marker's design caught Gael's attention with its near-spherical hand guard, which rested around the hilt.

"It looks like an ornamental blade," Gabriel commented.

"Not with all that rust it doesn't," Klein snickered. "One swing, and it's likely to break."

"Still," Mari mused. "It must serve some purpose."

"One of the Cabal's founding members died in this spot," Lang answered, having crept up behind them. "Or rather, a spot just like this one."

"So, the grave is a fake?"

"The grave, yes. The sword, though lacking most of its former power, is very much real."

"What sort of sword is it?" Gael asked.

"A rusted one," Klein joked.

"The sword is called the Hearthfire Blade. It is a relic that was forged long ago. If you wish to know more than that, you will have to ask that Zirennia woman. She spends many of her evenings here already. Strange woman that one."

Gael looked to the weapon which had been struck into the ground countless years ago. Resuming his practice, he took occasional glances back at the blade, making a note to ask the gnome more at the next opportunity.

That evening, head filled with questions, Gael made his way to the Great Hall, eager to speak with the Artificier about the story of the fallen founder. Unable to catch her attention prior to dinner, he kept a close watch on her movements during the evening meal. As the meal came to a close, he managed to capture her attention.

"Ah, Mr. Stryfe. How nice to see you," she said, hastily. Nibbling on numerous sweets, she moved past him.

"Wait a moment, Professor," he called, hurrying after the pink hair as it disappeared into the crowd. "I wish to speak to you about the Hearthfire Blade." At the mention of the fabled blade, Zerenia froze, hair shining like a beacon.

"Oh?" she asked, similar to the way an owl calls in the night. "I did not realize you had an interest in artifacts."

Quickly surveying his surroundings, he made certain his brother was not in earshot. "To be honest, Professor. I am much better at using artifacts than I am at casting spells. It is one of the few things I can do better than my brother. Like you, I also find them more interesting than talking about theories."

The gnome stared inquisitively a moment, her pink eyebrows arched. "You wouldn't be one of those boys who's obsessed with heroic tales, filled with tragedy, adventure, and glory, would you?"

Despite his pride and personal desires, Gael's eyes grew wide as Zerenia spoke. His grin widened as he recalled the various legends and stories held close to his heart further betrayed his secret. "I am," he replied, ashamed.

A small, sinister smile spread the tiny Professor's lips. "Follow me, young Stryfe," she ordered, turning about and walking away. "You may yet be useful."

"Useful?" he repeated aloud, staring at Zerenia's back. "How so?"

"Hopefully, as a brand new test subject. I have seen that you may have an affinity for my work."

Gael allowed the thought of being a favorite test subject to hang in the air. As his feet continued to follow the Professor, however, he prayed it was a result of poor social skills.

As he followed the gnomish professor back to her classroom, he caught Mari's eye, who, accompanied by Rinoa, stared at him curiously. He waved gently, still uncertain of his fate at the hands of the eccentric teacher. Both looked at him with concern before Rinoa resumed her disinterested gaze and walked on.

"Now then, where did I leave that book?" she said aloud, hanging precariously from the ladder in her classroom. Eyes scanning the shelves, Gael read many of the spines, ranging from old, faded tomes to personal notebooks. Reaching for an old leather-bound book with no title, he jumped as the gnome cried out with a high-pitched cheer.

"Alright, here we are," she exclaimed, dropping the book on the table, which boomed from the weight. A massive tome, one to give an energetic youth nightmares, Gael noticed several loose sheets of paper, protruding from the book in various directions.

"Do I need to read this?" he asked nervously.

Zerenia raised an eyebrow in response. "Parts. If you search through my notes, you will find bits of the legend you are searching for. I should warn you. To be my research assistant, you may need to read frequently."

"Research assistant?" he blurted, with no small amount of shock in his voice. "I was only curious about the Hearthfire Blade."

"Oh? That? By all means, then, follow me," Zerenia chirped, sliding down from the ladder and making for the door. Giving chase, Gael jogged for the door, desperately trying to keep up with the deceptively quick gnome. Reaching the arena, Zerenia made a straight course for the mentioned artifact, paying no attention to the groups of students on the field.

"What's a mutt like you doing here?" Gael's attention gravitated towards the young Reynald. "You're going to attract fleas standing out here." The entirety of the young man's social circle howled with laughter. Gritting his teeth, he ignored the jeers as he followed his instructor.

Resting off to the far side of the arena, the Hearthfire Blade remained stabbed into the collection of stones. Approaching the rusted sword, Zerenia removed a handful of herbs from her pocket. Smiling to Gael, she sprinkled the compound over the sword. As the herbs fell to the ground, they crackled with flame. A faint gleam of light rose off the blade as it consumed the fuel, setting off the smell of incense.

"The magic in the blade is still alive?" he asked, turning his head towards the smiling gnome.

"It is," she answered, nodding her head. "Touch it."

Eyes wide, he gawked at Zerenia. "Won't it burn me?" he asked, fearfully.

"What?" she asked, absently, eyes greedy with the thirst of knowledge and exploration as she stared at the artifact.

"The blade. Won't it burn me if I touch it?" The hairs on the back of his neck prickled as he realized an audience of less gullible students was amassing.

"Maybe. Touch it."

Again, he stared at the teacher and glanced at the spectators, who pretended not to notice him. Muttering a silent prayer for his hands, he reached out shakily. Extending a single finger, he gently brushed the hilt of the sword, which responded with the subtlest of vibrations.

"It's going to take more than a finger," Zerenia whispered.

He glanced back again, noticing the battle training had ceased. No fewer than a dozen battle pairs quickly turned away, pretending they were only stretching. Closing his eyes, he drew in a deep breath. Releasing it with a heavy sigh, Gael grasped the hilt.

A small crackle of flame lit the blade as it fed upon the surrounding stones and earth. He stared in awe at the sword, feeling it slowly draw upon his energy. It pulsed with a gentle heartbeat, until he released his hold and the gentle embers went out.

"Excellent work, young Stryfe," Zerenia clapped and cheered, excitably. "I think you'll make an exemplary assistant."

"Professor's pet mongrel, more like it." Reynald sneered from behind them. "I bet anyone could use that rusted piece of garbage if an unwashed beast such as yourself can."

From a distance, Professor Lang stood alongside several of the other students in the noble's class.

"Give it a try if you like," Zerenia smiled, motioning towards the blade with her right hand.

"I will. With or without your permission," He grumbled, shoving Gael in the chest. "Out of my way, Mongrel," he yelled, stepping in front of the blade. "There's no way a filthy-blooded, false noble can do this." Grasping onto the handle, Reynald gave the blade a pull.

Just as had been the case with Gael, the blade hummed gently. Reynald smiled as the sword continued to glow in his hand, thrumming with a lifelike pulse. As his grip on the blade exceeded the time Gael had held it, the boy's triumphant look grew.

"You see, everyone? It was just a fluke. The blade is barely hot at all," he cheered, pulling the blade. It resisted his pull, remaining firmly planted in the soil. Straining against the sword, beads of sweat began running down his brow. A moment later, a panicked expression crossed his face, before the sword burst into flame.

Reynald screamed in pain, lurching backwards as his hand was seared. Stumbling back, he fell to the ground, screaming as he clutched his hand. Fearing his death, he quickly attracted a large crowd.

"No need to fuss so, Mr. Reynald," Zerenia said calmly, waving off the boy's cries of pain. "I do not know of anyone who perished from such a small mana burn." Though she had stood opposite the arena, Lang was the first to the young man's side.

"I do wish you wouldn't encourage students to touch that damned relic," she growled. "I would have hoped your failure would have served warning enough." Removing her left hand from within her robes, Gael saw the multiple layers of bandages on Zerenia's hand.

"Progress is built on the failures of those before," she smiled, holding her uninjured hand to Gael.

Lang, producing an ointment, smeared it on Reynald's hand. Wrapping the wound, she turned her attention back to the gnome. "Don't try to make him touch it, too," she growled, turning her head to the still howling boy's entourage. "Get this boy to the Healing Ward," she barked. As the band scurried away, Professor Lang issued one final warning before returning to her class.

"Alright then, back to the matter at hand," the gnome said, excitedly. "Seeing as the sword doesn't burn you, let's have some fun." Rubbing her hands together, she poured over the artifact once more.

"How do you know it won't burn me? Reynald held it longer than I did, and he wasn't burnt at first."

"Was it hot when you first touched it?"

Gael considered the question before answering. "No. It was cool to the touch."

Pink eyebrows raised as the instructor smiled. "Touch it," she whispered again. "I've heard the rumors the same as everyone else. More than anything, you need to start a name for yourself now. Researching long-dormant relics would not be a bad place to start, Warden." The last comment was spoken so softly, Gael barely heard it.

"How do you know about that?" he asked, worriedly. "Professor Tarkan told me not to tell anyone."

Waving off the boy's concern, Zirennia smiled. "I'm not going to tell anyone. That's just how I knew you'd be a good fit, is all. You know, seeing as the last person to hold that weapon was also one."

"Who were the Wardens?" he asked.

"Who knows?" Zerenia responded, shrugging her shoulders. You find the mention of a few here and there in history books. Both good and bad however, the only times I have seen them mentioned are during times of major change."

Gael allowed those words to sink in carefully. At the same time, he considered a career as an Artificier. He often heard stories of people exploring the ruins of the old world. He knew of one such ruin beneath Lothren, which was still far from explored.

"I would like to learn more," he said softly. If you can trust me?"

"Young man," she responded in a firm tone. "My line of work revolves around the study of Kingdoms, which no longer exist. I have neither the time nor the interest to consider your loyalties. The Cabal accepts everyone."

A feint smile on his lips, Gael reached out unprompted and grasped the hilt of the sword. He felt steady vibrations flowing through the blade, the result of it pulling on his body's energy. The handle felt cool to the touch as it had before. Pulling on the sword, it came out of the ground with little resistance.

"Excellent," Zerenia cheered. "Now, let's see what it can do."

"Umm... How do I use it?" They stared at one another in confusion.

"Good question," she commented, thoughtfully gripping her chin. Looking back and forth between the artifact and the boy, she hemmed and hawed. "I do not know. That will need to be a portion of our research."

His stomach growing queasy, Gael thrust the blade back into its resting place. The flow of energy leaving his body subsiding, he placed his trembling hands on his shaky knees before falling onto his behind. As fatigue not terribly distant from what he'd experienced on the farm set in, Zerenia tapped his shoulder gently.

"That's fine enough for today. Get some rest while you can. As Phyllida has explained, your lessons will become much more grueling due to recent political developments." Nodding his head tiredly, he turned and moved away.

He dragged his feet the entire way back to the commons. He received several, disgusted glances from both his peers and the castle enchantments, while no fewer than a dozen insults were breathed his way from under another's breath. Though they were of little comfort, others still complemented him on his display with the Hearthfire Blade, while others thanked him for his father's contribution to a potential war between Dalmorithia and Altair

"See? I told you he would come back, eventually," Klein called, clapping Gabriel on the forearm.

"Where did you go?" his brother asked, closing his book. "You disappeared right after dinner."

"I wanted to talk to Professor Zerenia," he answered, sifting through the small stack of books resting on the shelf. Lifting the copy of *History of the Cabal*, which his brother frequently perused, he sat it down and opened the book.

"You're reading?" Gabriel asked, a nervous look on his face.

"Is that what you do with books?" hHe laughed, flipping through several pages, until he came to the chapter detailing several of the Cabals founders. Skimming through the pages, he read about the many founders but found nothing on the wielder of the Hearthfire Blade.

He read of the Enchantress, Catianna, who cast many of the mystical enchantments surrounding the island. With the help of the World Shaper, only known as Sai of the South, a great monolithic structure rose from the barren mounds. Their magicks are/were fueled by the ancient relics from the Warden's Guild.

Sighting this first mention of the Wardens who helped build the castle, Gael nearly poured face-first into the book. Continuing his interrogation of the information within, he traced his finger across every word, desperately seeking more on the Wardens.

"Once the castle was raised, born from the flesh of the mountain and the forest, erected to defend it, did work begin breathing life into what would soon serve as a sanctuary for those born with the power of the Lost Gods.

"With construction of the castle complete, war orphans possessing talents for the craft were brought by members of the Warden's Guild. Many magical outcasts soon followed, bringing their rich heritage to the halls of the Cabal. Soon, the first students of the Cabal worked alongside their instructors to further push the boundaries of magic."

Though the text moved from his inquiry, he continued to read on the history of the Cabal's first years. Within the pages, he recognized the names of many famous mages from his lessons with Rosalind. He smiled as he read of Kings, Queens, and fabled warriors, treated as mere legend, despite the rather real circumstances of their lives.

Even as tales of the academy further prodded his excitement, he turned another page and came to a new chapter. "The Mage Wars and the Sacking of Cabal Island." Curious at the title, he continued his reading.

"As Anon entered into the dawning of the Ruby Star, in the year 319 CC, the world was cast into turmoil during a civil war between mages. Previously, those with the blessing had remained neutral in man's conflicts as had been the practice since the Cabal's establishment.

"Forced to choose sides between warring kingdoms, each ruled by a former student of the academy, a line was drawn. Soon, soldiers for both sides of the war were recruited from within the school's hallowed walls. It was not long before the war found its way to the school, and bodies began to pile up.

"In the worst of the battles between the former colleagues, the fighting boiled over into the nearby city of Lordran, destroying over half of the lower city. Forced to defend themselves, the King and Queen of Altair struck back with their army, resulting in one of the most devastating losses of life either entity had seen.

"Seeing what had become of their academy, the leaders of the Cabal, alongside the King and Queen, worked to reform the Cabal. Thus, the Templar order was founded as a mediating party, keeping transgressions of a magical nature, far from the villages and towns."

As the hours rolled by and most of his peers turned in for the evening, he noticed Rinoa entering the hall. Closing his book, he watched the woman curiously, far from having forgotten seeing her strange power in the past.

"What a strange girl," he mused, watching out the corner of his eye as she sat down in front of the fireplace. Rubbing her hands together for warmth, she noticed his attention and snapped her head away.

"I don't see you reading often," she grumbled.

"I don't see many students return from the Dark Forest," he answered back as though entirely disinterested. The young woman grew silent as her eyes fell upon her peer. Flipping another page, he continued reading.

"You do not know what you are talking about," she snapped back.

"I do not much care either way. It's none of my concern whether you're eaten or not, Dark Empress."

Training her head upon him, eyes wild with anger. "I told you to stop calling me that, traitor!" She screamed, rising to her feet.

"Not likely, your Evil Majesty," he said, smiling as he rose to his feet, book in hand. "Try to keep it down when you conquer the world," he added, faking a yawn. Out of sight and ear-shot of the girl, as he traveled to his bed, he dabbed at his eyes with the back of his sleeve.

"I suppose Zerenia is right. I do not have any place left. I hope you are alright, Father."

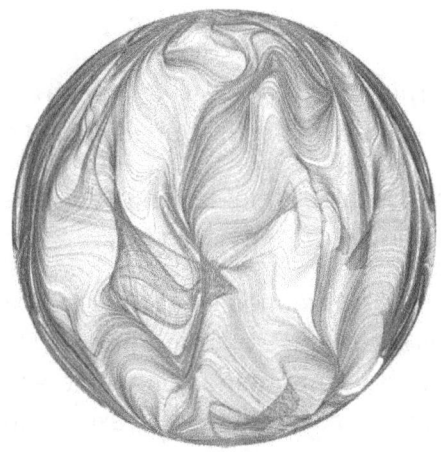

CHAPTER NINE

"It's horrible!" Klein wailed in the commons that morning, stuffing his face with last night's pilfered leftovers. "We're all going to die!" he complained through a mouthful of pastry.

"What's the matter?" Gabriel asked, standing in the corner practicing basic spells. Gael stared at him jealously as Mari took hold of Klein and shook him.

"Get a hold of yourself, Klein. This is a great opportunity for us," she cheered. "How often do we get real combat experience against more experienced students? And we get to use magic!" As she continued to cheer, the color slowly drained from the young man's face.

"Did you hear anything you just said?" he asked in exasperation. "Live combat against experienced fighters! Use of battle magic! We're all going to die, except maybe Gabriel. No offense, Gael," he added apologetically, eyeing the disgruntled looking boy.

"No harm done," Gael smiled excitedly. "When do we begin?"

****

"Good morning, everyone," Niferi called as she entered the room. "Is everyone ready to begin your advanced studies?"

"For goodness sake, Klein. Defend your face." Professor Lang yelled as she stared down at the dazed boy.

"Yes, ma'am," he groaned weakly. Across from him, Mari smiled wickedly as she swung at her opponent with reckless abandon. The second-year remained on the defensive, though it was clear he was far from serious. Overly excited from the combat session, Gael caught glimpses of the young woman's hands sparkling with small embers.

Looking from his classmates, he turned to his brother, who sat at the far side of the room. There, he displayed his raw talent for manipulating the basic combat spells they had learned over the past few months. Despite the impressive display, the blonde-haired boy wailed in terror.

"You might want to pay closer attention to me, dog," one of Reynalds' followers yelled, swinging their practice weapon at his head. Ducking down, he allowed the weapon to pass harmlessly over his head, before counter-attacking.

"Noble-born lackeys like yourself aren't worth your weight in manure," Gael yelled back, striking just inside the larger boy's reach. Lifting his sword pommel, he struck the boy in the ribs. Using the gap offered by his opponent's stagger, he swept his legs before holding his weapon in a killing stroke.

"Well done, Gael," Professor Lang called. "Glad to see you're good for something other than being a research subject." Walking past them, she moved to the next pairs. Seeing his brother struggling in his battle, he decided to watch from a distance. Observing his brother's outmatched opponent, he smiled as Gabriel played victim to his lack of nerves.

"I do not like that look on your face." He could hear a nail gratingly obnoxious voice jeering. Turning his head, he watched as Rinoa squared off against another returning student from the noble class he did not recognize.

The boy was slender but of a medium build. He had shoulder-length, sandy brown hair, which was finely combed. He had bright eyes, which gleamed maliciously as he formed his spell.

"I'm afraid the poor girl is in trouble," A voice to Gael's right said. Turning his head to the source, he came eye to eye with a young woman with bright eyes and well-manicured features. She sat, observing the match while twirling the long, curly strands of her sandy brown hair.

"Why do you say that?" he asked, suddenly amused at the two casters who continued to move about while spell crafting.

"Oh, it appears as though my brother Felix aims to summon one of his pets. I suppose I should inform one of the professors," she said with a disappointed tone. "He gets riled far too easily when it comes to our cousin, Rinoa." As she stepped back into the main portion of the arena, a dark ring formed upon the ground between Felix and Rinoa.

As those gathered around stared at the ring, Gael noticed a solid form growing within. Felix continued to stare maliciously, even as Rinoa trembled. As a hand, nearly the size of Gael's torso, reached out of the hole and pulled itself out, he noticed the young woman's gaze was angry.

"Be careful, Rinoa," he sneered. "You do not want people discovering what you are." The noble boy laughed. "You think they all hate you, now. Soon, you will not be able to show your face, again, without someone trying to burn you."

Gael looked to Felix, anger burning in his chest. Even as Rinoa looked at the enlarging beast, he rose to his feet, having tolerated the boy too long. As he reached the foot of the stairs, the conjured creature rose to its full height.

"What would possess you to summon a darkling, Felix?" Rinoa complained, rapidly gripping her hands as she contemplated her next move. "I will not do it, just to satisfy your sadistic appetite."

"I thought the agenda would be obvious. Uncle misses you."

Gael stopped briefly, awed by the impressive creature. Several other students screamed in terror as they fled. Only once he noticed the paling girl did he move forward.

"Leave her alone, Felix!" Gael barked, moving to the noble's back. The boy spit on the ground between them, before turning his nose up and sneering.

"Hasn't Reynald taught you common blood dogs your place? Go back to your hovel, filth. This is a family affair." The boy turned his back to Gael, who looked to Rinoa. Her eyes locked with his, even as the darkling loomed over her. She shook her head slowly at him, though the request was lost.

"Anyone ever taught you that wild dogs bite?" Gael growled, latching onto the boy's shoulder. Spinning him on his heel, Gael forced the boy to look him in the eye before driving his fist into Felix's nose. Both shocked and overwhelmed, the noble fell to the ground, blood trickling from his broken nose. As he howled with pain and indignation, the beast behind him bellowed.

"Now you've done it!" Rinoa yelled as the darkling continued to howl. As the beast stared down at him, its summoner, eyes wide with fear, fled.

"I was just trying to help!" he yelled, stepping backwards. "What did I do?"

"You've just set loose his darkling!" she yelled. "You idiot! The creature will retain however much energy it held, before returning."

The darkling took a step closer to him. Nervously, he looked around for Professor Lang, who was nowhere in sight. He stopped suddenly, nearly tripping over the small burial in honor of the arena's artifact. "So, what do we do?" he yelled, seeing Klein, Mari, and Gabriel standing watchfully to the side.

"Wait for it to run out of energy," she called, avoiding the lizard-like shadow's tail. The beast lunged forward, attempting to swipe at Gael with its front paws. Leaping back, he watched the shadow strike the blade by mistake. As it howled in pain, an evil smile crossed Rinoa's lips.

"Can you use that sword?" without hesitation, Gael leapt forward. Seizing the hilt in his hands, he pulled it from the rubble and gave it a swing.

The darkling howled once more as the small trickle of flames licked at its hide. Stunned, the darkling took one giant step back, forcing Rinoa to dive out of its path. Smiling, Gael swung once more at an angle towards his foe's head. Lifting itself free of the strike, another roar erupted from its throat.

"Try to hold it off a bit longer," Rinoa called. "I'm going to try breaking the summoning circle."

Unable to fully comprehend the last part, Gael shrugged his shoulders as he stepped into his opponent. Again, he swung towards the creature's head, praying that someone found a teacher. Shrugging one sluggish attack, the darkling leapt sideways. Fatigued from the sword's draw on his body, Gael's knees buckled as the darkling found its footing.

"Look out!" he could hear Rinoa yell. Looking up, he attempted to kick off the ground, only to drop to all fours. His body suddenly felt weightless as the beast swept him aside and paused.

Unable to feel the pain his body must be enduring, he looked up at his attacker. The creature stood, frozen in place, staring out into nowhere. He could hear several voices booming around him as he attempted to sit up.

"She's one of them!" he heard a student cry. "An Origin Magus. She's just like the Grey Mother!" Eyes glancing over his bleeding torso, he noticed Rinoa, her eyes closed in concentration. A moment after, flames rose.

"Get them back!" Tarkan roared, hand clasping the hilt of her sword. Gael swore he saw the bloodstone in the pommel gleam as the former Inquisitor swung. A second streak of flame rose the darkling's body, eliciting a second, pained howl. Collapsing to its side, the creature moaned pitiably before returning inside the black ring, where it vanished.

As though released from stasis, Rinoa dropped to the ground. Gael watched as she remained perfectly still. Turning to sit up, he felt a firm hand on his shoulder as his brother and friends converged on him.

"Rinoa's fine. Get Gael to the Healer," Tarkan ordered.

"Wait," he complained as he was gently, though painfully, lifted from the ground. "What was that? What happened to Rinoa?" he continued to shout as he was removed from the arena.

"You'd be better off avoiding her," Cornelius was suddenly at his side.

"When did you get here?" Gael groaned, watching as Tarkan bent down beside the collapsed girl.

"Who do you think got the professor?" he asked in response, eyes never leaving the scene behind them. "Did you even hear what I said?"

"Why?" he asked defiantly.

"Didn't you see that she's an Origin Mage?"

"So?" Gael asked again, much to the Dalmorithian noble's confusion.

"Origin magic? Void magic? Ever heard of them? They're only the most dangerous forms of spellcraft there are, and that girl is a conduit for one of them."

"Gael?" Gabriel said faintly. "I am not entirely sure, but I believe what Rinoa tried to do is called binding. She tried to make that darkling her slave."

"So? Reynald and Felix can summon darklings. You and Cornelius can summon creatures, as well. How is that any different?"

"Summoning gives a creature energy in exchange for borrowing it's power. Binding imposes the will of the caster upon another being. Had she succeeded, she would have completely enslaved that thing. Controlled it like a puppet." Cornelius explained.

"And if she had failed?"

"Then the darkling could have taken over her. It may have already, and we wouldn't have any idea." The older boy sighed. Gael considered the information carefully, though his attitude remained unchanged.

"Rinoa is fine. Tarkan said so." Cornelius looked at him with a concerned expression. Though Gael did not notice, his peers bore the same expression.

****

Gael was released from the Healing Ward the following morning. He was happy to hear from Klein that he had overheard Felix being forced to clean Professor Boon's animal pens for the next week. Still sore from the score on his chest, Gael kept from his

---

typical physical activities. However, Rinoa was nowhere to be seen.

****

"Why don't you practice holding that artifact?" Lang had suggested as he stood off to the side during their practice session. "You can make use of your time over there." She pointed to an unused space several paces away.

Grunting and groaning lightly, he slowly made his way to the edge of the arena. Turning back, he watched his classmates squaring off against their fellow students. Staring at them, he realized Felix was not among them.

"Stupid of my brother," Gael turned his head to face the blonde-haired woman from yesterday. Ignoring the girl, he gently touched the hilt of the sword. The blade responded with a gentle hum at his touch.

"I am quite curious about you, by the way," she mentioned as he continued to practice. Doing his utmost to ignore the woman's fixated gaze, he repetitiously activated the blade's power. Bored with the routine and confident with his control, he gently drew the weapon, watching the flames crackle.

"Do you know why my brother fixates on her so?" Felicia asked, eliciting a slight pause from the boy.

He could not see Felicia's reaction as he resumed his practice. However, he cursed himself for giving her the response she was hoping for.

"I assure you, he has no intention of harming her or seeing her come to any harm. In fact he may be more protective of our dear cousin than he is of me,"

Again, Gael found himself stopping.

"It's because she is an origin mage," The girl continued.

Finally, Gael turned to face her. "Your brother has a fairly twisted means of showing his affection," Gael grumbled. The woman smiled at him. Though she was naturally pretty, he could not help but imagine one of the many beautiful yet poisonous reptiles from his studies.

"I agree completely," she laughed, rocking in her seat. "I have been trying to convince him to leave her be for some time, now. I think she has proven herself to be quite an embarrassment to the family." He gritted his teeth once biting his tongue grew too difficult. The noble-born peer, however, continued.

"As I told you before, I am much more interested in you and that artifact of yours," she said, eying the Hearthfire Blade.

"It doesn't belong to me," he grunted, gently swinging the glowing blade.

"On the contrary, no one has wielded that sword in several hundred years. At least none I know of. Not everyone can have an affinity for relics, especially that one," she announced, pointing at the weapon in his hand.

"Not much to see," he grunted. "Swing the blade; it lights up, no big deal."

"No big deal?" she smiled at him. "I see you haven't learned too much about that blade, then."

"I am learning plenty. Professor Zerenia has given me several books to read through."

"And yet, you do not know the first thing about the blade's previous owner. Not even how he got the sword or how he died."

"Tamare!" Professor Lang called from across the arena. "Do you not have something you should be doing?"

Felicia smiled at Gael once more before she stepped down the stairs. "You should read up more on the Grey Mother," she suggested. "You might find it enlightening," she told him before walking away.

Staring at the girl's back, he shook his head, deciding to avoid her as much as possible. Her comment about the Grey Mother, however, stuck with him.

****

"Do you have any books on the Grey Mother?" Gael asked his brother, who stared curiously. A sharp gasp elicited from somewhere behind them, though the brothers paid it no attention.

"I do not think so," Gabriel answered, face scrunched up in confusion. "Why does that name seem so familiar?" Klein and Mari both eyed the brothers worriedly.

"Can you two please quit saying that name?" they whined, hiding their heads behind their books or, in Klein's case, beneath the lounge chair. "We're going to have nightmares."

"Because of someone's name?" Gael asked. "What's the big deal? I've heard people talk about the first necromancer, Necronos, without a room full of people panicking."

"How have you never heard of her?" Mari asked, dumbfounded.

"Exactly!" Klein chimed in. "She's pretty much the main horror story told to children. "Haven't you two ever been told a scary bedtime story?" Eying one another, the brother's responded with a mutual shrug. Mari and Klein exchanged a similar look before turning back on the brothers.

"We will discuss how bizarre that is later?" Klein began, only to have Mari, shaking her head despairingly, interrupt.

"No. We need to discuss this, now," she complained. "You can identify ancient creatures based upon their behaviors and habitats, but you cannot remember the most dangerous rogue magi known to time?" She paused to allow the severity of the situation to kick in.

"I have always been more interested in hunting than history." Gael shrugged. "I get bored easily."

"Likewise," Gabriel began. "I have always been more interested in spell theory and runes than anything else. Rosalind was always rather insistent that we needed to expand our knowledge."

"She is not wrong," Rinoa said, appearing in the back of the room. All eyes flipped over to view the young woman, whom they had not seen for three days. As Mari and Klein attempted to return to their game and Gabriel, his book as though nothing had happened, Gale perked up.

"Are you alright?" he asked, approaching her slowly. Glaring at him with the threat of death, Rinoa turned towards the girls' dormitory.

"Fine. Try not to stick your nose where it isn't wanted, next time." Vanishing into the next room, she left him in a familiar state of loathing.

"Well, she is definitely not possessed." Klein laughed through a mouthful of snacks.

"As vile as she acts, the demon may have been an improvement," Gael grumbled. "I am all done being concerned with her. And I do not care what Professor Tarkan says," he added, shooting a look at his brother.

Stomping away from the group, Gael moved for the hall. He could hear his brother call out to him briefly, though he did not answer. His feet and mind decided upon a single task, he quickly found himself inside the library. Lady Strauss, the librarian, eyed him curiously as he entered and made his way straight to her desk.

"Do you have any books on the Grey Mother?" he asked without restraint. Strauss choked, on what, he could not be sure, as she completely missed the book before her with the stamper. He heard an scream from the back of the room while he still stared forward, waiting for an answer.

"Did you say what I think you said?" she asked, adjusting her glasses.

"Yes. I was wondering if you had any books on the Grey…"

"Do not say it again," she shrieked. Somewhere, a disembodied voice made hushing sounds. Eyes were briefly flashing in the direction of the voice, and she slowly returned her eyes to see the boy staring patiently.

"Well, do you have any?"

Gaping at him as though he had combusted spontaneously, she swallowed, then nodded. "Follow me," she sighed, leading him away through the rows of books. He noticed the many floating shapes and formless figures moving about the silent room.

He looked on in a bewildering sense of wonder, looking on with appreciation for the collection the Cabal had gathered. Moving off to a separate wing, he saw many of his fellow students, reading leisurely or hastily scribbling on sheaves of parchment. Moving further beyond them, into a dimly lit section with a single table and set of chairs, the librarian stopped.

"Might I ask why you are looking for such a book?" she asked with a twinge of hesitation in her voice.

"I am Professor Zerenia's new research assistant," he said proudly. "I was told some information on *Her* might prove useful."

The librarian made a hissing noise at the sound of the gnome's name. Plucking two books from the shelf, she placed them on the table. "I believe these two might answer most of your questions," she began. "However, the character in question has appearances in many of the other books in this section."

"Thank you," he replied, eying the covers of the dusty tomes. Realizing one was a book of legends, he turned back to the librarian. "I am sorry, Lady Strauss. This one says it is a book of folklore and legends. I am looking for a book on a real person."

"Young man. That is a book of a real person. However, when an individual's deeds and abilities surpass what the common person can comprehend, their stories are filed under fiction."

Gael considered the statement briefly before looking back to the books on the table. Reaching out for the lamp, the object activated all on its own. Startled, yet intrigued by another, unique artifact, he admired it a moment before turning over the book cover.

Immediately, the book spoke to him of a region known as the Frozen North. He remembered a brief tale of the area and the woman who Uncle Drew claimed wrought havoc there. He had long dismissed the story as nonsense. However, he was surprised to learn the place actually existed.

He read about a lush, green sanctuary, shielded on all sides by mountains. Within the city center, a great temple was erected, housing the source of the region's prosperity. He read about The Eternal Flame, a great flame fueled by the natural mana currents on Anon. Local legends, ancient murals, and writings all depicted a variety of clues, dating the flame's origin to the time of the convergence.

Skimming through various, unrelated details about the city itself, Gael searched for more relevant information. His hand ceased its page-turning as he came upon a picture of the city. Despite knowing that the city he looked upon was ancient, he stared curiously at the remarkably modern-looking structures. More curious yet, the buildings had been drawn as though encased in ice.

Looking to the footnote beneath the scrawled drawing, he quietly read the text. "Artist rendering of the city of Eternia after the attack by The Witch." Examining the note and drawing the absence of the evil sorceress's name did not escape him. Even in a book as ancient as he held, people had still not dared utter her name.

Again, skimming the pages for further mention of the Grey Mother, he found nothing. Frustrated, he closed his book. Gathering his books, he marched to the librarian, whose expression was one of pain.

"May I please borrow these?" he asked, setting the books upon the desk.

A shiver ran the length of the woman's spine as she read the covers of the books. "Young man, I cringe to think of why you might be interested in that, of all subjects. However, as I maintain that knowledge should be available to all, you may."

"Thank you, Lady Strauss."

"Yes, yes, away with you, then," she shooed, ushering him away.

Study materials in hand, Gael made his way back towards the first-year commons.

****

"You're still trying to research *Her* of all things?" Mari gasped that morning at breakfast as Gael took to a little light reading.

Klein sat off to the side, pale-faced and shaken as he prodded his breakfast potatoes with a fork.

"Of course, I am," he answered between paragraphs. When skimming had borne little fruit, he decided to instead read through the book. Within its pages, he found himself captivated by all there was to know about the city of Eternia.

"Just, you know," Mari continued. "Do you have to read about *Her,* here?"

Closing his book with an irritable sigh, he looked up at his classmates. In the short time they attended the school, the Great Hall had grown much more crowded. He found himself grateful for the additional occupants as very few people knew of his relation to the Commander.

As his friends watched more incoming students, he left the hall and retreated to an empty corridor. Propping himself between two pillars, he stretched out. Enjoying the solitude that came with the diverted attention, he read in relative peace as he chewed on his sweet roll.

****

"How has your research been coming along?" Zerenia asked him later that afternoon, after class.

"I've been reading up on the Grey Mother quite a bit," he answered, eliciting little reaction from the gnome.

"A terse subject among your kind, to be sure," she commented. "You are indeed on the right track, however. Excellent work." She continued to speak in a monotone voice, clearly preoccupied with something else as she was want to do.

"Professor, is something the bother?" he asked curiously, setting the few notes he had scribbled on her desk.

Looking back slightly confused, she snapped from her disposition and smiled. "Oh my, I seem to have done it again." She waved the happening away. "I apologize, young Stryfe. No bother. I am just anxiously awaiting the arrival of a new artifact." She quickly grew giddy, laughing to herself.

"What kind of artifact?" he asked, curiosity piqued.

"It's called the Arcanus Orb." She breathed excitedly, her body trembling as she slowly lost control of her nervous energy. "I am afraid that you will have to wait for more details along with everyone else." Gael looked on with disappointment, despite Zerenia's enthusiasm.

"I promise it will not be too much longer," she winked. "I shall be leaving here shortly to collect the object myself. I already have the Headmistress's permission." She resumed her cheery pondering out the window as Gael gathered his belongings.

"Would you like me to come back, tomorrow, Professor?" he asked.

The woman remained silent a brief moment before answering. "No, young Stryfe. I shall be fine. Enjoy your free days. I shall see you again, for class." Nodding his head, Gael made for the Great Hall, certain to find his peers gathering for lunch.

"Where have you been?" Gabriel huffed as Gael made his way down the final flight of stairs to see his friends gathered.

"I dropped off my notes to Professor Zerenia," he grumbled back. "Where did you think I was?"

"Causing trouble," his brother continued to huff, shuffling his books as always. "I'm still not convinced you've suddenly taken an interest in schoolwork."

"Sounds like someone is jealous that they aren't the only bookworm," Mari teased, prodding Gabriel in the ribs.

"I like artifacts," Gael shrugged. "I don't know what else to say. I think everything about them is fascinating."

"Just don't neglect your other studies," Gabriel snapped, confusing Mari and Klein before brushing past them and leaving.

"Another letter came," Rinoa mumbled from the back of the group. "It came late this morning. He opened it earlier when he thought no one was looking." She paused a moment before saying anything further. "He was crying when he read it."

Alerted, Gael moved beyond their circle, following his brother. He found Gabriel tucked away in a resolute corner of the courtyard, not a soul nearby to bother him.

Approaching his brother, Gael stopped in front of Gabriel, listening to him snuffle. Gabriel looked up at Gael, tears in his eyes as he glowered. Gael remained silent, waiting to hear what his brother had to say.

"Inquisitors have moved into the Hunter's Bastion," Gabriel began, wiping his eyes on his sleeve. "Everyone is on lockdown; they are reading all our letters. Going through all our things. Anything, to find the Commander."

"Is everyone alright?" Gael asked, solemnly.

"As well as can be, I suppose," he sniffled, again. "James and Clarissa left. It's just her, Shayna, and the baby, Ruby."

"What about Zara and Bors?" Gael asked. "They were supposed to be staying to help out."

"They were recalled to assist in hunting down the Commander. They are trying to keep him from crossing the border into Dalmorithia."

"Good luck," Gael snickered. "You and I both know that they'll never catch the Commander. Zara and Bors aren't going to help them. If anything, Drew is already doing everything he can to mislead them. As far as Rosalind is concerned, a bunch of Inquisitors are not about to get her way."

The boy seemed to calm down as a smile creased his lips. "You're right. Fine, then. Let's get back to the others."

****

"You asked for me, Zerennia?" Tarkan asked, entering her colleague's classroom.

"You simply must see this artifact!" she cheered happily. "It is absolutely astounding what it can do." The woman poured over a small chest, which rested on her desk.

Unamused, Tarkan shook her head as she placed her palm to her forehead. "Not that I know what I am supposed to be looking at, but where did you find this one?" She feigned curiosity for her friend's sake.

"Borrowed it off another Artificier, whose studies in the north have run aground. Being an expert on the region, they've asked for my help." The words crawled from her lips slowly, spoken reflexively without any real consideration attached to them.

"I do hope you have permission from the Headmistress, this time?"

"Yes, yes, of course," the gnome grumbled, not taking an eye from the marvel before her.

Curious, Tarkan tipped her head from side to side, attempting to steal a peek. Guarding her prize jealously, however, the gnome gave the former inquisitor no ground from which to see.

"I shall let you get back to it, then. Great work, Zirennia. Take care not to forget to share your notes with the rest of the academe, this time." Shaking her head, Tarkan moved away from Zerenia, who had long forgotten her friend's presence. Staring deeply into the treasure before her, she muttered incomprehensibly to herself about the mysteries it contained.

****

Two figures entered the room, their cloaks pulled up tightly, their hoods shielding their eyes. Removing their hoods, they looked at a smaller figure, laying back on two legs of his wooden chair, his boots propped on the table in front of him. Looking out the window, he stared in the direction of Cabal Island.

As they approached, noticing the greatsword propped against the wall beside him, the figure whistled absently to himself. Breaking his line of sight, the relaxing figure sighed. "Has it been delivered, then?" The voice of the young man escaped his hood.

"It is. The artifact has made its way beyond the barrier."

"Good. Then our work here is done." The tips of the young man's boots bounced energetically as he resumed his whistling.

"And our payment?" one of the two men asked. The hood turned to face them. Both men, hardened smugglers, shuddered from the cold, icy stare whose presence emanated from beneath the hood.

CHAPTER TEN

"Now then, class," Zirennia began, her pink hair pinned tightly atop her head. "I have shown you many different types of artifacts. Some possess the capability of granting one special powers during battle. "Others will allow you supernatural abilities, such as sight in total darkness. Or the ability to scry people and things from a distance. Others still, can open you to entirely new worlds of possibility.

"What I wish to show you today is a particularly special artifact. An orb, mind you, which in the hands of a scholar, possesses an incredible learning potential. In the hands of another, it might prove a source of grand entertainment. I give you, the Arcanus Orb."

As Zirennia spoke to the mixed crowd of disinterested or enamored persons, she removed the silken sheet from atop the pedestal she had been hovering around. Beneath the piece of fabric rested a glassy blue, non-transparent orb roughly the size of the gnome's head.

The congregation before her, consisting of every first-year student, handfuls of the other years, and several instructors,

---

eagerly watched the gnome. Dancing around the altar, resting in the center of the arena, she traced her fingertips along the surface of the orb. A trail of light flowed across the surface of the orb, following the presence of her fingers. The audience stared in anticipation, eagerly awaiting more from the gnome. She smiled wickedly to herself, feeling every pulse of their impatience. Relishing in the focused attention upon her life's work, Zirennia returned to the orb.

"Now, you shall all be transported to a far-off realm," she began, carefully placing her hands upon the frosty surface. "Xavius Quanto Urek Orum." She began chanting, placing her fingers in different positions with each word. Gael felt a pull emanating from the orb. Leaning forward in his seat, he watched the swirling strings of energy within.

The swirling vortex of color within the orb rapidly changed, leaping from shades of blue to red, then yellow, and green. As the repetitious change in colors accelerated, rings fanned from the orb's epicenter. The amassed crowd "ooh'd" and "ah'd" with approval as the show of color grew to fantastic proportions.

From within the rings, grass began to grow up from the ground, with violet flowers intermittently rising amongst the patches. The rings widened, their colors growing more consistent. Interconnected columns of stone sprouted from the ground, shaping full scaled buildings. As the awestruck crowd held their collective breath, an entire village formed before their eyes.

Zirennia walked amongst the flora and the stonework, carefully examining each detail of what appeared to be an ancient construct, despite having recently formed. The orb glowed atop its pedestal, overlooking the town as it floated ominously above the village. Its web of influence, the spinning rings, faded into the fruits of its creation. From his vantage, however, Gael could still see the perfect circle the orb had formed.

"It's an illusion," he commented, looking at the border where the coliseum remained, and the green pastures began.

"But an impressive one," Gabriel mumbled, leaning forward as he carefully examined the growing scene. Though relatively small in size, the village within the orb's range of influence continued to grow. However, no signs of animate life were produced within the orb's realm.

"Using the Arcanus Orb," Zirennia renewed her lesson, "It is possible for us to glimpse at civilizations from long ago." A smile on her face, she turned her head to view the village behind her. "However, the ruins you see before you have been remodeled to match what I believe they once resembled."

Reaching out into an invisible expanse in front of her, Zirennia placed her fingers around the floating orb. Summoned back to existence, the orb reappeared before them. No one could hear the words the gnomish professor spoke next. However, the buildings soon lost their luster. The flowery pastures gave way to rot while powerful winds assaulted the high walls. The walls gave way as everything within fell victim to large drifts of snow. Within a short few moments, they watched as hundreds of years of wear weathered away at the city until the lustrous village scarcely resembled the marvel they had witnessed.

"I would like to introduce all of you to Eternia, the birthplace of the Eternal Flame." A chatter rose from both the students and faculty as Zirennia paused, allowing them their reflective period.

"Now, the illusion you see before you is only a portion of what the city once was. However, the image is a reimagining based upon a portrait. No living soul has ever seen the city of Eternia. The only glimpses we have of it, come from historical drawings."

A gentle hum vibrated Gael's hip. Reaching down, he placed his hand upon the hilt of the dull, Hearthfire blade and felt a longing warmth come from it. A hand shot up amongst the crowd, drawing the attention of the many people in the room.

"Yes, Mr. Rolands?" she looked up.

"Will the Arcanus Orb be used during combat practice?" he asked, causing a gentle ruckus amongst the excitable crowd.

Zerenia smiled. "I would hope so," she began. "There are many things we do not yet know about the orb. However, I have my colleagues' notes and will be doing experiments of my own. As soon as we are confident it is safe, we may very well make use of it during combat practice. Anyone else?"

Multiple hands all went up at once. Sweeping across them with her eyes, she smiled. "Yes, Miss Tallow?" she called.

Mari stood from her seat. "Yes. I was wondering if the Arcanus can be used to create an illusion of more than just places?"

"Excellent question," she replied happily. "Yes. The Arcanus can also be used to create the illusion of people or creatures. However, it is worth saying that none of the illusions can be touched, so it is not of much use for combat training in that regard."

Without her asking, CJ raised his hand, a mischievous smile on his face.

"Yes. Mister Ruthger?" she belted out with growing enthusiasm.

"Can someone use the Arcanus Orb to project whichever images of people they wish? However, they so choose?" The young woman in CJ's group indiscreetly jabbed him in the ribs as her cousin chuckled. Zerenia, sensing the boy's intent, narrowed her eyes.

"To answer your question; if one should possess enough control, yes. However, Mister Ruthger, only faculty shall have access to the Arcanus and shall therefore be the only ones to conjure illusions using it. Does that answer your question?"

"Yes, instructor. Thank you," he sat, a smile still on his face as the blushing woman at his side slapped him once more in the torso.

"I believe that shall suffice for the questions. I shall be certain to keep everyone up to date on developments with the Arcanus Orb. I expect to begin testing in the arena in the coming week. You are all dismissed." Without waiting for her students to leave, Zerenia turned on a heel and began studying the orb, muttering incoherently to herself.

"I can't wait to try it out," Mari chirped, punching invisible targets. "I want to fight on top of the Redanian Citadel during the Mage Wars." She spun, engaging her imaginary foes until she nearly trampled Klein.

"This is not the battlefield," the mousy boy squeaked, scurrying back to avoid further pummeling. Placing himself behind the brothers, he peered out as the young girl continued to flail excitedly. "Am I the only one that finds her scary?" he groaned.

"Let's go eat," Gabriel laughed, patting the boy on the shoulder.

The following morning, Gael rose early and headed directly for Zerenia's lab. The instructor was still marching circles around the room, head tipped in thought as she probed out at the orb periodically. The door unlocked, he gently crept inside.

"Professor? It's me. Gael Stryfe.," he called, walking in and shutting the door behind him. If she heard him, she paid no mind as she continued speaking to the artifact.

The orb began to glow ominously as Zerenia spoke to it. Gael watched as the waves of violet and blue rolled off from the artifact, painting a panoramic within the room. Grassy fields sprouted out from the center of the room while creatures crawled out from the earth to feed upon it.

He remained still watching as Zerenia's creation came to life before his eyes. Only once the magic working had ceased, did he move. His instructor, having made a revolution around the illusion, stared curiously at him.

"How very strange," she mused to herself. "I did not intend to create an illusion of a person." She paced around Gael, who, confused, remained perfectly still. "Seems awfully life-like."

"Professor?" he whispered, causing a slight jolt from the gnome.

"Oh? Yes, I understand, now." She began, waving away the illusion. "What can I do for you, Mister Stryfe?"

"I was just hoping to see if there was some way I could help with your research?" he began meekly. "Or if I could just watch?" The gnome thought a moment before looking out the window to see the rays of the sun greeting her.

"Might you be willing to run to the kitchens and fetch us both some breakfast?" she asked. "I had not realized how late it was." Enthusiastically, he moved from the corner of the room and made for the Great Hall.

Charging through the still vacant halls, he quickly reached the first-floor stairwell. Reaching the bottom of the stairs, he saw a set of doors off to the side of the Great Hall, which he couldn't recall. Curious, he slowed his pace, examining the doors when they opened.

He stood remarkably still, for as alarmed as he was, while three little men with rounded, frumpy bodies marched out. Two of them had skin the color and texture of white elm, while the larger of the two, looked to be a portly toddler with thick hands and an oversized head. The three looked at him and smiled a kind, yet jagged toothed gin.

"I, um," he began, remembering the smaller figures, imps, were flesh-eaters. "Was just coming to grab food for Professor Zerenia. I wasn't breaking curfew or anything." He attempted to reason with the halflings, hoping they were merely one of the many obstacles troublemaking students faced.

"Zerenia!" the imps cheered in their screeching tongue, throwing both hands joyously in the air. Looking to their portly friend, they repeated the cheer.

The evil-looking toddler locked eyes with him, maintaining the same, man-eating smile, and motioned for him to come closer. Trained personally by monster slayers, however, the boy did not budge. Next, the large doors to the castle grounds burst open as a loud "guffaw" threatened to rattle the stone works.

"Are you troubling the hobbs, again?" A deep, rumble of a voice called, jarring Gabriel's bones. The man threw a collection of massive, burlap bags to the ground as he spoke.

"Hobbs?" Gael asked, looking again to the little men who cheered as they ran to the man, whose visage was still cast in shadow. Footsteps approached him, casting the face of Professor Boon into sight.

"Hoy, you aren't Cavidius?" he grunted, squinting his eyes as he shook off the snow and ice from his massive jacket. "I thought you one of my wards, lad," he explained. "You're the Stryfe lad, ain't ya?"

"Yes, sir," he nodded vigorously, watching the halflings dragging the sacks towards the door. "I wasn't trying to cause any trouble. I am helping Professor Zerenia this morning."

"Zerenia!" The monstrous duo cheered once more, helping the large toddler, whom Gael could only imagine was the hobb, with the bags.

"Tell me that gnome stayed in her lab all night again," he sighed, slapping his massive hand to his forehead. Examining the appendage, Gael imagined his entire head could be enraptured by it.

"She did, sir," he gulped. "She asked me to fetch something to eat for the both of us since there will be much to do."

"Boy, don't you know there are no lessons today?" he asked in disbelief. "Shouldn't you be getting up to mischief with your friends instead of worrying about classwork?"

A fair point, he surmised silently. Any other time, he would have gladly shirked responsibility in order to run wild and free. However, with all eyes in the castle on him and his brother, the thoughts quickly fluttered away.

"Professor Tarkan specifically asked me to keep my nose clean," he answered. "I thought working with the professor might be a safer usage of my time."

"Safer. Probably not," the man said thoughtfully. "But, infinitely less likely to arouse suspicion, I suppose." He looked over to the three little men, who had managed the first of the bags but still struggled with the remaining two.

"Alright, you lot." Boon turned his attention to the imps and hobb. "Might you prepare a couple of platters for our young friend and Zerenia, please?" He pushed the bags into the room with no apparent effort as he spoke.

"Zerenia!" the imps cried again, quickly scurrying away. The hobb looked up at Boon, who smiled and patted the halfling on the head.

"Funny creatures, hobbs," he said, watching the tiny boy march into the room. "Inexplicably helpful," he continued, not the slightest bit alarmed as the door closed and completely vanished from view. Gael stood stunned, eyeing the solid wall.

"You there, boy?" he laughed, startling Gael.

"Sorry, sir," he muttered. "I was just surprised."

"I was telling you about the hobbs," he reiterated. "You'll learn a bit more about them during your studies."

"What exactly are they?" he asked, his purpose for being there forgotten in place of his curiosity.

"They used to be children. Like you or your brother," he said, looking solemnly to the door. "Sometimes, different beasts like goblins and their ilk keep our young instead of eating them. Raise them as their own. "No one is terribly certain how or why, but it does something to the children. Changes them. You wouldn't want to run into a hobb out there, though," he motioned with a thumb as thick as Gabriel's wrist. "No, they would eat just as soon as any goblin would." He spoke assuredly, shaking his head.

"Imps eat men, as well." Gael pointed towards the secret door. "Why keep them, here?"

"Well, imps and hobbs aren't all bad," he sighed. "The trouble is, not all hobbs can be changed back. Whatever corruption they go through takes hold after too long a time. They've got nowhere to go after that, 'cept here, that is. Mighty helpful and great cooks they can be."

No sooner had the words left his mouth did the trio of mystical men reappear. Between them, they carried two silver platters, which they happily ran with up the stairs. Charging past Gabriel, only the hobb remained, smiling innocently while looking between the two.

"Aye, that's a good lad," Boon cheered paternally, nearly sitting on the floor to look the creature in the eye. "Well done." He smiled, patting it on the head while producing a sweet from his pocket. With an excited gasp, the creature swiped the treat and waddled away on its underdeveloped legs.

"What do you find amusing?" Boon asked, seeing Gael laugh lightly as the hobb returned to the room.

"It reminds me of a little dryad girl I met," he said, smiling at the thought of Clarissa. "I didn't mean any harm."

"Well, that makes sense and all. That little one was taken as a babe. 'Fraid he'll be that way the rest of his life." Gael imagined he saw the giant man wipe a single tear from his eye. "Right then, that settled and all." He stood at his full height, brushing his hands together. "You best get back to your instructor, now."

Remembering his purpose, Gael turned and charged back up the stairwell. Quickly reaching the Artificier's office, he knocked before entering. Inside, he found the imps, dancing around the gnomish professor, who was showering the room with vibrant sparks from one of her many artifacts.

"Alright, you two," she smiled, looking to the imps. "You best return to the kitchens, now. Thank you so much for this," she added, motioning towards the platters. "Don't forget to stop by later."

"Zerenia!" they cheered a final time before running out the door, smiling at Gael as they passed by.

"Now then," Zerenia sighed, placing the artifact in her hand on the nearby end table. "Let's see, what is for breakfast today?" Lifting the lids on both platters, the room was quickly filled with the aromas of eggs, ham, and piles of sweet rolls, which began to tumble from their ridiculous stack.

"Those imps and their sweet tooth," she laughed lightly to herself, catching a roll before it fell to the floor. "They cannot get enough of them, you know. Now come on. Eat," she commanded, gesturing towards the food. "Can't eat this, myself."

They sat several minutes, enjoying a quiet breakfast save Zerenia tinkering with the illusions the Arcanus cast. Gael watched, transfixed as he was seemingly transported from one corner of the earth to the next. Zerenia, though less than talkative throughout their meal, stopped and looked to him.

"Anywhere you would like to see?" she asked, taking a bite from her third roll. The question instantly answered in his mind, Gael hesitated to ask. "If it is not too much trouble, I would like to see my home."

A smile crept across the gnome's lips as she motioned for him to come close. "Place your hand in front of the orb," she said softly.

Cautiously, he approached the artifact and did as his instructor asked.

She whispered a few, short words he could not hear, and the orb came to life. "Now, picture what you wish to see," she instructed.

Gael thought of the Hunter's Bastion, it's lush fields, surrounded by forest and mountain trails, save the one road leading to Leones. He thought of the high, stone walls and the fields they tended to during the warmer months.

"Open your eyes," He did as he was told and smiled broadly as he stared into the orb, seeing a panning image of his home within the orb. "It is a bit small to project in this room, but you could walk through those fields if we had the space."

He did not care. Seeing his home was rewarding enough for the time being. Responding to his thoughts, images of Rosalind, Clarissa, and the others began to appear within the orb, exiting the bastion. He swallowed a hard lump in his throat when his adoptive father exited, as well.

"A beautiful place to raise a child," Zerenia smiled. "Is that your mother and father?"

Caught off guard by the question, images of his birth parents floated into the back of his mind, their faces no more than blank, shadowy specters. "No," he tried to answer, the images coming faster as his attention was diverted. "My parents died when I was young." Flames leapt up, embracing the silhouettes. "I was raised by my sister before the Commander found me."

Without realizing it, Gael continued to cast what he saw onto the orb, captivating his instructor's attention. His sister's face was the next to appear within the Arcanus. Kindly and freckled, his sister was several years older than him. He saw the small home their parents had left them with the fields they worked to sustain themselves.

"Gael," he heard the gnome call from far away. The scenery shifted. He was under the house's floorboards, watching as his sister was thrown to the ground above him. The Templar with the jagged scar was there, too, grinning as he pinned her.

"Gael!" the gnome called again, pulling him free of the orb. His eyes snapped wide open, the vision of his home burning fading away as the artifact went dark. He looked to the gnome, who bore shame on her face. "I apologize," she whispered. "I didn't know."

"It was a long time ago," he grumbled. "I don't talk about it."

"Well, then," the gnome began, taking the hint. "Allow me to show you what I have learned." She took control of the Aracnus, drafting illusions of her own, entertaining Gael until long into the afternoon.

****

"Where have you been?" Mari asked as he sat at his normal place for lunch. "We were worried about you."

"She was worried," Gabriel commented. "I was reading."

"I appreciate your concern," Gael teased, jarring his brother with his elbow. "I was with Professor Zerenia, studying the Arcanus." No fewer than a dozen pairs of eyes turned to watch him.

"What can you tell us?" Emma asked, nearly knocking Lionel's lunch into his lap. "They've hardly let anyone see it since it arrived."

"You can use it to create all sorts of illusions." Gael smiled, seeing Aura and her entourage joining in, too. "The professor even let me conjure a memory with it." An excitable chorus rang out as they crowded as close as possible.

"What memory?" Gabriel leaned in, suddenly interested in chiming in.

"Just a memory of the Hunter's Bastion," he smirked. "It was like someone had placed it inside a bauble."

"So, it works like a crystal ball?" Lionel asked.

"Not exactly," Gael surmised. "So far, it still only creates illusions, but what we saw before when it changed the look of the arena, can also be done on a smaller scale. The professor believes there is more still that it can do."

"Are you going back after lunch?" Mari asked.

"Probably not. Why?" he answered in between bites of his cooling food.

"Klein doesn't want to play that silly game with me anymore. I thought maybe you'd want to get in some battle practice." She jokingly made fighting noises while throwing her hands in varying directions to emphasize her point.

"We all should," Triny chimed in. "I talked to Niferi, this morning. She and a couple of others are going to be practicing their warding so we can use magic." While the comment effectively warded off most of the more academically inclined students,

Gabriel's ears perked.

"They're going to be practicing warding magic?" he breathed excitedly. He received numerous glares and a shushing noise from a quarter of the gathering, forcing him to calm himself. All the same, it was difficult for them to contain their enthusiasm as they quickly decimated their food and bolted for the arena.

"You know I can only shield so many, right?" Niferi scowled, hands on her hips.

"I know Niffy," Triny sighed. "I just got so excited; I had to invite my friends." Niferi continued eyeballing the girl, unamused, while the others gaped at their classmate for their upperclassman's nickname.

"Just because we're related does not mean you should go out of your way to bend the rules." Niferi retorted. "If you can get a faculty member to sign off on this, then fine, but you are all taking turns," she continued to grumble, looking to the other two upperclassmen.

****

"I'm fine with it," Professor Lang grumbled, shuffling deceptively on her cane. "Be good to put you to the test before the battle games. I don't want any foul-ups, this year."

"Of course, professor," Niferi agreed, looking to the students.

Lang looked over the students while chewing the inside pocket of her lower lip. "Alright, there are seven of you. I want each of you to pair off, and we'll take turns. Niferi, you're instructing the lesson. You work with your pupils as you see fit. I'll manage the fighters. Someone will have to sit out."

"Actually, professor," Gabriel spoke up, raising his hand. "I am here because I am curious about the barrier magic. Is it alright if

I watch instead, and try to learn?"

Lang turned her head to look at Niferi, who shrugged her shoulders. "I'll see you earn extra marks if you can teach it to him," Lang said, looking to Niferi. "Never hurts to have an extra set of hands during war games."

The pairs stood; Gael and Mari, Lionel and Emma, with Triny and Aura concluding the pairs. Glancing to the side, he saw Klein sitting near to Rinoa, speaking to no avail as the strange girl stared forward with a look of disapproval.

"Now," Niferi began. "I shall take my cousin and Aura. Tails," she said, looking to the young, brown-haired woman to her side, whose hands had been consumed by an ill-fitting robe. "You work with Lionel and Emma. Finally, Nole, Gabriel, you two are working with Gael and Mari."

"Prefect Niferi," the freckle-faced boy known as Nole raised his hand. "If your new apprentice is casting as well, is there a chance for spell interference?"

"Not with a basic barrier. No," she answered. "Now, fighters. Hold still." Each caster raised their hands as they prepared to cast the barrier magic.

"This is going to be fun," Mari pulsed as she screeched lightly to herself.

"This might tickle," Tails warned in a soft-spoken voice.

"Oro murus." The three chanted in unison, startling Gabriel as a gentle thickness in the air announced the casting of the spell. Across from them, each of the battlers shivered and twitched as they felt the strange magic stretching over their bodies.

Happy with her spell, Niferi looked to Gabriel and her students. "You try, Gabriel," she said gently. "Look at your brother with a desire to protect him and cast your spell."

"You're assuming he doesn't want him bludgeoned!" Klein called from the stands, holding his sides as he did so. The others, save the brothers, shared in the laughter before Lang thundered her cane on the floor.

"That's enough. If anyone is getting bludgeoned, it will be you, slug," she growled at the meek boy. Klein shied behind Rinoa, who merely scooted further down the bench, leaving him exposed, rump in the air.

Ignoring the theatrics of his fellows, Gabriel focused intently on his brother. Gael stared at him, naked in comparison to the other barrier-clad fighters. Not a clue as to what was going through his brother's head, he waited.

"Oro murus," he said, pressing energy through his being and into his words. While the others had each emitted a semi-transparent bubble, which floated to their intended target, Gael produced nothing with his casting.

"Nothing?" the boy grumbled in frustration.

"Something made my skin tingle a moment ago," Gael attempted to help.

"Oh, sorry," Mari whispered. "You had a piece of fuzz on you. I was trying to be discreet." Gabriel furrowed his brow irritably as he overheard the exchange.

"It is nothing to be upset about, Gabriel," Niferi said softly. "Tails and Nole are in their second year here and that is considered advanced. Keep trying." She turned back to critique her students as Gabriel repeated his attempt.

"Gael, I will place a barrier over you for, now," she warned, quickly casting her spell. Gael jolted as the magic wrapped around him, forming a light, protective coating. He watched as it wrapped around his skin, only to see it vanish a moment later.

J.A. Bullen

"How do I know if it is still in place?" he asked, raising his arm to see. Doing so, he noticed the light bending around his arm, giving away the presence of the magic.

"Very well, then. Everyone seems to have a barrier in place.," Niferi continued, smiling at the boy. "Nole, Tails, be sure to maintain your focus at all times. If you slip up for even a moment, your barrier will vanish, and you will leave your charge undefended." The two nodded their heads as Gabriel walked off to the side to join Klein and Rinoa.

"Alright then," Lang stepped forward. "Suppose it is my turn." Let's begin by practicing with our chosen partners. Get used to battling within the barriers. Practice a spell if you know one. Once everyone is settled, we can begin."

As instructed, Gael and Mari broke off from the other pairs and collected training weapons from the rack. He grabbed his typical gear while his peer reached for a mace and shield. Smiling, they stared at one another, shields held to their chests, ready to begin.

"Remember," Lang began in her gruff tone. "Simply because we are employing barrier magic does not mean you cannot hurt one another. I will not tolerate any fatal strokes when instructors are not managing the wards. We do not want there to be an incident.

"That being said, there is little need to restrain yourselves beyond that point. This will be a great opportunity for you to practice your magic during a combat exercise. Even though this is your free time, I shall be taking note of your progress. Consider this an opportunity to earn a place in the more advanced courses."

At the mention of moving on to better and brighter things, a serious mood overcame the excited students. Mari grinned at Gael, waiting for Lang to begin their matches. With a clap of her cane upon the ground, three pairs of fighters charged at one another.

Mari roared as she flailed wildly at Gael. Despite having had little practice in combat before arriving at the Cabal, she moved more precisely than Gabriel. Gael focused on her movements as he kept on his toes. Reassured by the gentle flicker of light from the barrier around her, he stepped forward.

Catching her mace on his shield, he swept beneath his outstretched arm, grazing at her lower torso. Mari pushed backwards, jarring his blade down and to the side with the edge of her buckler as she attempted a follow-up strike. Using the momentum of her attack, he pulled his left arm in and pushed her weapon away in the direction of her swing.

Jostled, Mari overstepped from the ill-timed blow, allowing Gael to strike her shoulder with his own, stumbling her while allowing him an advantageous position. Eyes peering over her shoulder, Mari dipped down and rolled away from what would have been a strike high on her shoulder.

"Watch your forms!" Lang crowed to the entire assembly, banging her cane on the ground irritably. No matter where she struck, be it sand or stone, the enchanted wood boomed with a raucous melody. "Lionel, keep that head up. Aura, combat does not stop because you do."

She continued hounding each of the pairs as Mari and Gael both battled for position. Looking at his peer, Gael could see the girl rapidly tiring, the effect of her broad moves and overcompensating dodges. He could see the initial signs of fatigue as he slowly kept after her, pacing himself with every attack.

Gael again, using his body to press against his opponent, watched his weapon graze Mari's shoulder. She winced slightly, expecting pain but was instead struck with surprise as the magic surrounding her rippled, stopping the blade just shy. Looking at one another, they both smiled as their bout continued.

Likewise, Triny and Aura had resolved themselves to striking one another without much care to defense. They giggled each time they received a blow, the magic protecting them despite striking one another in the back, shins, or torso. Lionel and Emma, however, had begun actively casting what battle spells they could muster.

Gusts of wind began dispersing the earth, sending up puffs of dirt and sand towards the other two pairs. Showered with pebbles from Lionel's poorly aimed spell, Gael lifted his shield arm, exposing his abdomen. With a smirk, Mari swung backhanded.

Gael stepped sideways, suffering only a graze from the attack while responding with a horizontal sweep across his body. Mari's shield responded with a hollow clang, though she stumbled from the blow. Carrying through with a flurry, he managed to come down on top of his opponent, who lost her footing.

With a smile, Gael readied to end their match as Mari lit up and fire licked out at him. Jumping back, he staggered, his breath stolen from the unabated heat of the flames. Rising to her feet, Mari hooked the mace's strap on her belt and proceeded forward with a shield and flaming hand.

"Why haven't you finished the match, Stryfe?" Lang bellowed. An opponent cannot use magic when they are dead. Stop debating your movements and strike. Mari, show some heart girl. Do not allow him to control the battlefield."

Neither stopped to acknowledge their instructor's words as Mari continued her assault against Gael. With no battle magic, Gael found himself rapidly dancing around Mari's new attack. Though the jets of flame and small, tone-sized balls she threw were nothing to impress the experienced members of their group, to Gael, they had become a nightmare.

With each attempt he made to close the distance between them, Mari responded with a tiny trickle of flames. Worse yet, he could already feel fatigue settling into his legs as he fled from her attacks. With no discernable way to move on the girl, he continued backing further away.

"Maybe you could do more if you paid better attention during class," Gabriel grumbled, struggling on his own with the barrier magic. Klein sat by, unwittingly serving as the boy's guinea pig as he munched on whatever treats he had pilfered earlier in the day. Rinoa lowered her book to her lap and watched intently.

Another tiny cloud of dirt floated between them as Lionel and Emma dropped their weapons and were taking turns with simple wind spells. Triny and Aura had already given in, instead choosing to rest as Niferi gave her pupils instructions. As the cloud passed between Gael and Mari, he could not help but notice the partial dissipation of the weak flames.

"Do you want to take a break, Gael?" Mari asked. "I hope Klein realizes that he is sharing his food."

"Not yet," he grumped, ego wounded by his lack of efficiency in spell play. "I want to try something." Shrugging her shoulders, Mari watched carefully from behind her shield as Gael charged forward.

Waiting until he came well within range, she released her flame jet. Arcing out towards the boy, he already felt the heat as he threw all his body weight into a power slide. Right leg extended out in front of his left and shield guarding his face, Gael kicked up as much earth and sand as he could. Immediately, the heat from the flames was interrupted, and he slid inside of Mari's arm.

"Got you," he delighted, making contact with the barrier on the girl's exposed right side. Taking a light tumble from her shield as she attempted to defend herself, Gael rolled to the side before rising to his feet.

Mari fell backwards from the blow beneath her center of gravity and landed on her rear. "That was great!" she laughed, blowing dirt from her face and hair. "No one's ever tried that before."

"That's because it would not have worked against a stronger flame spell," Lang grumbled, leering over the two. "It was a good recovery, Stryfe. Your ability to observe your situation does not disappoint. However, if you hope to participate in more advanced courses, you will need to work on defensive and offensive magic or a means of countering it."

"Yes, ma'am," he sighed, the elation of his victory having passed before he had even felt relief from it. "I will work harder."

"And you, Miss Tallow," she reared on Mari, who still sat in the dirt.

"Yes, ma'am," she chirped, trying to rise to attention quickly but fell instead.

"That was an impressive use of magic for a first-year. Keep practicing. I will be pressing you harder from now on. You might just find yourself in the advanced course if you improve your melee ability. I will also inform your sponsor of your need for magical instruction."

"Thank you, ma'am," she replied, happily. "Thank you very much."

"As for the rest of you," Lang growled. "I expect each of you to take these extra lessons more seriously in the future. The opportunity to practice at a higher level does not often come to first-year students." With her usual pomp, Lang marched away from the group with a *harrumph.*

"That was a lot of fun, Gael," Mari smiled, looking over her shoulder at her peer, who sat nearby. "We should practice against each other more. Klein just runs away and hides."

"That's because you attack me in the hallways!" the boy bellowed. In die retort, he happened to notice Gabriel still attempting to cast a barrier spell and jostled away. As Gael looked up at Rinoa, he saw the girl had long since returned to her book, completely disinterested in her peer's affairs.

"I would like that," Gael answered, crawling to his feet and helping Mari to hers. "It might help me figure out a way around your magic."

"Have you thought about asking Tarkan to help you learn?" she asked, though Gael shook his head.

"I've never been much good with it," he complained. "Rosalind tried and tried, but I'm just not good in a pinch. I can cast some spells but nothing that will help me in a fight."

"We'll figure it out together," she smiled, clapping him on the back. "Maybe we can convince your brother to swap partners. He seems less enthusiastic about combat training, anyway."

"Yeah. He prefers the magic part. I'm afraid he got all the talent on that end," he grumbled, irritably kicking at a loose stone. "Hey, bookworm," he yelled, breaking his brother's concentration on Rinoa, whom he was attempting to fortify.

"What?" he growled, alerting his prey to his actions. With a *humph*, she moved away from him as well, doing nothing for his mood.

"I'm going to wash up and wander the castle. Want to go?"

"Go on ahead. I'm going to try to talk to Miss Niferi some more." His tone was agitated, though determination still burned brightly in the boy's eyes. Waving his brother off, he walked alongside Mari on their way back to the first-year commons.

That evening, all who participated in the battle exercises lay sprawled out in the lounge chairs. Gael, one of the few students who was predisposed to combat training, remained fairly functional beside Emma, while the others were spread out, near death.

"I never thought I would be so sore from a class," Aura groaned with every movement of her body, voluntary or otherwise.

"To think. Those of us who excel will be submitted to that every day," Triny chimed in. "I never realized how grueling my cousin's classes could be. It's no wonder she specializes in barriers."

"Are we sure we used barriers," Lionel said in a raspy voice. "It feels like every single one of Emma's blows struck their mark." His pained sobs only deepened as Emma slapped him nonchalantly in the ribs.

"Is that any way to treat the son of your Liege Lord?" he teased, coughing from the surprise.

"Blah, blah, blah," she replied, rolling her eyes. "This must be why Lady Isana said that you might need some help toughening up." The playful banter between the two quickly converted into a one-sided wrestling match, leaving Lionel further exhausted.

"I believe I've schooled you enough for one day," she laughed, brushing off her palms as she walked away. "See you all in the morning." Triny and Aura were close behind her as Klein and Gabriel played a round of Wizards, Warriors, and Rogues. Disinterested in their game, Lionel moved from his chair and took up the one beside Gael and Mari.

"Did you learn how to fight from your father?" Lionel asked without looking towards him. Both Mari and Klein looked up uncomfortably as both brothers cringed.

"Yes," he said lightly. "Our caretaker, Rosalind, taught us a fair amount, as well." An awkwardness quickly emanated from between the two as Mari stared between them.

"My dad told me a little about your family," he continued. "I do not know if the rumors about your father are true or not, but you don't have to worry about that around Emma and me," he smiled lightly. "That kind of stuff doesn't matter here, right?"

"Thanks, Lionel," Gael smiled while Mari released an unceremonious sigh of relief.

"Glad that's over," she sighed, wiping her brow. "That almost got awkward." Noticing that the room's attention had shifted from Gael and Lionel to her, she smiled uneasily. Rinoa, sitting in the far corner of the room, shook her head.

"I think I'm going to head to bed," Gael relented, stretching his body and making for his bed.

"Gael?" Klein said, looking between the two brothers.

"Yes?" he asked, eyeing the boy.

"It's just. What Lionel said. It's the same for me."

"And me," Mari replied happily, clapping him on the arm, before looking to Rinoa. Soon, both Klein and Lionel had joined in at staring at the young woman, who, with a shiver, looked up from her book.

"Hmm? Oh?" she began, alarmed at the glare she was receiving. "Me too. I understand." Closing her book, she made for the girls' dormitory before further stares could interrupt her.

CHAPTER ELEVEN

"Time to get up!" Gael woke to a pair of hands shaking him excitedly. Eyes searching, he saw Gabriel and Klein both staring down at him.

"What is it?" he asked, looking out the still dark windows. "It's not breakfast time, is it?"

"No. There is still quite a bit of time before that," Klein sighed with lament. "No. It's Rinoa. She's wandered off, again."

"So," Gael grumbled, rolling over onto his side. "What she does is her business. Not mine." Gabriel and Klein eyed one another before prodding Gael once more.

"But Mari followed her," Klein added, hoping to encourage his friend.

"What does it matter?" he sighed. "It's not as though she is going to be out doing something dangerous. She is likely out with an instructor." He pulled the covers firmly over his head, a last-ditch effort to drown out their complaints.

"We are aware of that. They do not know that Mari is following them, though. Are they going to be able to protect someone if they do not know they are there?"

Gael's eyes snapped open. "Where did you last see her?" he groaned, grudgingly rising from his bed and slipping into his boots.

"They were leaving for the front entrance," Klein squeaked. "I tailed them that far before heading back to get you guys."

"If you had all that time, why didn't you just convince Mari to turn back?" he grumbled on, fastening his cloak before marching towards the commons. Neither boy answered the question as he marched down the few stairs and exited the enchanted door.

"What took you all so long?" Tarkan grumbled, waiting for them in the commons.

"He's stubborn," Gabriel complained. "It took us a while to think of an excuse to get him out of bed." At a major loss, though grievously irritated, all the same, Gael turned his angry gaze onto his brother.

"And what was wrong with simply telling him the truth?" Tarkan asked hands on her hips. The two boys looked to one another, no words spouting from between them.

"What is this about, professor?" Gael asked politely, though the venom in his gaze remained on his brother and cowering friend.

"It appears as though Headmistress Caramoor intends on allowing first-year students to participate in this year's battle school. As your sponsor, I have decided to see that each of you undergoes special training to prepare."

"You want us to undergo additional training for a contest designated for more advanced students?" The entirety of the room, even the sleepy-eyed Rinoa, stared at Gael in shock.

"I would have thought you would be of the same mind," Tarkan mused. "Professor Lang tells me that you could use spell training in particular." Gael did not respond, though there was little need for the room to gather his thoughts.

"Let me be clear. None of you will be required to partake in this training. However, I have room in my schedule at this time if any of you should be interested. For those of you who wish to participate, you shall find me in my classroom. That is all." Turning, Tarkan left the room, Mari quick to follow.

"You're not going?" Gabriel asked, looking curiously to his brother as both Rinoa and Klein returned to their dorms. "I'm going to ask her to help me with barrier and summoning magic," he smiled. "I'll see you at breakfast." He clapped his brother on the shoulder before chasing after the professor and their friend.

Gael slumped into one of the many armchairs in the commons. Staring at the hearth, he closed his eyes, considering the offer. He thought of his bout with Mari, a bout that had brought his lack of competency to focus. As comforting as his bed sounded, he wished never to feel so inadequate again.

****

"Alright, then," Tarkan began, seated behind her desk, though in a mor relaxed position than what they had grown accustomed to seeing in class. She was eased back in her chair, one elbow on the desk as she looked at her three pupils. "I understand what one of you is looking for based upon Lang's notes. However, to tailor lesson plans, I need to know what it is that each of you believes that you need and what you wish to do with it."

Immediately, Gabriel's hand shot skyward, alarming his peers. Blinking her tired eyes repeatedly, Tarkan looked to the other two and grinned. "Yes, Gabriel. What do you wish to work on considering the upcoming competition?"

"Well, I am curious about summoning and barrier magic," he started, eliciting a raised eyebrow from the woman in front of him. "I understand these are advanced studies, but I cannot help but think that this is a perfect opportunity for me to learn."

"You are not wrong," Tarkan stated thoughtfully. "Those particular areas are much more advanced than our typical, first-year curriculum. However, it is not without possibility that there will be other first-years with such knowledge. Very well. I shall consider your request and speak with you again before the evening."

Sensing a flow to the meeting, Mari raised her hand next. "I want to learn better control of my pyromancy," she smiled.

"I suspected as much. I do say, your form could use some work. I will be sure to incorporate both into our private instructions. I shall speak with you later, as well."

"Thank you," Mari cheered, turning and leaving the room.

"And that leaves you, Gael," Tarkan said, as though this were the portion of the meeting which she dreaded. "I do hope you are aware why I insisted your brother and friend wake you?"

"I know," he groaned, refusing to look at his teacher. "I am incompetent with magic. I embarrassed myself the other day, during combat practice."

"Ah, yes. Lang did mention that," she replied. "However, you are incorrect."

Gael's attention was seized as he looked up with surprise. "Then why?"

"I want you to be on the team because I think you belong on it." She started in her typical, gruff, military fashion. "You've shown a good deal of potential in our lessons."

"But I am utterly useless with battle magic?" he retorted. "How am I supposed to compete with everyone else when I am so much less efficient in every field?"

"How indeed," she said, looking straight into him. "That will need to be a critical point of focus in our lessons from now on. You will need to learn how to defend yourself, whether you can or cannot cast magic."

"When would you like me to begin?" he sighed, seeing no other option than to give in to the professor.

"Now," she answered, slapping a book on the desk. His eyes grew wide as he stared at the massive tome.

"I have to read?" he complained. "On my free time?"

"Yes," she smirked. "Not everything can be achieved through bluntly blundering through life. Sometimes, one must also take the time to develop theory, as well. Inside, you will find some basic spells. I want you to take time each day, morning and evening, practicing them," she ordered, pointing at the book.

"I've learned several basic spells, instructor," he complained. "What does my lack of ability in battle magic have to do with these?"

"Gael, your ability to control the forces of chaos and creation is no different than a muscle in your body. If you wish to improve it, it must be strengthened and fed. Your lack of raw, magical talent like your brother or Rinoa by no means decides an inability to wield that power.

"Consider your magical muscle malnourished, incomplete. On your farm, have you ever encountered an animal who was not born as hearty as others?"

"Yes. All the time," he grumbled, crossing his arms as he glared at the assignment staring him down.

"And did you cull the animal, or did you nurture it?"

"Unless there is some form of disease or chronic malady, we do everything we can to nurture it back to health," he answered slowly, Tarkan's intentions growing clearer.

"That is the task we shall set to, here," she explained, again gesturing to the book. "You were born breached, Gael. An acute malady that you can overcome, should you nurture the underdeveloped muscle." She smiled at him.

"You know as well as I that as unpleasant a task as it may be, you can perform it," she continued. "Theory and practice, one hour in the morning and one in the evening, minimum. It may not accelerate your ability, but you shall improve. You might even enjoy the experience. I shall see you, tomorrow."

Rising from his seat, he turned from Tarkan, blindly reaching out and grasping the heavy tome in his arms. With a sigh, he reached for the doorknob.

"One more thing before you go." He stopped as a softer voice came from the battle-hardened teacher.

"Yes?" he asked, turning to face her.

"Zerenia spoke with me about the incident with the Arcanus. She told me that she may have seen some things you might wish to talk about," she paused momentarily, waiting for any reply. "Maybe about an Inquisitor with a large scar?"

"She was mistaken, professor," he replied hollowly. "She saw nothing important. Thank you for the book. I will see you in the morning." Leaving before she had the chance to stall him again, he made for the commons.

"What you got, there?" Gabriel asked, eyeing the book in his brother's arms while stuffing his face.

"Thought you of all people would know what a book was," he growled. "Did you happen to grab any for me?" Smiling, Gabriel handed a sweet roll to his brother.

"He probably just wanted to make sure you knew what it was." Mari and Klein both snickered at Rinoa's comment.

"Shove off," he snapped, moving to the far end of the room and throwing himself into a chair. The girl made some noise in her throat but quickly muffled it, before returning to her leisure reading.

He gripped a random collection of pages within the book and opened it. "Cleansing Water," he read. "Removes basic impurities from small amounts of water. Does not work in place of removing large, physical material."

"I can't exactly try this one, now," he shrugged and turned to the next spell. "Minor Spell of Warmth. Used to create the smallest of embers." As he read the instructions for casting the spell, he looked side to side and noticed the unlit candle near to the hearth.

Grabbing it, he sat it upon the nearby end table, which he dragged in front of his chair. Staring intently at his objective, he traced his finger along the instructions, carefully reading, before extending a lone fingertip.

"Fen," he whispered, willing energy to channel into the tip of his finger, which hovered just in front of the wick. The attempt produced no results, coaxing a sigh to escape the boy. "Well, I suppose this marks the start of a fun morning," he grumbled before attempting once more.

Thus began the long, arduous process of practicing baser spells. He managed to light the candle after several failed attempts but had yet to reproduce the result by midday. Frustrated after attempting two other spells, he stored the book in his personal trunk and went on with his day.

"I was wondering how long you were going to stay up there, today?" Gabriel asked once Gael surfaced for lunch. "We were getting ready to bring you something."

"Just working on my studies per Tarkan's orders," he grumbled to himself, wiping his tired eyes.

"Well, just be sure you don't take over this one's place as the designated bookworm," Mari smirked as she jeered towards Gabriel.

"Not likely," Both brothers said in unison. As they laughed together, the doors opened, and an entire gaggle of students trudged in, dragging their feet behind them.

"What's the matter, CJ?" Gabriel asked, noticing the boy and his entourage among the undead walkers.

"Professor Zerenia wanted to test out a new course she designed, utilizing the Arcanus," he said, eyes staring forward.

"Yeah? How was it?" Mari asked excitedly. Even Klein perked up at the question. He finally turned to meet them, his eyes wide and haunted.

"Eye-opening," he began, turning towards his compatriots, whose heads rested on the table. "I'm not sure how to describe it. As tired as I am, now, I cannot wait to do it again tomorrow." His signature smile finally surfaced as he moved to sit with his friends.

"We're going to die," Klein moaned, forehead smacking the table as he flopped.

"We're not going to die, coward." Mari laughed at the boy's disparity. "Stop being so dramatic."

"We're dead," he continued to moan into his folded arms as everyone around them continued to eat.

"What do you have planned for the rest of the day?" Gabriel asked his brother, who shrugged.

"Go through that book some more," he suggested. "I don't know."

"Alright. I have to meet with Tarkan later, but if you want some help. You know," Gabriel smirked.

"Thanks. I'm going to give it another try by myself, first."

After a quick visit to his room to collect his book, Gael scoured the castle searching for a quiet place to work. He eventually found a quiet spot inside a stone garden on the far side of the castle courtyard, opposite from where they traditionally gathered. There, the only company he enjoyed were the statues.

He looked to the several gruesome-faced gargoyles, and monstrous carvings, and wondered if any were enchanted like Perocles. Taking up roost alongside them, he opened the book upon his lap and thumbed absently to a new page.

"Life Detect. Briefly sense the presence of large animals. Can be used to find a lost child in the dark. The end-all in hide and seek." Reading the spell description, unfortunately, did nothing for his ego. With a heavy sigh, he read the instructions on how to cast the spell, which like many of the others in the book, revolved around channeling energy.

"Sure. Why not?" he smirked mockingly to himself. "See Shayna and Clarissa hide from me after this," he added in a sarcastic tone. Following the instructions for the spell, he channeled energy into the tip of his finger, concentrating upon it until he could feel it pulsing.

"Ente ven," he whispered, tapping his charged fingertip to his temple. There was a flash of light, where Gael's vision went blank. A surprised wail escaping him, he fell backwards from his seat and landed hard on his back. Fearing he had blinded himself, he cursed his luck, while fumbling to his feet.

Slowly blinking his eyes, he worked out the blur which had settled in before realizing the blur was a glow. Confused, he looked upward, noticing the cloud over his vision, trailing away. "What is going on?" he mouthed, lowering his gaze to the ground once more.

The moment his eyes met with his feet, the blur returned. He stumbled backwards, the cloudy shapes surrounding his feet following his paces. Stopping, he outstretched his hands, which glowed.

It worked," He laughed excitedly to himself. "It worked." He played with the new enhancement to his sight for several moments, staring back at the castle walls. While those outside of the castle could be plainly seen, regardless of what they stood behind. Those within the walls could not however, due to the castle's many enchantments.

Eager to see more, he looked through several other spells within the category. His practice session ran throughout the entire afternoon and into the early evening. Seeing his classmates gathering for the evening meal, he quickly his things and ran indoors.

"Enjoy yourself?" Klein asked, a stern expression on his face.

"I was studying," Gael said absently, looking to the others, who seemed their usual selves. "I cannot say that it was a wasted effort."

"Well, good for you," he grumbled, using his fork to swirl his mashed potatoes into every other food on his plate. "The rest of us weren't so lucky." Gael chose not to pursue the conversation as Mari leaned over their brooding friend.

"Professor Tarkan demanded I have a sparring partner for today's lessons. Klein was the first one I found."

The boy mumbled something incoherently to himself while shooting venomous, sideways glances at those around him.

"What was that, Klein?" Gabriel asked, moving slowly, nursing some kind of physical malady.

J.A. Bullen

"I said she set me on fire," Klein's voice cracked at the end of his complaint. "It was horrible." All eyes slowly trailed from the scarred boy, then to Mari, who shrugged.

"To be fair," she began, "It was only a small spot, and it was quickly put out."

"I was still terrified," he grumbled. "I'm better at sneaking around. Not being your magical test dummy. Even Tarkan couldn't fix the damage."

"She scarred you?" The looks Mari received bordered on condemnation.

Rolling her eyes, Mari slapped Klein in the back. "Show them," she barked, gently pushing him forward. Glaring at her, he leaned forward and presented a small, bald patch on the back of his head.

"Tarkan did not want to risk artificially growing my hair back," He moaned. "She said it could have an adverse effect on my growth."

"It's just a little bald patch," Emma laughed, touching the spot, causing the boy to flinch.

"It still hurts," he grumbled. "Tomorrow, she can give you a bald spot and see if you're still alright with it." Every girl in their immediate circle instinctively reached for their hair, confirming the point Klein had made. With a victory huff, he turned from the group and finished his meal.

That evening, as they readied themselves for bed, Gael moved from one end of the room to the other, extinguishing the flames in their sconces. Once he had, he returned to the still difficult task of reigniting them. Though he could not prove it, he was certain his brother and the other boys helped him.

CHAPTER TWELVE

The following morning, he rose early once more and began working on his new studies. Starting with his candle, he moved to the hearth after he failed to ignite it after several aggravating tries. Moving to the hearth, he lowered the candle to the flames, which ignited before he had drawn close.

"Good light, young man," A voice emanated from inside. Startled, Gael stumbled backwards, nearly falling over with the lit candle in hand. As he regained his balance, a face appeared within the flames.

"A bit jumpy in the mornings, are we?" the spirit of the hearth asked with a hollow cackle. "When you've been around as long as I, you must find ways to entertain yourself." It continued its disembodied laugh a moment before its face faded.

"Good light," Gael responded. "Thank you for the ember." The tongue licked out once more before he was certain the spirit had left. Examining the candle, he sat it back within its sconce near to the lounge chair. Crawling into the chair, he focused on the flame, aiming to bend it to his will.

Reaching out with his channeled energy, he squelched the flame without touching it. "First try, this time." He smiled, even knowing he was far from obtaining the level of mastery Tarkan expected.

"Now, to light it." He poured his focus into the candle wick, trying to channel his energy and bring it to life. The task was by no means as simple as extinguishing the flame, and he soon felt his temple pounding from maintaining such firm concentration.

His frustration only grew with each repeated, failed attempt. As his peers roused and began to make their presences known, he angrily closed his book and made ready to begin his day. His things stowed in their proper place, he washed his face and marched to the hall for breakfast.

There was little to be seen in the way of excitement as he sat in his usual seat, waiting for the morning letters to arrive and breakfast to begin. Of course, with the letters from home having ceased of late, the thought did little to ease him from his unpleasant mood. Once the morning had begun with post delivery and food, he picked at his plate with a melancholy disposition.

It came as a surprise to no one when Phyllida entered the room, in her typical fashion. A radiant, icy smile on her face, she entered the high tables with her fellow staff. In contrast to her colleagues, her smile did not waver.

"Good morning, students," she began, the frost in her breath sending out another arctic gust. "I trust everyone has enjoyed their advanced studies?" Several groans rang out amongst both the students and the teachers to this question. Unfazed by the lack of enthusiasm, the Headmistress's smile only deepened.

"I trust everyone has grown used to the effects of the Arcanus Orb?" Again, another round of groans escaped the crowd. "There is one other matter I wish to discuss with everyone." She paused momentarily, ensuring she held the attention of the room.

"I wish for all of our upper-classmen to stay after. First, second, and third-years; you will need to find your way about today, on your own." Gently clapping her hands, which thundered no less forcibly, she dismissed the room. Gathering up his books, Gael moved for the entrance, to be intercepted by Professor Tarkan and Lang.

"Young Stryfe," Tarkan began, "I would like you to come with us today." Eying the instructors cautiously, he reaffirmed his grip on his books.

"What about my studies?" he asked. "I have rune studies soon."

"Boy," Lang sighed. "Do you know your runes?"

"What we are presently studying, yes. I do not know the old dialects as of yet, though."

"Then I shall see that you are given full credit for today," Tarkan said sharply.

"Then what exactly am I to do today?" Lang eyed Tarkan a moment before turning her head away.

"You and I will have some private tutoring today," Tarkan answered. "It seems that other than your work on practical spells, it is about time you receive some proper instruction in the use of that artifact." Looking worriedly, he turned his gaze back towards his peers and relative safety.

"Where are we headed?"

"The Arcanus, of course," she answered bluntly, turning and walking away. Shoulders sagging, he dragged his feet as he followed. Reaching the center of the arena, he watched Tarkan approach the Arcanus. Placing her hand upon the strange, blue orb, the scene around them began to change.

Spirals of frosty wind swirled around them, covering the landscape with a thick and powerful illusion. Soon, the ruins of the coliseum transformed into the ruins of a mighty stronghold. Tarkan stood briefly admiring it a moment before reaching out her hand.

First, drawing a circle in the air, she traced a rune Gael did not recognize. A purplish hue shone from the rune circle, which deepened to black as she plunged nearly her entire arm inside. Watching appreciatively with no small among of shock, Gael witnessed the woman pull her arm free, removing the sword and scabbard he had seen her carry when they first met.

"Well then, Gael. If you would, I would like for you to grab the Hearthfire Blade." Nodding his head reluctantly, he strolled over towards the far side of the arena where the blade awaited him. Removing it from its resting place, he felt the familiar hum as the artifact resonated with him.

"Stand beside me," Tarkan said sternly. Sword stretching out in front of her, he noticed the jewel in the pommel flashing with a rubellite glow. Doing as he was told, he took up a stance beside her.

"Now, hold out your weapon like so and concentrate on its tip." Waiting for the boy to do so, she continued. "Slowly activate the enchantment on your weapon." A coat of flame came to life within the sword, causing licking tongues to splash out at random.

"Slower," Tarkan commanded. "Do not pour out everything you have. You must learn control. Otherwise, that blade is no more useful to you than it is for anyone else." Taking in a deep breath, he pulled himself away from the sword. The flames dulled, though gentle waves of heat were still visible.

"That's a good place to start," Tarkan said, turning to face him head-on. "Now, defend yourself," she ordered, swinging her weapon vertically towards his head. In a panic, Gael swept sideways, knocking Tarkan's weapon away.

The moment their blades connected, sparks sprang from the two weapons. Immediately losing his concentration on the flow of his energy, flames rose off from the ancient artifact. Tarkan sprang back slightly, dousing the embers on the sleeves of her robes with a word, and ceased.

"Get your energy back under control," she told him flatly, the reaction willing the flames to lessen. The moment they had, his instructor launched herself at him once more. This practice continued for well over half the day, until Gael could barely stand.

"You look terrible," Gabriel commented, watching over his brother as they ate lunch.

"It must be because you missed your morning nap in magical theory," Klein chortled. Gael grimaced at the other boy before laying his head back down on the table.

"So, did they have Rinoa practice with you?" Mari asked, staring at the top of his head. "She hasn't been in class today, either." A forceful grunt emanating from between the boy's entrenched face and the table was his answer.

As they spoke, CJ, along with several of the older students, entered the room, each looking haggard and worn. The noble from Dalmorithia, however, still smiled boldly as he spoke with his peers.

"I cannot believe you took that thing down by yourself," James, the small, reddish brown-haired member of his group, cheered. "I mean, it was massive."

"Cornelius, you need to show me that spell you used," Jessica, a cousin to James and similar in appearance despite being quite tall, continued.

"I suppose you will both just have to take your studies more seriously," he laughed with a smug grin on his face.

"Not fair, CJ," James complained. "Everyone knows that Darklings are a common nuisance in Dalmorithia. You must have seen dozens of them before ever coming to the Cabal."

"Perhaps a few. However, even with prior knowledge, you would be little better off than you are now with how badly you slack." James conceded with a smile, ending the conversation. No longer fixated on his friends, Cornelius took notice of the first-years.

"Does he always look that bad?" he smiled, pointing to Gael.

"Tarkan has him undergoing advanced studies," Gabriel answered, causing an instinctive flinch among the upper-classmen.

"I sure do not envy him," James commented. Closing the gap between them, Cornelius clapped the barely conscious boy on the shoulder.

"Do not take those lessons for granted," he warned. "Hard work and perseverance can always overcome raw talent. Just look at these slackers," he smiled, gesturing to his friends. "These two tested at the top of our class in practically every subject, dragging me along for the ride."

"Now, we're trying to steal tips from this dolt," Jessica smiled. "Hang in there, young man."

"There are no true shortcuts. You either fail, or you grow. In either case, you can learn to be stronger. Work your butts off, and you'll go far."

"What have you all been up to?" Gabriel asked, shrugging off the older boy's speech. At first, Cornelius stood, frozen in shock. As the first-years stared expectantly at him. Jessica and James began to laugh.

"The Headmistress has tasked us with training in the Dark Forest," she answered. "There has been a larger number of Darkling sightings of late, giving us a good opportunity to test our abilities."

"Has Rinoa been with you, then?" Mari asked. "We have not seen her since last night."

"Small? Purple hair? Looks as though she wants to burn the world?" James asked, receiving an elbow to the ribs from his cousin.

"That's her!" Klein cheered. "So, has she been fighting the Darklings with you?"

"She has been tending to concerns off the battlefield," Jessica replied sharply. "That is all that you need to know."

"She must know a lot about the Darklings, then," Gabriel said excitedly. Gently prodding his napping brother, he slowly shifted.

"Has she enslaved any?" Klein asked, earning a slap to the back of the head from Mari. "What?" he complained, rubbing the back of his head. "You were the one talking about Origin mages and their armies. Having one on our side could be helpful is all..."

"Klein!" Mari chided. "How thick are you?" Sensing her meaning, he averted his eyes.

"I am sorry. I wasn't thinking," he said, bowing his head penitently.

Jessica turned her head towards the entrance to the Great Hall and sighed. "I'm not the one you should apologize to," she commented as they each turned their heads to see a long flowing trail of violet hair vanishing up the stairwell.

"Now, you've done it," Mari growled, rising from the table and leaving the hall behind.

As the Dalmorithians moved on their way, the brothers and Klein rose from the table.

"What now?" Gabriel asked.

"Suppose I should go apologize," Klein groaned.

"Don't be too long, alright," Gabriel warned. "We still have our evening classes." Looking to his brother, who still appeared to be asleep, he sighed. "I'll help you stay caught up if you need to rest."

"Thanks, Gabriel," he groaned, dragging his feet as he marched off to bed.

****

Gael awoke a few hours later, rejuvenated and ready to continue the day. Leaping upright from his bed, he made haste to the lower levels where he hoped to join in on the evening fun. Before he reached the lower stairwell, he could hear his classmates cheering as they began their midday meal.

Already assembled, long before lunch was ready, several of his classmates formed a circle around their table. Squeezing his way through, Gael fought to a position in the crowd, where he might see what was happening.

"What's going on?" he asked, bumping into Aura, who was standing up on a chair.

"A couple of the older students are talking about the battle teams," she said without looking at him. "It seems as though anyone who wishes to join can sign up but the Captains shall choose the teams."

Gael felt a surge of joy floating into his chest. He had been looking forward to the chance to take part in the competition. He continued to squirm about, hoping to see more as raucous crowds began forming at the other tables, as well.

Across the room, he could recognize many of the older students. CJ stood, surrounded by a gaggle of girls, all wanting a chance to team up with the older boy for any length of time. He played ignorant to their plights, while his assured teammates, James and Jessica, helped people with questions.

Turning his gaze back to his table, he saw Niferi standing at the center of the group, calmly speaking with those gathered. He noticed very few people gathered around the signup sheets she laid out. Slowly inching his way closer, he saw his brother speaking with the prefect. Nodding his head, he signed his name and moved down towards the end of the table.

"I didn't think your brother was the type," Aura commented.

"Well, he must figure that he can lean on me," he smirked, stepping close enough to hear Niferi.

"As I told the last group, the battle games are entirely optional. Teams are comprised of four to six people. While first-year students are welcome to try their hand in the games with their sponsor's permission, they will not be permitted to create teams.

As usual, teams will be led by at least a third-year or faculty member. Faculty are not permitted to participate in the battle. Does anyone have any questions about what I have said so far?"

Gael watched as Lionel and Emma signed their names, along with two more of their friends. Somehow, Klein had managed to slip through the crowd and had took up a seat, scowling at Mari, who leaned over the documents.

"I hope we get picked," Aura smiled, seeing Triny at the front.

"Hopefully," he agreed, slowly moving through the line. "I did not think you would be interested in joining?"

She shrugged her shoulders without looking at him. "You never know. It could be exciting." They moved nearer, now nearly within reach of the lists.

"At the least," he sighed; his motivations were different.

"Or, we might distinguish ourselves," she continued. "First-years and already, we have the opportunity to make names for ourselves." He nodded silently, their intentions and thoughts matching. As he stepped forward, Niferi motioned for him to sign his name.

"If you are picked," she began, staring directly at him. "Your teammates won't be so forgiving, and your opponents will be vengeful."

"Yeah. I figured as much," he scrawled out his name and sat the quill back in the ink stopper. Moving through the line to the table, he sat next to his brother as Aura came through.

"I didn't expect to see you sign up," Gael started, prodding his brother, who grinned.

"I plan on working with the Niferi on maintaining the barriers," he smiled. "She said that I had to sign up first but that she could request I join her." The boy buzzed with excitement as Klein moaned.

"What's wrong with him?" Gael asked. "His burn still bothering him?" Gabriel and the others all smiled as the boy grumbled.

"I hope I don't get picked," he moaned into his folded arms, shaking his head. "I can't believe she made me do that."

"Wait?" Gael started. "Klein. Did you sign up, too?" The boy gripped his hair defensively, pulling at it as he continued to moan.

"Of course, I did," he whined. "Mari said she was going to beat me up if I didn't." Gael looked to Mari, who smiled.

"I did not threaten him with bodily harm," she stated. "I merely told him that he would benefit from the experience. I may have added in a touch of inspiration," she winked. "But just a touch."

"She scares me," Klein continued to sob, eyeing Gael. "I hope no one picks me for their team." He buried his face once more as the groups dispersed, and they settled in for lunch.

****

Their classes paled in interest to the allure of the battle games. The day stretching on, they struggled to maintain focus until they were released for the day.

"Hurry, Gael," Mari called, charging past him.

"What's the rush?" he called after her. She did not answer as she whirled around the corner, heading towards the arena. Gael hastened his pace.

"Excellent." Zerenia clapped from within the center of the arena. "More volunteers." Gael could not help but notice the seven students lying sprawled out on the ground, panting with exhaustion.

"I must say, Madame Zerenia," Lang began, walking in between her students. "That was a rather interesting test." The gnome continued to clap manically.

"Can we do it again?" she pleaded with the elder. "Fresh candidates." She pointed at Gael and the others as they assembled.

"Slugs!" Lang barked, forcing the ingrained muscle memory within each of the students to engage.

"Yes, ma'am." Twelve students instantly snapped to attention. She walked among their formation, making minor complaints as she tapped her cane and shook her head.

"It seems my colleague here would like your assistance in an exercise related to the battle games. It will be a grueling test and will no doubt show each and every one of you just how much competence you all lack. Is that something that interests you?"

"Yes, ma'am." They all bellowed in unison, unable to withhold their grins. Lang glared at their snickering faces a moment and tapped her cane.

"They're all yours. Try not to kill them," she limped off to the side of the arena.

"Right then," Zerenia clapped. "I would like for each of you to gear up or whatever it is that you do for this course." The grin on her face was borderline malicious. "I am going to use the Arcanus to summon a challenge for you. What makes this possible is…"

She trailed off on a tangent, describing in grotesque detail the inner workings of what she was about to accomplish. Immediately, the students found themselves at a loss as the gnome lectured. After a few moments, Lang's cane wrapped on the ground, echoing with a thunderous roar.

"To the point, Zerenia," she hollered. "These are soldiers, not Artificiers."

"Ah, yes. Quite right," Zerenia stammered, adjusting her glasses. "Just give me a moment, and we'll get to it," she said, turning her back to the orb.

A flash of light announced the activation of the device as swirling waves flowed from it. Zerenia maintained her grip on the bauble, forcing her magical reserves into it. A sheet of ice spread out along the ground, a wave of cold billowing up to greet them.

Instantly, the students took up the defense, the wintry chill biting into their flesh. The smirks and grins they wore a moment before left. Now, they each attempted to bind their clothing closer to their bodies.

"I did not think illusion magic could make you feel the cold?" Klein shivered fiercely.

"Untrue," Zerenia said, "Any form of magic, if fueled properly, can become physical. By using the Arcanus, I am going to create numerous colossi within the illusion. I will use the power of the Arcanus to help bolster their abilities and see how you all fare. Good luck," she closed with a giggle.

As the gnome began to speak words of power, Gael and Mari took the hit and bolted for the equipment racks. Their peers were close behind them as forms began growing out of the ground in front of the professor. Quickly shoving his head through a breastplate and grabbing a weapon, he stood beside Mari.

"Everyone ready," Mari called back, eyes locked on six targets as they grew taller and broader. Within a few breaths, they had grown to such a size they dwarfed the students. The colossi let out an angry roar as they took notice of the children in front of them.

"Quickly, everyone," Gael yelled, looking back to see their comrades still struggling to equip themselves. "Get yourselves ready!" he called, only Mari at his side.

"We're hurrying," Lionel grumbled, struggling with the clips on his armor.

Mari stepped ahead of Gael and reached out with both hands to produce a small amount of flame.

"That's it?" he complained, watching as the miniscule geyser lightly singed the creature's abdomen, which hissed as vapors trailed from its flesh.

"It takes me a while to get warmed up," she yelled, tucking in and rolling away from the bellowing beast's cumbersome retaliation. "I can never start a fight with my flames."

"How long do you need?" Gael complained, keeping his eyes on the others as they slowly approached them.

"I don't know," she yelled. "Klein. Where are you?" Eyes scanning the field, Gael noticed Klein sneaking behind their enemy, moving in the opposing direction. He waved to his friends and pointed further down the battleground.

"What's he saying?" Gael tried to understand as one of the massive snowmen pulled a wad of fluff from its body and threw a ball the size of a boulder.

"Incoming," Emma yelled, having reached their side. Everyone, fully equipped or otherwise, grabbed everything on their person and dove out of the path of the giant snowball. As the armor and weapons racks were obliterated, they could hear Lang screaming off from the side.

"Zerenia! I hope you plan on picking up all of that once your little test is over?" The gnome smiled awkwardly as she continued controlling her minions, hands placed firmly upon the relic in front of her.

"Gael. Come on," Mari declared, slapping him on the shoulder. "I think I understand what Klein is saying." Again, both of them threw their bodies to the side in order to avoid being pummeled by the frost colossi.

No sooner had she said it did Klein begin making a loud racket. His sensitive ears ordered his attention off to the side, though his eyes could still see the boy in the same position as before. The colossi, however, proved none the wiser as they turned their massive bodies and, scraping against one another, bumbled towards the source of the noise.

"Klein can throw his voice?" Aura asked.

"Not just his voice," Mari corrected. "Hurry. With a professor controlling them, they won't be distracted for long." She charged headlong, flashing past the elementals as the others struggled to follow suit. Close on her heels, Gael turned his head back to see their opponents already recovering.

"They've already caught on," he warned, as Lionel brought up the rear of the group and was caught in a lethargic, sideways swat. They each halted as they watched their comrade soaring through the air, unconscious before he struck the ground.

Reaching a hand out, Lang managed to slow his fall and quickly poured over his body. In that instant, the snow monsters already closed the distance between them. He caught a glimpse of Tarkan as he turned, and urged the remaining students to follow Mari.

Three more students were thrown aside and encased in ice as all six colossi continued towards the fleeing octet. Mari threw another bout of weak flames towards them, slowing them slightly but resulting in a chorus of angry roars. Reaching Klein's position, they stopped briefly to catch their breath.

"What is it, Klein?" Emma panted as Mari grabbed Gael by the arm and dragged him a little further.

"I was thinking we could attack Professor Zerenia," he explained, causing even Gael to look at him in horror.

"What?" The lot of them gasped as Mari stopped.

"Gael," she began, "We're going to need you to pull out that sword," she explained, pointing to it. "These creatures love ice and snow. It is the best way to be rid of them."

"You're right," he relented, placing his hand on the hilt. "What about the others?" They both looked back as Klein rounded up the others, keeping his eyes on the slow elementals.

"We're not actually going to harm her," he explained, peeking up to make sure they were still safe. "We'll just break her concentration, is all."

"She could lose her grasp on the magic, weakening or even disbanding the creatures." Aura filled in the rest as she turned back, watching the creatures which encircled the gnome. "Alright then, what do we need?"

"A proper distraction," Gael interrupted Hearthfire Blade in hand. "Mari and I will keep them busy. Klein. What else?"

"Right. I will need everyone to disperse a bit. Divide the summoner's focus. That will make it easier for me to get behind her. She won't be expecting us, which will make it easier."

All nodding their heads in agreement, they dispersed, Gael and Mari leading the center charge. They spread out, forcing the titans to distance themselves from one another. Gael focused on the blade's edge, as Tarkan had taught him, and swung low and wide as he drew in close.

The snow colossi howled with anger as a fair portion of its shin hissed and melted. It swung for Gael but buckled over its injured leg, toppling it off to the side. Falling wide of its target from its own weight and momentum, it collided with its nearest fellow, whom Mari was keeping distracted with tufts of fire.

The two creatures wailed as they fell to the ground, their melted parts attempting to freeze, fusing them in places. They stumbled awkwardly while attempting to divide themselves, giving Gael a chance to look at the others.

Triny and Aura were both running circles around their targets. He was uncertain about what types of battle magic the two utilized, as they frequently hurled tiny wisps of light. They appeared to be holding on well enough, though opposite of them, he saw Emma struggling on her own against the remaining two giants while Lang's assistants were collecting her teammates.

"Gael, look out!" he could hear Mari call, breaking his focus as he searched for Klein.

Eyes quickly rising, Gael quickly threw his body sideways, avoiding the large snowball their adversaries had shoved in his direction. Scrambling back to his feet, he ran around to the outside, forcing his opponent to adjust its position to see him.

"Emma needs help," he called, unable to see a friend. "Try to break away and help her." He clipped at the monster, gently peeling away at it while trying to make his back over to Emma.

As he ran, he saw an enormous shadow floating overhead. Looking up, he watched as the entire sky fell towards him. Throwing himself once more, he was clipped sideways and tumbled, losing his grip on the sword in the process.

Deep, biting, piercing cold attacked his limbs as he numbly searched for his feet and weapon. He ran too close to his opponent in his distraction and allowed it to swat at him. He could feel ice flowing up his body, rapidly dropping his temperature.

An idea suddenly struck him, and he looked down to his numbing limbs. Remembering the book Tarkan had loaned him, he focused on the flow of energy through his body. Forcing it to travel to his legs, he remembered the candlewick and willed his body to feel the warmth.

Though the feeling he gained was far from relief, he felt a trickle of warmth flowing to his legs. Only a breath later, however, course, stabbing pains flooded into his legs as he thawed. Fumbling around as he grimaced in agony, his hand struck something metal, which filled his arm with warmth.

Sword in hand, the weapon's flames roared to life once more, a dull ember that added a gentle warmth to the spell he had just cast. Turning himself to sit on his bottom, he scooted backwards and away from the colossi. To his surprise, he gained distance as the creatures grew stationary and began to melt away.

"That will be enough," Lang's cane thundered, jolting all of them to their senses. "I daresay, I never expected anyone to think to attack an instructor."

All heads turned to see Klein, lying on the ground near Zerenia, unconscious. The snow giants melted back into the ground, and the illusion the Arcanus created was gone. Gael looked around and saw Mari helping Emma to her feet while Triny and Aura rested their hands on their knees as they panted. The others had all been dragged to the side of the field, where they were wrapped in blankets and holding steaming mugs.

"I do believe that was what you might call an excellent strategy," Zerenia chuckled merrily, brushing off her robes. "I did not see that one coming." Looking at the red gel stains on her robes, she brought a fingerful to her nose, sniffed, and licked. "Oh, excellent. Strawberry is my favorite."

"I am sorry, jelly tarts," Klein mumbled, still playing dead. "I sacrificed you for nothing."

"On the contrary," the gnomish professor continued. "I think the idea was brilliant. By distracting me, you managed to disband my creatures and save your friends. After five previous groups, you're the first to come up with it."

"Whose idea was it?" Professor Damcian appeared on the scene. The students' mouths all clammed shut, fearing the punishment, which surely approached. Gael locked eyes with Klein, who had managed a seated position. The boy's eyes were filled with fear.

He thought carefully of what it would mean for him to create further trouble. What Tarkan would say. What his brother would say. Still, swallowing hard, Gael made his decision.

"It was me, Professor," Mari yelled before Gael had even raised his hand, taking the blame. "It was my idea. I didn't think we could win otherwise."

Klein's gaze widened as he looked at his red-haired friend. "No, professor," Klein mumbled, eyes already watering. "It wasn't Mari's fault." His body trembled. "I did it," he mumbled.

"I am sorry," Professor Damican growled. "I did not hear you."

"It was me," he squeaked, his courage quickly leaving him. "It was my idea. Please don't punish the others." Gael and Mari looked at the boy with a newfound sense of respect.

Silence reigned until Professor Damcian stood over the boy, glaring at him. "Who is your sponsor?" she demanded, causing all color to leave his face.

"P...p... p... Professor Tarkan," he stammered.

"Can you stand?" she asked.

"Yes, ma'am." He glanced over to Mari and Gael, who looked on with horror at what might befall their friend.

"Come with me, please?" Damcian helped him to his feet and walked with him.

"It's not his fault," Mari pleaded. "He wasn't trying to hurt anyone."

Professor Damcian turned her attention to the other children and smirked. "I am not here to punish the boy. I am here to collect him." Klein's expression dropped even lower as he was dragged away.

****

"Heard you all had yourselves a good time in the arena today?" Gabriel started that evening at dinner. Lionel and the others who had been frozen stiff by the ice golems had not joined them. Klein had not returned from his talk with Professor Damcian, either. With so few of them having pulled through the fight together, their table felt lonely somehow.

"You can say that," Gael answered hesitantly. "It was a pretty difficult test, to be sure."

"Yeah. If not for Klein, we would have definitely lost," Emma chimed in. "And if not for Mari, I'd be with Lionel and the others in the Healer's Ward. Thanks again, by the way," she smiled at Mari, who blushed.

"It wasn't a big deal." Mari struck the tip of her nose as she smirked proudly. "Still. I wonder what is taking Klein so long."

"Perhaps I can answer that," Tarkan approached their table, A rather sullen vision of Klein at her side.

"Klein!" They all cheered, looking at their deflated friend.

"What did they do to you?" Gabriel asked.

"Did they torture you?" Mari added. All eyes turned in a daze at the question. The boy snuffled in response, adding weight and concern to what they perceived as a joke.

"Worse," he sobbed, his head hanging low. "They're making me participate."

"Participate?" Mari asked. "As in the battle games?" she exclaimed, eyes growing wide. "Klein. That is great."

"For who?" he whined. "I'm going to get beat up and tortured and have to train. It's all going to be horrible."

"We'll let you eat all the jelly tarts your stomach can hold?," Tarkan added in lightly.

The boy rounded on her, his attitude suddenly serious and tempered. His eyes narrowed as he stared down the much taller adult. "You don't have the tarts," He said with a growl. "No one does."

"Allow us the opportunity to try." She smiled at him, patting him on the shoulder. "As of now, Professor Damcian has selected you to take place in the games. Once the Captains have chosen, you will be assigned a teams."

Turning away from the group, Tarkan left to sit with the rest of the faculty, as cheers went around for Klein. He, however, seemed less than enthusiastic until Tarkan snapped her fingers, and a tray full of jelly tarts appeared before the boy's seat. Immediately, his elation exploded as he tore in with both hands and began to devour them.

"It seems that his courage is easily bought," Aura laughed.

"But far from cheaply," Mari stared on with wonder. "That many tarts would surely break an army's back."

"Nonsense," Triny argued. "We have tarts every day back home." Both Klein and Mari turned their gaze to their naïve peer. Aura, clearing her throat, shoved her in the ribs.

"Forgive her," Aura smiled. "However, if it gets him to take part in the battle games, I am certain whoever chooses him will be happy."

Triny, massaging her ribs, looked on apologetically. "Yeah, Klein. You're going to be great," she coughed. "I hope I get in, too." The remainder of their meal passed by without incident.

That evening, they saw preliminary sheets for the battle games posted in the commons.

"Have everyone's teams been determined?" Klein gulped, too afraid to look.

"Just some of the noble-born teams," Mari commented, eyeing through the lists. "Your name is on here but not under any team. Must be they need more time to decide."

"Well, it's only the first day," Lionel, who had finally returned to them, snuffed. "Hopefully, they won't finalize anything until more of us get a chance to show off."

"I daresay, they cannot do any worse than you did. Lord Icicle-," Emma teased, swatting her friend on the shoulder. "Keep performing like that, and you'll be helping us find a spot, instead." She continued to laugh, drowning out his protests.

"Sounds as though a few of you could use the help," Rinoa mumbled, watching Mari playing a round of Wizards, Warriors, and Rogues with Emma.

"She makes a point," Gabriel chimed in. "The stories we heard were less than favorable."

"As if you would have done better," Gael grumbled. "We didn't do too bad."

"Wasn't half of your team wiped out?" his brother retorted. "Besides, I was complimented for my activities." He turned his head up, a proud sneer on his face. "If you looked closely, you would see my name is already on the board." Gael stared dumbfounded at his brother. Glancing over at Mari, the young woman confirmed the story with a nod.

"I didn't see you out there," Gael eyed him. "Whose group were you in?"

"I was working on my barrier magic," he smiled. "I can do it, now."

"Show me!" Mari and several of the others swarmed around the boy, who suddenly grew quite uncomfortable beneath the gaze of his peers.

"Well, it takes a lot of practice," he stuttered, looking around at the many eyes upon him. "I don't have it completely down yet. I still make mistakes, sometimes."

"Gabriel," Mari began, deadpan staring at him, "This morning, I accidentally bit my tongue while chewing. Klein, drooled paste all over his shirt when he was brushing. Mistakes happen."

"Alright," he sighed. "Just don't get too uptight if I mess up." Gabriel hovered over the many things on the table before him.

Clearing the table, one object at a time, he began making a space for himself as Triny dashed the table clean.

He took a piece from Maria and Rinoa's game board and placed it in the center of the table. Staring intently at the object, he breathed deeply and spoke the words for his spell. A gentle gleam appeared around the piece as Gabriel smiled confidently.

Pointing towards the piece, he urged Mari to test his barrier. Reaching out, she gently stroked the piece, the magic vibrating in response. "It feels so cool to the touch," she gasped, tapping the game piece several times over.

"It is cold," Emma added as the rest of their entourage joined in. Only Rinoa and Gael sat apart from the group, both reading.

"So, you are going to be participating in the games, after all?" Mari smiled.

Rinoa glanced over at the spectacle and, rolling her eyes, turned back to her book. Likewise, unimpressed, Gael closed his book and made for the dorms.

J.A. Bullen

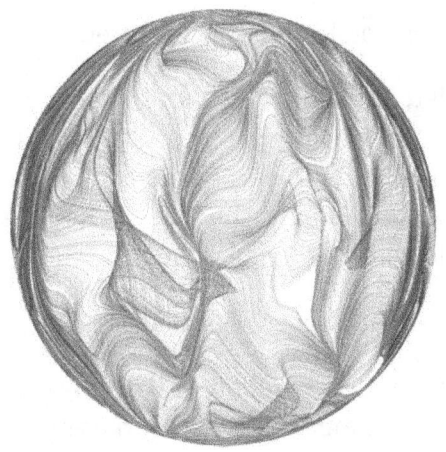

CHAPTER THIRTEEN

Gael continued chasing his newfound routine and was sufficiently agitated with his studies before breakfast. Grumbling over his failings, he reluctantly made for the lower levels, thoughts of ham steaks and jelly tarts on his mind.

They sat, enjoying their morning meal as the telltale calls of the morning post arrived. A new wave of excitement reached them as the enchanted carriers swopped into view as a floating sea of ruby wings, delivering letters, which fluttered down to anticipating hands.

One letter fell to the boys, the first in weeks. They stared at it fearfully, their anxiety unnoticed by their fellows as they tore into their own deliveries. Gabriel held the envelope at arm's length, trembling as the birds gathered above them once more.

"A second letter?" Gael asked aloud, turning his head skyward. This bit of mail came on a darker bit of paper, as though it had been exposed to char or contaminant. Curious, he stood and reached up for the letter.

"You needn't worry about this one, Mister Stryfe," Tarkan smiled, snatching the letter out of the air. "These sorts of things sometimes happen. The Post being delivered to the wrong person."

She strolled away, moving back towards the High Table where she deposited the letter in front of Phyllida. The Headmistress looked over towards Gael and his brother, cross expression on her face. Finally, she inclined her head to Tarkan, who tucked the letter away.

"What was that about?" Gabriel asked.

"I'm not sure," Gael replied, still eyeing the duo across the room. "She said that it must have come to us by mistake." Both brothers looked on in confusion a moment longer before looking back to their letter.

"What's it say?" Gael asked, leaning into his brother.

"Give me a minute," he shoved back. "I haven't opened it yet." Turning his back to Gael, he broke the seal on the letter and read carefully.

"Well?" Gael pried, disrupting the silence that was coming from the boy. "Any news?" He placed his hand on his brother's shoulder as the boy stood up.

"Here?" he said softly, and walked away from the table. Curious, yet frightened, Gael grabbed for the letter and held it tenderly at arm's length, fearing some monstrosity might rear its ugly head from inside. Carefully folding the paper over, he slowly read what Rosalind had written them.

"Dear Boys,

I do hope that your time at the Cabal has been a wonderful experience for you. Though brief, I know my years there were some of the very best. It pains me greatly to inform you that Lady Kirin is dead. There is still no tangible news on your father, though I suspect from our regular visits from the Inquisition that he is alive and well.

What we do know is that he seems to have crossed the border into Dalmorithia. While Father and Zara have been dispatched in the search for him, Uncle Drew has gone missing. James has been taken into custody, but Grandpa Amadeus assures me regularly that he is being treated well. Clarissa is still here at the Bastion and is growing into her own just fine.

Still, I wish you to know that Shayna and I miss you both something terribly. She, the baby, and I are all doing well and want you to know that we love you both. I am inexplicably proud of you boys, and I hope you take your studies seriously. I will be testing you when you return in the spring.

With love and consideration,

Rosalind"

He was unsure when it began but he noticed as he folded the letter, tears peppered his hands. He gently turned, avoiding eye contact from his peers as he gently dabbed the corners of his eyes with his sleeve. Stowing the letter into his pocket, he looked up from his lap and saw several eyes upon him.

"Are you alright?" Mari whispered, tears of empathy glistening.

"Yeah," he flashed a smirk. "Just news from home." With a nod of her head, the young woman turned to converse with Klein. Four seats down from her, he noticed Rinoa's eyes linger a moment before she rose and left the table.

"Suppose I should get ready," he sighed, pushing himself from the table. As he rose, he immediately noticed Duncan looking at him with a vile smirk. Eyes locked on him, the boy rose and walked towards him.

"There you are," Cornelius boomed out of nowhere, wrapping his arm around Gael's shoulder. "Just the guy I was looking for." He loomed his head in the direction of the Reynald boy, who scowled before returning to his seat.

"What was that all about?" he asked, hastily moving with the much taller boy's broad strides.

"Nothing," he said, patting Gael on the shoulder as Jessica and James hastened to their side. "I just wanted to ask you about the Arcanus and your practice bout the other day."

"Yeah," Jessica smiled, tapping Gael's elbow. "I got to watch some of it. You kids are incredible," she smiled.

"We were wiped out in just a few minutes," James groaned. "That play for Zerenia, though," he added a laugh as he spoke. "She's taking a much more active roll now."

"Got any tips for us?" CJ asked, leaning in closer. "Anything special about the Arcanus that could give us an edge on our training?" Gale thought a moment about the brief bits of research he had taken part in

"Well, the Arcanus does not just project illusions," he said. "It can also be used to enhance magic, just like with the professor's golems." He continued his walk through the halls, making his way through a previously unexplored region of the castle.

"We sort of suspected as much," Jessica started, "But what about the weather changing? What is that all about?"

"Again, the Arcanus feeds off the image projected by the caster. The professor still suspects that it holds additional capabilities, but as of now, she has said the weather changes are in relation to the Arcanus channeling the user's magic into the illusion."

"Alright. Makes sense." Cornelius released Gael and gripped his chin. "So then, the Arcanus could be used to manipulate the weather of any region displayed in the illusion?"

"Yes," Gael nodded, looking at the foreign decorations and illustrious new views as he entered the third-year commons. "I'm not supposed to go any further," he said, stopping short of the archway.

"Oh, it's alright," James smiled. "Tarkan told us we should have a word with you somewhere private, anyway. You're safe with us. If anyone complains, Jessica here is our prefect." He smiled.

"Yeah. Completely fine," Cornelius agreed. "Anyways, is it possible to conceive other effects inside the illusion?" He led Gael to a chair, where his three upperclassmen pulled up chairs to surround him.

"Well," he started, considering the question at length. "I suppose that depends on what you mean?"

"Well, would it be possible to change the terrain of the battlefield? Say, add an obstacle or make something feel real?"

"It is possible," he concluded. "It is not so different than the weather changes. The rain feels real. The snow feels real. I do not know how realistic it would feel compared to a real tree, but I believe that it would be possible to make someone believe they were touching something."

The conversation continued at length until noticing the time, and the arrival of several of their peers, Cornelius and the others rose from their chairs. "Thanks for your help, Stryfe," they said, each patting him on the arm or shoulder.

"Yeah. We appreciate it," Jessica added. "We need to get ready for our battle practice. If you want, I'll take you back to your commons?"

Rising from his seat, Gael smiled. "That's alright. Thanks. I know where to go." Taking one last eyeful at the luxurious commons, he left to prepare for his classes. Gathering up his things from his trunk in the dorms, he moved downstairs and made for the exit for the first-year commons.

"Hey, Gael." He turned on his heel, seeing Rinoa looking at him, shyly.

"Yes?" he asked, looking around cautiously in case he had missed something.

"That letter from earlier. The one that Professor Tarkan took."

"Yeah. She said it was a mistake. It got delivered to us by accident."

Rinoa nodded, though she averted her eyes several times, before continuing. "I know, It's just that, I thought you should know..." She stopped herself, wringing her hands. "Those types of letters are usually sent by the Inquisition, personally. I just thought you should know that they would not contact you by accident."

"You're saying that the Inquisition wants to speak with Gael and me" The question of "why" came into his mind, though it was answered before expressed. "They have to know we don't know about our father."

"I just thought you should know," she called, scurrying from the hallway.

Scratching the back of his head, he forced the thought to the back of his mind as he made his way to his morning classes.

"Fall in line, slugs," Lang bellowed her afternoon greetings as she sized up their formations. Checking to ensure each of them had equipped themselves properly, she continued to holler. "I am sure you're all aware by now that we shall be regularly using the

Arcanus during our combat training."

Loud groans emitted from the group, interrupting their instructor. Opposed to lecturing them, she smirked lightly. Tapping her cane, she brought everyone back to order and resumed.

"That being said, Professor Zerenia is making use of the Arcanus today and shall not be able to loan it to us. Instead, we shall be participating in live combat. You may have also noticed the many spectators sitting off to the side. "They are some of the sponsors, who have started their own teams, faculty included. They are here to observe your progress in order to help them form their teams. Now, pair up, the lot of you."

Klein shied away from the main group, trying to avoid participation until Mari seized his arm. He yelped in fear and surprise as she stubbornly dragged him away, a cross expression on her face.

"Gael?" Gabriel asked, kicking his brother's boot. "You want to? You know. Team up?" he looked away, looking at his other options.

"You know I never had a chance at looking good, anyways," he smirked, clapping him on the shoulder.

"You? Look good? Never." They shared a smile as they paired off. Lang marched through the teams, nodding her head in approval as she observed the pairings. She flashed a glance to the upper level of the arena, where Professor Damcian stood and nodded.

"Alright then, slugs. Each pairing will be facing another pair. Everyone turn to your nearest pair. They're who you are dueling." Looking from the professor, they slowly spun in a circle to find their nearest pairing.

"This should be fun," Emma smirked as they came face to face with her and Lionel.

"Yeah. I can make up for last time," Lionel smirked. "You guys ready?" With a nod, the brothers readied themselves. While Gael drew his sword and shield, Gabriel took a step back and held out his hands.

"Begin." Gael lunged forward, swinging aggressively at Lionel, who leapt backwards. As he moved out of reach, Emma attempted to clip Gael from the side. Light on his feet, Gael stepped to the side, avoiding the stroke and swinging up and over his head to strike her weapon down and away.

"Gael." Already knowing what his brother had planned, he backed off. Lionel followed after Gael as he backed down and was nearly struck to the ground as Gael's spell activated. Hit in the stomach by an invisible force, he slowed his approach as Emma swung at Gael.

He blocked the attack, catching her blade above his head. Sweeping it down, he swung wide as she danced around his stroke and caught a weak thrust from Lionel, which he easily knocked away. Behind him, Gabriel contorted his hands as he spoke words of power.

"Just keep them back for me," the boy called, pausing briefly between consecutive castings as he prepared for their victory. With a grin, he focused on just that. Playing defensively, he kept his opponents in front of himself without allowing them to move towards his brother.

Meanwhile, Klein and Mari battled against Aura and Triny. A fleet-footed battle between four proclaimed Battlemages, they took turns throwing bouts of amateur magic at one another.

Dodging and rolling to remain clear of the back and forth assaults, Mari and Klein crept nearer to their opponents, Mari serving as the front line. Klein, two blunted daggers in hand, fought with the skills that had kept him alive in the gutters of Lower Lothren.

Both Triny and Aura fought with a combination of two different sized blades, doing their best to shift from defense to offense. Mari, playing defense for Klein, kept her shield busy, batting away the weapons of the others while stabbing and thrusting herself.

Lang sat back, cursing under her breath at each inefficiency she witnessed. Snarling at every break in form, she twisted her hands around her cane, planning grueling rounds of torturous education for the slack performance.

Professor Damcian loomed overhead, a disappointed look upon her face. The groups of students poured with sweat as they fought their hardest. Metal clanging and magic sparking, the students were unaware of the many sets of eyes upon them.

"Gael. Move," Gabriel called, giving his brother enough time to drop to the ground before he felt another burst of lesser battle magic. Looking up, he saw Lionel upon the ground, nursing his stomach.

"That's not going to work on me," Emma called, striking back against the web-like strands of magic that floated in front of them.

"You got anything else?" Gael growled, struggling to keep up with the rapid strikes from his peer.

"I'm spent," Gabriel huffed. "There's only one, now. You should be fine."

"I've been dealing with two this entire time," he called back. "What do you want from me?" They continued bickering at one another while Gael fended off Emma's brutal attack patterns.

"Are you planning on helping me at any point?" Emma yelled over her shoulder to her prone Lord in waiting.

"I cannot move," he groaned, fidgeting wildly. "He struck me with some enchantment." Emma buckled slightly, dividing her attention between the two of them.

"Gabriel. This is our chance," Gael cheered, both he and his opponent nearing the end of their strength. "We can both make it into the games." They fought lethargically, their weapons swinging uselessly, while their counterparts had already ceased.

"That will be all for now," Lang bellowed, banging her cane on the ground. Covering their ears, they each dropped their weapons to the ground and turned to eye their professor.

"I have seen all I can stomach for today," she continued, one arm behind her back as she leaned over her cane. "There is much you all need to work on."

Bodies already aching with fatigue, they brushed themselves off and gathered their equipment. Placing everything in its proper place, they shuffled off. Professor Damcian marched to the center where Lang awaited.

"Did you find what you were looking for?" Lang grumbled in her usual tone. "You've certainly made yourself known to my students."

"They've some potential, those students of yours," she smiled. "Course, you'd never let them know that."

Lang spat unceremoniously. "No more than you or any of the others did at that age." She continued to grouch, her feathers more than a little ruffled. "You still haven't told me why you are spying on my students."

"My apologies, Teacher." Damcian softened her tone and inclined her head. "I merely wish to make a spectacle of the games this year. You happen to have several promising students in your ranks. Not to mention more than one of them that is famous."

J.A. Bullen

"A bit of a lineage problem, I would say," the elder corrected. "The matter is quite unfortunate for each of them. They will spend their entire lives trying to live down the legacy of their parents."

"The battle games will be good for that."

"And this has nothing to do with your own, personal agenda? Don't you have people you are attempting to impress?"

"Yes, yes," Damcian rolled her eyes as she waved off her colleague's concerns. "This has little to do with them."

"You are not convincing anyone with that attitude of yours," She grumbled. "I will not tolerate you conscripting amongst my students to appease the orders of any King."

"Professor," Damcian started, placing a hand upon the elder's shoulder, "You have my word. I will not attempt to conscript any of them. I do desire a spectacle, but right now, I am most concerned with prepping our students. Dark times are nearing, and we must prepare them."

"Be certain your disposition does not change."

****

"I got in!" Mari screamed, forcing everyone to jolt with surprise.

Gael, who had been practicing with his candle, knocked his things to the floor, scattering hot wax across the carpet. Quickly patting out the small embers, he looked up at Mari, who was still buzzing, excitedly.

"They actually picked you?" Emma charged the post, smiling brightly as she jumped up and down alongside her friend.

"Am I on there?" Lionel asked, edging in closer.

Emma turned and glared at him, a disappointed expression on her face. "Do you honestly think they would have chosen you?" she asked, hands on her hips.

"You don't need to be so mean about it," he grumbled, turning away. "I'll get on that list, yet."

"Good for you, Mari." Klein smirked. "If we are on the same team, you can protect me."

"And if we're not, I'll crush you," she teased, raising a clenched fist to the boy while maintaining an executioner's smile. The boy crumbled like a paper doll as everyone else joined in the laugh. "Come on, silly," she prodded. "You know I'm just kidding."

"Easy for you to say," he sighed, placing his hand over his stomach. "All this anxiety is going to ruin my appetite." A second round of snickers traveled the room as everyone left the commons to begin the day.

****

He sat facing towards the fireplace, exhausted from the day's exertions. He was alone, in the middle of the night, too tired to sleep. The week's activities had been unforgiving on his body, while the distressing news of his family and the Inquisition had performed equal numbers on his mind.

The heat and gentle flowing light from the flames calmed him, though it did nothing to lure him to sleep. Scooching his chair closer, he stretched himself in front of the warmth, feeling his bones pop and crack. Looking to the side, he fumbled with the books on the table, before rising with a huff.

"This isn't getting me anywhere," he growled, throwing his book aside. "I'm never going to make it."

"Quit being so hard on yourself," Emma said, a groggy tone in her voice as she stretched. She scratched herself, walking with a slight hunch as she curled into the chair nearest to Gael. "What are you up so early for?"

"Practicing," he grunted, pointing at his book. "Tarkan has me focusing on the basics. She said it would help me learn battle magic."

"Why not stick with what you're good at?" she suggested. "That's what I do. I am best with deflecting and projection magic."

"But I'm not good at anything," he groaned. "The only thing I can do well is this." He looked over to the candles he had lit and held out his hand. Focusing on his fingertips, he imagined smothering the flames, which immediately snuffed out.

"Oh? That's great," she gasped, leaning forward. "It takes me forever just to extinguish one. How did you do so many at once?"

Gael's eyes sprung open wide as he stared at her. "Is it that special?" he asked.

"Yeah. Is there any way you can make use of that during training? You could probably ask Tarkan to let you use artifacts, too."

A broad smile spread across the boy's face as a strategy developed itself in his mind.

****

"What makes you think that I am going to allow you to use any of those in my arena?" Lang growled as she looked at the relics Gael had borrowed.

"I cannot use battle magic," he started, "This is something I am good at."

Lang's eyes narrowed as she observed the hopeful student. "I shall consult with the other instructors so that you might utilize them in the battle games. Currently, against your peers, no. We do not have the proper defenses in place at this time."

"This could be my last chance to prove myself," he insisted.

"If your only option is to rely on an artifact, then you were a lost cause to begin with?"

He released a sigh, nodding his head as he moved away from the instructor to join his friends.

"Gael," Mari whispered, doing her utmost to remain incognito. He slowly turned to face her. "No. Do not look at me. Look ahead." Following her instructions, he faced forward.

"Klein and I can take a dive for you," she whispered, again, urgency in her voice.

He nearly choked on her suggestion as it struck him. "No. I have to do this on my own," he resolved, shaking his head. "One way or another."

They were paired off, Gabriel and Gael versus Triny and Aura. As they eyed one another, he and Gabriel both prepared themselves for battle.

Gripping the hilt of his sword tightly, he prepared for the call to begin. He glanced back to his brother, who smirked at him while maintaining a relaxed posture. At the sound of Lang's call, Gael charged forward.

Immediately, Triny threw out her hand, several tiny bursts of light flew towards them. Swinging his weapon, he managed to knick one of the blades, which chipped at his sword. The other blades moving off to his side, he continued his charge forward.

Aura waved her hands, emitting a wave of force that flashed its way towards the brothers. Shielding himself, he felt the magic flow around him. Blocking a stroke from Triny's weapon, he could see a semi-transparent bubble flickering around him. In response, a repulse wave flowed out from behind him.

"How are you defending and attacking at the same time?" Aura yelled, watching Triny buckle as her left arm dropped to the side. Gabriel, smiling, shrugged his shoulder as Gael shoved Triny back.

"We can finish this quickly," Gael called, swinging his blade but barely missing the young woman. Triny bounded backwards, using her right hand to continue throwing daggers of light. Raising his shield, he felt the daggers striking his shield arm.

The shield fell from Gael's grasp as his arm went limp. Dangling beside him, he swung out with his weapon, again, attempting to entrap his opponent. Two more gusts of magic shot out from behind him as he lashed out. Triny, much quicker on her feet than either of them, managed to avoid both magical bursts as she moved back towards her partner.

Aura leaped forward, throwing out both hands. Strands covered with little flames webbed out at Gael, eyes opening wide. Triny dropped to the ground, avoiding the net as it passed over the top of her. His eyes imagining the flickering wick of his practice candle, he stretched out his numb hand and squeezed.

Aura's magic evaporated, leaving both she and Triny baffled and confused.

"Move, you dummy." Confused himself, Gael only snapped to as his brother yelled at him from behind. As he charged forward, vines crept along the ground beneath him, slithering their way to their opponents.

"What are you two playing at?" Aura yelled, throwing down her strips of flame to impede the vines. Stumbling backwards, the duo threw out their hands, attempting to strike out at the brothers as they moved closer.

Stepping around their attacks, Gael threw out his hand again, squelching a portion of the barrage thrown at him. More vines passed through the gap, grappling around Triny's legs. The girl fumbled backwards, leaving her open to a tap on the shoulder from Gael.

The girl rumbled her frustrations, crossing her arms and looking away as Gael chased down Aura. Throwing out both hands in frustration, she sat in the dirt and watched the fighting continue. Aura dipped down and leaped backwards from Gael's attack.

As she attempted to cast another spell to hold him at bay, Gael reached out with his empty hand and focused on suffocating her magic. He felt a pressure resisting his own, and watched as her hands lit up, producing a diminutive result. Sidestepping the magic, he closed the distance between them and swiped.

"That's enough," Lang called, ending the bout. "Stryfe." She eyed him. "Someone would have a word with you." Fearfully, he looked at the professor, who impatiently motioned for him to follow her.

"What did you do?" Gabriel mouthed, to which he shrugged. He repeated his silent question to their competition, who reacted with the same response. Entirely confused, he looked pleadingly to the rest of his peers, who had each frozen in place.

They marched to the tunnels beneath the arena, where Lang turned a corner he had never been down before. The route took them straight through the dungeons, where chains hung from the dank, damp walls. At the end of a particularly long tunnel, Lang stopped, pointing towards the light at the end of it.

"Mister Stryfe," Tarkan stood, hands on her hips at the end of the tunnel to greet him. Just beyond her, numerous students stood at attention, each baring arms he instinctively knew to be artifacts. "I hear that you are causing a bit of an uproar above."

"I wasn't trying to," he exclaimed, looking back towards the tunnel. "I was just doing what you told me. I've been studying out of that book every morning and every night after our practice sessions."

"Oh?" Tarkan spoke with an edge to her voice. "And how are our lessons proceeding?"

He frowned in response to her question, head hanging low. "I still can't use battle magic," he sighed, despairingly. "I can barely light the candle."

Tarkan's expression remained unchanged as she looked at her student. "But you've managed at least once?"

"Yes, ma'am." Tarkan's students remained at attention, waiting for her to call them back to practice. Glancing back at them briefly, she looked at her younger student again.

"Excellent. I want you to continue practicing. Is there anything you would like to tell me about your duel today?"

"Did I do something wrong?" he asked, unsure of what to say.

"Did your father or caretaker never teach you manners? Answering a question with a question. Tell me about your duel."

He detailed the proceedings as she listened intently, without interruption until he finished. "That is all I needed to know. You may return to your friends. Head back down that tunnel and take your first left to reach them."

Nodding his head, Gael fled from his instructor in confusion. He made his way through the tunnels and back into the lower levels of the castle for dinner. As his friends joined him in the dinner hall, they bombarded him with questions he could not possibly hope to answer.

As the evening came near its close, he sat in the commons with the others. Gabriel was learning a new game from Lionel involving various colored gemstones that produced weak magical effects. He paid no attention to their games as he read from one of the many books Zerenia had given him.

He continued to read until late into the night when most everyone had turned in for the evening. After finishing his chapter, he closed his book and looked ahead. Staring absently, his attention was drawn towards the battle team posting.

Leaning forward, he watched as ink started running across the paper. He drew in a sharp breath as his lungs tightened. Slowly, the ink trailed along the paper until it had formed his name. A tear in his eye, he smiled as he looked forward.

Chapter Fourteen

"You were selected, too?" Gabriel gasped excitedly as he looked at Mari.

"All of us were," she smiled, proudly holding up the announcement list.

The entire commons was in an uproar, save Klein, who sulked in the corner with his arms folded across his chest. "Yay. Go us," he grumbled.

"When do we learn whose team we are on?" Aura asked, pumping her arms up and down in excitement.

"It doesn't say," Mari answered eyes squinted as she carefully read the page.

"I'm going to breakfast," Klein scoffed, hands folded behind his head. "It's a free day, and I'm not going to waste it worrying about some battle games."

The commons erupted with a chorus of grumbling bellies as Klein left the room. Clutching their growling tummies, they soon found themselves following. As they reached the Great Hall for the early meal, a cacophony of excited voices met them.

"They're going to announce the teams today," Several people screamed cheerfully.

"Stryfe." The brothers turned their heads sharply, hearing the call. "You're with us, Stryfe."

"CJ?" Gael spoke, seeing the upperclassmen approaching him.

"Hey. Yeah. That's me. You're on our squad," he grinned. "With you on our team, that gives us four. Hopefully, we can find one or two more." His grin only broadened as he clapped the boy on the shoulder.

"I don't know what to say," he answered, gently stepping from the older boy's reach.

"Nothing to say," CJ's eyes scanned the potential candidates as they scaled the stairs. "Already spoke with your sponsor, and she signed off on it. You're officially a junior member of Team Ruthger."

Again, Gael found himself at the mercy of the boy's gangly arms. "I won't let you down." Gael smiled, looking to his brother for help. With a shrug of his shoulders, Gabriel left Gael to fend for himself.

"Are you already scaring away our new teammate?" Jessica smiled luminously as she pushed her way through the crowd.

"Yeah, CJ. You know if you scare him off, we'll be short a person," James smiled as he nudged the larger boy in the ribs.

"No. I was just letting him in on the good news." He rubbed the back of his head as he smiled sheepishly. "By the way. We practice bright and early tomorrow. Say, West Courtyard, an hour before breakfast."

J.A. Bullen

The trio walked away, leaving Gael in relative peace. Gently prodding his way through the crowd surrounding the roster, he swam for his table.

"And here I had down that you weren't going to make it," Gabriel smiled, already munching at his breakfast.

"You just cost him his jelly tart," Mari laughed, mouth containing food as usual.

"Can you swallow, first?" Rinoa sighed, handing the girl a napkin. "You're drooling jelly."

Mari smiled as she accepted the napkin. Dabbing at her cheeks and taking another bite, she turned back towards Gael.

"So, anyway," Mari resumed her hedonistic conversing, Rinoa burying her forehead in her palm. "Figure out who's team you're on?"

"Cornelius just told me that he's already asked for me to be on his team," he smirked. "At least I got picked."

"I don't know yet," she jittered with nervous energy. "I cannot wait to see who picks me."

As she finished her statement, a gush of flame announced the spirit of the hearth as it prepared for the morning's announcements.

"Good day, students," it roared, quickly calling in the stragglers from the hallway. "I trust everyone is excited to learn their fates?" Cheers rang out from near half the students.

"Oh? Never mind, then," the voice said, sarcastically as the flames flickered. "I'll come back, later." As the fire in the hearth faltered, the chorus of voices returned with a wail. "Ha ha, I heard you all like that joke." Every eye in the hall rolled.

"Alright then," the spirit continued. "For my next trick, I would like for all the team Captains to step up to the table."

The students watched as CJ and several others marched to the front of the hearth. They stood, huddled together, pouring over the rosters, though each bore a confused expression. Turning their gazes over to the flames, something akin to a smile appeared.

"Oh my, how embarrassing. I see to have forgotten to fill them out." The spirit said as the entire table burst with light and flames rose several hand lengths. Many of the team Captains stumbled backwards, landing on their posteriors. As the flames quelled, the disembodied voice of the hearth could be heard laughing.

"My apologies, everyone," it began, glancing at the agitated faces of those on the floor and the faculty nearest the table. "My attempt at humor, you see. Now, if you will all collect your rosters, we can be on with the rest of the day."

Squinting, Gael could see that instead of a single roster detailing each of the teams; there were now several pages. Each Captain stepped forward, helping their peers off the ground. Eyes focused on Cornelius, Gael watched the boy lift his paper and smile.

"Captains, assemble your teams and begin your preparations for the battle games. The opening ceremony will be held next week." As Cornelius and the others moved back towards their tables, the face within the fireplace winked and was gone.

"Stryfe," CJ called, a childish smile on his face as he held up the paper.

Gael smirked back and waved at the upperclassman as he sat back with his friends and showed them the list. Glancing about the room, he saw several older students moving to tables that they did not usually frequent. One such Captain approached Duncan's table, while another stopped in front of theirs.

"Mari Tallow? Klein Rolands?" Gael recognized the woman immediately. Tiana Odaren or Lady Odaren, as she introduced herself, stood eyeing her piece of paper as she waited for the recruits to introduce themselves.

"Here, ma'am," Mari leapt from her seat, performing a full salute. Klein continued to munch as he lethargically followed suit. "Thank you for having me on your team, ma'am," Mari continued. "I won't let you down."

"That's good," Tiana muttered, an eyebrow raised as she observed the duo. "Meet me at the arena tomorrow, before breakfast." She glanced nervously at the two once more, before moving towards the table on the opposite end of the hall.

"I'm pretty sure you can sit down, now." Gabriel laughed, looking at the stern expression on both Mari and Klein's faces.

While they both sat, Lionel, Emma, Triny and Aura were each approached regarding their battle teams. The excitement only swelled, even after the morning meal came to a close. Surging into the hallways, students poured out in droves. Others were quickly collected by the members of their battle teams and steered into the courtyards for practice.

"Where do you think you are going?" Tarkan asked as Gael exited the hall.

"The commons?" he said slowly, eyeing the instructor with no small amount of suspicion.

"If you have the time available, now would be an excellent opportunity for you to show me some of what you have learned," she counter-offered. "Or maybe provide a few pointers."

He thought to the constant aches his body endured from his regular training sessions, in addition to his private lessons in the use of the Hearthfire Blade. Now, he had morning workouts with his new battle team to top it off.

"Just one lesson?" he asked, tired, bemoaning tone in his voice.

"Just the one," she smiled. "Follow me," she instructed. "You might enjoy this one."

****

"You're going to carry around a magical sword in school?" Mari cheered, excitedly. All eyes were on Gael as he stood in the commons, relic safely within the sheath on his hip.

"Not at all times. Just during the afternoons. Professor Tarkan also says that some artifacts will be allowed during the battle games." His enthusiasm could neither be contained nor quantified. He stood, visibly vibrating with energy as he delivered the news.

"That's great news!" Gabriel cheered, the most excited he had been for his brother in weeks. "With artifacts, you'll be able to make up for your skill in practical magic."

"That's what I thought," Gael replied, scowling slightly at his brother for the offhanded comment.

"I wonder what types of relics they will allow?" Klein smiled. "Maybe I can find something useful."

"Do not get too excited," Rinoa interrupted. "While being able to use artifacts will be helpful for many students, there simply are only so many available. While the rule clearly favors Gael, some teams might be placed at a disadvantage."

"Can you please mind your business, for once?" Gael grumbled, his joyous mood severely dampened. "You're not even participating. What do you care?"

"I don't," she answered pointedly. "I just didn't see the point in letting you or Klein have false feelings about the ruling. Even if everyone manages to get their hands on exactly the artifact that they want, there is only so much time available to practice, and you are the only one capable of wielding that one." She pointed at the sheath on his hip.

"But you suspect me of receiving favoritism?" he complained.

Tensions in the room rose as Mari stood between them. "I think we can leave this argument unsettled," she smiled, jarring Gael in the shoulder. "You got lucky. Good on you. Rinoa's just voicing her opinion."

She steered the two further apart as Gael maintained his glare. However, come dinner time, all was well and forgotten between the two. Returning to their typical habit of ignoring one another, the day concluded peacefully and without incident.

CHAPTER FIFTEEN

They awoke the following morning, ready to begin their day. CJ's battle games training turned out to be every bit as brutal as Tarkan's and less forgiving than Lang's. By breakfast, Gael slumped at the table and required several rounds of nourishment before resembling a living being.

Their last free day, before another round of lessons and countless, grueling battle practices, they savored every minute in the hall. Neither did they waste any time returning to their typical playgrounds. Gael, with little to do, casually strolled towards the western courtyard to watch Gabriel practice magic.

"Why are you following me around?" he heard an irritated, female voice.

"Oh, you know me. Just concerned about my little cousin, is all." The second female voice had a taunting tone to it. "You know how furious uncle would be if I didn't look after you."

Gael carefully crept forward, trying to hone in on the voices while keeping himself hidden. Coming up around the corner of the castle leading to the western courtyard, he could see Rinoa and Felicia Tamare.

"Well, you've done your job," Rinoa huffed, clearly not noticing they were being watched. "Run along now and report back to that man and let him know I am just fine."

"You know him," Felicia responded with an air of disappointment. "You know that's not good enough for him." She tipped her head to the side, forcing Gael to shrink back behind cover. A wicked smile crossing the girl's lips, she turned to face Rinoa.

"Listen," she resumed, "Mostly, I just want to warn you that they are planning something."

"Such as what?" Rinoa grumbled, still not facing her cousin.

"I don't know," Felicia responded, assuming a defensive stance as she placed her fingertips to her heart. "I know that something is meant to happen soon. That is all."

"And why would you want to warn me?" Rinoa scoffed. "Won't you get in trouble?"

"Please," Felicia laughed wickedly. "You know how I feel about you. I would just assume they decide that they don't need you."

"So that you can take my place?" Rinao laughed back. "By all means. Take it. I don't want it. Never have."

Felicia glanced back in Gael's direction once more before shrugging her shoulders and resigning in defeat. "Have it your way, then," she sighed. "Just try to keep your guard up. For both our sakes."

"There you are," Gael immediately adopted a look of horror and betrayal as Gabriel ran into view. "Professor Zerenia wants to show everyone something with the Arcanus." He eyed his brother's mortified expression and stopped himself, mouth partially open.

Felicia and Rinoa, looked at the blonde-haired brother in confusion. Looking to one another, Felicia inclined her head forward. "Are you talking to us?" she barked, a volatile tone in her voice.

"Well, yes," he sheepishly replied. "She said any of her students should come and see her demonstration after lunch. It's about lunch time, now."

With an eye roll intense enough to make a four-eyed raven dizzy, the girl stamped towards the castle, bypassing both brothers entirely. Rinoa, looked to Gabriel and at the small chunk of the wall near to him.

"How long have you been standing there?" she snarled.

"I just wanted to make sure you were not in trouble," Gael said, stepping out with his hands held high.

"Well, as you can see, I am perfectly capable of caring for myself," she snapped, collecting her things and stomping off in the same direction as Felicia.

"I'm sorry," Gabriel whispered, stumbling as he was unexpectantly shoved in the shoulder.

"Let's just go see what Zerenia wanted," he grumbled. "Where did she say to meet her?"

"Oh? Felix just told me that she was waiting in her classroom. We have time. We could grab lunch first."

"Fine," Gael grumbled, slowly marching back to the castle. "Let's just go eat."

Their conversation at lunch proved rather solemn. Mari and Klein spoke in excited whispers about what Zerenia planned to show them. Gael and Rinoa contributed nothing to the conversation as the two repeatedly made eye contact, only to reject one another with glances of disdain.

Agonizing over his careless eavesdropping and eager to be done with the day, Gael forced it from his mind, placed his hands on the table, and rose. "I'll see all of you in Zerenia's class," he said lethargically.

"Why are you leaving so early?" Gabriel asked as Gael rose from the table.

"I have to get the Hearthfire Blade," he sighed, ready to start the long trek back to the arena. "Tarkan said every day, between lunch and dinner."

The others all waved him off as Gael started hastily moving through the castle. Despite his full stomach, he felt he made the journey there in fair time. Collecting the weapon, he carefully attached it to his hip and gripped its hilt, feeling its steady connection with him. Proud that he could do something no one else could, he hastily moved back through the castle to see Zerenia's presentation.

"Oh?" Zerenia smiled brightly as she watched him enter the room. "So glad to see you've come to watch the demonstration," she cheered, motioning towards Felix Tamare. "I was just discussing with Mister Tamare about an intriguing breakthrough in my research."

"There are several others coming, Professor," Felix smiled. "I spoke with many of my classmates. They are all eager to see what you have to show us."

His smile felt unsettling to Gael. However, annoyed with the boy and his twisted family, Gael moved across the room. Taking up a place on the far side of the Arcanus, he leaned against the wall, folded his arms, and waited.

They all assembled around the Arcanus as they had countless times before. Eager for the gnomish professor at the center of the room to impart her knowledge of the artifact, they crowded into her classroom. With the upcoming battle games approaching, their eagerness to know all there was ~~about~~ the relic grew exponentially.

"We have learned a great deal about this artifact through everyone's duels~~.~~," Zerenia began, a cheerful smile on her face. "I must say, we may have learned more in the last month than the college has learned this past year. I cannot thank you enough."

She placed a hand to the orb and chanted the key words to bring it life. The ball ignited with energy, projecting images across the four corners of the class. The images projected were of an ancient city, lost beneath the earth hundreds of years ago.

"Today, we will be studying the lost city of Katra, it's remains resting beneath the capital city of Lothren. Before you are images from the actual research site, a closely guarded secret of the Royal Family of Lothren. These images come from my memories, as I have actually visited the ruins during my studies."

Gael marveled at the images surrounding them. Tall, triangular towers, reaching towards the earthen ceiling, which glowed with bioluminescence. Craning his neck, he traced tall pillars lining long roads that ran the course of an aqueduct.

"The entire city was built within the belly of the earthen peaks, which house the capital city of Lothren and is believed to be connected to other parts of the city on the mainland," Zerenia continued her explanation.

Nearly all the first-years huddled together, enjoying the demonstration, save many of the more snobbish nobles, who stood to the back, examining their fingernails and casually throwing insults to their "lesser" peers. Gael stood, shoulder to shoulder with Rinoa, smiling at the images. He held his artifact vertical, running along his hip to keep from knocking anyone with its sheath. Mari and Klein stood opposite them~~,~~ while the Tamarians loomed nearby.

"Discovered by the Templar, Duncan Wrotar, during the investigation of several disappearances within the city, Katra was thought to have been built by the Druegen or the ancestral dwarves. We do not know how the Druegen came to be wiped out; however we do know that a lamia was found, using this once great city as her home."

"This is a waste of time," Reynald complained from the back of the class. "Who cares about a bunch of mole men digging in their tunnels. All the better that they are gone, along with the rest of the primitive races."

"That will be one demerit for a Mister Reynald," Zerenia said casually, her lesson otherwise uninterrupted. "While the denizens of Katra are long since gone and clues to their departure are scarce, researchers believe there is more to be found beneath its surface."

The Arcanus pulsed lightly as the image they were viewing shifted. Soon, they all found themselves delving deeper within the tunnels beneath the city. Massive archways connected by expansive bridges ran unfathomable distances. As the students watched in awe as they journeyed through the perceived innerworkings of the lost city, the entire image shimmered.

The Arcanus flickered a vibrant shiver that flowed through the entirety of the illusion. Zerenia wrinkled her brow momentarily but continued her lesson as it stabilized. "There are entire passageways that are now flooded with seawater from the bay." As she spoke, she pointed to images of flooded buildings and roadways. The image flickered again, and with it, a chill wafted into the room.

"These areas," she resumed without pausing for the happening. "Correspond with the locations of the Alistair Memorial Bridge and Lower Lothren. It is believed that there was a series of tunnels connecting to another city, which exists beneath Upper Lothren."

Again, a chill wind struck the class as the images flickered. "Forgive me, class," Zerenia said irritably as she poured over the Arcanus, looking with wonder at the malfunction.

"Is something the matter, professor?" Felicia Tamare asked, voicing the question on everyone's minds.

"It is nothing, dear," Zerenia answered, tapping the orb in various places, attempting to reproduce the error. "Just a strain on my magical connection, I am certain." She smirked, rubbing the deep shadows forming beneath her eyes.

"Now, then. Where was I?" she asked the class as Katra began bleeding from the walls. Their heads whirled about curiously, watching the tall towers, flooded passageways, and bioluminescent flora run together, a ruined painting streaking across its canvas.

"Professor?" Gabriel said.

Gael looked down to his hip. The artifact in his hand pulsed lightly. A song drifted lightly into the room, whispered into the ears of the students nearest to orb. Four, haunting notes, repeated andante.

"What is that?" Mari whispered to Klein. Lionel and Emma, leaned in close, trying to hear the tune. Gael's hip pulsed again. He looked beside him to Rinoa, who stared forward, entranced.

A flash of light emitted from the orb, stunning everyone a moment. Blinking her eyes, Zerenia turned away from the orb. "It might be best for everyone to exit the room," she said calmly. "Come now, do not push."

"Professor?" Gabriel spoke. "What is that?" Tall, ruined spires encased in ice began to appear on the wall with each flicker of the orb. Another blinding flash and half the class stumbled backwards, halting the escape. The forms on the walls receded, though Gael could see them within the sphere.

Slowly, the overpacked room began to empty itself, progress delayed by the curiosity of the students. Another gust of wind, stronger and shriller than those previous, coursed through the room, blowing stacks of papers from the professor's desk.

"Hurry now, children," Zerenia called calmly, her attention now focused on stopping the orb. "We mustn't delay." Another burst of wintry chill struck them. "Quickly, now."

Slowly, the orb began to rotate, no longer controlled by the gnome. Light radiated from it as the wind shifted, presumably in response to its new life. Now, the room became interested in emptying. The students began pushing to get those nearest the door to move. Their efforts only slowed their escape.

"What is happening?" Gabriel shrieked as the Arcanus's glow intensified, blinding all who looked upon it.

"I am not sure," Zerenia squeaked, doing her utmost to place her body between the rampaging artifact and her students. "Everyone please move for the exit. Gabriel, grab Professor Tarkan and the Headmistress."

As Gabriel took flight, Gael looked over to his other classmates. Papers flew about the room, caught in the tempest that was the day's lesson. Many of his classmates opposite to him, quickly ran out into the halls, following his brother.

Those unfortunate enough to have stood with their backs to the wall, slowly shuffled towards the exit. Pressing their bodies against the wall, they attempted to squeeze themselves past the orb's growing sphere of influence. Watching over his fellows, he noticed Rinoa and the Tamares were frozen in place.

"Rinoa. Come on," Gael called, holding out his hand. Taking another step, he gently grabbed her hand. "We have to get out of here." Despite his calling, his peer remained entranced by the orb's glow. Her lips trembled slightly as though whispering. Similarly enthralled, Felix and Felicia both reached forward.

J.A. Bullen

"Don't touch it," Zerenia yelled, careful not to touch the orb, herself as she slowly made her for her students. However, even as she spoke, Felix's arm slowly rose.

"Felix! Don't!" Gael called as the tip of his finger grazed the orb. A flash of light and the spinning of the orb intensified. Rings of light revolved around the orb, shifting position between vertical and horizontal. Gael, blinded, stumbled backwards, losing his hold on the paralyzed girl.

The rings flashed in unison, causing his retinas to burn from the glow. Shielding his eyes, he peered a moment after and saw no trace of his classmates. Across the room, dropped to a similar position, was his instructor.

"Young Stryfe, are you alright?" Zerenia asked gently, her voice trembling.

"What has happened?" Professor Lang came quickly around the corner, Mari in tow.

"It took them," Gael muttered, staring at the orb, its violet lights continuing to spin, slowly. "Felix touched the Arcanus, and it took them." He shuffled to his feet, keeping his back to the wall as he remained focused on the artifact in front of him.

"We must determine a way to bring them back," Lang announced, turning to Zerenia. The gnomish professor was already deep in thought, muttering aloud. "Eleanor!" Lang snapped, breaking the gnome's concentration.

As the two professors debated amongst themselves, Gael stared deeper into the orb. His hand clutched at the hilt of the blade on his hip. One final glance to his instructors, their eyes met. Before either could voice the words rising through their throats, he reached out and touched the Arcanus. Hands outstretched, Lang and Zerenia watched as the boy, along with the last traces of the violet rings, faded.

Chapter Sixteen

The violet spinning whirl of the Arcanus finally ceased, throwing Gael face-first into the unforgiving snow. Turning about in the tunnel his volatile landing had burrowed; he flailed his limbs, dislodging himself. Scraping his body painfully as he wriggled his way through the tunnel, he pressed his head out to see the fading light.

The winds churned with a primal bloodlust, the likes of which he had only heard of in old stories. Shielding his eyes as he peered out from his burrow, he strained to see only a few paces outside. Already feeling a chill upon his exposed skin, he reached for his compass.

"It's possible that I was sent to the Eastern pasture," he said aloud to himself, scarcely able to hear his thoughts over the howl of the storm. Pulling his clothes as tightly around himself as he could, he pulled the collar of his shirt over his face and slithered from his hiding place.

The flowing waves of ice pained him the moment his body became exposed. The cold stinging his eyes, he stumbled blindly, traveling north. It only took him a short few minutes before the feeling began bleeding away from his limbs.

"I cannot stay out here much longer," he grimaced, continuing to drag himself through the walls of snow. "Hopefully, the castle isn't far." Maintaining his charted course, Gael eventually made out a large shadow up ahead. Knowing what it must be, he hastened his pace, quickly feeling his lungs tighten.

On the verge of collapse, he buckled to his hands and knees. Crawling the last several lengths, his hand touched upon the cold stone at the threshold. Reaching the top of the steps, he leaned against the ratty old door he found there. Pressing his entire body against it, the aged door swung slowly, the hinges squealing with discontent.

Collapsing to the floor, at last, he dragged his nearly lifeless body inside and kicked the door shut. Body shaking feverishly, he scooted himself further into the dimly lit room. Noticing a series of snowy footprints, he lifted his head.

"Hello?" he called out hoarsely, his voice echoing from some expanse in the darkness. "Is anyone there?" he called again. Still receiving no answer, he willed his aching limbs to lift him up.

Balancing on wobbly knees, he dragged his feet forward, making his way deeper into the darkness. The Hearthfire Blade clapped tightly to his side; he drew it from its sheath and willed a gentle flame to rise from it.

Warmth and light flooded into the room as the artifact responded to his touch. With the gentle flames lighting his way, he looked out at the derelict halls of a long-forgotten mausoleum of a building. Holding his blade in a parry position, he turned about.

"Where am I?" he said softly. A loud, metallic clang rang down the hallway. Pivoting on the balls of his feet, he oriented himself to face in the direction of the noise.

Working his way down the hall, warmth slowly trickling back into his limbs, his senses slowly returned. Beyond the growing agony in his limbs, he could hear someone or something further down. Mindful of his surroundings, he reached the next corridor, ready to strike out at anything that moved.

"Is anyone out there?" he called out. Only his voice answered back. Walking further within cast a faint light into the next room, where a quivering form lay.

"Rinoa!" he gasped at the sight of violet hair lying over her face. Rushing to her side the best he was able, he reached out and touched her shoulder. Half frozen to the touch, lips, and skin off-color, Gael tried to wake her.

"I have to get you warm," he said aloud, taking up his sword and stabbing it into the ground. Flames rose from the ground crackling wickedly as they consumed anything within their reach.

Quickly gathering up as much of the dried refuse and broken, aged furniture lying about, he began piling the pieces around the blade. The flames around the blade leapt up excitedly. Basking in the heavenly warmth and glow, he carefully jostled Rinoa's back and shoulder.

"Rinoa, you need to wake up," he said urgently.

The young woman stirred uneasily, shifting her body closer to the warmth. Her eyelashes fluttering, she stared at Gael blankly before shooting upright. "Gael! What are you doing here?"

"I got drawn into the portal, as well," he told her, averting his gaze as he said it.

"But I thought it was just the twins and me," she moaned. She shifted herself slightly as Gael surveyed their makeshift camp.

"We are going to need water and food. Do you have anything?" As he waited for her answer, he lifted a bucket from the floor and began wiping out countless years of accumulated dust.

"Not much," she moaned. "What are we going to do?"

"First, we need to get warm. You can stay here by the fire. I'll go fill this with snow, so we have some water."

"What about the others?"

"I'll look for them after I fill the buckets."

"And leave me here?" she growled, her stern expression betrayed only by the fearful look in her eyes.

"I am just going to look around. You need to warm yourself by the fire."

"What if you need your weapon? We both know you are lousy with magic."

Narrowing his eyes, he grumbled under his breath a moment. "I will manage," he finally answered, turning and walking away. Rinoa stared at his back as he left, regretful of what she had said.

Guiding his path with the old candle, Gael walked the desolate halls, which proved to be just as void of life as before. Large nets of deteriorated drapes and curtains dangled from the ceiling. Pressing past the skeletons of that forgotten place, he stepped out into a large open room, which exited back out into the frigid wastes.

"Is anyone else here?" he yelled, carefully opening the door. There came no answer, save the blustering cold as he opened the door. Quick to gather as much snow into his bucket as fast as he could, he quickly slammed the door shut. Shaking feverishly, he lifted his pail and hurried back to Rinoa.

"Did you find anything?" she asked, eyes wide.

"No. Looks like there is another building across the way. How are you feeling?" he asked, though he could still see her trembling.

"I am just fine," she grouched, still curled into as small of a ball as she could compress herself. Gathering a small amount of the salvaged kindling, he pressed it to the blade's base and sat beside Rinoa.

"What is it?" she grouched, shifting away from him.

"Do you have any idea where we are?" she remained silent a long while, neither meeting his gaze or otherwise implying she had any idea.

"None," she finally growled without facing him. "Weren't you leaving?"

"Are you going to be alright?" he asked.

"I'll be just fine. Just do not expect me to come save you," she grumbled, turning away from him.

"I will do my best," he answered with a sigh. "I will not be long." Rising to his feet, he moved to the far end of the building. The freezing wind whistled to him through the cracks in the time-weathered door. Slowly opening the door, he tightened his clothes around himself, shielded his face in his collar, and ran.

The strength of the wind had only risen in the short time he had taken shelter. Stumbling from the sudden, sidelong burst, he fell to a knee, before righting himself. Making straight for the next building, he threw his shoulder against it.

He could hear something break away as the door swung free. Stumbling into the tiny walkway, he braced himself against a solid, wooden bookcase. Eyes quickly scanning the room, he found this new building differed little from the previous one.

"Hello?" he called out. Before his echo answered, a glowing streak of purplish light hurtled in his direction. Throwing himself to the side, he tumbled behind the bookcase. "I am unarmed," he began, looking for a weapon. "My friends and I are lost. I was just looking for help."

"That you, Stryfe?" A familiar, silky tone spoke.

"Felicia?" he called back. Next, he heard the scurrying of hastened footsteps as the young noble came into view of his hiding place.

"It is you. It's about time someone came to get me." She eyed him curiously. "On that note, what are you doing here?"

"I was drawn into the portal shortly after you were. I found Rinoa in the next building," he said, pointing. "Have you found your brother?" He imagined he saw a tear in the young woman's eye as she shook her head.

"That idiot. Ran off without me, going on about hearing someone calling him."

"All the same, let's head back. Rinoa is waiting for me. We have a small fire," he added, seeing the way the young woman shivered.

"I suppose, I must," she scoffed. "You would all be in terrible sorts without my aid." Rising to her feet, she stomped towards the door and glared back at Gael. "Well? Are we going?" Gael growled in the base of his throat as he walked to the door.

"Sure. It's right this way," he continued grumbling to himself as he lead Felicia to the door.

"Where have you been?" Rinoa snapped upon seeing Gael enter the room.

"Get out of my way!" Felicia yelled, shoving her way past Gael and setting herself opposite the fire from Rinoa. Taking a brief moment to warm herself, she glanced over at her scowling relative. "Hello, Cousin. How good it is to see you well," she hissed in a snide tone.

"Likewise," she leered in no less disgusted a tone. "I must say I had begun to fear the worst." Gael looked between the two of them a moment before examining their bucket of melted snow.

"You will not kill one another if I leave again, will you?" he asked, gently tipping the bucket and taking a small drink.

"If I was in the mood, I would kill you both here and now," Felicia said with a nonchalant giggle. "But as it stands, you may both prove far more useful alive." Rinoa stabbed Gael with an irritated glance as he groaned internally.

"Do you know which way your brother went?"

Shrugging her shoulders, Felicia smiled. "I told you all I know already. I was resting, trying to recover, when he started on about some woman talking to him. When I woke up, he was already gone." She ran her hands across her torso in a vain attempt to warm herself. "We about froze to death trying to figure out that map."

He eyed the woman curiously, having missed the mention of her map previously.

"How long have you been here?" he asked, looking between her and Rinoa.

"If I had to guess," Rinoa started. "Not quite a day."

Flinching slightly at the thought of the difference between their arrival and his, he shrugged. "A distortion?" Gael mumbled aloud.

"Why?" Rinoa chirped. "How long have you been here?"

"I only came in shortly after you, and I just arrived. If you have already been here a day, I believe it is safe to say we cannot just wait for rescue. We will run out of provisions long before we are extracted if time truly runs so differently."

"Then what do you propose?" Felicia asked.

"I think we need to at least determine where we are," he said. "Maybe we can find some way back to the Cabal from there." Rinoa and Felicia shared a tense glance before looking back to Gael.

"It is difficult to say. However, I believe we may have found ourselves in the Frozen North." Tears slowly streamed down Rinoa's cheeks at the guess.

Gael looked between them curiously before speaking. "Then that would make this?"

"Exactly. Eternia." The city made famous by the Grey Mother." Felicia sighed.

All color drained from Rinoa's face, only rousing Gael's curiosity further.

"But she died centuries ago. The first necromancer destroyed her himself." Gael argued.

"You read that in a book?" Felicia scoffed. "From what I have read, her power was too great for Necronos, so he sealed her away. After extinguishing the Eternal Flame, he cursed her to remain in Eternia, forever."

"But still, she cannot still be alive, can she?" Gael's voice was softer, the weight bearing down on him.

"Gael?" Rinoa spoke faintly. "I think we can assume we need to escape from here as quickly as possible."

"First, we need to find Felix," said Gael.

"He's chosen to go off on his own. I say let him figure it out."

"Felicia, you know we cannot just leave him behind." Gael chided.

"Are you sure?" Felicia smiled. "The Grey Mother could be lurking anywhere, waiting. Every moment wasted is another opportunity for her to claim Rinoa, here."

Gael could hear Rinoa sniffle, though he could not take his eyes from Felicia. "What did you say?"

The noble looked between Gael and her crying cousin as if stunned. "I thought that you knew. Rinoa here represents a rare opportunity for the witch to return. Why else would she be on the run from her family?" Now, it was Rinoa who could not meet Gael's eyes.

Ignoring the revelation for the moment, his mind reverted to the matter of their survival. "Do either of you know of a way to contact someone on the outside?" Both girls shook their heads. Growling internally, he weighed his options. "Let's build a small fire. If we are in hostile lands, I may need a weapon."

"But you are not the only one who is armed," Rinoa growled. Gael and Felicia stared curiously at the kneeling girl.

"Are you sure you want to go out there?" Gael asked.

"It might be true that the Grey Mother will come for me. However, I will not sit here and cower when others take risks in my place." She carried an angered tone, her face fierce with determination. Glancing at Gael, she narrowed her eyes. "Well, are we going or not?"

"Yes. Let's get going," he answered, removing the sword from the stonework. The gentle flame dissipating, Felicia growled unhappily.

"We do not even know where to start looking," she complained. "He could be anywhere, while we haven't the faintest notion of where we are."

"We have some idea where we are," Gael said. "Currently, we are in an old storehouse. I would guess that places us on the outside edge of the city. I suggest that we travel further north. That's where the rest of the city will be."

"Good. Let's go," Rinoa grumbled, marching for the doorway. Gael hastened after her, with Felicia reluctantly following behind. Weapon at the ready, he thrust open the door and stepped out into the blizzard.

Chapter Seventeen

"So, what you are telling me is that the Arcanus resonated with one of the students, before engulfing them?" Phyllida asked, staring inquisitively at Professors Lang and Zerenia.

"Yes. Three students were taken with a fourth following a short time later." The head enchantress gripped tightly at her temples as she groaned.

"A short time later?" She repeated the words aloud. "And pray tell, how did the student manage to enter the portal 'a short time later,' if you two were here?" Lang's head drooped into a solemn bow while the lights in Zerenia's eyes grew alight.

"You see, Phyl," Zerenia began, causing everyone to ~~flinch~~. "While Lang and I were working to stabilize that collapsing gate, there was a fourth resonance."

"A fourth? Which student was it?"

"Young Gael Stryfe." Immediately Phyllida's right hand returned to the task of therapeutically massaging her temples.

"What a troublesome family. Their father was enough of a handful for the lot of them. Now, his sons seem to be just as troublesome, if not more so."

"Headmistress, if I may," Lang began, "Only Gael went through the portal. Young Gabriel is working with Professor Tarkan to help find a way to reactivate the gateway."

Phyllida's eyes quickly enlarged at the comment. "I do not want that boy anywhere near that portal, am I understood?"

"Yes, ma'am," both professors in unison.

"Good. That child, in particular, would benefit greatly from an otherwise dull life. He smells too much of the Witch Woods for my liking."

Neither instructor uttered a word in response as they returned to their study of the silent Arcanus.

****

"What about this one, here?" Gabriel stood at the top of a ladder, peering at the highest rows of shelves as he plucked a particularly old tome from the shelf.

"Let's see it, then," Tarkan called, turning from her careful screening on the ground. Nodding his head, Gabriel dropped the book, which came to a stop, and hovered in the air at the level of the professor's waist. Setting down the book she was currently perusing, Tarkan placed it back upon the shelf and moved to collect the next one.

"Hmm…" she mused, thoughtfully. "This could be bringing us closer, however, the trouble with Melstrom's ravings is that they must be taken with a grain of salt." Having already slid his perch down to the next set of shelves, he removed another book.

"I thought maybe it could be compared to the findings in this one," he added, dropping another book before sliding gracefully to the floor. Lifting the book, he carried it over to the table and opened it.

"If we compare the two of these," Tarkan mused, looking over the two books, "They may just give us a general overlay of the Arcanus." She thumbed through the first several pages of both books. Glancing at what he could, Gabriel made out the early origins of the arcane relic.

"How are you hoping to find them?" Gabriel asked.

"I am not certain. If we can learn what caused the interference, we might be able to replicate it."

"How will you know where they went? Has the Arcanus ever been used as a teleporter in the past?" Tarkan's only response was a subtle shake of her head as she shrugged her shoulders and continued flipping through the pages. The room grew solemn as the two continued their research.

"Let's take what we have here.," Tarkan suggested. "It may not be much, but it's a start."

****

"You're right, Aurelia," Zerenia squeaked. "We should try something to get those children back." They walked through the halls, heading away from the library. Gabriel carried a stack of books in his arms as he chased after the surprisingly quick gnome.

"We will find them, Zerenia," Tarkan began, "We just need to discover where they went and reactivate the orb." Forcing the doors open, they stepped into the Artificier's classroom.

"The problem is, we do not know where to start," Zerenia grumbled, thoughtfully tapping a single fingertip to her nose.

"I believe that I can be of assistance, there." All heads in the room swiftly turned to face several figures entering the room. Upon seeing them, Tarkan's hand immediately shifted to the hip where she typically wore her sword. Sensing the rise in tension, Phyllida took a half step in front of the former Inquisitor.

"And what can we do for an emissary of the Inquisition?" The figures fully entered the room, revealing five of them in total. Their leader, wearing a similar hood to Tarkan's trademark, stepped to the front, the plates of her armor rattling as she walked.

Her troop followed close behind her, similarly dressed. The non-existent eyes of the identity-concealing hoods stared directly at Tarkan, returning a matching aura of malevolence. Likewise, the troops standing behind the Inquisitor placed their hands upon their hilts.

"You will find that to be quite unnecessary," Phyllida said calmly, even as a chilling aura fell upon the room. "Again, I ask what we might do for an emissary of the Inquisition? May I remind you that our organizations separated some time ago."

"I suppose there is no harm in talking, for now." The five stood down, though the tension was far from dissipated. "As you know, we have been surveilling this place for some time."

"I hadn't noticed," Tarkan growled sarcastically. "It is not as though you've shown yourself and threatened my students numerous times."

"Be that as it stands, it appears to us now that a malevolent artifact has been activated." The leader turned their gaze towards Zerenia, who, despite her already small stature, shrank considerably. "By the power invested in me as an Inquisitor and agent of the Templars, I am taking the magus, Zerenia Chambers, into custody."

"You will be doing no such thing," Tarkan growled, placing herself between the Inquisitor and her despairing friend. The other four inquisitors drew their blades as Phyllida raised her hands out to her sides.

"That will be quite enough," she said in a soft but no less demanding tone, likening her to the calm of a storm as the temperature of the room rapidly dropped. In the pause of a single breath, a fog rolled from their mouths, and their bones chattered beneath their armor.

The woman before them glared menacingly with eyes of milky white as gentle streams of power rolled off from her outstretched hands. "Zerenia dear, I do believe you have work to do," she maintained her calm demeanor as she tilted her head back and looked to the gnome from over her shoulder.

"Yes, ma'am," Zerenia squeaked, wiping her tears and turning her focus back to the now silent Arcanus. Gabriel, meanwhile, privy to the entire confrontation, squeezed himself into as narrow a corner as could be found in the entirety of the castle.

She placed her hands to either side of the orb, tiny fingers gripping at the pedestal it rested upon peacefully. Staring deeply through the Arcanus, eyes searching for something beyond it, Zerenia called out the activation phrase. The artifact remained silent; all signs of its magical luster were gone. She continued muttering incoherently to herself as Gabriel crept from his corner.

"What do you need?" he asked her, their gathered resources nearby.

"I need to understand what happened? How was the orb activated? We need to discover what went wrong," she muttered. Furrowing his brown, Gabriel reimagined what happened.

"Why were Rinoa and the Tamares taken? They were not the only ones close to the orb." he asked, snapping Zerenia and Tarkan to attention.

"Zerenia, dear?" Tarkan said, stepping closer to her colleague, who turned to face her.

"I know, Aurelia," The gnome sighed. "Headmistress, I think I know where they are." Phyllida and the Inquisitors all turned their eyes to Zerenia and waited.

****

"Please tell me we do not need to go back out into that blizzard," Felicia whined, curling herself into as small a ball as possible, as she attempted to warm herself.

"I do not… know," Gael panted, quickly readying a small flame. "I certainly hope not." Rinoa sat quietly, shivering feverishly, attempting to warm herself.

"Well, I most certainly will not be," Felicia continued. "I could have died out there."

"We still need to find your brother," Gael said, readying their water pail as he, too, inched as close to the fire as he dared. Sitting in relative quiet, Gael periodically glanced at Rinoa out the corner of his eye. Felicia grinned as she observed the two, her thoughts, her own dark secret.

"How are you holding up?" he asked.

"I'll be fine," Rinoa grumbled, not bothering to look up at him. "How long do you plan on resting?"

"Not long." He tried withholding a groan. "It looked as though the next buildings were just ahead."

"So, is your plan to just run between the buildings and hope you do not freeze to death on the way?" The shock on her face grew ever more apparent as the sickening realization of their hopeless circumstances deepened.

"Pretty much, but should you come up with a helpful alternative, I am all ears."

"Nope. None here." She turned away from him, hands raised in the air. "Have fun out there. Build a snowman. I do not care." Shaking his head as he turned away, Gael made for the door, sword on his hip.

"Gael. Wait," Rinoa called, already on his heels. "I am going with you. I cannot just wait here." Nodding, he turned his head to see Felicia prodding at the meager fire.

"Good luck," he called. "We will be back once we find your brother." He could not make out what she said in response. Considering it unimportant, he and Rinoa each drew in a deep breath and charged outside. Running headlong into the blizzard, they both searched for a doorway.

"Here!" Rinoa called, tugging vainly upon the frozen handle of a large framed door. She continued fighting with the handle as Gael struck at the ice on the hinges.

"It's no good," he panted, in no small part from the chill in the air, starving his lungs. "Frozen shut. Do you know a spell?" Nodding, she held out her right hand, palm facing the handle with her left arm steadying it. Closing her eyes, she spoke a word of power.

"Fuero." A small trickle of flame poured onto the door, spreading out over it. Though simple, Gael could see the strain of the spell creasing the young girl's brow. Staring at the ungiving portal, he grabbed the blade at his hip and forced the pommel to the door.

His whole body vibrated from the strike, but he swung again. Clenching his chattering jaw tight, he continued to hammer at the ice as Rinoa maintained her spell. As the ice slowly chipped away, Gael drew his weapon.

As though a ward against some hex, the ice hissed and squealed as it retreated from the blade's embrace. Sprinkled by the cracking shards, they both covered their eyes as they continued to push. A shrieking wail permeated the air, drowning out the call from the raging winds.

"By the lost gods, what is that?" Gael howled, nearly dropping his weapon as he jolted. Rinoa stared out into the winds, shaking despite the relief offered by the looming building. Listening intently for a long pause, Gael tapped her gently on the shoulder.

"We need to keep moving. I would not want to be outside when whatever that was, comes this way." Nodding, she scurried inside. Closing the door behind themselves, they both carefully scanned their surroundings.

The interior of the building proved itself much larger than the previous ones. What once served as a grand welcoming room now proved a tomb for the denizens of the lost city. Slowly making their way through, he looked upon the faded murals and reliefs.

"I think this building served as some sort of temple," Gael commented, running his hand along a featured column.

"It is," Rinoa mumbled. "We are in the temple district of the city. If we follow the corridors towards the center of the city, we should find the brazier of the Eternal Flame."

"Is that everything you know or is there anything else you would like to tell me?" Before Rinoa could retort, they could hear something howling from outside. Quickly motioning towards one of the upper ledges where more statues awaited, they climbed above and hid.

Hugging one statue, Gael gently peeked his head out around and waited. The howling only continued, though it now existed separately from the wind. As they stood, shoulder to shoulder, the door began to slide open.

At first, Gael saw nothing but the light drift of snow coming through the door. They heard nothing save the dampened howling of the wind. Easing slightly, the sight of what entered the room made their renewed tension exponentially worse.

The door creaked again as a whining snarl could be heard against the wind. Something within the corridor shuffled closer, its feet dragging across the floor as it drew nearer. Fully within the

J.A. Bullen

room, the creature released a howling shriek, which echoed painfully through the room.

Continuing to peer out from behind the statue, he noticed as the creature shuffled into view. The creature's skin was a putrid color, resembling something which had crawled from a sere of one of the lesser developed cities. The monster was tall, despite walking hunched over and had long, gangly limbs.

It swayed heavily from side to side as it walked, slowly making its way forward. Gael could also not overlook the methodic gibbering of the monster. A series of clicks and high-toned whistles moved with it. Anxiously fixating their eyes upon the beast, Gael and Rinoa watched as it made its way through the room.

"What was that?" Gael finally whispered as he released his withheld breath.

"That was a howler," she answered, shuddering. "It is a type of Darkling that sees using sound."

"Like a bat?" he asked, to which she nodded.

"Yes. Exactly like a bat. We will be in a great deal of trouble if it should happen to spot us."

"I assume it is not going to be half as slow or cumbersome as it appears, is it?"

Rinoa shook her head. "We need to keep moving. Clearly, it is aware that something else is here. The further away from the Darkling we can get, the better."

"We still need to find Felix," he said pointedly. "Although, with as much trouble as we had getting in here, I doubt he is in here."

"I am not so sure of that," Rinoa commented. "Summoning Darklings is hardly a common practice. There is a chance that he did summon that thing. If what has been said about the legends of this place, then you know who should have the power necessary to start summoning such things."

"What are you suggesting then? You think we should follow the howler?"

"I am not so certain we have any other choice." Silence grew between them as they considered their options.

"How can we be certain it will not notice us following it?"

"We probably cannot be sure. However, by listening for its clicks and whistles, I think we can probably follow with enough distance to avoid detection. If you hear it howl, I would suggest running away very quickly. The storm will help conceal us if we run to another building."

"Alright then. I am convinced," he sighed. "If your cousin did summon this, can we agree that I get to punch him when we find him?"

"I have no objections to that plan."

"Good." He drew in a long, nervous breath. "Suppose I will go first." Gently dropping to the floor, he slowly walked in the direction the howler had taken. Rinoa right beside him, they fought against the dark of the room with the simple light spell they had gained during their studies. He only hoped it would prove to be the only thing they would need to utilize.

Moving through the nearly silent hall, they listened for the telltale clicking that led them closer to their objective. As they approached a large set of doors, they paused. The Darkling traveled further away as they stood in deliberation.

"We should go through here," Gael suggested, pointing at the footprints in the dust.

"Do you think Felix passed through here?" Rinoa asked, crouching down over the tracks.

"I know that someone did. Whether it was Felix or not, I could not say." He continued to mutter.

"What if it was someone else?" Gael placed his hand on the hilt of his sword and slid it partially from its sheath. Looking at Gael with wide, frightened eyes, she swallowed. "Could you do it? If it came to that?"

"I do not know. I know neither of us are dying here. As far as what happens to ensure that happens? No use worrying about the details. We do what we have to." He pulled open the double doors and peeked inside. Carefully glancing around the seemingly empty room, he turned his head back to Rinoa and nodded.

"We should close this door behind us just to be safe," she suggested. "The fewer traces of where we've been that we leave, the less likely we will be followed." Nodding in agreement, he cast his simple light spell and walked further into the room.

"Rinoa. There are more of those footprints leading this way."

"It has to be Felix," she answered, quickly hastening to Gael's side. Following the footprints deeper inside, they looked upon a series of long silent sconces, trailing a path to a large set of stairs.

"What are these tracks?" Rinoa asked, pointing to where the footprints turned to large streaks. Tilting his head to the side, Gael furrowed his brow.

"Looks like something was dragged," he mumbled, pouring over the tracks, which traveled up the stairs. Stepping onto the stairwell, they both yelped as Gael's werelight vanished.

"That is not funny, idiot," Rinoa growled, throwing her hand out blindly to strike his shoulder.

"I didn't do it on purpose," he grumbled, ignorant to her attempted assault. "It just went out."

"What do you mean 'it just went out?'"

"Exactly like I said," he snarled under his breath. "I cannot summon another one," he complained, holding out his empty palm.

Unleashing a snarl of her own, Rinoa extended her hand, producing no result. "I do not understand," she hissed. "I can feel the energy flowing, but nothing happens."

"I might be able to explain." Their eyes shot forward as the male voice spoke. "You see, my lady has lost most of her magical strength due to a rather nasty curse that has been placed upon this place." With the snap of a finger, the sconces began to ignite with blue, spectral light.

"Felix, what exactly are your intentions?" Gael asked before the final lights ignited to reveal the boy.

"Why, to serve the agenda of my family, of course," he sneered.

Rinoa stepped beside Gael, shaking her head. "He has become enthralled," she whispered. "She is twisting his thoughts to force him as her hand." Looking at her cousin, she raised her voice. "Why does your master use you as a puppet instead of assailing us, herself?"

"Dear cousin," he smiled. "You must be quite foolish to have not guessed by now. My master has been sealed away in this place for too long, drained of her magical energies by the very seal you have just described.

"It is for that reason my master requires a new vessel. One suitable to contain her soul."

"Then why not offer your own? If she has already taken you in your mind, why not your body, as well?"

J.A. Bullen

Felix's smirk wilted faintly, another sign that he was no longer the one in control. "I need a suitable vessel. One which is comparable to my own. Another power rises, which stands to challenge the very power I once held. For this, I must obtain a vessel, which may hope to surpass my former life."

A dark presence loomed into the edges of the room. Acutely aware of the encroaching shadows, Gael stepped in front of Rinoa, drawing his weapon. All around, a hissing announced the shadow's disdain for the weapon in his possession. Slowly fanning the sword, he sensed the subtle retreat of the darkness.

"Speaking of relics of a forgotten past, I find it strangely ironic that blade has found its way home." Felix's voice carried an unmistakable tone of malice, though if he, or the one controlling him, held any interest, it remained concealed.

"I heard this blade was forged here," Gael muttered, still not taking his attention from the shadows. At the back of the room, the double doors drew open.

"There you all are," Felicia called as she entered the room. "I see you have found my idiot brother. Does that mean we can all leave, now?"

"Felicia, quick. Come up here with us," Gael called. "That's not your brother, right now. This entire room is surrounded by darklings, just waiting to pounce."

Looking about, Felicia hastened to their side. "What has become of him?" she asked, hiding between Gael and Rinoa.

"He has been taken over by the Grey Mother." Rinoa flinched at Gael's words. "She aims to use Rinoa as a means of freeing her soul from this place. The seal on her magic has rendered her body useless."

"I see that even someone as fluff-headed as you can grasp such a simple concept," Felix replied, glaring at Gael. "I wonder, if you have discovered the obvious."

Looking with confusion at his classmates, Gael barely noticed a flicker of light from behind. Quickly turning about, his eyes were filled with a vast light as he felt something striking him between the eyes.

"Felicia! Why?" he heard Rinoa cry as Gael slumped to the ground.

"Why indeed." The young woman smiled, snapping her fingers as she placed distance between her and Rinoa.

"You are aware of the Altairan Shadow Court, are you not?"

"Of course. Your family serves as a multigeneration head on their council."

"And you are aware of the existence of a rogue element who oppose the council."

Gael struggled against the invisible bonds holding him, working to claim control of his limbs. He caught Rinoa's eyes briefly as she continued her interrogation.

"I am aware. Last I knew, the court had taken the initiative to weed out such rogues."

Remembering Rosalind's lessons, Gael attempted to deduce a means of escape. He knew that he had fallen prey to a curse.

"They have. In fact, you might say this little adventure is another piece in that puzzle."

"You do not believe she will help you, do you?"

Felicia shrugged her shoulders as she shook her head. "It does not matter what I believe. What matters is that I have orders. The rogue mages must be stopped at any cost. We cannot survive another Neravor."

"What do you know?" Rinoa asked, still gazing at Gael, who had managed little more movement.

"Just what I suspect. It is news to no one that we cannot survive another mage war."

"So, you hope by resurrecting a terror of the old world, you can prevent one?"

"Do not ask me. I am just following orders."

An unnatural breeze blew from deeper within the room. It carried with it the smell of decay and rot. Seeing the hilt of his sword within his grasp, Gael wriggled the best he could before being frozen in place by another horror.

"Bring me the girl," a dry, moaning whisper seethed at the back of the room.

"Of course," Felicia answered, turning her gaze towards the back of the room. Before Rinoa so much as spun about, the shadows had loomed closer.

"I would not try anything, Rinoa," Felix said. "It would be a shame if we were forced to take our anger out on Gael."

Rinoa froze as she looked upon her friend. The wild, daring edge in her eyes dulled, even as he tried to bolster her. "Please do not hurt him," she replied solemnly. "None of this has anything to do with him."

"Step forward," the dusty voice said.

Obeying the command, although hesitantly, Rinoa slowly stepped forward.

Grimacing the best his predicament would allow, a smile creased Gael's lips as the flat of his left hand touched the blade. Pressing his will upon the edge, he allowed his essence to flow within.

A bellow escaped his throat as the blade ignited, searing the flesh on his left hand. Free from the incantation's hold over him, Gael quickly rose to his feet, allowing his left arm to hang at his side. Smiling, Rinoa jumped to his side.

"Slaves!" the voice growled. "Kill the boy and bring me the girl. Do not allow that accursed relic to come up here." Felix stepped off from the steps as Felicia called for her summoned minions.

A sudden burst of light announced the start of the confrontation. Rinoa quickly raised a barrier, shielding herself from her cousin's initial attack as Gael turned on the darklings. Before the first of the creatures had sprung on him, Gael swung. The darklings cried angrily as they staggered backwards in surprise.

"Felix. Deal with him," Felicia growled, resuming her assault on Rinoa.

"Rinoa. We need to move back to the main hall," Gael began, placing his back near to hers to cover her. "I do not think you will last long like this." Nodding her head, they both shuffled to the front of the room. As they did, Felix drew a weapon from near the top of the stairs. Though the weapon in his hand appeared ancient, Gael imagined it would still rend flesh.

"You two are going nowhere," the voice called. "None shall serve as a witness to what has happened here." Noticing no reaction from either of the twins, it became obvious that both were fully enthralled.

"Keep backing away," Gael whispered, doing his best to hold the blade at length while fanning it threateningly at the shadowy monsters.

"Felix, do not be such a coward," Felicia snapped, drawing nearer to their other side. "One-handed and exhausted, he probably cannot swing that blade, let alone fight you."

Without responding, the boy lurched forward. Throwing out her hand, Rinoa muttered a few, hasty words and their attacker was struck backwards.

"Can you open the door?" Gael asked, pressing his back to one of the two. Pushing with his legs, his heart surged with a deeper panic as it refused to budge.

Eyes wide with panic, Rinoa threw her shoulder against the door. "It won't budge!" she yelled, speaking a quick few words of power as she extended both hands.

"I told you, none of you are leaving here alive," the voice of the Grey Mother cried. Gael caught sight of a haunting form in the far back of the room.

The ghostly visage lingered within the shadows, emaciated flesh, and withered hair. Lifting an arm into the air, Felix played the role of puppet. Words of power flowed off her lips as Felix provided the necessary energy. Spectral light poured from the corpses' fingertips as the cloak of death fell upon Gael and Rinoa's shoulders.

The two collapsed, warmth fleeing from their bodies. Gael's weapon fell from his hand as his strength flowed from his body. Dropping to his knees, then all fours, he continued to sink until he feared his death. At his side, Rinoa held on, though far from steady.

"Child of Origin, step forward," the voice bid. Seeing Rinoa take a step forward, Gael reached out weakly and gripped onto her leg. Unable to shake the hands of fate from her entangled strings, she shuffled forward, dragging Gael two paces before he could no longer hold on.

"Rinoa. Don't," he moaned, pressing against the ground with a single hand. Falling again, he watched as she drew closer to the altar.

"Child of Origin. I have waited long for you. Waited for you to answer my call and release me. Waited, for one such as you, to return me to power. I have glimpsed within the hearts of these children and am sickened by what I have seen.

"Our kind are persecuted, hunted as beasts for slaughter. In my time, we were feared or worshipped as Gods. Now, the most capable of you serve as little more than court jesters and fools.

"I shall return us to the highest seat of glory once more. All shall again live in fear of our power. None shall dare oppress us, again."

"Thy will be done-," Felix and Felicia called, dropping to a knee and bowing their heads. As Rinoa reached the top of the altar, shrouded in shadow, she, too, kneeled.

The ancient magus kept from fully entering Gael's view. Chanting inaudible words from an incomprehensible tongue, both her and Rinoa's forms slackened. Inching forward, Gael continued to moan for Rinoa to waken but was stilled by a clap of thunder, which left him deaf.

He could not hear their reactions as the twins suddenly jolted upright. He felt a surge of vibrations flowing through the stonework again. Tracing their source to the door, he did his best to roll his head away and defend it with one arm.

The door cracked and splintered with subsequent thunderings. As the enthralled twins moved to heed their master's orders, a sprinkling of chips fell from the door frame. Clenching his body tighter, he felt a strong gust of wind thrusting against him as the doors were forced apart.

His hearing returned suddenly, an unfortunate affair, which left him reeling. Fragments of the door blew out in various directions, tackling the twins who remained on the ground. The light hum of chanting continued as dust wafted into the room.

"Release the girl, Croan!" A genderless voice loomed. Gael turned his head to see a metal boot crash beside him. "Gael, can you stand?" Looking up at the figure's red and black armor with faceless hood, he smiled.

"I will be alright, Professor."

"Good. Try to lift your sword. The Grey Mother might still prove herself a difficult opponent."

"Yes, ma'am," he groaned, attempting to lift himself, once more. His body cried out in protest as he attempted to rise. Joints creaking, he reached his knees and swayed over his weapon. Arm unsteady, his fingers wrapped around the hilt. The metal singing as it scraped across the stone, he propped the blade on his forearm.

"An Inquisitor?" the voice said, an amused tone in her voice. "Your gift of power is most appreciated." Lifting her arms, Felix and Felicia's limp bodies rose from the ground. Both thrust out their hands, serving as the Undead Sorceress's dolls.

Drawing her blade with a flash, Tarkan surrounded herself in a thick, sanguine-shaded barrier. Both blasts arced to either side of Tarkan and collided with the wall. Carefully eying the glowing gem in the blade's hilt, Gael watched it shine brilliantly with each parried attack.

"Come, Gael. I need you to get Rinoa out of here. Zerenia and Phyllida are working to keep the Arcanus active. Get Rinoa to it. I will do what I can for the twins."

"I think the Child of Origin shall remain here," Rinoa said, stepping down from the altar. Behind her, a spectral image of the Grey Mother floated overhead.

"Rinoa?" Gael gasped as Tarkan stepped back. Gripping his weapon with renewed vigor, he stumbled forward. "Rinoa, you need to fight back. Do not let her win." Even as he struggled to reach the base of the altar, the twins' darklings stepped in between he and Tarkan.

"Disperse!" Tarkan yelled as she struck her sword horizontally through the air. Flames burst at the level of her strike, erupting across the chests of those nearest to her. Those that did not fade back into darkness wailed angrily as they jumped forward.

Swinging his blade, Gael felt the weapon make contact with his enemy's torso. Stumbling back, an agitated snarl was its response as it touched the ruined center of its chest. Quickly recovering, the darkling charged through Gael, flinging him sideways.

Landing hard against the lower steps, he gasped as his lungs were flattened. Ignoring him entirely, the darklings continued towards Tarkan, who maintained her assault on the magical demons. Trails of fire streamed across the room as Gael raised his head to look upon Rinoa's wolfish smile.

"All of you are insects," she seethed. The ethereal puppet master spoke through her. "Be gone from my sight!" she bellowed, waving her hand sideways. Magically lifted into the air, Gael felt his weightless form being discarded. Landing hard on the stone floor further down, he was surprised to see he still held his weapon.

"These young ones contain information about you, Inquisitor," Rinoa spoke, slowly approaching the desperately outnumbered Tarkan. "They tell me your order was birthed to aid in the suppression of magic. You yourself have served as an instrument of oppression." With a single hand, immense amounts of energy were released through Rinoa and her cousins.

Buckling to a knee, Tarkan held herself firm, streams of energy breaking apart from the orb surrounding her. Painfully, Gael turned his body about to observe his surroundings. Residing midway up the stairs at the far end of the altar, he saw a faint light, glowing red beyond the sea of blue lights.

Looking down at his pulsating blade, he extended his arm, kicked with his legs, and pushed himself up the stairs. The sound of Tarkan's last stand continued to echo through the room, vibrating the stones beneath his belly. Dragging himself further along, he grew fixated on the tiny flame calling out to him.

The room took on an unnatural calm as the noise from the battle vanished. Suddenly engulfed in a feeling of emptiness, Gael reached deeper for the sole source of life. As the fledgling flame sang for him to draw nearer, the pulse from the sword grew stronger.

"Are you the Eternal Flame?" he whispered, reaching the top of the stairs unnoticed. "The Grey Mother fears your power. Can you save my friend?" The flame flickered as if responding to the question. The blade in his hand continued to sing. Raising it just barely off from the ground, he slid the weapon into the bowl containing the flame.

"Stop him!" he heard Rinoa order. Bereft of strength, he released his grip on the weapon. The ringing of the blade broke out into a full chorus as the weapon slid into the bowl. Clatter and clan, the tip of the weapon struck the bottom of the basin. Standing upright on its power, the sword and the dying flame became one.

A ribbon of fire wove itself around the blade. One by one, the blue light of the flame sconces was extinguished as their power was consumed as his proximity to them would suggest, he felt as they drank from him.

He could hear a two throated cry, both voices feminine, shrieking. Shielding his ears, the best he could manage, he folded into himself as his magical strength slipped away. A tranquil song rose to fill the violent void, bringing with it a sense of peace.

He could no longer comprehend what took place behind him as the swelling flame continued to grow. Somewhere, far away, a shrill cry echoed within the abandoned halls. Something fell to the ground at his side. Lazily rolling his head to the side, he saw Rinoa.

As his consciousness drifted on the edge of darkness, a memory came to him. He was running through the woods, desperately trying to catch up to the young woman in front of him. His short legs, unable to keep pace with the teenage woman, he found himself tripping and stumbling repeatedly.

"Hurry, Gael," the young girl called, tears falling from her eyes. "The Inquisitors are coming!"

"But sis, the Inquisitors protect us," he yelped, tripping again and being pulled several feet.

"Not these ones," she continued to cry. Focused on keeping her brother close, the young woman could not manage a proper defense of her face. Low hanging branches and brambles deeply into her bare arms, face, and legs as they ran.

Silently, Gael followed obediently the best he was able until they reached a lone cabin at the far end of the woods. Throwing open the door, his sister forced him through the doorway, before slamming the door closed. Quickly bolting it shut, she turned to face the cowering boy.

"Here!" she yelled, leaping across the darkened room. Dropping to her knees, she wrenched on one of the floorboards off to the side of the room. Pulling it free, she produced a small opening, barely larger than a hunting dog.

"Get inside, Gael," she commanded. "Get down as far as you can go and keep quiet. Whatever you do, don't make a sound and don't open your eyes."

"But sis?"

"Promise me," she ordered.

"I promise," he answered, slowly squeezing his body into the hole. However, his promise was not to be kept. Once the Inquisitors arrived, they quickly blew apart the door.

He could only see as a moment later; his sister was forced to the ground. Crawling on all fours as she was assaulted, she placed her body over the hole where she concealed her brother. Despite their abuse, she held on to that single point, hiding his presence.

For all her efforts, he could not see the horrors that were wreaked on her body that day. The entire time the Inquisitors unleashed their form of judgment upon her, she kept her eyes on him. Tears fell freely onto his face, even as she maintained a strong smile. She mouthed something to him, the memory fuzzy; he could not make out the words.

"Rinoa?" he moaned, pushing himself closer. She looked feverish to him, her face decorated by beads of sweat. She cried weakly, unconscious as inhuman bellows still rang out. His strength long deserted; he pulled his body over hers and shielded her.

"I am sorry," he groaned, whispering close to her ear. "This is all I can do." Eyes closed as the scenes from his past played out; he felt a hand on his shoulder. Ignoring the warmth of the touch, he clenched tighter.

"You've done well, Gael," Tarkan's true voice spoke. "Now, it is time to head back." Again, he was embraced by the feeling of weightlessness as they were taken back to safety.

Clinging to consciousness, he drifted slightly outside the edges of darkness as a brief excursion in the cold returned them to the warmth of the castle. With great haste, they were rushed to the Healing Ward where their wounds were poured over, laboriously. Shortly after the rush of the many bodies subsided, did Gael finally succumb to the warmth of his bed and slept.

Chapter Eighteen

I am just saying," Klein began, talking through a mouthful of sweets he pilfered from Gael's bedside. "Between a swine farmer trampled in his own pen and you, I think the farmer got the better end."

Mari slapped the boy unceremoniously as she looked at Gael. "The teachers explained what happened to us last night," she said, softly. "I am... I mean, we are all very glad that you are alright," she finished, wiping a tear from her eye.

"Where's my brother?" Gael asked; Gabriel nowhere to be found.

"He is resting," Klein answered, looking through the amassed sweets on the bedside table for his next conquest. "I do not think he has slept for at least three days."

"Sounds like him. Worry wart," he laughed lightly before glancing around the room. Noticing the three of them were the only ones present, he frowned.

"What about, Rinoa? Is she alright?" Mari and Klein exchanged a nervous glance, which they maintained briefly. Seeing the panic crawling across their friend's face, they both snickered.

"She left yesterday with the Headmistress and Professor Tarkan. The Tamares left the evening prior, whisked away by their family, before the Inquisition could torture the truth out of them, no doubt."

"Mari?" Klein gasped, staring wide-eyed. "I did not expect something like that from you?"

The girl folded her arms as she turned away with a sulking expression. "Well, someone needed to say it. It would not surprise me if they were the cause of the Arcanus malfunctioning."

"But to just come out and accuse them like that," he said in disbelief, shaking his head. "That's bold. Even for you." As though imagining the severe punishment rendered upon offenses against a noble family, Klein returned his sweet to the offering pile.

"So, it is all over, then," Gael sighed with relief, a smile creeping across his face.

"Such a statement could not be further from the truth." All eyes turned to see Headmistress Phyllida standing in the doorway. "However, for now, it appears a great deal of the immediate danger has passed. Young Stryfe, I must ask your friends to take their leave for now. There are matters I would discuss with you."

Both Klein and Mari rose from the foot of the bed.

"We'll see you later," Mari smiled.

"Yeah, I still need to pack, anyway," Klein added. They quickly hastened from the room, closing the door behind themselves.

Waiting for their footsteps to fade down the hall, Phyllida turned her eyes on Gael. "I will have you know the Inquisition is having a field day with all of this. Had you not already grown accustomed to their added attention, I would caution you of it, now."

"I do not think I will ever get used to that. Did they discover who tampered with the Arcanus?"

The Headmistress shook her head. "Everyone has their suspicions. However, there exists little evidence to accuse anyone. Unfortunately, for the time being, Professor Zerennia has been taken into custody."

"Why?" Gael gasped, his entire body jolting from shock. "What did Professor Zirennia do wrong?"

Phyllida's initial response was a saddened gaze at the floor. With an aggrieved sigh, she returned her eyes to the awaiting boy. "It was Zerennia who brought the Arcanus through the Cabal's protective barrier and into the school. She was questioned after the incident, but no trace or record of her contacts can be found. To the Inquisitors, it seems as though she orchestrated the incident in recompense for previous offenses against her kind."

Gael knew all too well of the extreme racism that existed between the various humanoids. It was even worse between those of the magical variety. "She would never do that," he argued though he knew his words meant little.

Phyllida placed her hand on Gael's shoulder and nodded in agreement. "I know, perhaps better than you do," she began. "The matter is out of your hands at this point. Professor Tarkan and I shall do all that we can through the process. When you return after the harvest, you should expect to see her here, once again."

"I hope so," he sighed.

She patted him once, before removing her hand. "With regards to that other matter. I will have you know; I have already contacted your guardian and informed her of what has happened."

"Are Rosalind and the others alright?"

"They are. You shall see your friend before it is time to return home." Phyllida's gaze trailed off momentarily.

"Is there something else you wish to tell me?" Gael asked, nervously.

"Wish, no. However, I feel it imperative you be made aware. Despite Professor Tarkan's best effort, she could not destroy the spirit of the Grey Mother."

"I feared as much. Is she still trapped inside of Rinoa?"

"No, but Rinoa shall always be in danger, I am afraid. Her life will not be an easy one. Many shall seek her death for one end or another."

"Will the Cabal protect her?"

"Measures have been taken. Yes. There is another matter I wish to discuss with you."

"I am sorry I disobeyed your orders. But I am not sorry that I went to help."

"Not that. No, I wish to ask you about the Eternal Flame."

"What about it? I do not know much about it."

"How did you know to return the Hearthfire Blade to the altar?"

Gael contemplated the question a moment before answering. Remembering the impulsive gut instinct, which guided his actions, he stared into the professor's eyes. "I do not think I knew. Rather, I felt as though I needed to return the sword. I think it asked me to."

Phyllida nodded her head thoughtfully at the answer. "Do be sure to watch after yourself, young Stryfe," she added, moving away. "It might be best for all parties if you and your brother, keep from attracting too much attention." The woman turned away and left the room.

****

Later that day, all their things gathered and loaded back onto the boats, Gael ventured away to meet with his peers. The crowd roared through the halls, all eager to be on their way home. Moving away from the first-year dorms, he made his way to the lower courtyards for some well-earned peace.

"There you are," Gabriel shouted cheerfully, two slings of books over his shoulder.

"What is all of that?" he asked, staring frighteningly at the bundles.

"Just some books the librarian said I could borrow. You know, for a small bit of light reading."

Eying his brother, Gael shook his head. "Anything interesting?"

Gabriel furrowed his eyebrows, the sign of his cataloguing mind at work. "Just a couple of books about defensive spells, relics. That sort of thing. Probably nothing you would be interested in." Gabriel smiled.

"I am not so sure," he answered, looking over his brother's shoulder. "A little light reading might not be so bad."

"Are you headed for the boats?"

"No, I am going to head over to the courtyard. Take some time, before we leave."

"Just do not be late," Gabriel grumbled, moving on his way.

Stepping out on the courtyard lawn, he moved towards the shaded side of the hill. Rounding the last of the stairs, he saw Rinoa, already perched on the hill.

"What do you want?" she snapped. Ignoring her tone and attitude, he sat down beside her. Without answering her, he laid down upon the grass and stretched himself in the sun.

Turning her head to complain, she stopped at the sight of his closed eyes and broad smile. Quickly, she turned away, a slight blush to her cheeks. Slowly, a smile spread across her face, as well.

"So, what now?" he asked, without showing the slightest sign of being awake.

"We go home, of course. What else?" Rinoa said, shaking her head at such an obvious answer.

"But it's not so simple for you, is it?" he sighed. "You cannot just go back to a home that isn't safe." He remembered crawling out from that awful hole in the floor where his sister gave her life to keep him safe.

****

After whimpering her name softly for hours, he finally decided to escape from his prison. It was past nightfall before he managed to escape out from beneath her body. As he rose to his feet, he was covered in the vital fluid which had flown from her veins and through the floorboards.

He stared down at her disheveled clothing. Much of it had been torn away. Signs of abuse he could not comprehend at such a young age, were apparent.

He lay by his sister's side for several hours more, until he could hear the whiney of a horse outside. A pair of boots touched the ground a moment later before a man appeared in the doorway. Discerning eyes scanned the room without missing a single detail.

"There is nothing we can do for your sister, now, save honor her courage." Extending his hand to Gael, the man looked sympathetically to the boy. "If you wish, you can come live with me. It will not be the same, but it's safe there." Accepting the hand, Gael had started his new life.

****

"I know it doesn't begin to help, but I understand."

Rinoa remained silent a long while before nodding her head in agreement. "It's not a terrible thing," she started, "To be understood. What are your plans?"

"No clue," he scoffed, shrugging his shoulders.

Rinoa's head snapped towards him, jaw slightly ajar. "You are quite irritating; you know that?" she continued to grumble, despite maintaining a full smile.

"Mmm Hmm," he mumbled in response.

"Perhaps even intolerable."

"Naturally," he replied nonchalantly. She snapped another quick glance before laughing lightly. Hearing her laugh, Gael's stern expression melted away just as the last traces of winter.

"Thank you for what you did," she said, leaning in and kissing him on the cheek. His eyes sprang open in shock, and he found the burning red shade of his cheeks matched hers.

"It was nothing," he stuttered. "I mean, we almost died, but I would do it again. Help you, that is. We are friends, right?"

She gently grabbed his hand. "Of course, we are," she laughed lightly as she spoke the words. Involuntarily, he breathed a sigh of relief.

"Would it be alright to keep in touch?" he asked, looking down to his knees shyly.

"Do you mean write each other?"

"Well, that too, but maybe if you find yourself near Leones, you might visit? Or perhaps Gabriel and I could visit you?"

Her smile flushed again. "I would like that."

Returning home, eager to see his family and regale them of his time at the Cabal, Gael had already planned his first letter.

****

As the carriage moved into the city square, they saw Rosalind, Clarissa, and Shayna awaiting them. ~~The~~ brothers burst from the carriage, leaving their belongings behind. Baby in her arms, Rosalind rushed to meet them halfway, Shayna and Clarissa beside them.

Without exchanging words, they wrapped their arms around one another, their heads bowed as they exchanged tears. "Rosalind," Gael groaned. "You're getting me wet." He wiped the tears away.

"Shush," she grumbled, swatting him with her free hand while holding the baby close. "You'll be just fine."

"Are you certain? They still look like a couple of ruffians to me." Stepping back from one another, the boys saw their grandfather's head steward, Sophie, smirking. The boys ran from Rosalind, and wrapped their arms around the little woman, who barely stood as tall as they.

"But we're your ruffians, Miss Sophie," Gabriel sobbed, overcome with emotion. Everything they had felt while away came to the surface in a flash. Their joy. Their anxiety at leaving. The terrible news of their father and step-mother-to-be. All of it came out with the tide as they held tighter to the tiny, yet stern woman.

"It will be alright, boys," she whispered, motherly to them, patting them on the backs. "We will find our way through the storm."

"Where are Grandpa and Uncle Torran?" Gael asked, looking around. "Or the others? They promised they'd be here."

Sophie's eyes saddened as she casually wiped away her tears. "They are still in Lothren," she replied. "As for Bors and Zara," she paused. "I am certain you already know. No one knows about Drew." Nodding their heads sadly, they turned back to face Rosalind.

"Hey, Clarissa," Gael smiled, eyeing the halfling dryad girl. "Do you remember me?" Stepping away from the folds in Rosalind's dress, she stepped out and smiled, several tiny, sharp teeth showing. Without warning, she broke away from Rosalind and ran to Gael, wrapping her arms around his waist and burying her head into his stomach.

Surprised, he looked to the others in shock as Gabriel approached Shayna. Gently wrapping his arms around the girl, he smiled in turn. The girl backed away from him and quickly reached into the folds of her simple outfit, and removed a small candy.

"For me?" he asked, as she extended her arm, a toothy grin as her response. "Thank you."

"What do we do, now?" Gabriel asked, looking around for an answer.

"First, how about everyone come inside the Manor for some treats, and you boys can tell us all about the Cabal?" Sophie suggested, motioning towards the vast gates of Stryfe Manor.

"That sounds great," Gabriel chirped, looking to the others. "What about you, Gael?"

He thought about the question a moment before answering. "Sure. But afterwards, could I please have some stationary? I need to send a letter."

CHAPTER NINETEEN

"Then the experiment was a success?" A small but imposing figure spoke, leaning back in his chair casually, feet up on the long table. Beside him, resting along the back of a chair, was a large broadsword. Within the figure's hands, he held a hooked knife.

The room had been emptied, all except for a few figures that sat in the dark, their faces concealed by the touch of shadow. A conference table, easily able to seat fifty, stretched the length of the room.

"By success, you mean we failed to resurrect the Grey Mother, then yes." One of the shadow-clad figures spoke from the side of the table. "Between that and Tristan evading our assassins at every turn, I would say things could not be worse."

"They could be much worse, were any to overhear us, you fool of a Count," the man sitting opposite of him hissed. "It is all we can manage at the moment to keep the rest of their troublesome family from ruining our plans."

"If I might intrude?" The young figure at the far end of the table spoke, toying with the edge of his knife. "I understand that in Altair, the Shadow Court is quite the talk of the town. However, I am afraid I just do not care."

"How dare you speak so out of turn, ruffian?" The man seated to the right rose from his seat but did little to reveal his identity.

"Reynald," the man at the head of the table at last said. His tone was soft, though nonetheless dangerous.

"Forgive me," The man said, returning to his seat as the man at the head of the table spoke once more.

"While it is true that the outcome of events has been less than favorable, it has little to do with your involvement." The man removed a small pouch from his robes and tossed it across the table. "The gemstone is yours. It is of no importance to us. However, I must ask. What does it mean to your Queen?"

The figure planted his feet on the ground and rose from his seat. Absently reaching behind his back, he collected his broadsword, which he effortlessly flicked onto the hooked holster on his back. Marching across the room, he stopped halfway between he and the three members of the Shadow Court and collected the pouch.

"You could say it is part of a collection," he mused, opening the pouch and removing the small, carefully cut gemstone. In the darkness, it appeared to be made of shadow. The diamond, was shaped as a squat cylinder. Satisfied with the gemstone, the young rogue smiled and stuffed the pouch into his robes.

"Might I ask your assistance in another matter?" the man at the table's head asked.

"Not likely," The young figure sighed, placing his hands behind his head. "I am afraid my Queen has no other use for you." He turned his back to the table and prepared to walk away.

While the other two at the table rose and reached for the weapons on their hips, the third man remained seated and halted them with a single hand. "And what of your interests? Is there ought we might offer to rouse them?"

"Sorry. Beyond my Queen, my only interests are my brother."

"I see." The man's tone changed slightly, capturing the hooded figure's attention.

With a shift of his stance and a single flick of his wrist, the broadsword was pulled from his back and cleaved through the table. Without touching the floor, the blade stopped and was returned to the holster. "I would advise you to leave my brother be. While his involvement with your daughter has been troublesome for you, I will not forgive any interference from your Court. Good evening."

As the young man left the now silent room behind, those remaining could only wonder what devil they had contracted.

J.A. BULLEN

J.A. Bullen was born in 1988 and grew up a country boy in a small town. He learned to read at an early age and began his storytelling journey shortly after. He finished his first novel at the age of eight, though it has yet to see the light of day. Alongside his wife, daughter, and son, he continues to be a scatterbrain and dreams of impossible things, daily. Book preferences tend to lean towards Fantasy, Horror, and lately, LitRPGs (weird). Reader, author, gamer, and nature enthusiast. Pretty fond of food, too.

Follow J.A. Bullen's writing career on his website at **www.JABullen.com**. He can be found on social media at Facebook, Instagram, and Twitter.

Signed copies may be purchased through a direct website request; and all books are available in both print and ebook formats on Amazon.com.

Also Written by J.A. Bullen

Legends of Valoria:

- The Last Paladin of Highmoore
- Rise of the Divine Knight
- The Shield of Aneira

Blood In The Rain:

- Blood In The Rain I
- Blood In The Rain II

The Unbound Series:

- Unbound
- Betrayer (Coming Soon!)

Tales of Anon

- Beyond The Amaranthine Vale
- The Brothers Stryfe

The Adaptables (Coming Soon!)

www.ingramcontent.com/pod-product-compliance
Lightning Source LLC
Chambersburg PA
CBHW061931170626
46813CB00006B/2360